UNFOLDING

Other books by Jonathan Friesen

Aquifer

Both of Me

Middle-grade novels

The Last Martin

Aldo's Fantastical Movie Palace

UNFOLDING

A NOVEL

JONATHAN FRIESEN

BLINK

BLINK

Unfolding
Copyright © 2017 by Jonathan Friesen

This title is also available as a Blink ebook.

Requests for information should be addressed to:
Blink, 3900 Sparks Drive SE, Grand Rapids, Michigan 49546

ISBN 978-0-310-74833-5 (hardcover)

ISBN 978-0-310-74886-1 (softcover)

Cover design: Ron Huizinga
Interior design: Denise Froehlich

Printed in the United States of America

18 19 20 21 22 /DCI/ 20 19 18 17 16 15 14 13 12 11 10 9 8 7 6 5 4 3 2 1

She dropped from the Oklahoma sky.

A gift. Proof of the Almighty's existence.

But the Miracle Baby could not have descended with less fanfare. The citizens of Gullary, huddled in bathtubs and hidden in shelters, missed her arrival. Their collective heads were face-to-floor as seven tornadoes danced through the night.

The tornadoes traveled over five hundred miles. They teased and jabbed their twisty fingers toward the earth, only to rear back and punch through the green with a fury rarely seen previous, and only once since. And on one such strike, heaven—or hell, depending which side you're on—opened its fist and gently stole a child before pulling back up into the angry sky.

How far the swirling clouds carried the child is anyone's guess. But that she was set down with the care of a new mother is a *fact*, one my parents emerged to when the wind paused and the rain fell straight. She was wide-eyed and peaceful, still in her cradle, calm beneath soaked pink swaddling.

Ma found her first. Ms. Pickering, our neighbor, was a close second, though this detail contains some wriggle room. She joined Ma in leaning over the baby girl, and in the moment of that child's deepest distress . . .

"Martha Pickering, get on inside and see to your own!" Ma muscled Ms. P out of the way. "I'm caring for this babe."

"No. The rights to her are mine. She landed on my property." Ms. P paused and looked to heaven and whispered, "He has seen my sadness and sent me a replacement child."

As was customary, their argument raged until Dad intervened. He eyeballed the cradle. Our neighbor had a point: Everything but the child's feet rested on Ms. P's unmown front yard.

"Come on, more storms are comin'," Dad said, tugging on Ma's arm. "Martha says she's gonna deal with her properly. There's no denying where she landed."

Ma pursed her lips and swiped wet from her brow. Her gray-tinged hair, normally kept on the straight and narrow, swept wild and matted across her face. I envision her here an overweight John the Baptist, straight from the wilderness. "Well now, I suppose, as Solomon is not present to solve this dilemma." She rose and stomped toward our trailer home while Ms. Pickering gently carried the baby next door.

I've often wondered how life would have been different had God's finger nudged that cradle six inches eastward, had Ma carried the little one into our home, where I lay two months old and sleeping in the bathtub. Would she have shared a tub with me, Jonah Everett III, her first night in town?

Turns out the girl landed along with a dowry. Morning revealed a living cow and a grandfather clock also settled on the Pickerings' lawn, cementing Ms. P's claim on the baby's care.

News of the miracle traveled quickly. Hordes of reporters recast our town as more than the hardened home of a Supermax prison. A columnist from *The Oklahoman* penned it best:

Here in Gullary, Oklahoma, surrounded by devastation, one can feel the innocence. A word for the ground? Blessed.

Overly poetic, yeah, but this tiny arrival had that effect. Our trailer park became a campground of news vans and satellite dishes. The story of the airborne baby with raven-black hair hypnotized our state and eclipsed other storm-related news, such as the destruction of the aforementioned prison and the disappearance of several fearsome inmates. But looking back, Gullary got it right. Violent escapees weren't nearly as unnerving as this one, beautiful girl.

At least to me.

Great lengths were taken to discover the child's rightful home. Claims on a clock, a cow, and a baby girl were few, and the fistful that did come in ended up bogus. Days turned to months, and finally the courthouse spoke. Ms. P was granted rightful guardianship, and added another to her family.

"Look at that peacock." Ma hissed the words beneath her breath whenever she saw our neighbor outside with her three-year-old son, Connor, and the dubiously obtained child.

"I was given the feet of that babe. I should've had say in the choice of a decent name."

Ma's opinion never did change. In fact, she blamed the name for much of what followed. But I'd say Ms. Pickering pegged Miracle Baby with the only name that made sense, given her unique arrival.

Stormi.

CHAPTER 1

One week after the storm, Ma planted a cotton-wood out front of our trailer. She later explained it as an act of defiance. Ma was sinking roots, declaring that no tornado could dislodge our family from Green Country, the eastern wedge of Oklahoma infiltrated by the Ozark's mountainous tentacles.

Defiance or not, the cottonwood was woefully out of place. Gullary nestled in the Henshaw Valley astride Gullary Creek, which flowed easily from Lake Gullary set higher up and on the far side of the Arkansas border. Oak and Black Hickory found the creek and our town to their liking. Aside from Ms. Harrison's renegade apple tree, Gullary tolerated no other varieties.

"So why'd you have to plant a cottonwood?" I asked Mom this every spring, when the cottony fluff set my eyes to watering.

"You understand the principle of sowing and reaping. All these wispy seeds will take flight, take root, and one day change the look of this valley."

"You don't like how it looks?"

Mom never answered that. She'd eye that cottonwood, and the seeds swirling in the wind. "Sowing and reaping, Jonah, it's inevitable. A law of God."

My first photos of that tree evidenced a slender shoot, aiming straight for the sky. But somewhere along the way, its trunk had second thoughts and took a detour. The tree twisted, gnarled.

Bent.

But the cottonwood still grew leaves, broad leaves that fell green and full and hid the abnormal growth, and Ma called it lovely.

I have no leaves.

And it may not be a law of God, but the law of teen-hood is near as unshakable: senior year doesn't hide anything.

"This way, folks." I stepped in front of the mural, beneath the "Gullary's Glorious History" sign. While the most recent addition to the tornado museum, this display was also the ugliest—Kelli McCann's best fifth-grade, sidewalk-chalk effort at a prison, a twister, and a little cradle.

I reached into my back pocket and removed my cheat sheet. It had been so long since we snagged a visitor, I forgot most all of my fancy lines. I cleared my throat, peeked at my notes, and plastered a stupid smile on my face.

"Our town was once known for more than storms and babies dropping from the sky. Long before that night, Gullary meant lead—lead and zinc, but also chat, the pulverized, toxic leftovers we dug up and then dumped. Like nearby towns, mining placed Gullary on the map, and then blasted a hole beneath it.

"Sinkholes ate buildings. Slides trapped miners. And a bustling town nestled into the Ozarks gave up its soul. Fifteen thousand mining jobs packed up and left, along with the scratchers willing to drop into that hell."

I paused for dramatic effect and gestured around the museum.

"It happened all over. Treece. Cardin. Picher . . . where sky-blue Tar Creek turned red with iron. Contaminated. Poisoned. Dead. And when people leave, Feds always come. They declared our town a toxic waste site.

"But here in Gullary, a few hundred people remained. A few hundred very determined people, including my grand-parents. A handful of folks and a whole lot of chat.

"Those two hills, the chat piles you likely saw on your way in, still stand as reminder of what happens when you dig too deep. 'In Gullary, the past best stay buried.' Those were my granddad's words."

I moved on and tapped the black-and-white picture of four grim miners, emerging from their hole with their faces cov-ered in grime.

"Now, I mention Gullary's mining ghosts because it explains this town's reaction when the Feds first threw us a lifeline in the form of a new Supermax prison facility, SMX for short. Hundreds of the most violent criminals on earth moved into our neighborhood. You'd think it would cause fear.

"Not here in Gullary. We saw the promise of jobs, and lots of them. Soon we all relied on SMX—my ma was the cook—and Gullary was reborn on the shoulders of rapists and murderers." I scratched my head and shrugged. "Strange way to bring life back to a town."

My tourist couple exchanged glances, and the wife cleared her throat. "And then the tornadoes came?"

"Not right away, but yeah, we can't catch a break." I gestured toward the next photo, a snapshot of the largest funnel, taken by Greasy Jake while crouched behind his garage's dumpster. The twister bore down in the background while a hubcap took flight in the fore. Priceless.

"An F5," I said. "Nothing survives a direct hit from an F5."

"But those chat piles out there did. You did." Wife let her gaze travel my frame. "Is that how you, I mean, did that tornado bend your . . . oh, I'm not sure how to say it."

Husband grabbed her arm and glared. "Then don't. You don't ask about personal matters." He turned to me. "Sorry, your situation's none of ours."

I gritted my teeth, and crumpled up my lines. "No. Storms don't give kids scoliosis."

It was time to conclude this tour.

"The first of many tiny twisters struck at bedtime eighteen years ago, pushing most of the town underground. Our people survived that night, but the prison didn't. Usually, F5s take everything. But this one was different. It had . . . mercy. When that monster landed, it seemed bound and determined to claim only one thing, the complex. Once it wiped the foundation clean, it stopped on a dime and turned back the way it came. In the aftermath, the chat piles were undisturbed, but not one stone of this former building was left on another. The crews couldn't even find the remains of most of the inmates.

We needed jobs, so we rebuilt it, but the government cut funding, and SMX never reopened. Now here it sits. A fully operational Supermax prison that houses only this small tornado museum, and employs exactly one person: me." I opened the front door and peeked toward the courtyard. "Well, that's it."

I placed my mouth on autopilot. "If you've enjoyed your tour today, please consider a gift to Gullary's Tornado Gallery." I gestured toward the plastic, coin-collecting funnel. "Any contribution is mighty appreciated."

The gentleman smiled and dug in his pocket, pulling out two twenties. His wife gasped and slapped his shoulder, but he stepped toward me and shook the bills. "Life can't be easy all bent like that, and I want to tip you, but first, I've been curious about something the whole time. This entire joint is white and gray . . ." He pointed over his shoulder. "Except for that. What's behind the bright red door?"

I exhaled long and slow. For forty bucks, I'd tell him I wet the bed until twelve years old, and that I spent hours gawking at photos of Stormi. I'd name every drunk in town, and whisper the places they go when the moon is full. For a tip, any tip, I'd spill all of Gullary's secrets.

But I couldn't tell him what was behind the red door.

"Sorry." I shook my head and forced a smile. "You now know more about Gullary than some of its residents. Best keep one detail private."

He tongued his cheek, and gave the bills a final shake before stuffing them into his pocket. "Fair enough."

I stood in the doorway and watched my money walk out the main entrance—past the guardhouse, through the electric fencing—and vanish beneath the wide Oklahoma sky.

First visitor in a month, and so close to getting a tip for my time.

I sighed and shook my head. Describing pictures in a one-room tornado museum barely hinted at employment, but in Gullary, few eighteen-year-olds could boast of any income, so I never complained. Final exams and our upcoming graduation did little to brighten the future. Gullary was a house of mirrors. Everyone thought they knew a way out, but decades later, all the same faces remained.

I spun back into the museum and slammed the door behind me, breathing in the bought air. I peeked at the clock. 12:30.

"Lunchtime."

I lifted a tray from beneath the counter and removed the plastic wrap. Ma went all out today: fried chicken, mashed potatoes, gravy, and cranberries.

Too bad it wasn't for me.

I gentled aside my 35mm camera and grabbed my crushed brown bag, offering an exaggerated eye roll. Likely the usual: knockoff peanut butter and Aunt Josephine's tangerine jam.

I carried both lunches toward the red door and paused. This part of my job description never felt right. Stormi always said danger lurked where I was about to go, and I, more than most, knew the folly of ignoring her prophesies.

But in this matter, I had no choice.

Though heavy metal, the door swung open easily, and I slipped inside. Leaning into it with my knee, I slid a brick along the floor and propped it open. But that much steel had a will of its own. I stepped away and listened as the weight pushed that brick right out. It closed with a clank, and my shoulders slumped. I wouldn't be leaving the way I came in. There was no keyhole or handle—not on this side—and I stared down the well-lit hall.

"Locked in SMX. I don't get paid enough."

"That you, Jonah? You're late." Ahead, a pair of hands waved me nearer.

"Yeah. I got held up. A couple lost tourists wandered into the gallery." I marched forward, stopping in front of cell 117. Tres's cell.

"Boy, you know a geezer like me got needs. If you have visitors, they need to clear out of my house before twelve thirty. I thought we had that straight."

"Sometimes prisoners don't get their way."

Tres whistled. "Ain't that the truth?"

How do you tell museum visitors that the Gullary town council secretly keeps a guy locked up behind the red door? I'd never found the words to work it into my presentation, especially as I wasn't sure why myself. I asked Dad my first day; right after Ma handed me two dinners.

"Jonah, I'm not at liberty to discuss the matter. That's Circle business. But as the Max's only employee, your responsibilities include mowing the grass and feeding Tres, its only prisoner."

"At least tell me what he did. Am I feeding a serial killer? Some Hannibal Lector/*Silence of the Lambs* type? You do know I'm there alone with the guy."

"Do the job. I don't expect you to understand." Dad winced and slapped my back, as if I had a lot of growing up to do. "You're just a boy."

After that first shift at SMX, I locked up the joint and beelined it to Greasy Jake's Garage. Stormi was there, working late. Without pay.

"Just a boy, huh?" Stormi handed me her wrench and straightened. "Your dad's a piece of work." She folded her arms. "Ever seen such a beauty?"

"No."

I was supposed to be admiring the engine, but as usual my gaze was fixed on Stormi. She was my own age—at least that was our best guess, given her appearance upon arrival—however, similarities stopped there. There was a confidence that animated her words. She was free, free and wild. Gullary had no hold on her. It felt like she was here by choice, which made no sense. Whatever seed grows certainty had taken deep root.

"Jonah?"

I blinked free and shifted my gaze toward the hood. "It's a cheap V6 engine," I said.

"Look beyond that. She came to me as a monster. She's a kitten now."

Stormi was Jake's right hand. In truth, she was both of his hands. No car could hide its mystery ailments from her, and after two years of her dedicated employment, Jake owned the only garage in town and was a very wealthy man. Wealthy enough that he could spend his days with his new shoes kicked up on his new desk playing his newest video game while Stormi ran the place.

"Did you know there was a guy locked up in the Max?"

She reached for a rag and wiped her hands.

"Am I the only one who didn't? Why is he in there? I mean, what if he's some psycho person-eater who could hypnotize me and trick me into opening his cell—"

"He's not a zombie." Stormi took firm hold of my cheeks, then released. She bit her lip, dipped the rag in mineral spirits, and dabbed at the smudges on my face. "He's an old guy who's been there forever."

"What did he do?"

"I don't know. Something awful, I'm sure." She threw down the rag. "You need to feed him, right? You can do that. Just walk in, drop off the food, and walk out. Like you're feeding a puppy. Without the petting." She grinned and I didn't and she exhaled. "Listen, I don't know why he's there. I know it's for a reason, so don't, you know, do what you do."

"Which is what, exactly?"

"You listen to people and believe them and then you get hurt."

"So, I'm naïve." I stepped back and folded my arms. "You're calling me naïve. Just a boy. Same as Dad."

Stormi was silent and shifted on her feet.

"That's not me," I continued. "And it's not fair. You know I don't trust *him*."

"Well, your dad's a piece of work. I don't see how your ma puts up with it. But he's only one in a very big world."

I paused. "Connor!" Silly how triumphant I felt at the remembering. "I don't trust your brother either. So that's two."

Stormi leaned over the hood, her voice suddenly tired. "Add the prisoner to that list and you'll be fine."

I opened my eyes and shook free from the memory. I'd kept my guard up for about a week, but time slowly whittles away concern. Tres was perpetually good-spirited. I enjoyed his company. But Stormi's words plagued me when our visits became lengthy. Stormi was never wrong, while I rarely had ideas of my own. Ignoring her never sat well with me.

Tres smacked his parched lips. "What did Lizza cook on up? Oh, Lord!" His eyes grew. "It must be Thanksgiving. Is it Thanksgiving, son?"

I slid Tres's food into his cell and took my seat in the chair across the hall. We were in the only well-lit section of SMX. Here, locked behind traditional bars, a prisoner felt much less confined, unlike the rest of the units, where solid steel doors and a four-inch window were the norm. Tres flourished in minimum security, or so Dad said.

"No. But the thought of you must've brought Ma extreme joy. You are experiencing last night's leftovers, and the meal was incredible. I tried for a second helping, but she whacked my hand with a ladle. 'Jonah,' she said, 'you best learn now to leave some for the unfortunates in this world.' That always means you. Now, when it comes to me, Ma's extreme joy must disappear." I shook my brown bag in the air. "Peanut butter again."

Tres paused, his fork halfway to half a set of teeth. "Growin' boy like you? You know I'm willing to make a barter—"

"No, you go on. Remember, that's both lunch and supper. I can't complain. Besides, you don't own anything I need."

I glanced around Tres's cell. Bed, toilet, desk, books, and chessboard.

My chessboard.

A gift from Stormi, but I'd never learned to play. At least now it was getting use.

My gaze landed on Tres and I chewed and stared and chewed some more. I put him at seventy, but it never felt right to question. He was tall, and built with enough muscle to cause apprehension. Tres said he was nothing but a drifter; he said we were doing him a great kindness by providing him food and shelter. I couldn't figure out how a drifter could be happy locked up, living a solitary life, but here again I never probed. I rarely had the chance. Our lunch talks focused on only two people: Stormi and me.

"That girl of yours is comin' up near eighteen, if I'm right." Tres gnawed on a drumstick.

That girl of yours? I wish.

I took a mouthful of sandwich. "It's kind of hard to say, given that she didn't blow in with papers or a birth certificate. We'll go out for ice cream again on July fifth, seeing as Ms. P never sees fit to celebrate."

"Still." Tres swiped grease from his mouth. "I'm certain her actual eighteenth is coming up. Does she look it?"

"I don't really follow what you're asking—"

"Oh, sure you do, fool. Is she pretty?" Tres showed his teeth. "Like me."

I started to rock in my chair. "Well, pretty doesn't really touch it. I won't go into what *you* are, but Stormi—"

"Finish that, now." Tres scooted forward on his bunk. "You usually don't make it this far. But Stormi what?"

It's not like the truth would go anywhere; it'd bounce around a cell with an old man.

"If you could see her. She walks into a room, a packed room, and suddenly she's in hyper focus, and everyone and everything else blurs in the background. And then she looks at you, and her image gets sharper still. But you can't hold her gaze long, and just like that you realize you're gawking at her lips or neck or . . ." I cleared my throat. "Maybe I'll bring a picture sometime."

"I'd like that. Very much."

I stared off down the hallway. "She knows me, knows pretty much everything. Maybe everything."

"Everything? That's a poor stratagem. Strapping lad like you must have the ladies falling at your feet." Tres gently placed his tray on his bed, and his voice softened. "Trusting everything to only one puts a man at a disadvantage."

"Disadvantage? I know her better than anyone. And she shares everything with me too, so it's not one-sided, or not totally one-sided. I don't think." I glanced down. "But we're close. In every way except for . . ." A heavy sigh escaped. "Except for the way she's close to other guys."

It gets really quiet.

"But what should I expect, right?" I tried to straighten, and winced as my back screamed. "Why would she want to be with deformed me?"

Tres scratched his head. "What do you mean 'other guys'?"

I slapped the floor. "You need it spelled out? She goes out. A lot. And when those guys fill the locker room with their talk, I can't bear to stick around and listen. But based on the number of times her name flies around, I can only imagine she's probably not saying no too often. To anyone. Not that I know for sure, I mean, how could I know? No. Oh no." My fingers tingled. "Oh, God."

My eyes blurred, and I slowly lowered myself to the floor. The ringing in my ears overpowered.

A seizure was knocking on my door.

"Jonah, calm down, kid. I was just clarify . . . What's go . . . on . . . ?"

My hearing muddled and Tres's syllables fought through in staccato bursts. The chair slid away, and my body curled, fixed and fetal, on the ground.

I fought my fit for a while, like I always did. I searched for something that made sense, something clear, but when my vision failed and my right eye fell blind, I let the monster inside have its way with me.

Idiot seizure. Leave me alone.

It wouldn't, not for another twenty minutes of mouth-foaming, eye-fluttering misery. I was kidnapped, whipped by the brain meant to serve me. My hands clawed and my head jerked rhythmically against the tile floor.

I felt nothing.

But I heard.

Screams. Girl screams. Boy screams. Ghostly shrieks. A seizure had never brought such terror with it before.

And then feeling returned. A warm breeze swept over me, and the rhythm of my head slowed. Another minute, and I lay face down, gasping, my back aching, but my body and mind at rest.

The room stilled. My seizure had gone. But not my tears—they puddled on the tile.

"You okay, kid?" Tres's voice was gentle. "You done beat yourself up pretty good."

It would be minutes until my legs supported me, and I uncurled and stared at the ceiling. I touched my face, splotched with a combination of nose blood and peanut butter.

"I'll be all right. Happens once a week or so. Old Rickety decided to interrupt our lunch, is all. I'm surprised he hasn't taken me in here before now." I wiped my eyes and forced my head to the side, and frowned. In my distress, I had traveled clear across the hall. My shoulder pressed against cell 119, the one that neighbored Tres's. A chill worked its way around my neck and weaved down my twisted spine. I glanced back at Tres, his face visible in the mirror he held out through the bars.

"How'd I get over here?"

"You scooted, all jerky-like. Old Rickety? That was a seizure, right?" Tres set his mirror down on the table. "Why did you name it?"

I fired a glance into the empty cell, the one that spooks me whenever I pass. "You can't hate something that doesn't have a name."

"Oh, I don't know about that. I do know your brain and your bend must weigh as heavy burdens. I also know life ain't fair. These next days'll be hard on this town. Cryin' shame that a good kid like you should have to pay for what's been done." Tres clasped his hands on the outside of the bars.

"'What's been done'?" Even in a post-seizure fog, the words struck as ominous.

"Jonah, you've been right kind to me. Since your first day, you've treated me well. I took notice, son. It's been noticed. Remember that." Tres spoke quietly, so quietly I wasn't sure if his voice came from the inside or the outside of my head. "Don't be afraid."

Understand that in Gullary, biblical admonitions floated around like cottonwood fluff. Tossed liberally into earthly conversations, like table salt, so overused they lost their impact. Unfortunate, really.

"Maybe next time, let's keep our conversations about Stormi." I pushed up to a sit. "It's preferable to this little morbid path you're walking."

"You're right. I'm sorry, son." Tres's strong baritone returned. "But, now, get on up if you can. You done your piece with me, and the gallery needs ya. I'm figurin' you'll have a visitor waiting."

"Two tours in a day? Not likely." I raised myself to my feet, picked up the chair, and glanced at the mess on the floor. "I'll be back to clean this tomorrow. You okay with that?"

Tres smiled. "Oh, and next time you see her, tell Stormi hello, and, if you would, give her this." He opened his desk drawer and pulled out a necklace, gold and beautiful. He stroked it and then reached it out to me. "Seeing as I'm in here and she's not, I'm thinkin' she'd probably not accept it if'n she knew where it came from, but maybe if you was puttin' thought on a birthday gift, it could come from you. But it's your call." He sighed. "Nothin' asked, nothin' required."

I stared at the necklace. "It's really . . . wow, it's um . . . but how did you get it, and why would you, and all that?"

"Shut up and take the necklace."

"She'll know this wasn't from me. She always seems to know."

"Take it!" He closed his eyes, and his voice softened. "Try. For me. For you. While you can still head it off."

Looking back, Tres left a breadcrumb trail clear enough to follow through the thickest of the Ozarks. No, I don't reckon I could have pieced it all together, but I should have recognized the puzzle. Unfortunately, hurry, perception's greatest enemy, had me by the neck.

He dropped the necklace and a napkin into my hand. "You might want to use them both."

I sighed at the mess I'd made, and the mess I'd become.

"Say, kid, do me one more favor." He gestured at my chessboard. "Get your brainiac friend's next move—the quicker the better." Tres took a deep breath. "This match is takin' too long. It's been days since you've brought me Arthur's play. Not much else to look forward to, if you get my meaning." He walked over, lifted a pawn, and slowly waved it in the air. "We're entering the endgame, you know." He gazed into me and then closed his eyes.

"Who is?" I asked. "You and Arthur?"

"We all are, Jonah. We all are."

My exit involved a slow weave through the most controlled section of the prison to the opposite end, where the magnetic card in my pocket would free me through the service door. Though my vertebrae balked at the distance, I knew I could gut it through; I'd locked myself in before.

Which is why I knew the terror of cell 119. How could an empty cell create such dread? I hadn't a clue, but that chamber was evil, as sure as the day was long.

A bit of history: Reconstruction of the SMX had spared no detail. Following the twister, it was reborn, a twin to the original. The first prison had four wings, as did the second. The first, four courtyards, as did the second. The first, two hundred cells—two hundred sequentially numbered cells.

But here another breadcrumb fell unconsidered. The rebuild tweaked the cell numbers. There was no cell 118. It had been skipped, like floor thirteen of a hotel, and the oversized unit was given the number 119 instead.

A little thing. Probably an oversight. No big deal.

Except that the misnumbered cell always felt dark. Foul.

Chilling enough to send a post-seizure tremor through my body.

I lumbered away from Tres and the cell that haunted me, and emerged at the far end of the prison. It was a warm fifteen-minute walk around the perimeter back to the front entrance. I didn't travel it alone; those screaming voices still echoed in my head.

I shook them free and hurried to the museum door, which stood ajar.

I peeked inside. Stormi slid off the counter and swept back her hair, brushing back the few dark strands that clung to her lips. Her hair was wild—not unkempt, just wild—and her complexion tanned. Surrounded by all that smooth darkness, her white teeth glimmered. "I got here as fast as I could." She cocked her head and let her gaze roam my face. "Peanut butter again. Looks like I'm a little late."

"You're never late. Admit it: You were out here when I was seizing in there. You could've come in." I stared at her hard and unforgiving, noticed her penitent sadness, and kept on. I had a goodly reservoir of righteous anger. "If you had, there would be no blood and no peanut butter, and maybe I would have heard your voice instead of screams."

She exhaled, and my hot air balloon floated gently back down to earth.

"I can't figure out why Tres frightens you," I said. "He's locked behind bars. He's forever old. A puppy. You told me yourself."

She stepped up and wiped my chin with her thumb, her touch setting my body on fire. "You don't have to believe everything I say. Listen, can we get out of here?" Her face brightened. "I have a surprise for you, so grab your camera. I'm inviting you to a private birthday party."

That girl of yours is coming up on eighteen.

I bit my lip and peeked at the red door. "Your real birthday. You think it's coming up soon?"

"Today." She kissed my cheek. "Eighteen today."

CHAPTER 2

I followed Stormi out of SMX and round Windy
Road. A word on Gullary: US-59 brings you in, US-59 leads
you out. But if you're willing to risk your life, there were
plenty of smaller routes out of town.

One being Windy Road.

As the name suggested, it twisted its spongy finger deep
into the Springfield Plateau. Thin, overgrown with forest, and
blocked when the rains came, it was a path rarely followed. I'd
walked it as far as the Gullary-Green River split, though not
without considerable lumbar discomfort. Beyond that, though
only two miles from my home, the Windy went rogue and
became an uneven trail.

With a brain eager to rise up and throw me to my knees,
the river always seemed a safe place to stop.

"Keep up, Jonah! I'll be nineteen by the time we get there."

"How come suddenly you know your birthdate for certain?
Another prophetess moment? You never knew your birthday
before."

Stormi glanced back over her shoulder, smooth and tanned
in that green strapless top that hugged so well.

"No. This is different. This year I *feel* my birthday. I felt it when I woke up, and by noon there was no doubt." Stormi shrugged. "It's today."

How does anyone feel a birthday?

She reached the moss bridge over the Green, slowing to gloat with a voice full and free. "You're always falling behind."

I slowed further still. "If you'd told me we were going to walk into Arkansas, I'd have stolen the truck. I've no desire to hike that far."

Stormi gripped the bridge railing, her body swaying back and forth. Hair splashed down on those shoulders and once again I knew: I would follow my best friend anywhere.

"Then how far do you want to go on my birthday?" She cocked her head and licked those flawless lips.

Don't answer that. You always lose this game.

"Jonah?"

You listen, you believe, and then you get hurt.

"Are you talking distance, or are you talking how far, you know, well, when a normal girl asks a normal guy that . . ." My voice lowered to a mumble. "I don't mean that you're abnormal, but a person might think you were asking about something more personal or physical or . . ."

Her eyes were wide, but her face gave away nothing.

"You know, maybe let's forget this last minute. I thought maybe that was a real you-and-me question, but I can see on your face . . . I can't see anything on your face. Let's go to Arkansas."

It's hard to love your best friend. Over the years, the Line of Friendship is drawn, thickened, deepened, until it becomes a freakin' canyon. Maybe if I would have grabbed her hand early on, in kindergarten, before my back twisted and my brain rebelled. Maybe that would have built a bridge to get across.

But time solidifies the status quo. It was too late, and I was stuck on my side, lobbing idiotic emotions across the chasm, hoping she'd bite. I couldn't tell if she saw me as friend or beast or charity case, but it didn't matter.

I only needed her to stick around.

I raised the camera from my chest and focused the lens on Stormi. She smiled broadly, and I zoomed in and took a perfect shot. Definitely a bedroom-wall keeper.

"We're almost there, Jonah." Stormi's eyes were pure light. "The spot is right ahead."

She bounded across the river, turning to wait on the far side. I took a deep breath and approached the moss bridge, some twenty feet above the water. My head lightened. It would be a bad site for a seizure.

The river hadn't always caused dread.

Not when we were young. Second-grade young.

Strange that our parents let us wander as they did; seven years old and we had the run of town and beyond, though how far we strayed remained our secret. We loved the moss bridge for the elven realm we were certain lay across it, hidden deep in the forest. Like all kids in Gullary, we were fantasy junkies, dreaming of worlds far away. We watched *The Fellowship of the Ring* until we could recite the lines, until they were no longer fantasy, until they became our own. Stormi was Arwen from the House of Elrond, and I was her Aragorn.

I saved her from a thousand restless orcs, rescued her from Sauron's clutches time and again. And once, while splashing about in the river, my heel brushed against a small, smooth object in the sand. I dived down and emerged with a ring.

It was rusty, but we scrubbed it until it glinted silver in the sunlight.

"You found the Ring." Stormi's eyes grew. "The ring of power."

My thoughts always tilted a bit more toward reality. "I think it's just an old ring."

"No." She shook her head solemnly, and reached the prize back toward me. "It's yours to keep. When you're in trouble, you'll need it."

"Nah. Take it."

She thought a moment, and slipped it over her thumb.

The next day, Stormi arrived at the bridge and held out a necklace. "I'm giving this to you." It was her shark's tooth on a leather string.

"Why are you giving me your—"

"It's in the movie, stupid. Arwen gives Aragorn her necklace. It's like a heart."

"It's like a tooth."

She kicked my shin and tied the leather string around my neck. It never did come off.

After the discovery of the ring, our Hobbit dramas became more extravagant. Stormi would toss the ring from the bridge, and I would dive in after it, reviving hope and saving Middle Earth.

And then, July five happened. Stormi was eight, and I was late to our adventure. Ma had me cleaning my room, and I reached the bridge in time to hear the splash. Stormi had jumped.

I dove in after, because for all Stormi could do, the girl could not swim. I found her a foot beneath the surface and dragged her to shore.

She coughed and sputtered. "Get my ring!"

And I did. I saved both her and the world, which were basically synonymous.

In time, our Hobbit games faded, until last month.

"Remember when I used to throw my ring." Stormi had leaned over the bridge's edge. "You always found it."

"Yeah," I called up from the bank.

Stormi bit her lip, removed the old band from the finger it still rounded, and tossed it in. "Save me, Jonah. For old times."

"Seriously?"

She gave no answer.

I exhaled, stood, and waded gingerly into the river. Three steps, and the seizure took me, threw me back onto the bank. When I came to, Stormi had not moved. She stared down at me, her face disappointed.

"I'll get it." She dove and soon swam toward me, ring in hand. She never wore it again.

How far I'd fallen.

But now, eager to forget recent failures, I followed her. Old Rickety had mercy, and once again Stormi laughed and took off running. I set out in hot pursuit, a term you'd deem mighty generous had you seen my lurch. I stumbled around the bend and barreled into her.

I tried gamely to both keep her upright and hold myself vertical, but it was an either/or. My spine landed hard on a gnarled tree root.

Stormi knelt, wincing at my misfortune. "That was very sweet."

"Oh," I groaned. "The part where I crushed you or the part where I crushed me?"

"Both. But more than the crushing, you kept me standing."

There are few conditions that render a body more infantile than a bad back. Should you hear of someone complaining of the ailment, it ought to immediately draw forth all manner of sympathetic prayer. The pain is akin to a knife, plunged deep into bone and marrow, and then twisted, once and again. I tried to shift, to rise to an elbow, but the blade twisted, and I rejoined the earth. Stormi laid a hand on my chest. "Don't. Stay there." She lifted my head onto her lap, and gently stroked the dirt from my arms, my shirt. Her hair swished across my face while her hands paused above my heart.

Had this been the first time I'd felt her healing touch, I'd have endured agony and flipped over quick so as to hide the sudden and dramatic effect she had on certain personal parts of me, but I had spent considerable time with my head on her lap in the past, recovering from a seizure's sudden arrival.

This is because of her "knowing," and perhaps here is a good time to clarify. There is a knowing borne of experience. Old Gantry used fifty years of this variety of understanding to turn fishing on Lake Gullary into a pitiful affair. Those fish had no chance. Stormi possessed no such insight; she owned *foresight*, a frightening ability to see beyond experienced time. Her mind's reach into the future extended into most matters, but when it came to me, it stretched farther. She knew when Old Rick was coming, knew where I was, knew how to find me. Stormi saved my life multiple times after my brain threw me down in places wild and remote. Stormi was my soldier, the one battling the creature caged in my skull. Though I wanted her more than life itself, maybe it was best not to disturb our delicate friendship balance.

Even if her smile filled every pleasant dream.

Minutes later, the grip on my lumbar eased, and I hauled myself up. "Well, lead on. I don't know where we're going."

"We're here. This is it. This is where I wanted to celebrate. With you."

"On this path?" I lowered myself back down to my knees.

She glanced around, shrugged, and nodded.

"But we fell by chance. This can't be what you had in mind."

"I don't believe in chance." Stormi dug into the front pocket of her cutoffs. "You know what I want? What I've never had?"

No, but I'm willing to oblige.

She yanked out her hand. In it, a pink candle and a book of matches. "I want a wish. I'm eighteen, and you know my mom's paranoia about celebrations, and I can live with that, but a girl can't live without making a wish."

I grinned. "No, I'd say that's mandatory." I grabbed a stick and twisted it into the dirt, pressed the candle into the hole, and mounded dirt around its base. "Allow me."

Soon Stormi's eyes glinted in the light of a tiny flame.

"Now close your eyes," I said. "That's right. And make your wish. But you can't tell me what it is."

"Thank you for the tutorial." Stormi cracked an eyelid. "Did you really think I was going to?" She squeezed her eyes shut and blew.

Flame out.

"Can I tell you my wish after it comes true?" she asked.

While that seemed unnecessary, I acquiesced. I sat and watched the wisp of smoke rise from the candle and circle around Stormi. A minute later I risked her gaze. She stared at me and my eyes darted.

"Hold me."

I raised my brows and pointed at myself.

She nodded slowly.

I started to scoot near and then paused. "Have you ever knocked down dominoes?"

"What?"

"You know, set them up in a row and pushed the first over and then watched all of them tumble?"

"No, I haven't."

"That may be the problem. See, in dominoes, there is a trajectory. Things go down in a specific direction. You set 'm up, push the first, and the others fall in order. I think what you and I are missing is trajectory."

"Trajectory," she repeated.

I repositioned my spine, summoning all the courage I owned. "We're together a lot, you and me. A *lot*. But it feels like maybe some dominoes haven't been knocked down, some key relational dominoes."

"Relational dominoes."

"Yeah, relational dominoes. It's as if we've been playing a chance game like Yahtzee, when we should have been playing dominoes. It seems, at least from what I can tell, when a guy and girl spend this much time together there usually comes a first push, a noticing—you know, interest. That starts the trajectory."

"Fascinating analogy." She reached out and stroked my hair. "So first the push of interest. And then?"

"Well, then might come a more tangible event between them, maybe an event that makes the interest very, very clear."

"Hmm." She leaned forward, crawling slowly toward me. Her arms rounded my shoulders and she eased in, whispering, her lips brushing my ear. "Next domino, please."

I wriggled. "This is the problem. The next domino might be a bigger deal, you know, that they would remember for a long time. Sort of a key—intimate, if you want to use the word—only-between-them kind of domino. But between us, this domino won't fall over. And I get it, I mean . . ." Her warm breath caressed my neck and I gathered my thoughts, lost them, and picked up what I could.

"Why should you want to knock over a domino with a bloody, peanut-butter-covered me? It's just that when you say stuff like 'hold me,' this stupid domino can't figure out what you want from it, er, him, I mean me."

"I see. How about this? When she says 'hold me,' she wants you to hold her."

"And uh, that's it, right?" I bowed slightly, resting my forehead against hers. "Hold you. Our game ends in a holding pattern. Nothing falls after that?"

Stormi thought for a moment. "How long does it usually take for all the dominoes to fall?"

"Normally, it happens pretty quick."

"That's the problem," she said softly, and caressed my chest with her cheek. "Wait for me."

This was not fair. This was agonizing. If you've ever been banished to the friend zone—which holds confusions similar to the twilight zone—and the perfect object of your desire presses into you, you know this wasn't fair, not even on a birthday. But I didn't dispute. Right there on that path, for the first time, a piece of my own wish was granted, and I reached my arms around Stormi and drew her tight. As the sun stretched long shadows over the Ozarks, and the evening breezes brought with them the scent and rustle of hickory, I still held her. We lay on that dirt path, every now and then her body shifting against mine.

For a deformed epileptic, I guess this is as good as it gets.

Stormi nuzzled my neck and whispered words imperceptible. With anyone else, this would be a beginning, but with me it marked an end, and no matter how much my heart ached, I would not ask for more. She was at peace; I felt it, though I did not know why, and I daydreamed into a memory.

CHAPTER 3

I recalled last December's annual spinal measurement. One of the few times I'd ignored Stormi. The doctor had placed his hands on my twisted, leafless trunk.

"Twenty-one degrees forward, ten degrees to the left. The bend is accelerating. It's like I've been telling you." He scratched his chin and then his balding scalp, likely pondering all manner of delicate words. But he was speaking to Dad. No gentle message would do. "Jonah's back is a sight to behold. Never seen such a dramatic case of scoliosis."

That word always sounded sinister. Maybe the Latin name for a dying tree, like *E. deforma monstrus freakosis*, or some ancient curse like *Forevis Screwediosis Bendicus*.

"Please. Take the young man's warped back to Mayo." Dr. Only-Doctor-in-Gullary-Who'd-Never-Before-Seen-a-Back-Like-Mine exhaled hard in Dad's direction. "And best sooner than later. My guess? They'll crack it, rod it . . . who knows, maybe fuse it. I've heard young bone grows fine around rods and bolts."

Mom teared up and Dad frowned down and I tried my darnedest to sit straight. *Screwediosis Bendicus*? A rotten lot, but survivable. The thought of young bone—*my* young bone—fusing around parts from Lurvy's Hardware?

Pretty much the end of the world.

Turned out, Armageddon was quick in coming. The operation schedule was determined. And so was Stormi, right up until the night before the trip.

"Don't let him take you." Stormi pressed into my shoulder, shivering in the night. From where we sat on my family's front step, the moon hung orange and low, a glop of color clinging to a black canvas. It looked about to fall.

"Why are you telling me this the night before?" I peeked down at her face. My, Stormi had turned out beautiful.

"Because if you go tomorrow, if you go through with this, everything will get worse."

"Pretty cataclysmic sentiment, Stormi. You see the curve. I'm not thinking worse is possible."

She drew a breath and rose, lingered on the top step, staring across the lawn at her trailer. "Why do you think I landed here?"

"I was pretty young. I didn't get a chance to ask the tornado. But I'm not sure why we're talking about you right now. Can't we focus on my trip and how everything's going to be fine, and my spine is finally going to be straight—"

"It's not your stupid back I'm worried about." Stormi's voice was flat, emotionless.

"What then?" I jumped up and grabbed her shoulder. "Are they going to screw up some procedure and leave me vegetated?"

She turned, faced me, reached out, and held my cheeks in her hands. "Procedure? Oh, Jonah, you won't make it that far."

"Okay, this time I need you to explain your little premonition, 'cause you're talking death language, and if there's one thing I do not need to hear, it's death language, not the night before."

She squeezed me tight. "It's my turn to wait for you." Stormi backed down the steps, turned, and stepped slowly toward her trailer home. "Someday you'll return the favor."

I cupped my hands and called, "You'll wait for a happy, living me or a not-so-cheery, dead-type me?"

Stormi paused at her door. "Both." Her door clicked shut behind her.

From anyone else, I'd have chalked up her concern to over-protection. But when Stormi gave a prediction, you didn't bet against her, and you certainly didn't risk it.

Not after she brought flowers to Jason Murphy's house ten minutes *before* two military officers arrived to give the tragic news of Jason's sacrifice.

Not after she invited Ashley for a sleepover the same night a gas line explosion leveled her friend's double-wide.

You didn't question Stormi. I, especially, should've known.

Yet, pain tilts otherwise reasonable thought. Under duress, I understand why prisoners spill their secrets to the enemy. Unrelenting agony overshadowed Stormi's words, and I climbed into bed after she left, falling asleep to thoughts of flagpoles and skyscrapers—proud, straight things. I would soon be counted among them.

On Christmas Day, Ma kissed both my cheeks European style, and Dad and I climbed into the 1984 Ford F-150. We chugged six hundred mostly silent miles north to the Mayo Clinic in Rochester, Minnesota.

That trip to Minnesota was cold. Stupid cold. Inside and outside the truck.

My "correction" began with what hospital folks called a work-up—or, better put, *Testicus-up-the-Butticus*. There were CAT scans and PET scans and MRI scans. After all that scanning, we consulted with ten different doctors, none with a sense of humor, and each with the word *neuro* in his or her title. Meeting with *neuro*surgeons—people who sawed skulls and poked brains—made me want to vomit.

Those doctors put their humorless heads together and developed my "treatment plan." That term sounded so gentle, so nurturing.

Don't believe it. It's code for freaking *surgery*, likely the first of many. Turns out Dr. Only-Doctor-in-Gullary was dead-on. My treatment plan included a violent spine crack, five vertebra shaves, cartilage rips, a hip bone harvest, and finally a white-knuckled fusion. Add a few rods and pins and, in three months, I would be titanium straight.

Hallelujah.

The afternoon before found me lying in bed, fiddling with my 35mm, taking random shots of the bedpan and flower arrangement on my bedside table.

"Jonah Everett the third . . . that's a fancy name. You rich?"

A pleasant looking blond in green scrubs stood in the doorway, leaning on the handle of her mop.

"Sure," I said dryly. "Why not."

She smiled and peeked back out into the hallway. "I'm supposed to say 'Housekeeping.'"

"If I have my own housekeeper, I must be rich." I waved her in. "Feel free to keep house."

She moved easily about my hospital room, beautiful, effortless. She smelled good and paused often, most disconcerting. I felt her presence—not intense or weighty like Stormi's, but light, light and free, like so much fluff. It would be lying to say that scrub had no effect on me.

"I'm going to ask." She eased nearer the bed. "Why are you here? You don't look like the ones I usually see."

"How are we different?"

She quickly moved toward the door, shut it, and leaned her back against it before hurrying to my side. I instinctively made room on the bed and she plunked down.

"Well, for one thing, they don't have this."

And here she stretched out her hand and worked it through my blond hair. Honest. She touched me.

"And they sure don't have these." Her hand slipped down, stroking the contour of my shoulder, pausing on my bicep. "You're not hospital-typical."

"I'm not sick. But I'm here."

"You are."

At this point, I forgot my personality. Blame it on the fear of death. "Would you mind if I took your picture?"

"Go ahead. Wait, with that?"

"Yeah." I raised my 35mm to my eye. "Much better than a phone selfie."

What started as a dying man's last request morphed into an entire photo shoot. She posed, in ways both tempting and uncomfortable. After thirty shots, I let the camera fall to my side and leaned back.

"So, you're not sick." She tapped my forearm with her finger. "What are you, contagious?"

"Not contagious. Twisted."

The scrub smiled slyly, leaning over me. "I don't know if that's all bad."

"No, that's not, I'm actually—"

"Ahem."

The door was open, and Dad marched in.

I shifted, pushing myself higher. "Dad, meet . . ." I winced at my new friend.

"Hannah."

"Yes, Hannah. She's . . . well, she's apparently part of my spontaneous treatment plan. An important part, actually."

"Hmm," Dad said. "She looks to be at that."

I placed my hand on Hannah's. "Thank you for the encouragement. It was . . . encouraging."

Hannah's eyes twinkled. "You are most welcome, Jonah Everett the third."

She left and I fiddled with my shark tooth necklace, racked with guilt, as if I had gone behind Stormi's back. Feeling wanted is a powerful thing.

That evening, hours before the knife, I met with a bunch of other pre-surgical teens also in the final stages of their treatment plans.

Eight self-absorbed patients filed into a room and sat down in plush chairs to discuss the "emotions of the moment" and to celebrate our "oneness and inner wholeness." To everyone's credit, nobody said a darn thing for the longest time. With no facilitator, we sat there completely alone, and I thought that maybe this part of the treatment plan would work, since I could use a little peace.

My mind circled Stormi, remembered her leaning on my shoulder, and wished she were here. I replayed our last conversation. She'd never been wrong until now. Surgery definitely qualified as a procedure, and my wristband screamed full steam ahead.

I glanced around the circle, wondering if the other kids had their own Stormis, because none of them seemed present in the room. There were no jokes, and in the silence, a strange weight fell. Yep, I decided, it was a good group, every last one. Strange how the real possibility of premature death improves manners.

"What are we doing here?" said the kid sitting across from me.

Turned out his name was Gabe, who, like most gathered, was an epileptic awaiting brain surgery. Their seizures grabbed them and flung them to the ground too, or so Dad had said.

"Shut up. I'm searching for inner wholeness." This from Francis, a pretty girl from the face up. Another warped cottonwood, she kept peeking at me—or, more accurately, at my feet, since that was the direction of her gaze. This I only caught in my periphery, as I couldn't bear the sight of her straight-on. It's tough to gaze at yourself.

"How's that wholeness working for you?" Gabe smirked.

Francis shrugged. "I think I found some in my shoulder. My left shoulder. That feels pretty good right now."

"Ankles," another boy blurted. "My ankles are golden."

"Solid elbows." I touched each one. "Left, right. Solid. They screw up my elbows tomorrow and there's gonna be a lawsuit."

Ankles held out his fist and we bumped. "Where you from, Elbows? That's some accent."

"Nowhere, Oklahoma. We don't have an accent."

Ankles laughed. "Fair."

"Talk about wholeness, I have the healthiest back in the room. Wow, does my back feel good!" the nerdy guy with frames the size of Dad's windshield blurted, and the room fell quiet. He glanced around, clueless. "What? It does." He turned toward me. "My back feels awesome—Oh crap."

All eyes shifted to Francis and me.

"Well, Mr. Gold-Medal Back, my *brain* never felt better." I risked a peek into Francis's eyes. "How 'bout yours?"

"Perfect."

I laughed and she laughed and everyone else laughed and a nurse walked into the room and we all stopped laughing.

She sat down, found her somber face, and quickly had the room properly depressed.

"My name is Nurse Kalan, and it would be understandable if you kids were a little bit afraid. Your surgeries are major; I won't lie to you."

Why not? Now would be a really good time to tell a whopper.

She continued, "This time is your time to come together. To share your hearts."

My heart was another piece of me that worked perfectly. There would be zero chance of me sharing. The others must have felt the same.

Except for Holly.

Quiet until now, she burst to the fore.

"I'm Holly"—we all knew this from the dumb *Hello* badge she alone was wearing—"and this will be my fifth brain surgery. I'm not scared because it's my fifth. My first was scary though. Really scary. During my last surgery, I made it to the anesthesia count of ninety-six. That's kind of the game, and if any of you beat me . . . Well, none of you will, because you'll be out at ninety-eight. The anesthesia is seriously weird. Between that and the narcs, most people conk out or say something stupid before they even get to the counting, but not me, not this time. I'm going to lie there and count backward and still be lying and counting when I hit ninety-five."

She glanced triumphantly around the circle as if she had discovered her purpose in life. Ankles stared at me, his eyebrows raised. I shook my head. There was a girl in our midst living to reach ninety-five. Well, backward.

Nurse Kalan glanced at me. "Jonah? I noticed your response as she shared. Care to share *your* thoughts?"

"About Holly? No. You know, I hope she makes it tomorrow. To ninety-five, I mean." Nobody spoke. They all kept waiting and waiting, and they were probably just thinking about my perfect elbows, and I shouldn't have felt compelled to say any more on the eve of a near-death experience, but their eyes wouldn't shut up, so I said it. I thought of Stormi's words and I said it.

"I don't want to die."

And like that, Gabe flung forward. He hit the ground with force, his eyes rolled back, and he started to seize. It was fish-floppin' something. Kate, seated on my right, must've felt an intense kinship with him, because she joined him in a communal jerk-and-writhe session on the floor.

Now, epilepsy is not contagious, but I tell you this spectacle shook me. Ankles and Francis and the nerdy guy, they all dropped to their knees. Were they helping? Was everyone taking the oneness thing to extremes and seizing? I closed my eyes and listened to Nurse Kalan call for calm. Her voice muddled, morphed into gibberish, and my fingers tingled. A metallic taste filled my mouth and a ringing strengthened inside my ears. I tried to stand, to flee, but my legs were no longer my own and I struck the ground, feeling nothing.

A felled cottonwood, having his first seizure.

When I came to, I was gowned and bedded. Dad stared down at me with venom, quickly lowered the rail, and began to dress me, groggy as I was, in my own clothes.

"We're leaving."

It was all he said to me; all he said to the nurses and the doctor who attempted to dissuade him.

Dad had come to get me fixed, and this place had not only stolen his money, it had doubled his troubles. Three days after Christmas, he led me out into the frozen Minnesota night, helped me into the truck, and the next day we were back in Gullary.

I had two more seizures on that ride home, and following the second, miles from the Oklahoma border, I thought to tell him of Stormi's words. But it was too late. I'd already paid the price of ignoring her prediction.

Ma greeted us at the door, frowned at my back, and drew me close. "I'm not sure I understand."

"Doctors," Dad hissed, flinging his keys onto the table and vanishing into the back room.

I stood in front of my mother, watching her cry. I tried to straighten, but it hurt and I wasn't sure that it mattered anymore.

"I'm a monster," I said quietly. "Stormi won't want anything to do with me."

"Oh, honey, you're the most peaceful child I know."

"Wait," I whispered. "You haven't seen the nightmare."

Stormi shook me back to the present. "Off the path, Jonah. Quickly."

We crunched into the forest of hickory and oak and crouched behind a fallen log.

"I liked it *there*. Why are we here?" I whispered.

She shook her head, and I rolled my eyes.

Five minutes. Ten minutes. Then voices. Deep and hushed, men's voices joined the symphony of frogs and crickets from down the trail. The trudging of feet crackled the bracken, approaching, walking back toward Gullary.

Sun gave way to moon, and night shadow stole their faces from me, but it didn't matter; I knew these voices well.

"You know my stance on the matter. He doesn't need to be stayin' in Gullary no longer." Mr. Cartwright. "Nothing he said would hold weight."

"He does no harm inside. Can't be sure of anything if we let him out." Dad. *Dad?*

He continued. "Haste never provided us any benefit. It's why the mess started in the first place." Their feet paused on the holy ground where I'd held Stormi, and then three more men gathered. "I don't hear from Jonah that Tres is complaining. I say if it ain't broke—"

"And Stormi. What of her?" Men murmured and Cartwright's voice lowered. "My Gina says she's unnatural."

"Do we have a law against that?" Dad asked. "What would you have me do?"

"Many things can be done. Have been done." Mr. Cartwright pulled Dad nearer. "Shoot, I know Jonah's taken a likin' to her. And heaven knows that boy deserves some good his way. I'm startin' to think he's the reason you don't act."

Dad grabbed Cartwright by the shoulders. "I don't act because Stormi's done nothing wrong. Unexplained intuition is no reason for concern. You're on a witch hunt, and, David, I know why. It hurts. But what's done is done. We can't go back."

"Dang you, acting all innocent, Mr. Mayor! You've got chat under your fingernails like the rest of us." Cartwright shoved Dad, and then along with Mr. Tennyson pounded away across the moss bridge over the Green.

Dad swiped his hand over his head. "Men, this is going to get worse before it gets better. But the Circle must stay united. You understand the importance of this?"

Murmurs and nods, and together, three men plodded into the night.

Stormi took a deep breath. "Now would be another really good time to hold me."

I did, and she squeezed my arms tightly around her. What struck me as odd must've sounded a deeper chord in Stormi. An hour of mosquito-slapping minutes passed before she finally broke free. "It's safe now."

"What were they talking about? Unnatural? You haven't committed any crimes." I forced a chuckle, and my face hardened. "Have you?"

Stormi looked at me with those piercing browns; it was a sad look, both hopeful and resigned. The same look I got from Ms. Aldermaky when I failed trigonometry.

"Not yet."

"Not yet?"

She took my hand and pulled me back onto the path. I thought about that answer clear back to Gullary.

Stars appeared in the east, while the sun gave up one last streak of gray across the western sky. The lone cloud hovering above the hills caught the glint and whispered pink around its edges—a lot of beauty floated over our angry town.

"And why were they talking about Tres?" I asked. "Do you know about that?"

She hugged me and whispered, "Thank you for my birthday wish."

Birthday. Oh, birthday!

"Stormi, I have questions about what I heard, but I'm setting those down for now."

"Thank you."

"Yeah, no problem." I squinted, and rocked. The lie I was aiming to tell and the gift I was thinking to give were both out of character. "I'll be straight with you. I wasn't certain when your birthday was coming—we never knew before—but I thought I better be ready."

I dug in my pocket and pulled out the necklace. "It's real gold, I think. I thought it would look pretty on you, if you want it. I mean, I want you to want it—the necklace, that is. Oh, here."

I dropped the necklace into her hand, and she examined it for a long time, her face unreadable. Finally, she nodded. "Yeah, this is right." Then she exhaled, long and slow. "Put it on me, would you?"

"Sure." I fumbled with the clasp and her hair and the feel of her neck, but in time, I achieved my goal. "I think it's really good on you."

Stormi stroked it and stared toward SMX. "I'm scared, Jonah. It's like this whole town is holding its breath. A storm's coming, but I can't see it. Why can't I see it?"

"A storm? A funnel?"

Stormi winced. "I think worse. See you Monday morning, Jonah." She jogged away toward our trailer park.

I kicked at the dirt, experiencing none of Stormi's usual afterglow. In its place was dread, an anxious claw that ripped at my thoughts.

Cartwright. Dad. Stormi.

Not yet . . .

Worse?

CHAPTER 4

Sunday was dark.

Dark clouds billowed overhead. Dark questions ran through my mind.

It was dark with the memory of Dad and Mr. Cartwright in heated debate. Mr. Cartwright was a "bag o' wind," even Ma broke Christian charity to say so. But the fact that I had been involved in the debate sat sour with me, as did his flimsy concern for my well-being, which could blanket the truth no more than plastic wrap over a pig.

Mostly, Sunday felt empty because I didn't see Stormi.

I spent a fair piece of the morning gazing alternately at the hundred-plus photos of Stormi plastered on my walls and out my bedroom window at the Pickerings' trailer. As self-absorbed as I admittedly was, I worried all the more about Stormi in that double-wide. This because Connor lived there, and where I had trouble speaking clearly when Stormi was near, Connor expressed his perverse passions with ease.

He wasn't safe. I told Stormi as much.

"I know," was all she'd say.

So, on days when Ms. P had the 5 a.m. at Sophie's Diner, I watched, knowing nothing but Stormi's knack for the prophetic would keep her from harm's way.

"Sorry, Mr. E!"

Connor's voice cut through the open window, and I frowned and scampered to the front of our trailer. I cracked the blinds.

There was Dad, tossing a baseball to Connor.

I loved baseball.

They stood thirty feet apart, nodding and firing. Nodding and firing. Their gloves swallowed each ball with a thwack. I tried to leave, but I couldn't pull free from that stupid window.

Couldn't take my eyes off my happy dad. My happy, talkative dad.

"You've got a good arm, Connor. You're a strong kid—young man, I should say."

Thwack.

"You know, son, I forget how much I miss this."

Son?

Thwack. I heard Connor's throw strike Dad's glove. *Thwack.* And I felt Dad's words nail my gut. *Thwack.* And I thought to dig for my mitt and join them, to show them I could play. That I was worth playing with. That I wasn't some cripple.

"You know, son, I'm heading out fishing tomorrow." Dad gestured toward our trailer with his head. "Can't really risk him on open water. Have any interest?"

Thwack.

I retreated from the glass, the sound of the ball and Dad's words tossing about in my brain. *So, Dad, you found a replacement.*

I hauled my defective self back to my bedroom. Ten minutes later, a knock at the door. I made no move to answer.

Dad peeked in. "How long are you planning on eyeing our neighbors?" He plunked beside me on the bed, mitt still on his hand.

I boiled. Even before I saw him with Connor, Dad had that effect. All my classmates had long ago snipped their umbilicals, but not me. Not with the seizures. Without a driver's license, I needed Dad to shuttle me, Ma to buy my medicine, both of them to speak gently when Ol' Rick took me at home. Yeah, I needed them—hated needing them. I found rage much easier to bear than shame.

"You know . . ." Dad leaned into my shoulder—granted a fatherly gesture, but I was simmering and muscled his weight off me. "We live too close for you to ogle the day away. That type of surveillance isn't healthy." He glanced at my photos, the ones that captured every nuance of her. That's what I was, a nuance collector.

"Not sure your obsession with her is healthy either."

"Neither is *Connor's*, your baseball buddy. And you know his sick thoughts," I hissed.

Dad gently set his mitt on the floor and folded his hands. Two minutes passed. Then five. I peeked over at the man. He exhaled slow and loud, and then tousled my hair.

It takes a fair piece of energy to hate a person for any length of time. Maybe if this had been the first time I'd seen them together, I could have stoked the fire, but it wasn't and I calmed.

With the anger went my wonderings about the secrecy and mystery of the night before. I was with Dad. A jerk sometimes, yeah, but as decent a dad as could be found in Gullary.

I tracked a silhouette, followed closely by a larger shadow, moving behind the Pickerings' kitchen shade.

"Oh, I know Connor's a scoundrel." Dad chuckled and lowered his head. "I see it each time he mocks you. And believe you me, if I hear of that young man causing trouble in there, I will . . . well, I'll force the Circle to move its hand. How's that?"

The Circle. Five men with the authority to pass judgment on the citizens of Gullary. My father was the unpaid mayor, but it was his position in the Circle that gave him power.

Dad often told the story of an out-of-control former mining town and Granddad's solution. A Circle with the town's blessing to act as judge and jury. With the SMX at their disposal, there was no need to involve the courts or outsiders. Gullary could take care of its own problems.

The Circle, accountable to no one, was effective, and soon there was no crime in Gullary, a source of pride even today. Gullary still did not employ a single police officer.

Dad's arm rounded my shoulder, tried to straighten my spine. "But I don't think we'll need to get involved. Time's on Stormi's side. The two of you are weeks from setting school behind you. I don't figure she'll stick around our quiet town after graduation." He paused. "Do you?"

The room was silent. A little too much so.

"What's wrong with Gullary?"

"Oh, nothing. I'm not saying that. It just seems like a young lady with so much going for her wouldn't find much purpose here." He gave my chest a thump. "Best let her go now. People like Stormi have a bigger place in the world. You'd do her a favor to tell her that."

Bigger place than me, huh?

"Why do you think she landed here?" I asked.

"Ma would say Providence, but there are other forces at work in this world."

I rubbed my face, frowned. "Like what?"

"Oh, painful forces without names. But they come without warning. There are times when life is going well, when you're headed in a wonderful . . ."

"Trajectory?"

"Exactly right, Jonah. A wonderful trajectory. And from out of nowhere, the unbelievable happens, and all you love gets turned upside down. You keep breathing. That's all you can do." His voice trailed off. "Keep breathing."

I felt certain that one of Dad's unnamed forces, thick and weighty, had settled in my bedroom.

"Now come on." He forced a smile, and gently backhanded my shoulder. "Mom'll be back from church soon, and I promised her the place would be spotless. That's a two-man job."

Spring cleaning took the rest of the day, but I glanced through the curtain each time I strode by the window. Someday Stormi would need me like I needed her, and, once again, Aragorn would be there.

CHAPTER 5

If Sunday was dark, Monday was flat-out inky.

Rain fell in sheets, and I splashed through mud puddles, bounding up the Pickerings' steps. I raised my hand to knock, but never struck wood. Stormi burst out, slamming the door behind her.

"What's going on?" My, but she was shaking.

"Do you think your dad, your mom, might take me in?"

I squinted. "What's he doing to you?"

"Do you think they'd take me in now?"

"Ma took in that stray German shepherd last year, so I don't see her objecting. Dad would be tougher, but if there was a reason." I paused. "You have to tell me. Is there a reason?"

Stormi gathered herself straight, offering a mighty body shake. Then composure returned.

"Well, let's give it some thought. Connor isn't bearable any longer." Stormi reached out her hand, and let the rain splash against her palm. "Beautiful day." She squeezed my forearm. "Get me away from here."

Again, the door flew open.

Connor stared at Stormi. Of all the emotions a soul can string together, contempt and want are the most terrifying. I tell you, that is what I saw. He turned those eyes toward me, and good old-fashioned disgust took over. "So, Stormi, we're done, huh?" An evil heart says those words while looking at another. "That was all?"

"We never started. We never will." Stormi's hand worked its way into mine, and Connor's jaw tightened.

"Hey, Fish. No flopping yet, huh? Well, the day's young."

"I, I don't—"

I never stuttered, unless I was near a Pickering. Stormi, out of adoration. Connor, from sheer hatred.

"What's that?" Connor leaned forward, bent down. "I missed what you said. Were you talking to me or the ground?"

My mouth opened, shut, and I shook my head. Connor was twenty-one. Connor was an idiot. He had no job, unless alcohol consumption could be considered an occupation. But Connor had good looks on his side, and in Gullary that stood for something. I'd seen most every girl in town climb into his truck. Except for one. The one he couldn't have.

The one I knew he wanted most of all.

Connor reached for Stormi's arm and she recoiled.

"Easy, sis. Why don't I drive you to school? Heck, Hunchie can come too. We'll throw the beast in back."

Stormi spun me around and ducked under my umbrella. "Let's go."

We left slowly beneath the pattering of raindrops and the occasional peal of thunder, and though Stormi relaxed, I admit the exchange had wounded me. Those for whom you have no regard shouldn't know the ways to skewer your heart, but with a word, Connor Pickering could leech blood like no other.

"Finals today." Stormi broke the silence. "World History and Psych. Should be passable."

"For you." I glanced over and noticed that she still wore the necklace, the one I gave her. "Hey, you're wearing the—"

"Connor saw it and went a little crazy. He guessed who it came from." She touched it gently. "I think this gift might cause both of us some problems. Do you want me to lose it?"

"It's not the necklace he hates. It's the you-and-me, right?" She said nothing.

"And I can't lose that."

Stormi leaned her head on my shoulder. "He can't figure us out."

"Nobody can." I paused. "Neither can I. Everyone stares at perfect you—"

"Not perfect."

"And then they look at *Deformicus flopicus fishicus*—"

"I hate when you do that stupid Latin thing."

"Point is," I said, "you can obviously spend your time with anyone you want and you pretty much hang with me. Someday, possibly, you'll tell me why?"

Maybe I didn't raise my tone at the end of that sentence. Or maybe she didn't hear me beneath the splat of raindrops overhead. Either way, she left my question dangling unanswered. "You know," she straightened, "we're a little early to head to the bus stop. Let's take the long way, around the chat pile."

I shrugged, and we huddled and walked, listening to the pound of straight-down rain bouncing off the umbrella.

We reached the first heap and Stormi grabbed my hand. "Hold up here."

She stared at that pile, ten stories tall and mixed with fine tailings. When it rained, those tailings traced grooved streams down the mound.

Stormi peeked down at her feet, at the toxic pool forming around us.

The slop filled my shoes. "You, uh, you want to keep standing in a poisonous pond?"

She shushed me with her finger and kept staring at the ground.

She's unnatural.

The words popped in, and I pushed them out. Unusual, maybe, but not unnatural.

"Do you ever feel there's something you should be doing?" Stormi stared straight ahead. "Something important? Do you ever feel like you're wandering through life, walking in circles, running from something, when right in front of you is this big thing?"

"Like a chat pile?"

She glared.

"Sorry," I said. "No, I, uh, I don't. But you'll figure it out. You always do. Even Dad thinks so. He says you're about to leave." I hadn't planned on bringing Dad into this, but he sort of fit. "Are you, you know, leaving Gullary?"

"Yes."

I kid you not; right here a rumble of thunder shook the sky.

What do you do when half of your heart sprouts legs and decides to walk out the door? How does half a person live?

"Where you going? Is it far?"

"From you? Not so far." She stepped out of the sludge and shook her feet. "It's time. We better get to the stop."

We walked to Washington Ave. and swung onto 2nd Street. In the distance, the bus stop was alive with drippy laughter. A puddle fight beneath a lightning storm. The senior class was soaked, except for Gina and Yolanda, who stood on the far side of the street.

Such was school for seniors in May. It kicked the maturity level back a few years. Which probably explained the rash of parking lot vandalism at school the previous week. Which absolutely explained the principal banning all students from driving to finals. Which unfortunately meant a special, early bus had to be sent to Gullary solely for the senior class.

Which was the reason for the impromptu water fight happening at the bus stop.

We eased up, and Stormi squeezed my forearm. "I no longer need the umbrella, Jonah."

I frowned and stepped away, still thinking about her departure. Rain fell hard on Stormi's upturned face, and she closed her eyes. She always said she listened better beneath clouds, and if true, whatever she heard today would fall loud and clear.

The bus to Waxton-Gullary Senior High hydroplaned to a stop in front of us, sending a swath of water onto jeans and bare legs, but nobody cared.

Especially Stormi.

We boarded, all except for my friend, who stood as a statue, palms raised, jaw set.

Unnatural.

Hank, the bus driver and a stickler for time, offered two honks. Late to school was forgivable. Late for finals, a different matter.

"Commune with the world after you graduate!" Hank held a newspaper above his head and poked his baldness out the bus door. "I give you ten seconds and then I'm leavin' without you."

She didn't move.

"Stormi!" I hollered out the window. "Come on!"

Hank turned to me. "Sorry, Jonah. Whatever's gotten ahold of her can't throw me off schedule."

I sighed, the brakes hissed.

And Stormi jumped in front of the bus.

"Whoa!" Bus brakes squealed.

Stormi leaped around and slapped the accordion door, which quickly opened. Chuckles faded to strange silence. Stormi hopped up, scanned our faces, and rubbed her own.

"All of you, off the bus," she whispered. Her breath was heavy, and she grabbed my arm, her voice gaining strength. "Off the bus! Everyone!"

"That girl needs medical attention." Hank levered the door shut and pulled out. "Enough theater. Sit down."

Stormi stared at me, wild-eyed. I knew what she was asking.

Right now, I'd sure appreciate a normal best friend.

I took a deep breath and walked up the aisle. "No, Hank." I jammed my foot on the brake, and again we screeched to a stop.

"Foot. Off. My bus." Hank reached down and lifted my leg.

"Why not open up? Give the kids who want to get off the chance."

He squinted, massaging his temple. "You're letting affection warp good sense. Mayor's going to hear of this."

"I know. Believe me, I know."

Hank smirked and opened the door. "Well, I remember a time when I would've done the same for a girl. Been a few years now."

Stormi quickly walked down the aisle, touching the shoulder of every classmate except for Gina, who swatted her with a math textbook. When she again reached the front of the bus, her voice was calm and settled and held more authority than I thought possible.

"I will tell you one last time." She pointed at the door. "Get off this bus."

Her eyes turned terrible, so terrible that I almost didn't recognize her. So terrible that seventeen kids risked failing finals and stepped into the rain. When finally the bus did pull out, only one face remained pressed against the glass. Gina Cartwright.

It was the last time I ever saw her.

⌇

"Cat Jones had a view of the whole thing." My legs felt weak, and I slumped down against the cell opposite Tres's. "You know the pole bridge over Limon River? How that turn onto it comes out of the blue? Well, due to the rain, Cat was shutting down his irrigation, and our bus came screaming by fast. Way too fast, given conditions. Cat jumped the fence and stepped onto Washout Road in time to see the bus squeal, misjudge the right, crash straight through the old fence, and drop from view. Cat hauled after it and peeked down into the river. The bus landed on its head. Hank, Gina, they didn't live."

Tres stared at his dinner tray.

"Only one kid on that bus?" His voice sounded far away. "That was a stroke of fortune."

I shook my head and tapped the floor slow and rhythmic. "That was the unnatural part."

Tres's gaze shot up. "Some got off before, didn't they?"

"Some."

"And it was Stormi." He whispered, "She knew."

"I can't find her. Haven't seen her since. The rest of us got off that bus and drifted back into town. But not Stormi. She wandered after the bus, crying, I think. Stormi never cries." I sighed hard and pointed at his tray. "If it wasn't for her, there'd be no chili in your cell."

Tres stood and paced. "There shouldn't be chili in this cell," he muttered. "That crash finally would've ended it." He pounded the wall.

"Ended what? My life? Yeah, it would have. It would have wiped the senior class of Gullary off the face of this earth. And you seem to be taking the accident's side." I stared at Tres. Maybe he'd been locked up so long, he misunderstood key portions of my narrative, but I still thought seeing me alive would provide him a little happiness. "It's strange. Walking around today. Coming here today. It feels almost wrong."

Tres sighed. "Here." He shoved Ma's cooking back into the hall. "I ain't hungry no more, and you deserve a good meal. You were on death row, all right, and Stormi done issued a last-second pardon."

Tres opened his drawer and pulled out a sheet of paper, ripped it in two, and scribbled a quick note. He glanced at the rip, shaved little bits off the torn edge, and held it up to the light. "Close enough. For you. Pocket it and set your eyes on it later. After things calm down 'round here."

I rose and nodded, took the note, and trudged slowly toward the red door.

"Hey, Jonah!"

I stopped but did not turn. "Yeah."

"I am mighty glad you got off the bus."

I closed the red door behind me and glanced around the gallery. Another ripped note, this one from Stormi, rested on the counter.

Need to get away for a few days.
Please, come see me.

Take the birthday path to our place.

I lumbered home and into my room, where I began a frantic stuffing. Extra clothes, wool hat, and a flashlight all went into my pack. Who knew how long we'd stay?

"Jonah."

I spun around. Dad and Ma stood in the doorway, their faces somber.

"Where is she?" Dad asked.

"She? Can you be a bit more specific?"

"Jonah, not the time for that."

"Kinda is. Stormi, then?"

Ma walked in, glanced at my pack, and sat on my bed. "There are some questions that beg answers. And right now, I think she is the only one who has them."

"I don't follow."

Ma started to speak, but Dad shushed her and took a step forward. "David Cartwright lost his daughter in a bus accident that, by all accounts, Stormi had foreknowledge of." He glanced at her photos covering my wall and stuffed his hands in his pockets. "This is no small thing. How did she know? Unless she knew who meddled with the brakes, Jonah, she could not. We both know she lives in an . . . unstable environment."

"Brakes fail. By themselves. No meddling required. And buses lose control in storms. This isn't the first time she's predicted a tragedy." I paused. "Wait, you said 'unstable environment.' You're saying Connor did it."

"More likely—and don't take this wrong—it was Stormi herself. Greasy Jake confirmed that she worked on that bus in his shop not more than a week ago. Mr. Cartwright is convinced she's the one."

Of all the stupid sentences my dad had strung together over the years, these were so far afield I could hardly speak.

I straightened as much as I could and walked toward my father. "You should be thankful for what she did this morning. She saved the entire class. She saved me."

He winced, and I wanted to smack him.

"Speaking of you, son, from your classmates' reports, it sounds like you had a hand in the proceedings as well."

"Well, yeah, I stopped the bus by stomping on perfectly good brakes. Can we agree that's a good thing?"

"I think what your father is trying to say is that he needs to know who knew what, and how they knew it." Ma sighed. "Please, where is she, Jonah?"

I peered around my room, thinking on what to share, what to hold. "I'm going to see her now, and in a few days we'll come back. And when we do, you can talk to her." I lowered my voice. "Stormi's done nothing wrong. Unexplained intuition is no reason for concern." I peeked into Dad's eyes. "Isn't that how it went?"

Dad glanced sharply. "Yeah. That's how it went." He folded his arms, and the muscles in his jaw tensed and then loosened. "If you can convince me that your return will be imminent."

I dug in my pocket and yanked out a note. "Doesn't sound like I can convince you of anything, but . . ." I unfolded the sheet and flattened it over my knee. It wasn't Stormi's handwriting. "Oh, wrong note." Stormi's came out next, and I laid it on my desk.

Dad read the words. "Her birthday? I didn't know."

"Neither did I."

He pushed his hand through his hair. "All right. I'll appease David. I trust a private message from Stormi to you reveals her plans. But you may not leave before the funeral. All the Everetts will pay their respects to Gina. It's only right. Stormi can wait."

I stared at my pack. "But I can't contact her. There's no reception at the . . . You know what? Fine. Deal."

"Deal." Dad exhaled hard. "Now can I see the other note?"

"It's not from her," I said.

Dad raised his eyebrows.

"What?" I frowned. "It's not!"

He reached out his hand.

"I'm an adult. You can look at it, but next time trust me a little. I haven't read it yet myself." I threw it in his direction.

Dad bent over, scooped it up, and placed the sheet below Stormi's. "Deceit helps nobody, Jonah. Has she given you still more?" He tongued his cheek.

I walked to the desk, reached down and flattened the pieces of paper. The tear lined up perfectly. It was more than the same note; it was the same sheet. Given to me by two different people.

"But that can't be." I leaned over the words. "How did Tres get the other half? I saw him rip it and write it. And she won't go near him."

"Tres. You got the bottom lines from Tres?" Dad glanced at Ma and then back to me. "Did you tell him what happened?"

"Not that specific detail. He couldn't have known the number."

Dad spun and strode out of the room. Ma placed a trembling hand over her mouth, stroked my head, and then followed him out.

I blinked and reread the entire note.

> Need to get away for a few days.
> Please, come see me.

> Take my birthday path to our place.

> I should never have saved any of those
> eighteen kids.

> It would have been a fair trade.

> I didn't do my job, and that's because
> of Jonah.

CHAPTER 6

I woke early to the crisp lightness of a blue sky, a hinting at the clear day to come. But it did not feel clear. I grabbed my camera, hoping to take some shots, eager to find beauty through my lens and return to normal. But as I stepped out the trailer door, the weight of some unnatural fog settled over me. It turned out that I wasn't the only one.

Confusion surrounding the accident drew Gullary's students together.

Signs and banners sprung up outside houses, on storefronts.

WE ARE GULLARY

REMEMBER GINA

Truth be told, nobody cared much for Gina while she drew breath, and it pains me now even to mention it. Death muddies the realities of life. Unexplainable words began to circulate about her final moments on this earth, words recounting heroic actions and steadfast convictions. Had she not remained resolute, while the rest of us fled the doomed bus? Like a captain, sacrificing her life as her crew escaped on lifeboats, wasn't that Gina?

The high school called it quits three days early in light of events; final exams were administered via the postal service.

That day before the funeral, I saw all but two of my class-mates: Gina and Stormi.

The senior class floated aimlessly through town in small patches beneath that cloudless sky. What were we doing? Why were we wandering? I can't say, except that whenever I saw one of the fortunate ones who exited the bus, I knew they felt as I did.

We were the walking dead. Those who should not be alive. Mortality had come to Gullary in search of victims and, finding only two, decided to take up residence. It clouded my thoughts, troubled my dreams. None of us knew how to handle it.

Least of all me.

I couldn't stay inside the museum, and after making a silent six a.m. food delivery to a sleeping Tres, I locked the gallery and shuffled through town, hoping to meet my class-mates. Usually my mockers and tormenters, the sight of them held no dread; without Stormi to make sense of my feelings, isolation was my only enemy.

Strange. One life ends and the living cling to each other all the more.

Wally, six foot seven and the closest thing Gullary had to an athlete, hailed me from behind while I meandered down Main Street.

I stopped, and he jogged up to me. "Jonah, I, uh, thanks, man. Yeah, that's it. No, thank her too."

I couldn't remember the last time Wally had spoken to me. It felt good, and for an instant, I mattered. Had I not been the one to slam the brakes? To plead our case before Hank, and save everyone but Gina? But pride is fleeting, especially when unjustified. It had been Stormi, and Stormi alone. Had I been alone, we'd all be dead.

"I'll tell her, if I see her." I glanced over his shoulder. Carly and Madison fast approached, their faces puffy and red.

A word on Carly and Madison: They existed at the top of the food chain. Girls, Stormi excluded, fought and scratched for the pair's approval. Guys seeking bragging rights hungered for more than that.

Both gave Wally a hug, long and real, and then turned to me. Awkward moments ensued.

"Can't stay inside today," Carly finally said, rubbing her eyes with the heel of her hand. "It's so totally depressing. It's like suffocating or something." She paused. "I mean, what if I would've stayed on the bus? I could've sat there. There was no reason to get out. It was raining and we had finals. How did you and Stormi know that would happen?" she asked, but did not wait for my reply. "I mean, I know she knows things."

"I didn't have a clue—"

"It doesn't matter. I'm not believing Dad. Stormi wouldn't do that to Gina, and she warned her too. It's so weird today." She scuffed the sidewalk with her sandal. "We're still alive, right?"

In that instant, Carly passed from know-nothing to deep thinker, at least in my book. She nailed it, the question we were all asking, and the reason we were walking the streets.

We wanted to feel the warmth, the breeze. We needed reassurance our feet still touched the earth.

Carly gave me a hug. Maybe it wasn't as long as the one Wally received, but it counted nonetheless. Madison, two notches harsher but five notches more attractive, followed suit.

A stranger to appreciation, I found it as awkward as a group shower in phys ed, and stuttered some drivel about thanking Stormi when I see her and feeling in shock and wishing Gina was still here.

The mention of Gina's name extracted a fresh round of tears from the girls, which was followed by more hugs for me.

My presence had a very different effect on adults. Even those whose kids Stormi had saved cast wary glances my way. I had become an Other, like Stormi. Suspect. No longer homegrown Jonah with an unfortunate back and brain. No longer one to pity.

One who left Gina to die. One who could have done more. One to dread.

My wanderings carried me into the DairyWhip, one of the few open businesses, and I plunked down my dollar.

Mrs. Contulky emerged quickly from the back, drying her hands on her apron. "What can I get for—" Our gazes locked, and I offered my most pleasant smile. Her face pruned, and she slowed and swallowed hard, her lower lip pinched between her teeth. "Can I help you?"

I frowned and lowered myself onto a stool. "Well, yeah. It's me, Jonah? Same as always. Cone. Vanilla. A little caramel?" I cast her a sideways glance. "Please?"

She peered at me a moment before slowly reaching for the bill and turning toward the soft-serve machine.

"People treat you strangely." This from Arthur, sitting at the far end of the counter. "That was an eleven-second stare she gave you. Your regular order has never garnered you an eleven-second stare."

He hopped up and hunkered down next to me. Arthur Bales was the one person I did not want to see today.

A senior like myself, he had also been on the bus, but not even death could faze Arthur. Was he happy? Was he distraught? His face offered no tells. Of all the students in Gullary, he alone, as far as I could recollect, had never mocked me. Maybe because hiding behind the largest glasses in town was a kid who had taken his own lumps. Or perhaps his eyesight was so poor, he simply hadn't noticed my hunch.

Arthur was odd, his affect rarely matching the moment. Socially, he was lost in this world. But he was brilliant, claiming to have an IQ of 160 or some number in the stratosphere. Still, he failed English Lit and Chemistry and Health, instead choosing to master all of life's minute details, which pretty much made his IQ irrelevant.

"Hey, Arthur. Some day, huh?" I stared straight ahead and reached out for my cone. Mrs. Contulky set it down on the counter and walked quickly into the back room.

"It's a beautiful morning." Arthur took one last slurp of Cherry Freezie. "Where's Stormi?"

"I'm not exactly sure," I lied.

Arthur nodded, reached for a pepper shaker, and slid it across the counter until it rested between us. He squinted at that shaker, and finally nodded. "I've been thinking about this for some time now. I have decided on my next move."

"What next move? Oh no. Your little chess match will need to wait. I fed Tres this morning and I'm not going back to see him for a while."

"I need you to make the move." Arthur started a nervous tap on the counter. "I need it done today."

"No."

Arthur shook, as was his custom when presented with a curveball. "Bishop to G5," and then louder, "Bishop to G5. Zugzwang. Yet again, he's done it to me. The evils of zugzwang."

"Zig—"

"Zugzwang! He forces me to make a move, but every move weakens my position. This man is an expert at placing me in zugzwang." Arthur leaned over. "Are you sure I'm not battling a computer?"

I laughed. "No. I wish you could see the man you're playing. Imagine a severely tooth-deficient old guy. But our agreement needs to hold. Tres can't communicate with the outside world. You're playing completely under the table. No mentioning him except to me."

"I haven't been illegal!" He pounded the counter. "Move me! Zugzwang. Zugzwang!"

I glanced at Arthur, picked up the shaker, and sighed. How strange our minds were. His brain was brilliant, but he couldn't handle the slightest change of plans. My brain, completely unbrilliant, yet it hurtled me to the floor whenever it chose.

"I tell you what. After tomorrow's funeral . . ." I took a slurp of melting ice cream. "I'll head over and see Tres. There's an unusual note issue we need to discuss, and I'll inform him of your move then."

Arthur's eyes glazed. He seemed to retreat deep inside himself, to a lonely land I didn't want to visit. His eyebrows furrowed and his lips tensed. He shook free and quick glanced my way. "Yes. That will be fine." I smiled and patted his straight back. On a day filled with confusion, the predictably quirky behavior of Arthur calmed me.

I glanced at my cone. It was no longer appealing, and I pushed off the stool and tossed it into the garbage.

"Have a good day, Arthur. And you too, Mrs. Contulky!"

No response from the back, but as I exited the door, Arthur called, "Remember the move. Bishop to G5."

I stepped into daylight with Arthur's words on my mind. He wasn't the only one in zugzwang. Me, Stormi; it seemed like every move we made angered somebody. Dad, Ma, Mr. Cartwright . . . somebody. I couldn't wait to see my beautiful friend, but already I feared our eventual return home.

She'd be asked to explain how she knew, and she'd give the answer she always gave, the one that was frustrating and evasive, and never satisfied: "The truth unfolds. It just unfolds a little faster for me than it does for you."

Zugzwang.

I spotted the perfect kicking stone on Main Street. It was red limestone and the size of a golf ball and it stayed with me all the way home to A Street, where I gave it one last kick toward our trailer. It bounced off the gravel street, and skipped across the grass that long ago took over the driveway. It came to rest beneath our lean-to, beneath the lawn tractor.

My blasted lawn tractor.

Trucks were the standard set of wheels for teens in Gullary. Not for an epileptic. As a seizure-free year seemed an impossibility, Dad downgraded expectations and traded five chickens for an orange Husqvarna riding mower.

He washed it up, and, with great ceremony, walked me outside with his paw over my eyes.

"I bought you something. Every kid needs a set of wheels."

"You're kidding me!" In that moment, all Dad's faults were forgiven. "But I can't drive!"

He removed his hand, and rounded my shoulder with his arm. "Sure you can. You didn't think I'd be so cruel as to buy you something you can't use."

I stared at that stupid tractor.

No, I would never think you could be cruel.

"So, is something wrong with the push mower?" I asked.

He walked over and leaned against the Husky, kicked the tire. "You misunderstand. This is not for work, this is for your transportation. *This* is for pleasure."

"Pleasure."

"I'm not as old as you might think. I remember the freedom a good set of wheels can bring."

I coughed. "So this is for dates, and road trips, and all that freedom stuff."

"Might take a few modifications, but this deck here, that'll support a bag of groceries, your meds." He walked back, a twinkle in his eye. "Can't say that this might not improve your prospects around here. Girls like a guy with his own wheels."

I knew he was trying—in his own way, he was trying—but I could not endure it.

"It's a flippin' mower! I can't drive this around Gullary. So, what, I go on a date, and five hours later we pull in to the Waxton drive-in, blades blazing? We make out, cut the lawn, make out some more?"

"Calm, son. It's for transportation, not procreation." His face fell. "Things are different now. You're different now. The quicker we accept that what you aren't . . . that you aren't . . . you know—"

"No, I don't. What am I not?"

He looked off. "Normal."

Dad left his abnormal son standing alone, staring at his ride. One week later, I drove my tractor to the drugstore. Two weeks later, Stormi removed the blade and replaced the engine. She turned it into a 40 mph machine, able to reach top in-town speeds.

But I never did take Stormi to the drive-in.

Only jerks could do that.

I turned my gaze from my tractor, and stared at our trailer. Silent. The hills swallowed all sound in Gullary, and with Stormi gone, it seemed quieter still.

The outside of our home was falling apart. Shingles hung crooked, and the screen door sported one hinge. Dad lacked the basic handyman skills common to most men in town. Even the mailbox stood cocked.

Mailbox. I wonder.

I walked toward the Pickerings' and peeked inside. One letter. Stamped and outbound.

A letter from Stormi.

Tampering with the mail was a big-deal offense, but every so often, generally late at night, I took the risk.

I removed the envelope and quick-stepped inside. I hurried into my room, plopped on the bed, and stared at the writing. They were always addressed the same.

Mom

1111 Wherever St.

Home, KS 51111

Kansas. Do you know that?

I slid my finger beneath the flap, and fell onto my back.

Dear Mom,

It was great to see you.

Eighteen, it was a really special birthday. Glad you took some time out from your busy life to come see me. I felt we shared some nice moments. Oh, you know, the moment we didn't have together watching the sunrise. Then there was that nice moment we didn't have hiking toward the Green. Oh, and then my candle moment; that was another nice birthday moment we didn't share.

Don't worry; Jonah took your place. Again. He always does. He always will. That's who he is—dependable, caring, concerned—all the things a mother should be.

Sorry. It's just that I really could use you right now. Right now I'm messing up in every way possible. Right now, Connor is out of control, and I won't give him any more space in this note. Right now, everyone in Gullary thinks I messed up by doing something good, and I'm starting to believe them.

But not Jonah. I keep coming back to him, but he keeps coming back for me. I can't lose him; he's all I have. I used to feel that way about you.

I wish you two could meet. He'd show you how a mother should be.

Your daughter,
Stormi

p.s. What did you name me?

I gently folded the note and opened my bed stand drawer, slipping it alongside ten other Stormi letters resting there. I pounded the wall, and enjoyed the throb in my hand.

Dependable, caring, and concerned. All the things a mother should be.

Again, I hit the wall, and felt a maternal ache.

CHAPTER 7

Two occasions typically animated the entire town of Gullary: funerals and the Fourth of July. This year, while one committee planned to celebrate the birth of our country, another, with equal fervor, planned to mourn the death of a girl. The irony was not lost on anyone, and the town was buzzing.

Yet something was lost: all talk of Hank the bus driver. For nearly forty years, he shuttled kids back and forth, safely running his daily routes. Three generations of residents had seen the inside of his bus. In life, he was an institution.

In death, an afterthought.

His quiet service in neighboring Waxton received little mention, even in the *Gazette*, the local paper quick to report every stubbed toe and skunk sighting. Gina's photos filled its pages, even warranting a special memorial issue to honor "Gullary's precious lost jewel." This attention, of course, was due to her young age and her father's status on the Circle.

Dad was right. What the Circle wanted, the Circle got.

But not Mr. Cartwright, not today, and it was easy to feel for the man.

Gullary squeezed into the Baptist church, which seemed to please Deacon Holmes.

"Welcome, welcome. So glad you're here." He worked the somber crowd in the foyer. "It's so nice to gather, isn't it?"

For all the homage paid to Gina, there had been no wake, no open casket—no chance to say good-bye. Mr. Cartwright had not allowed it. Instead, he requested that the entire senior class receive special seating in the front two pews.

Painfully hard, those forward pews. Pitched over in the packed second row, my bulging vertebrae knobbed against the straight oaken back. I scooted up an inch, giving in to my natural bend, and rested my forehead on the seat in front.

Directly behind me sat the Pickerings, minus Stormi, of course. Ms. P and Connor seemed amazingly at peace, given they had no clue where Stormi had gone. Then again, Ms. P gave up on parental involvement long ago. Connor was proof of that.

The church was thick and silent. The nasally organ that accompanied these affairs had also been nixed by Gina's father. There were no whispers. No crying. Just the occasional cough or creak of wood.

Mr. Cartwright seemed determined to put all of us through a near-death experience.

On the casket rested one yellow rose, and beside it, in front of the stage, a large framed photo of Gina from seventh grade. She was smiling, without a care, her braces glinting. Gina never looked that good in real life.

Mr. Cartwright strode before the rows of sardine-packed seniors. He looked at each one of us in turn. It was a fearsome gaze. A how-dare-you-be-alive gaze. He paused in front of me.

"We will have words following."

I peeked up and nodded, and he turned and took his place across the aisle.

A tap on my neck. "Man looks serious," Connor whispered. "Don't envy you, explaining to Cartwright why you and Stormi axed his daughter."

I spun around. "What the heck?"

"Shh!" Ma's hushing reached me from the back of the church. I rolled my eyes and reassumed my position.

Only stupid Connor. Let it go.

"Now would be a good time for one of those seizures. A real big one," Connor's whisper again floated to my ears. I swatted the air to quiet him, but he was determined to see my party trick.

"What comes first? Ma says its dizziness. Or is it tingling?" He leaned way forward. "Stormi says your vision blurs; yeah, in our moments she tells me everything." He ran his fingers across the hairs on my neck. "Are we tingling? Is it blurry yet?"

The power of suggestion is a mighty weapon, and Connor knew how to wield it. There, resting on the pew, I turned my head, and needles prickled my fingertips.

Not here.

Had I been at home, maybe it would have stopped there; maybe I could have ignored the sensation and my mind would have quieted.

But in the church, cramped, tense, and on display before the entire town, Old Rickety eased onto my lap.

I closed my eyes tight, and when next I opened them, Carly, seated to my right, was fuzzy, as if someone were taking a giant eraser to her edges. I blinked hard, and she doubled, not sideways but up. One Carly floated on top of another Carly.

Old Rickety reached inside.

My hand clawed, and Carly scooted away in horror. I quickly stood and stumbled over her legs, desperate to escape. I reckoned I had about twenty seconds to make it out of the church.

I reached only the aisle. I crashed to the floor, and there, for the next ten minutes, the entire town of Gullary witnessed my funeral, my little death. Only there was no casket in which to hide, and I didn't die. Not completely.

I remained partly conscious throughout my thrashing. Those were always the tough ones. Thrown about, while my mind suspended me in that middle place—like the murky end to a nightmare. Terror has you bound and you can't wake up.

My thoughts were still my own, and while on the floor they traveled from Connor to Gina to wondering how pissed Mr. Cartwright would be that I stole the show at his daughter's funeral. I wondered about my positioning, how visible my hunch was to the audience, had I struck oak on the way down, and if so, was my pressed white shirt now stained crimson.

I wondered why the God of this good universe took time to fashion a freak.

My body finally stilled and my vision stabilized.

Crap.

The easel and Gina's picture frame lay in splinters beneath me. There was Ma, crying softly at my side. Dad sat on the stage and gently cradled my head. I wished Stormi would appear, and on the heels of that hope, I wished I would vanish. But neither happened and there I was, spread-eagled on the floor.

The Monster. The Spectacle.

The Funeral Thief.

As I rose, people slowly retook their seats, all except for Connor, who glanced at me and winked. He clapped slowly and quietly, mouthing, "Well done, my good and faithful servant."

I was too exhausted to care.

Dad wrapped his arm around my warped back and hoisted me up, led me down the aisle, parting a sea of faces I partially recognized. He herded Ma and me into the last open row. "You okay?" he whispered.

"Yeah, but I can't stay here now." I panted. "I've messed up enough, haven't I?"

Dad exhaled hard. "I need to sit up front with the rest of the Circle. We'll leave right after the service."

I rubbed my face. "Yeah. Whatever." *Ashamed to sit by your freakish son, huh?*

Likely concerned that this change in plan might alter the created order, somehow circumventing the ham sandwiches that normally followed proceedings, Pastor Hildegard beelined for the pulpit. He opened his notes and his mouth, and at that instant the congregation came alive with mumbling. I'd heard that this type of ruckus occurred in Waxton Pentecostal, but never here, and good pastor Hildegard peered up and, after adjusting his glasses, squinted at the entrance behind me, the epicenter of the disturbance.

I forced myself around, and watched three men walk into the room. I'd never seen them before, which in this interconnected town meant nobody else in the room had either. They were old and jittery and dressed in identical black suits and hats. Creepy. Dad rose and, for the second time in minutes, walked down the aisle. He whispered to the first visitor, who took hold of Dad's elbow.

"Came to pay our respects." His reply was gentle. "News reached of the accident." The old guy sighed, like he really cared. "Shouldn't end this way for anyone."

By now, Mr. Cartwright had joined them in the aisle. He set a hand on Dad's shoulder, face aglow that even strangers would honor his daughter.

"You got that pegged right. You're more'n welcome to stay." He glanced down at me, and his eyes narrowed. "Move over, boy. Have you not been taught to make room for gentlemen?"

Truthfully, I had not. My appearances in church were few, usually following some inconsiderate behavior by Dad on Saturday night. Like the time he forgot to pick Ma up from Tulsa, after choosing to worship at the shrine of Sooner football. Did we not rise early the next morning to atone for his sin?

Ma and I slid to the wall, and soon the three creepies sat next to me. It wasn't long before they had all discovered the wayward wanderings of my spine.

If you've an infirmity or deformity and have endured harsh and obvious gawks, you know that pride somehow survives.

"What?" I hissed. "Never seen a back like this before?"

"No, Jonah, I guess I haven't," whispered my neighbor dressed in black. He paused, leaned over. "Where's Stormi?"

Oh, the power of a name, my name. It caused a deep, unsettled quaking. I blinked hard. "How do you know me?"

The pastor interrupted and launched into the remembrance talk. Filled with left-us-too-soons and we-don't-really-understands, the sermon was respectable, if not predictable. At least what I heard of it. My thoughts were fixed on the man seated to my left. He was dressed like an undertaker, and I didn't appreciate him knowing me so early in life.

The aroma of ham and potato salad wafted into the room, and the pastor brought the service to a speedy close. He hurried out the side door while those gathered mopped up with a very depressing rendition of "We Shall Overcome."

The last note sounded, and I turned to the stranger. "Okay, so now you can tell me how you know Stormi."

He glanced down at his hands. "She hasn't told you?"

"Told me what?"

"Good-bye, Mr. Everett."

He stood, fitted his hat, and slipped into the exiting flow.

"Hang on," I called.

The men did not turn, and by the time I hauled my body into the large meeting room, all three visitors had stepped out the front door.

I stood surrounded by crowds and conversation, conversations again sprinkled with my name. Twice, members of the hospitality committee offered me plates of food. Twice, I turned them down. Old Rickety had dampened my appetite. The strangers stole what remained.

"Jonah, what a dramatic opening to a funeral. Unusual." Arthur pushed toward me, caught me, shook my shoulders, and then quickly let go.

"You liked that?" I offered a quick smile, and lowered my voice. "Just trying to liven things up a little before I leave town tonight."

"Tonight? You do remember your promise—"

"Yes, Arthur. Your precious move." I pointed at the door. "Did you see those old guys?"

"Yes."

"Have you ever seen them before?"

"No."

"Right. And did you find them . . . unnatural or unusual or—"

"Unexpected."

"Yeah!" I grabbed his arm and he quickly pulled free. "Sorry, but they *were* unexpected, weren't they?"

He sighed as if my questions were boring him. "Yes. And they left because they didn't belong and they didn't know anybody."

I folded my arms. *Nobody except Stormi and me.*

"Jonah, come now!" Ma called from near the door and quickened her good-byes. She tugged on Dad, who looked tired of fielding seizure questions. They beckoned intensely and I grabbed a pillow mint and almost reached the door.

"Boy!" Mr. Cartwright and his wife weaved through a sociable crowd. Potato salad and ham sandwiches do wonders for the downtrodden. He planted himself squarely in front of me. "Where is she, son?"

First Creepy, now Cartwright.

"We had this talk already." Dad stepped forward. "You're not the only one eager to reach the bottom of this. When Jonah and Stormi return, we *all* have questions."

"We *all* didn't bury daughters," Mrs. Cartwright snapped.

"No," Ma said, her jaw tight. "Today, we didn't, but I can grasp the grief. There's nothing Jonah can do to ease it. He's had enough of his own pain today. You saw it yourself."

Mr. Cartwright grabbed my wrist and I grabbed Dad's, who grabbed Cartwright's. We stood there for a moment, firm gazes all around. Slowly, the pressure eased and I extracted my arm.

"You know what? Here's the ridiculous thing: Stormi didn't do anything to harm your daughter. She didn't," I said. "She tried to *save* Gina. But you can't wait to blame her for something. And you're in the Circle, so she's officially screwed." Ma tried to touch me, but I stepped back, my face hot. "Stormi tried to get everybody off that bus, including Gina, but Gina wouldn't move. In fact, she smacked Stormi with her textbook. There's the truth. Wasn't in the paper, but there it is. Your girl isn't here because she didn't move. That's all I know."

"Come, Jonah." Ma rounded my shoulder and whisked me out of the church, with Dad protecting our backside. "What's gotten into you?"

"Who else is going to stand up for her?" I spit out my mint. "Not Ms. P, not Cartwright, not Dad—"

Dad squeezed my shoulder, spun me, and stuck his finger into my chest. "Enough, Jonah."

"Well, are you?" I lowered his hand. "Sixteen kids told the Circle *exactly* the same story. And you're still going to put Stormi through an inquisition. How many witnesses do you need? Why are you so afraid of Cartwright?"

Dad's jaw tightened, and then loosened, releasing an exhale long and loud. "There are things in motion that you don't understand."

"*Bingovis! Absolutus!* So tell me, 'cause it seems really clear to me: you have seventeen breathing kids who owe their lives to Stormi."

Dad glanced at Ma. "Gina would have made eighteen."

Silence fell heavy, and I plodded home, knowing there would be no more words.

CHAPTER 8

"Your father and I have been thinking." Ma set the cling-wrap on the counter. She'd been following me around the kitchen. "Four seizures in one week. It's best you not head out alone."

I grabbed a root beer from the fridge. "Uh-huh."

"I'm also not tickled that you're heading out at night. Why not wait till the sun rises?"

"Uh-huh."

"Jonah! A little attention. You don't need to understand us, or even like us right now, but pay heed to sense. Let your father drive you to wherever you two are meeting."

"Oh, no." I stiffened. "You know every inch of my life, except this place. Wait, so tonight, you're hovering because of my seizures? You're worried about my safety?"

Ma leaned against the doorframe. "I'm hovering because you're in *my* kitchen, and I needed to prepare a tide-me-over for Tres." She paused. "And yes, contrary to what teens think, kids' seizures do steal a mother's sleep." Ma twisted her face around. "Is there another cause for concern?"

No. No, there wasn't, and the fact made me ill. Ma, self-appointed moral compass for the entire town of Gullary, and the unyielding, righteous buckle of the Bible belt, had no problem sending her eighteen-year-old son on an overnight with a beautiful eighteen-year-old girl.

How many times had she passed judgment on Connor for his nightly exploits? How many criticisms of Ms. P slipped from her lips, such as "That woman need keep a tight rein on that boy," and, "We all know what pulls at the bit of a young man"?

I blinked hard, and Ma rubbed her hands on her apron. "You all right?"

"Sure."

I was not, and as I stared at Ma, rage took root. She *shouldn't* feel at peace about Stormi. Wasn't I also a young man? Sure, I was deformed, and I'd been recently compared to Stormi's mother. Sure, I flopped and gagged, but I was still a guy—a good-looking one at that, aside from my torqued torso—and guys get ideas.

I'm a dangerous young man with dangerous urges.

I sighed. Or maybe not. Certainly my parents did not think it true. To them, I was barely male. I was a pitiful, lurching, castrated child, and Stormi another cute babysitter. No, Ma didn't say the words, but they rang clear in my mind: *My poor Jonah Everett. Take good care of my monstrous eunuch.*

I spun around, grabbed Tres's covered plate off the table, and walked by her outstretched arms. "Hug some other kid. I'll be back for my things. Don't wait up." I slammed the front door behind me and slumped back against it.

"Who am I kidding?" I thumped my head against the knocker and winced. "What right does a monster have to Stormi's affection?"

"I've never given thought to rights of monsters."

I jumped, temporarily losing hold on the tray, allowing corn to mingle with burrito meat. I calmed and rubbed my face hard when I saw it was Arthur. "You can't do that. You can't stand outside my home. That's called lurking"

His face was unaffected. "This is called assuring that my move will be made. I'm coming with you."

Arthur looked so determined, so settled on his course. He shifted his feet, as if bracing for a fight. Having been stripped of my manhood, no fight remained, and all I could do was sigh.

"Okay, but you need to stay in the gallery while I deliver the food and your instructions. That's a rule. Nobody follows me back there."

Arthur scrunched his face and adjusted the bridge of his glasses, fighting to loosen hold on his resolve. "That sounds reasonable."

We reached SMX, imposing by day and downright ominous beneath a pale moon. The yard lights stretched and warped my hunched shadow, enough so that Arthur stopped and pointed.

"You're basically a walking boomerang. A boomerang carrying a plate."

"Thank you, Arthur." I tongued my cheek. "You wanted me to move your pawn, right?"

"No. No! You can't mess this up!"

"That's what I thought." I smirked and removed the shark tooth necklace bearing the museum key from around my neck. I pushed into the gallery. "Here's where you wait." I switched on the lights and gestured around. "Feel free to browse. I won't be long. Odds are he's already asleep."

I opened the red door, and slid the brick in the crack.

"Jonah? That you, boy? Mighty late for a visit. Closin' in on midnight," Tres called. "You know how I be needin' my beauty sleep."

"You got that right." I shuffled to his cell. "Listen, I'm going off for a day or two. I don't know exactly who'll come to take my place—probably Dad—but Ma threw together a plate to hold you through in case provisions don't arrive in a timely manner. Burrito, I think."

"Mighty generous." He rose from his bed. "Where are you going, Jonah?"

"I can't say exactly, but I'm going to see Stormi."

"She left then. Without saying nothin'. No words. Nothin'."

I frowned, pushed my hand through my hair. "What was she supposed to say? She said enough in the note. Wait, that note. Yours and hers. They were the same."

"Huh." Tres began to pace. "Fancy that."

I set down the plate. "The same paper, Tres. Two halves, the same note. Can you explain that?"

"Not in a way that will bring you satisfaction." He glanced around the cell, cursing. "You done it now, Stormi."

"That's exactly what Stormi would say—well, the first part, not the cussing."

I watched and waited for Tres to explain his note trick, but minutes later he was still pacing.

"You know, it's late, so forget it, okay? Not a big deal. Probably a coincidence, that note." I stretched and released a mighty yawn. "The funeral took it out of me. Old Rickety showed up."

Tres slowed and took a deep breath. "I'm sorry 'bout that, Jonah. Really am."

"He wasn't the only visitor. Three old guys showed, never seen them before. They sat by me the entire time, and they knew me. At least my name."

"Hats?" Tres stopped pacing and looked off, gathering thoughts from somewhere else. When next he returned, his voice was a hair above a whisper. "Suits?"

"All."

Tres grabbed the bars and pressed his face through the opening, his eyes filled with urgency. "Do you trust me, son?"

I stepped nearer; don't know why, but I did. "I guess as much as any guy can trust a person he's known for six months, who's been locked up forever for doing some hideous thing, and who never shares a lick about his own life or what he's done or where he's been or . . . I mean, I trust you as much as that."

"That'll have to do." He reached out through the bars and his hand settled on my shoulder. Strong and gentle at the same time. "Time to lead. It's time for *you* to take the lead. She doesn't have courage without you."

Warmth spread down my arm. A good warmth. Wait, a seizure warmth? I quickly dropped to the floor just in case. "Crap. I gotta up my Tegretol. Two in a day? It's not helping a bit." The room spun and I closed my eyes. Shrieks and laughter invaded my dark, pressing so close, I felt the weight, the weight of a horror I didn't recognize.

And one voice that I did.

Tres.

"See you soon, Jonah."

I came to, aware I was on top of a bed. How I had traveled home was a mystery. I rolled over and wiped foam from my mouth and opened my eyes.

No.

Arthur sat staring at a chessboard, the chessboard inside Tres's cell, the cell that now held us and only us.

"Why are we here and where is Tres and all that?" I cleared my throat and tried again. "Are we locked in?"

"It would appear so." Arthur spoke, but did not turn. He was lost in the world of the game. Our incarceration was secondary.

I raised myself to an elbow, and then swung my feet over the edge.

"This can't have happened. What happened? Arthur! Look at me."

He rose from his kneel and rolled his eyes, as if releasing a prisoner was an acceptable outcome for the evening. He reached me a peanut-butter cookie, but I slapped it out of his hand.

"There's no need for that." He breathed deeply. "I had no choice. He told me I had no choice. He placed me in zugzwang."

"Don't start in with all that chess—"

"But I need to, because it explains our present situation." Arthur sighed and started to rock. "I did wait in the gallery, but you didn't come out, and didn't come out, and so finally I came in, and you were balled up on the floor."

"I know that part. I was occupied. But go on."

"I ran to help, and I met Tres. He wasn't at all like you described him. We talked for a while—"

"While I lay there jerking by your feet?"

"It's not a picture I would have chosen, but what was I supposed to do? Tres showed me the chessboard on the dresser, and told me it was nailed down. So I told him the move, and he said I must have forgotten the scheme. He said that I could not legally make that move. Jonah, I never forget the field of battle."

"No, I imagine you don't."

"But the pieces were too far away to prove it. He told me to come in and take a look. He told me there was a room where I could unlock all the cells."

"And you gave no thought to the fact that a prisoner was inviting you behind bars? Your powerful brain didn't think, 'Wow, what kind of idiot does he think I am?' or 'Maybe I should wait and ask Jonah?'"

Arthur glanced down and folded his hands. A puppy returned to the pound. My shoulders slumped. "Okay, I didn't . . . I really didn't mean the idiot thing."

"Yes, you did," he said quietly. "And I'm not. But Jonah, he said I was illegal, and I wasn't illegal. I would never be illegal." Arthur wiped a tear, and continued. "I opened the cell and showed him that it was fair, but he didn't care and quickly countered and then, well, he lifted you. All by himself, that old man lifted you gently onto that bed. Then he shut the door and left." Arthur pointed to the game board, now lowered onto a stand. "It wasn't nailed down."

"No."

"Maybe I am an idiot. Everyone says so. Even you."

"Not true." I tried the bars, and gave them a kick. "You are the most intelligent person I know. But we may be here for a time. Don't imagine Dad will come by until late tomorrow, and Ma will think I left straight away."

"That's fine. It will give me time to analyze his hasty play. See, I took his bishop. But then he took mine. It's a fool's move. It's a desperate move. He was winning. So now, with an exposed queen, he's conceded. At least I think he's conceded. Nobody that brilliant sacrifices a queen without cause."

"Jonah?" Stormi's voice echoed down the hall.

My heart leaped, and I pounded the bars. "Stormi! In here!"

"Is Tres?"

"No, he's gone."

Stormi's footsteps neared, and she froze in front of the cell. She glanced from our pen to the foul one beside it.

"Where is the old guy?" she asked, her gaze flitting down the hall. "Tell me you moved him to another cage. Tell me he's still in here somewhere."

"He's, uh, still in here somewhere."

I stared into her eyes and bit my lip. She already knew. "I didn't see it happen, Stormi. Honest. Old Rickety came and Arthur, well, it doesn't matter how Tres got out. But it would be really nice if you could open this cell." I quieted, searching as young men do for words, though words will never do. "It's good to see you."

Stormi threw back her hair and boot-kicked the bars. Once and again. "I can't believe you let this happen. Always trusting. Don't you ever *use* that crazy brain of yours? Does it, like, think? Like complete thoughts? Ever?"

Did my shoulders sag a little more? Did my heart shrivel? Of course, she was right, and I slinked back down onto the bed while Arthur told Stormi how to unlock the unit.

Five minutes later, she returned. Though my heart was no longer set on release, I slumped out and leaned against the wall across from the cell. Arthur hadn't moved. He scratched his chin and muttered at his game.

"You should have come to the old farm right away."

"I started to, and was unexpectedly delayed . . . You know what, forget it. You're right."

Stormi's face tightened. I'd never seen her cross, at least not with me. "We need to leave now, before daylight. And we can't go to the farm anymore, it's too nearby, what with the old guy loose. Do you know some place far away where we could disappear?"

We. She said *we.* She was furious and I had been stupid, but she still wanted to be with me. I stood and straightened, well, as much as possible.

"Yeah, disappearing is probably best. Wait. What? Disappearing from Gullary? For how long?"

Stormi said nothing, but reached her hand toward me, eyes pleading.

I stared long at her gently beckoning fingers. My friend needed me, and for no other reason that should have been enough, but it wasn't. My hand balled, grasping familiar, anxious thoughts. Will I seize today? Tomorrow? My heartbeat quickened. Vanishing was all well and good for Stormi; what daily battles did she fight?

How little I knew.

I opened my hand too slowly, and Stormi's flopped to her side. "I need you, Jonah."

"Oh!" Arthur shot up and tossed me a balled-up sheet. "Tres told me to pass this on. He said it's his next few moves."

"I'm kind of in the middle of a moment. Besides, I doubt he's coming back." I tossed the paper back.

Arthur unfolded the paper and scowled. "Guys?"

"We need to leave." Stormi stomped toward the red door, pausing to cast me a hopeful glance before disappearing into the gallery.

I sighed and gestured to Arthur. "A little speed. I have to lock—"

"There's a problem." Arthur adjusted his glasses. "It says, 'Truth with three hats and suits. Avoid Q to prevent more loss. Suggested next moves: J3 and S1 to Bishop.'"

"So what's the prob—Wait, three hats and suits? What color are you playing?"

"Black."

Black.

"Okay, so make his move, and what would be your next logical play?"

"That's the thing. I can't follow his directions." He stepped out of the cell. "There are no chessboard squares labeled J3 or S1."

I rubbed my face and shook my head. "I, uh, have to let this craziness go. Stormi is waiting on me and—"

"But, I do have some friends with those names," Arthur said quietly. "J3: Jonah the third. S1: Stormi the, well, the first, I guess. Looks like Tres wants you to go to Bishop."

"Bishop, Oklahoma? That's hundreds of miles away. In the panhandle."

Stormi poked her head through the door. "Jonah!"

"Coming."

Arthur and I walked briskly down the hall. He paused to press the captured black bishop into my hand. "So what's your play?"

I glanced at the piece. "Are you ever afraid?"

Arthur frowned, and I waved him off.

"She said we need to disappear, someplace far away . . ." I tucked the bishop into my pocket. "I never would have thought of it myself, but now I think I know the place."

CHAPTER 9

Stormi was beautiful when angry.

Beautiful, but not quiet.

I was the recipient of a strange peace. Stormi's yellow pick-up sped west out of Gullary, and miles quickly separated me from the oddness of the funeral and Tres's escape. The anxiety that plagued me seemed somehow connected to the fabric of Gullary, and the more I ripped free, the less weight remained to smother me. Stormi's mind clearly found no similar rest, racing in bursts around the same chaotic track. Fits of rage gave way to nervous chatter, followed by lengthy pauses. Rage, fear, repeat.

I hoped for a moment that Stormi might return to herself, to someone I knew. I hoped and sat silent. What do you do when the rock in your life turns buoyant and starts bouncing in the waves? You hunch forward to relieve the pressure on your vertebrae, lean hard against the door, and wait.

At least that's what I did.

". . . Jonah! Are you even listening to me?"

"Okay, yeah." I straightened, sort of. "I've been lost in thought. Sorry. But definitely listening to you while I was lost in the thoughts." I rubbed my temple, urging away an oncoming headache. "Are you okay? I mean, I can't remember you ever losing it like that."

"You made me lose it!"

"I was writhing on the floor. You can't cut me a little slack?"

"You want sympathy."

"No, I just don't think I deserve *all* the blame." I folded my arms. "Maybe two percent, two percent of the blame."

Stormi opened her mouth to speak, then closed her lips.

"I'd go as high as six percent," I said.

"Six percent," she repeated and shifted, and for a moment her anger ebbed. "There are things I haven't told you, Jonah." She glanced down, and the truck swerved. When we regained the road, Stormi had all but lost her voice. "A lot I haven't said."

It was my turn to get upset, and I really tried. After all, I told Stormi everything . . . well, except for my postal felonies. She took my secrets and she held back. Thief! Liar! But none of those accusations worked. I felt no betrayal. I glanced at her face, and a new shade had taken over, one not seen in all my years of studying and yearning.

She seemed frail, broken . . . human. I wanted to touch her—not for the fantasy it promised me, but for the comfort it might give her. Somehow, her being human made me more human too.

"You could tell me a secret or two now, if you wanted. It's just us."

Nothing.

"Or you could ignore the *Deformicus beasticus* at your side—"

"Shut up."

"Or you could verbally abuse the deformed beast at your side."

Stormi slammed the brakes and swerved onto the shoulder. She turned and stuck her finger in my chest. "*You* aren't a beast." She poked harder, her nail discovering soft tissue. "*You* never were." She fisted up and smacked my shoulder, deadening my arm. "It's me. I'm the beast. Can't you see it?"

None of what she was saying made a lick of sense, but I kept my tongue planted.

She collapsed into my chest, and I awkwardly placed my arms around her. Such foreign territory. I had nothing to offer. There had been strange moments before when she'd requested closeness, but it never felt like *I* was required. I was simply the nearest armed creature.

But not here. No other set of headlamps was in sight, and with the wind shuddering the truck and an odd fear filling her words, I felt suddenly as though it was me she wanted. No one else. The idea was strangely warming.

"I can't see anything, Storm. You know that. You said that." I buried my face in her hair. "Besides, I'm six percent responsible for this mess. I'm the gullible one, remember, the crooked painting that'll never hang straight. But you, you're the beauty, at least that's how I figure it."

She tensed in my arms, but did not pull away. "Promise me that when you find out, you won't leave me."

"Find out what?"

"Promise me."

"Yeah, I promise."

She scooched away, and wiped her eyes with the heels of her hands. She reached forward and gently lifted my chin. "Jonah, you are gullible."

We eased back onto a different road, me and the stranger beside me, the one who looked like Stormi but who spoke in confused tones like mine. Confused words. Unhinged words.

Morning came, fled, and we sunk deeper into the dryness of afternoon. Although it was still spring, the horizon shimmered in the heat. With no AC in the truck, it was too hot to talk, and the distance between us lengthened. Another hour passed, and the heat flat-out baked away whatever affection Stormi's midnight embrace revealed.

"I'm going to pull off for gas," Stormi said.

"Yeah, I could use a stop."

Stormi looked at me with questioning eyes. Our relationship was changing, but I couldn't figure how.

The Wanaka exit fast approached. Wanaka consisted of one Shell station, Wanaka Liquors, and Jethro's Antique Emporium, and we sidled up to the lone gas pump. Another truck was mid-fill on the opposite side, and Stormi exhaled hard.

"You pump, I pay, or . . ."

"Naw, I need the facilities inside." I pushed out. "I'll cover it. Put in thirty."

"Be quick," she called with urgency.

An odd command, as one has limited control over a bladder's demands.

Odd commands. Stiff red flags I rarely ignored.

Rarely.

I strolled through the door, pausing to stretch my spine, before tracking down the bathroom. I slumped inside. It's a mindless affair, standing before a urinal after hours of languishing in a truck. Thoughts drift over the miles, and this trip provided little to latch on to. Stormi had come strangely unglued, which unnerved me, yet not as much as I would have thought.

Business done, I washed and power dried and wandered out toward the bubble-gum-chewing kid behind the counter. He couldn't have been older than me, and he certainly paid me no mind, lost as he was in his Superman comic book.

Two scruffy guys jostled around the freezer, and I suddenly felt sick, strange sick. Like I was in a scene from a movie sick. It wasn't the scruff—I was familiar with dirt and wear from a life in Gullary—no, it was the volume. No-goods who possessed the decency to hush their antics, well, there was rarely much harm in them. It was the others who, like Connor, felt no shame and broadcast their no-goodness. That's who you had to fear.

In that instant, I thought to check on Stormi, but I was hypnotized, my gaze captured by a couple of idiots laughing and shoving.

"What you staring at?" The older one turned and took a step toward me.

I broke free. "Nothing. Staring spell. Go on back to whatever." Eager to be out and done, I glanced at the counter and the door, and was once again captured.

Posted smack in the middle of the glass, right above the *Sorry, We're Closed* sign, was a poster the size of a newspaper, a Wanted poster.

Though hastily printed off by a machine badly in want of toner, the three faces were frighteningly recognizable.

The largest mug belonged to Tres. Tres Cantor. The warning stretched beneath his name.

Considered armed and dangerous. Do not attempt to apprehend. Call Authorities immediately.

Beneath Tres, side by side, Stormi and me.

"Stormi Pickering. Granddaughter of the above. Jonah Everett III. Friend of the above."

I backed away from the counter, and glanced over my shoulder at bubble-gum boy still lost in his comic. I quietly removed the poster and pushed outside. "Stormi! You've got to see—"

Stormi was pressed up against the pump, arms pinned above her head, a defiling knee wedged between her legs. The guy from the other truck moved against her, his head performing such acts with her neck that to think of them still makes me wince.

Thoughts flew through my head. The no-goods would soon be here, making escape impossible. Bubble-Gum couldn't see, didn't want to see, any of this. Rage filled me.

"Hey!" I lurched toward the scuffle, scanned my options, and grabbed the nozzle from Stormi's truck. I yanked the rear of the Defiler's jeans with all the authority I owned, and jammed the pump nozzle down deep into the back of his pants.

Words I will not record flew from his mouth. He spun, first to swing at me, and when I ducked, he fought and clawed at his backside.

"Go! Go!" I hollered, and Stormi raced around to the passenger's side of the truck, while I leaped his wildly swinging gassy tail and pitched myself into the driver's side. From the building, voices exploded as the other two raced out, shouting.

Ignition. Gas pedal. Our tires spun in the gravel as the Defiler finally extracted the hose. Treads caught and we fishtailed forward. I checked the rearview. Bubble-Gum was jogging toward the three, all of whom pointed in our direction.

I drove. Kept driving. My breath fought out, while my heart beat wildly.

"I can't believe it! Stormi, I couldn't hear you. I didn't hear your scream, or I would have been there quicker, I should have . . . I got lost in there, and then there you were . . ."

"I didn't scream. Did you pay for the gas?" Stormi asked quietly.

"What? Gas? No. Who cares? Are you okay? That guy, I mean those guys would have, you know, he didn't look like stop was on his mind."

"He wouldn't have been the first."

117

Jonathan Friesen

I knew what she meant. And then I didn't. "Wait, he wasn't the first to try, you know, or he wasn't the first . . . period?"

"Look at me," she said softly. "What do you think?"

There was a right answer. I knew there was. I also knew this was a time for listening and being there and all that crap you learn in psychology. I should have been thinking only of her, of what she went through, but anger brought out the ugly and twisted all goodness. My eyes stung.

"So why do you climb in the car with every stupid guy who asks? There's me and Connor off that list, but that's pretty much it. Do you think they care, like, at all? Do you know how guys talk and what they say? Well, I don't, because I can't handle listening to them. What do they tell you? That they need you? Love you?

"If you don't believe me, listen to the guy who you think of like a mother. How can you see everything and be so dang blind?"

"Oh. My. God," she whispered.

We drove for two silent hours. There was no way to fix it, fix us. I drove and hoped for a seizure to come and end the misery.

"Do you enjoy my letters?"

Her voice so cold, so distant.

"No . . . yes. I read a bunch of them." *Stop. Stop. Leave it.* "I thought you'd be happy. At least they reached your mother." I shook my head. I couldn't stop digging.

"Good. I'm glad you enjoyed them. Since we're coming clean, you selfish ape, I go out to prove to myself that my *no* still works, to remind myself that I'm worth . . . I'm worth it. You should stick around and listen to the fools in the locker room. Listen to what they say about me. Listen to what they can't say."

"Who says you're not worth—"

She glanced sharply at me and swallowed hard and I knew.

Had Connor been here, I would have at least tried to kill him. But he wasn't. It was just me and my pain, and I didn't know how to kill that.

"Connor tries to take," Stormi said resolutely. "But if you speak his name again, I will find some way to kill you."

"You just did."

Stormi blinked hard. "It shouldn't be hard to forget him. We're not going back."

"Whatever." My mind whirred. "Wait. What about my parents? Ms. P? Of course we'll go back." I veered off the road, regained composure, and slowed. "Won't we?"

Stormi reached down between us, gently lifted the poster that had found its way into the truck, and flattened it over her thighs. She placed it so I could see it. "You didn't pay for gas. Now they have our license plate for sure, they know this truck, they'll know where I live. They'll look for us there, and when they do . . ." She pointed at the photo of Tres. "We'll have bigger problems."

"How is he bigger than what happened? And Con . . . the nameless guy? What is going on?" I rubbed my face with a gas-scented hand. "What bigger problems?"

She was gone again, and I swallowed hard. How many hurtful things can a guy say in one conversation?

"And Tres." I forced a smile. "What idiot thought he was your grandfather?"

In the distance, a lit-up squad car screamed nearer. It raced by, leaving a trail of sound.

"Stormi? I'm sorry, Stormi."

"Turn off when you can." She straightened. "It's time that we talk."

Clouds gathered quick and ominous, and we drove off the main road, deeper into the hills. We'd left the wombing cover of the Ozarks back in Gullary, and I knew what lay west: they didn't call it No Man's Land without cause. Red dirt, tumble-weed, stretches of flat, and winds that stole your sight. A chest flutter sounded an anxious note. I was leaving all I knew, risking a future on the girl I suddenly didn't. Not going back?

This hadn't been part of my plan, well, Tres's plan.

We wound through the gentle hills. My mind felt solid, but my dumb heart was broken.

Connor. I knew it.

Stormi scanned this way and that, asking me to slow at each rundown farmstead. I wasn't sure what she was looking for, but one peek at that sky and I knew we didn't have time to be choosy.

The storm gust hit, pushing the truck off line and onto the chatter strips lining the shoulder. Stormi jumped.

"Keep on the road, Jonah."

"We need to get off the road. There's swirling up there. We need shelter."

Stormi closed her eyes. "Turn in to the next place. It'll be vacant."

I took a quick right and snaked onto a property so decrepit, fears of breaking and entering vanished. We scrambled out and blew toward the boarded-up front porch.

"Busted window!" I pointed.

"Go inside." Stormi pushed me forward. I wedged my spine through the opening and tumbled in, landing with a thud on hardwood. Stormi did not follow.

"Stormi?" I winced and stared out the window. She walked into the distance, lit like a strobe in the afterglow of lightning strikes. Rain poured down on arms spread-eagled. Her face was upturned, soaking in the wet.

"You'll get killed out there," I called, but my voice was feeble.

She needs you.

I heard it, plain as plain, but my legs were rooted. The next bolt cracked nearby, and by this time Stormi had fallen to the ground. She pounded the earth again and again, screaming into the night. I'd spent hours staring at her curtain, but this felt so private, so agonizing, I couldn't watch, and slumped down to the floor.

Stormi fell apart, and I was afraid.

She needs you.

When next I peeked, she stood at the window, soaked and shivering, tears streaming down her face. I backed up as she crawled in and fell into my arms. We found the corner and huddled, as ancient boards creaked with each gust.

Forever passed, and in the blackness of the main room, I stared up.

"Do you think she'll hold?"

Stormi's breath came in staccato bursts. "Yes." Her hand found my arm in the dark.

There are places filled with memory, where the past hangs thick like dough. This old place was like that, refusing to crumble, though countless storms had certainly come to call. Ma would say the spirit was strong in those walls. Stormi seemed to be fighting that spirit. Finally, the words.

"Let me talk, and don't interrupt. Let me get this out while I can, here, where you can't see me."

"Yeah, sure."

She smacked my arm, but in the darkness her fist glanced off my shoulder and cuffed me across the jaw. "I said, don't interrupt." Again, Stormi gripped my forearm.

"But—"

She released me long enough to smack again, and I held my tongue. Soon she softened, laying her head on my lap.

"Have you ever felt summoned?"

"Dad was summoned for jury once, down to Tulsa."

"Shut up!"

"Sorry, it just sounded like a question."

The storm crackled overhead, and above us, the busted chandelier tinkled. Each remaining shard of dew-drop glass reflected the sky's light show, creating a disco ball effect. The flashes were tough on an epileptic, but my mind remained my own, and I waited, and waited.

"I got the first letter when I was ten. Remember Danny?"

Of course I did. Dad fired him from the gallery without cause—well, without good cause. Truth is, Dad needed a job for me. Danny was gone from Gullary the next day, and nobody had heard from him since.

Stormi continued, "He hand delivered it."

"I'm not following." I slapped my hand over my mouth.

She sighed. "Tres wrote to me. When I was a little girl, he introduced himself. Of course I showed it to Martha, and she had the test done immediately."

"Test?"

"A grandparentage test. It turned out Tres was my grandpa after all."

I winced my back into a new position. "You're kidding! Well, that's great, right? I mean, you actually know someone from your family! You know, maybe a violent-convict-type of family member, but still . . ." She was silent. "That is great, isn't it?"

More lightning.

"His letters started coming every week." Stormi tapped my thigh, slow and metered. "Each one ended the same. 'Do your job, Stormi. And whatever you do, don't get hooked up with that Jonah.'"

"Me?"

"No. The other Jonah. Of course you." She exhaled, and her voice softened. "But I did. I fell for Jonah."

"Me?"

Another smack. "Don't go there. Not now. Tres wrote more than once that you'd keep me from 'carrying through my summons.' He said that the more I felt for you, the less I'd see. The less I'd let myself see." Stormi paused. "But I was ten. None of it made sense. It does now. Tres was right. I feel it. I was summoned, and I think Tres was the one who called me, called me to do something, something big and important and terrible, but I can't see it, Jonah. I still can't. And you're all rolled up in it. But all I see is you."

"Me?"

"Could you use another word?"

"Uh—"

"Then you took over at the museum. Tres took to you. He was pulling you in, and it scared me, but I figured, what could he do to you from behind bars? But now . . ."

I tried to reason out her story, but I kept getting stuck at the same point.

"You felt for me?" I asked.

Stormi sat up. "Seriously? That's all you heard of what I said?"

"Well, not all, but it seems to be the sticky part—good sticky, you know? Well, sticky isn't really the right word. Maybe consequential is a better word. Consequential with hopeful implications. Right? Or not."

She started to stand and I grabbed her arm. "Hang on, I'm pressing out the me part and now do recall the rest. Let me get this straight. We're running from Gullary, because toothless Tres, from inside his cell, called you forth from wherever you came from and placed you down in a sleepy town to do something terrible, but you couldn't do it because of me. Now you're scared that, what, he'll find us and gum us to death?" I chuckled. She didn't, and I cleared my throat. "You said it yourself—he's just an old guy."

"He's more than that."

I shivered. Because I knew she was right. Like Stormi, he also knew too much. He may have slept behind bars, but I couldn't recollect a conversation in which he wasn't in control.

The door rattled hard, and Stormi scampered to her feet. "He's here," she whispered.

"The wind is here," I whispered back.

She pulled me into the kitchen, and then beneath the table. "No, he's found us. He's been following us the entire time."

From outside, "Jonah." My name swept away with the wind, but I had heard it.

"Tres." I sustained the whisper. "Your grandpa is not going to kill us. He had a chance and he didn't."

I climbed out from beneath the table, walked toward the window, and froze. A silhouette, dark against dark, stood in the room.

"I tried the door, but you didn't answer, so then I tried the window. This might be illegal. I've never been illegal before."

"Arthur? What are you . . . ? How did you . . . ?"

He shifted, and in the dark I could tell he walked on unfamiliar footing. "You're a friend. I have to warn you. You and Stormi are in a fierce zugzwang."

CHAPTER 10

"Something murky is happening in Gullary."

Arthur sat at the kitchen table, staring out the broken window. The wind and rain relented, and we joined him in the darkened room.

"The older ones are scared. My parents. Your parents. And those older still. Everyone is scared, and everyone is talking about you and the prisoner. A bunch have set out after you. Some want to bring you back, and then there's Mr. Cartwright." Arthur pulled a candy bar from his pocket, removed the wrapper, and took a large bite. "He's why I'm here."

"Cartwright?" Stormi tensed; I could feel it even in the dark.

Another big chocolate bite. Arthur nodded. "He was going door to door asking everyone if they knew where you were. I couldn't have him ask me. I would have had to tell him what I suspected."

"Why?" Stormi asked.

"He just would," I answered.

"So I had to leave, because I knew."

"And you found us in an abandoned house?"

His chewing slowed. "I don't have a good explanation. I drove past a gas station, saw commotion, and knew I was close. I knew you'd get off the highway. But I kept driving until the storm and, I don't know, I felt summoned. Then there was Stormi's truck."

"Summoned? By who?" I turned to Stormi, who slowly shook her head.

"So Arthur used a familiar word, a really unusual, coincidental word. It doesn't mean anything. It doesn't mean Tres had anything to do with him finding us. And, Stormi, none of what you said means we should be afraid of the guy, but Gullary is. Do you know anything else? What did he do? What does he know?"

Ringing in my ears drowned out her answer, and I slumped to the floor. Old Rickety was also summoned, and had his sights aimed directly at me. He struck with a force I hadn't experienced in years. There was no gradual lead in—no easing into hell—and my brain raised the white flag without a fight.

I was out.

I came to in the truck, with my head bouncing against the passenger side window. Stormi drove with purpose, and Arthur sat squeezed in between. Control of my mouth didn't return to me for some time, but thoughts that made little sense flooded in.

Arthur found us.

Tres was looking for us.

Stormi hated Tres.

Stormi liked me.

Stormi liked me? A drip of spittle fell from my mouth, traced down my chin. All her teasing was real? No, locker room stories about her; they were real. How could she fall for the monster? She deserved someone better. Or maybe I did.

I am never going home.

The thought rattled around in my mind. A life on the run. A life with Stormi. Never going home. The idea didn't shock me. It didn't frighten me, and the wildness of it would have made me smile were I in control of my mouth. Bonnie and Clyde. Stormi and Jonah.

With faithful sidekick Arthur.

We bumped on through the night.

"There." Arthur pointed at the turnoff. "There's the sign. Bishop, Oklahoma. That's where we need to go."

Stormi lowered her voice. "Why Bishop? Jonah still hasn't told me. He only said he knew a place."

I peeked at Arthur. I could see him thinking, trying to find a truth that wouldn't get me killed.

"It just played out that way."

Stormi was quiet. "Okay, then."

Well done, Arthur. Well done.

Bishop, Oklahoma
The Jewel of Red Carpet Country
Population 102

Stormi rumbled to a stop at the hand-painted sign on decaying wood, ominous in the headlamp's beam. "Are you back, Jonah?"

I blinked my eyes. Sleep must've found me, and I pushed myself higher, peered around.

"Yeah, that was a tough one. Sorry. Can you see the town?"

Stormi slowly shook her head. She knew what I knew; we'd reached the end of the world, the Oklahoma panhandle.

Though I'd never been, we spent a good deal of time discussing the panhandle in school. That Bishop was nowhere to be seen on any map did not surprise me; panhandle history was filled with places that were, and then weren't.

Okie towns disappeared for many reasons. Those in the northeast vanished due to the poison man dug up. But panhandle ghost towns, they just blew away. Some started as Native American settlements. Tribes held the land gently, loosely, letting the ground shift like the sand dunes near Beaver. White folk thundered in, determined to fix those towns to earth. The lack of trees should've been the tell; panhandle roots don't stretch down deep.

When times got hard, when the dust came, people blew away, leaving remnants, remnants of lives. Soon the wind reclaimed the remnants, leaving no trace of man.

Except perhaps this population sign.

Arthur spotted it first, a dot of light in the distance. After a nod from me, Stormi eased toward a bar that seemed to rise out of the earth. We pulled up, our truck awash in dust, and joined near thirty others parked every which way, headlamps on full. That was it. This was the dramatic culmination of Tres's plan.

Bishop consisted of one bar.

Moonlight refracted in the glimmer of those headlamps, casting mini rainbows all around. When the wind died, it shone down large and bright, and to each horizon, the world turned flat. No hills to cover us or valleys to shield us. No trees. Just space, wide and dark and lonely. And a lit-up bar.

"What exactly made you think this would be a good place to hide?" Stormi chewed a nail.

I couldn't tell her that we were here because of Tres, because he had suggested it.

"I knew Bishop was in the panhandle, that it was far away without being too far." I waited, knowing Stormi would sense the stupid in my answer. But she didn't. She scanned the jostling kids—most of them seemed a whisker above drinking age—bit her lip, and shrugged.

"Tell me where to go," Stormi said quietly.

"I think inside."

And with the direction came the thought. I had no idea why we were here. Not one to follow without cause, I had done so given Tres's directions. In that way, he was a bit like Stormi—authoritative—and I hadn't questioned.

Until now.

We pulled into the parking lot, which looked little different than the plain around it, and quieted the engine. Stormi and Arthur both turned to me, and I forced a smile. "This can't be all of Bishop, right?"

I pushed out of the truck and stretched. Long drives took a toll on my spine and I forced it vertical. I weaved through the laughter. It wasn't directed at me, I knew that, but it cut just the same. A lonely hurt. An outside-looking-in hurt. It had been that way in Gullary, when kids would gather and I would stumble on their mockery.

Here, the three of us passed through like ghosts. Unseen. Unnoticed.

"Hey, girl!"

Well, two of us passed on through.

Stormi's hand found mine, and she pulled me onto the porch and inside.

We stood blinking in the doorway. It was silent, motionless, as if the place had somehow been turned inside-out. There was a bar on the right, a bartender reading a paper behind it, and three haggard men sprinkled about the tables.

I shrugged and wandered up to the barkeep, still gripping Stormi's hand. "Excuse me. Is this Bishop?"

"Pretty much." The guy didn't look up. He shifted his readers, stroked his gray stubble, and yawned. "Can leave 'm on the pile."

A stack of church bulletins, stained and dog-eared, rested to his left.

"I don't have one."

"Hmm. Your loss. What didn't happen in church this morning, we'd have got done for you tonight. Free drink in exchange for your church bulletin. Maybe go find one and come on back."

I'd never seen a man so wholly disinterested, so vacant, but I had questions that needed answering.

"If we wanted to find a place to stay nearby, where'd we look?"

"That be dependin' on your definition of nearby." He removed his glasses and set down his paper. Checking us over, his gaze landed on Stormi and stayed there. He glanced over my shoulder at the men seated in the bar and lowered his voice. "You seem a piece more desperate than most drivin' to Cimarron. Plenty o' places you shouldn't stay in these here parts. Move on. Quick and quiet. There's a Super 8 in Boise City not sixty miles west, near the mesa."

"We could make that," I said, turning to Stormi. Post-seizure exhaustion was sinking in, and my judgment was turning foul. Sure, I had originally chosen Bishop, but Stormi counted on me to provide safe quarters, especially after the events at the station.

"Seems quite a trip this late. You look tired."

We spun around in time to see a clean-shaven man in his thirties rise from his table. I hadn't noticed him before.

"I know a place not eight miles from here. It's no Super 8, but it provides two beds. And believe you me, it's private."

I glanced at Stormi and back, mustering my strength. "We need three beds. We're not really together."

He let his gaze run over Stormi. "There's a shame."

"I mean in the sense of together that you might think we're, or two of us are, together—"

"Two beds would be wonderful." Stormi wrapped her arm around my twisted trunk.

A whisper in my ear. "You don't want to be going where he'd be taking you. Death there." But when I turned, the bartender was back behind his paper.

"What's the name of the place?" I asked.

The man walked up to us and reached out his hand, first to Arthur, then to Stormi, and finally to me. "Names are nothing compared to what it offers. Seclusion. A place for the weary to find rest." He gestured toward the front door. "Out away from the world and all that comes with it. It's up to you, of course, but there'd be minimal cost and you could up and on your way whenever you so choose." He paused. "Nothing asked. Nothing required."

I froze. I'd heard that phrase before.

"So it's not a hotel? How do we know it's safe?" Arthur whispered far too loudly.

"Safe? Is that what you're looking for? I s'pose you can't know for sure. But young folk don't come out here to be found, they come out here to get lost, and that, friends, I can guarantee."

The three of us huddled, but nobody spoke. It was a horror movie set-up. But our truck would soon be located, which meant a hasty shipment back to Gullary, and Stormi would have nothing of it.

"What's your name?" Stormi asked.

"Sixty-one."

"Your name's a number?" I asked.

"Your given name," Stormi asked, her voice firm and terrible.

His face twitched, as if fighting a return to some place he should not go. "Winston."

She stepped toward him, holding him in that horrible Stormi gaze. "Nothing asked."

He smiled. "Nothing required."

Stormi turned to me. "We need to go where Tres will lose our trail. This is our chance."

"I thought you didn't believe in chance."

Stormi peeked at Winston. "We'll follow you."

Arthur and Stormi wandered toward the door, and behind me a paper rustled furiously. I glanced over my shoulder, and the bartender caught my eye. "Be gone by morning. You don't want to meet Q."

I frowned and followed my friends out into the night, my fingers grasping the chess piece in my pocket.

Q. The queen?

Avoid Q to prevent more loss. Tres's note read itself in my mind.

This was my second warning. Yeah, by morning we would be gone. One way or another.

Our destination snuck up on us like a star-eating mass, a dark collection of lightless structures that blocked out horizon-hugging constellations. We followed Winston's truck to a row of garages, and he hopped out and lifted a door. He waved us in, and Stormi obliged, parking behind a white Chevy. Winston quickly pulled in behind us.

The garage was built three cars deep, and we were wedged in the middle.

We would not be gone in the morning.

"I don't like anyone who gives his name as a number. Is that even legal?" Arthur shook. He was losing it. "I don't like staying with strangers. I don't like anything about—"

"Arthur!" Stormi said. "It'll be okay. Jonah brought us here. It'll be okay."

"Now hold on, there's a little error in that narrative. You okay'd the sleeping situation. You said, and I quote, 'We'll follow you.' It's not like I had much to do with us coming *here*, as in, right here. Bishop, yep, but I was tilting Super 8. But you, when you get all confident and Stormi-voiced, it usually means, you know, you have it under control."

Stormi stroked her necklace. "I don't have anything under control, Jonah. I can't feel anything. We're following you."

"I'm following you, Jonah. I'm right behind you."

I had been on my way home from Percival's, Gullary's food mart/video store/dry cleaner. Folded over my left forearm was a suit, on the eve of my first suit-wearing occasion, the spring formal.

The dance had once been a prom—at least in the old yearbooks, it was called a prom—but something foul must have happened in 1980, because in 1981, there was no yearbook, and in '82, the event had become a highly militarized spring formal. It remained so right up to my senior year.

I wanted to survive it, survive my first and only trip to it.

Of course I was going with Stormi. She would look beautiful. I'd forced in the thought of her, and pressed out the voice of Connor, striding three feet behind me. Why he was trailing me home, I could not say, other than the cruelty of man.

"They have strobe lights. Strobe lights cause them seizures, right? That would be embarrassing."

Think about Stormi.

"It'd be a sight, seeing you foam all over her."

I stopped and turned. "Why? Why do you do this to me?"

Connor licked his lips, reached out, and snatched my suit. He gently laid it on the ground, and dug his muddy heels into it. Again and again. Then he carefully picked it up, folded it over my arm, and walked away. "Have a nice evening, Hunch."

Why had I watched? Why didn't I make a move to protect what was mine?

Why had I been so weak?

I showed up at the dance two hours later, my black suit blotched with oil, my red tie and once-white shirt the same. Yeah, I wore the outfit. I felt I deserved it. That somehow the grotesque covering matched the gruesome interior.

Chaperones manned the three escapes from Gullary Golf's nine-hole public clubhouse. Chaperones wandered among the dancers, enforcing the bodily contact rule with vigor. But it still appeared to be the highlight of most students' year.

Stormi stood by herself beneath the disco ball. I think the other girls kept distance, as compared to her, all their fashion efforts paled. She stood waiting for me in a short, deep red dress, which swished gently over her beautiful thighs and was hemmed beneath her knees. I figured right there that the red dress would pretty much destroy every other couple's chance at enjoying the event; for a guy, to see Stormi that night was to want her.

I know I did.

It mattered little. Old Rickety took me by the punch bowl before the first dance. Soon I was drenched, tinted orange, and carted home by my dad.

Apparently, Stormi stayed and danced the night away.

I'm glad she got to enjoy the senior formal. It was a really pretty dress.

I came to in blackness.

Stormi had hold of my left hand, the one I could feel. The right was still numb, along with that side of my body.

"Welcome back." Stormi smiled. "Sorry we didn't get that dance." Her voice softened. "I'm also sorry I didn't stay with you. It still could have been a great night."

I glanced at her, my mouth unable to speak. She must have been recounting the night of the formal. Somehow her words pressed in, even while I writhed in the garage.

"How would . . ." I fought through the fog. "How would it have ended?"

Stormi leaned over and kissed my ear. "With you and me."

"It always ends with you and me, but it never starts that way."

Her head paused, her hair falling over my face. "Don't start this now."

"I never do."

Stormi straightened and gave my hand a squeeze. "No, you don't. You could have a thousand times, but you don't. You're the only gentleman I know."

"It hurts to be me."

"I know, Jonah."

We fell silent in the dark, and I thought I might have caught her sniffing, but my senses still weren't trustworthy, and I lay still beneath her touch.

"Well, Winston wasn't lying. Two beds," Stormi whispered, and nearby Arthur snored. She looked off. "The other is already claimed."

I was so tired, the implication didn't strike me until morning, when I woke with Stormi nestled in the crook of my arm.

How could she see me at my most disgusting and still come near? How could she embrace a monster? That kind of affection only lived in moms and God, and I wasn't even sure about that.

But she was here, and I leaned over and smelled her hair.

"Do you enjoy irony?"

Arthur stood in the corner, posture impeccable, his hands folded in front of him. Maybe he was off somehow. When it came to Arthur, maybe God had withheld or given too much or just plain got tired of cookie-cutter personalities. But his back; it was beautiful. He was beautiful. Straight and solid. Vertebrae lined up like soldiers at attention, ready for any order.

Sure, I held the girl, but in that instance, would I have traded my support for his?

I'm ashamed of my answer.

"Irony," he continued, far too loudly. "You came to this place to flee Tres, who you think brought you here."

I frowned. Put like that, it was clear: Tres had hopped off the edge of my life and run to the center. He was the reason for everything. I slowly pointed toward Stormi and mouthed, "She doesn't know that."

"Irony number two. For the second time in as many days, you and I are trapped in a cell together."

"I wouldn't call this a cell. It's comfortable enough."

"It's a cell. What kind of people get a place to stay for free and aren't asked to do anything?"

"Uh . . ."

"Prisoners, which makes this a cell. It has a pretty girl inside, but it is still a cell."

"I think you're jumping to conclusions."

"And, since nobody walks into their own cells—"

I thought of Mom. Presumably, she chose to walk down the aisle with Dad.

"You're wrong."

"No, I'm not. Nobody walks into their own cell. They are always led."

"You're still wrong."

"So," he continued, "we've not been choosing. We must've been led, and people who lead need to know a little more than those who follow. We've been led by someone . . ." He lowered his voice; not low enough, "Who knows events before we do."

I squinted and pointed at Stormi. "What? Storm—? No. She's terrified. She's running. She's following me. Said so herself."

"She followed *you* here?"

"Well, it's not quite how I remember it, but she said she did."

Arthur grinned a very knowing grin. "I think you may be in bed with the enemy."

"Shut up. Stormi is not the enemy."

"I think, if you keep following her, pretty soon you will be on a poster."

"We *are* on a poster."

"Not a wanted poster, a missing poster. That's irony number three. You're about to have your picture on two different kinds of posters."

I puffed out air and Stormi rolled, her peaceful face inches from mine.

Arthur doesn't trust you. Sleeping with the enemy.

Did you lead us here?

The door burst open.

"Up! All of you." Both the voice and the face were weathered and husky. "Welcome to the Hive."

CHAPTER 11

The old man disappeared outside, shutting the door behind him.

"The Hive. So, are we bees now? What does that mean?" Arthur spoke to no one in particular.

"Bees work." I stood and stared around the room. I'd not planned well for an extended trip.

Outside of my ill-fated sojourn to the Mayo Clinic, this registered as the longest I'd been away from home. Well, aside from April's Boundary Waters fiasco.

Oddly, the only pleasure trip I'd taken had also sent me north, way north, up through Wisconsin, creeping west to Minnesota, ending a stone's throw from Canada. There, you find the Boundary Waters, aptly named as they form the watery barrier between us and the Canucks.

I had no will to camp, but Ma looked online and located a Boundary Waters expedition specifically for epileptics. Strange, my warped spine had dominated early teen-hood forming the misshapen trajectory of my life and dominating Ma's concern. But when Old Rickety moved upstairs, my back and its limitations were often forgotten. Which is the only excuse I can think of for sending me alongside eight able-bodied campers and a doctor for a ten-day canoe trip.

There was little in Oklahoma to compare to the Boundary Waters. Oh, the Ozarks has its share of lakes and streams, but the sheer volume of water, the pristine quality of the Boundary Waters—you could drink straight from the lakes without worry of amoebas—this was unheard of, and I admit, climbing into the canoe, I thought it: who knew Minnesotans and Canadians had a corner on heaven?

Five minutes in, I discovered that heaven carries a steep price. With a sixty-pound Duluth pack strapped to my twisted back, we prepared for the Grand Portage, a mile-long hike through the forest, during which we'd be hauling all we owned. Our goal was to achieve the next lake.

My fellow campers were an odd collection, bound only by the sickness dormant in our minds. Three girls, two of whom displayed a radiant kind of beauty, were among our number, and pride set in, a disastrous visitor for the feeble.

"Yeah, I can carry a pack and a canoe."

This was the line that did me in. To my credit, I managed for half a mile. Hunched forward, I carried the canoe upside down—an oversize captain's hat concealing my head— stabilized by shaking hands. Aching shoulders felt the weight of the crossbar, but the unusual hunched position provided a strange relief to my lumbar.

At the midpoint I reached a summit, glanced down at a treacherous path, and met Old Rick. He took me at the top, flinging me forward. I do not recall the tumble, and in fact have but flimsy memories of the next two days. That I fell is certain, as Kylie, the prettiest of our group, snapped a photo of me laying face-first at the bottom of the hill, my body eclipsed by canoe, arms stretched out on either side.

Dr. Medroni forced me to sleep in his tent for the remainder of the trip, like a needy child requiring constant observation. From a distance, I witnessed love blossom between four campers. Perhaps it was an appropriate penalty for thinking of other girls beside Stormi. But I returned home feeling less, believing that adventures were not for me.

Still, this trip felt different; I felt different. And not even Arthur's ironic distrust of Stormi could mute that fact. I was leading. Well, maybe leading, while Stormi maybe followed. She had done more than share a tent; she felt at peace in my bed. That had to count for something.

Stormi flattened her hair and straightened wrinkled clothes.

First thing, take my medicine.

Crap.

"I don't have meds, Stormi."

"None?" She paused and looked at me with impatience. "You didn't pack any?"

"Yes, I packed them, but I was hurried out of Gullary, remember?"

"Fine. I'll figure something out," she said, heading toward the small sink. How quickly the girl I held all night could turn.

In truth, seizure meds—items compulsively hoarded back home—were the least of my worries; they didn't work anyway.

However, my lack of fresh clothes felt urgent, as I still smelled faintly of gas. Stormi, too, appeared lost as she washed her face and stared vacantly into the mirror.

A tiny wooden shack, with two windows propped open for ventilation, containing two beds, a toilet, a sink, and a small desk and chair. That is all there was.

Okay, so maybe it is a cell.

"Hurry on, miss." Our wake-up caller reappeared. He sounded tired, though morning was barely upon us. He slipped inside and eased himself down on Arthur's mattress. I didn't imagine there was much hurry left in his aged, arthritic fingers.

Stormi wiped her face and set down the towel. "Ready."

We stepped out into morning, for the first time taking in our surroundings. "Well, we're still in Oklahoma," I said. All year long we'd run fifteen degrees above normal. This was made clear by my skin, not my eyes. The unusual heat came quickly, as it often did in Gullary, but this heat felt different; it was a saturating heat, and I wanted nothing more than to duck back into shade. To the right, Oklahoma stretched out forever, and in this forever, there was a refusal of anything to be hidden. One could see for miles, from the deepest, bluest sky down to the reddish hue of the horizon; it was the uncovering of all things. And I felt uncovered as well.

"The cells are ours, the cabin is yours. Name's Eleven."

A gust of wind swept over our cabin and Eleven raised the red handkerchief from his neck to his face, filtering out the dust.

"Eleven," I repeated, and glanced around the compound. I saw no difference between their cells and our cabin. All identical wooden log construction, with two windows, and large enough for a large man, or two really little ones. Thirty cells surrounded a center courtyard, which boasted only two other buildings.

"Them's the meetin' house, where you'll be eatin' for now," Eleven said, eyeing the direction of my gaze. "And that on the left is the prayin' shed. You won't be goin' in there for any reason." He looked at each of us. "Clear?"

"What if I want to pray?"

Stormi and I turned toward Arthur. It seemed a strange question, as I'd never seen him before at service.

"You won't catch flack for that." Eleven bent over and fisted a handful of reddish dust and threw it into the wind, which drew it back into the sky. "Maybe God'll hear ya. But not in there. Not in *our* prayin' shed."

I had no inclination to pray; this was Ma's territory, and I'd yet to see her prayer on my behalf produce any change to life or limb. I was, however, human, susceptible to all the temptations prohibition brings. Do not go in there? Why not? The shed instantly became the only place here I wished to go.

Eleven winced and shifted his weight. I recognized the maneuver, and felt for him. "Hope you enjoyed your tour, and your sleep-in. Tomorrow I reckon you'll be on detail, but of course that all be up to Q."

"No, we were promised we'd be gone. Any chance we can see Q now?" I asked.

"You will not refer to him by letter. You'll use his name. First and last. And no, not now. He workin' with the men. I's only here as my leg makes me fall behind." He cocked his head, examining me from a different angle. "That back keep you from work?"

"Some, not all." I straightened. "I can do pretty much whatever—"

"Winston told us there'd be nothing asked, nothing required." Stormi interrupted, like I was so much dust. "We need a day or two to sort things out."

"Ain't heard of a Winston, not in here anyways." A swirl of sand up and surrounded us. Arthur and I instinctively lifted our T-shirts to cover our noses, but Stormi stood statued in the dervish, unaffected by the choking swirl. Eleven hawked and spit, squinting through the earth. "What are you sorting, girl?"

The gust moved on. Stormi glanced at me and shook her head, and I read her silencing cue.

Arthur did not. He lowered his shirt and spit, and then blurted, "We're on the run."

Shut up, Arthur!

"Course you are. We all run from something. What you all running from?"

I stepped hard on Arthur's foot, but truth was on a roll.

"Gullary. It's a small town, so you may not have heard of it."

Eleven's face twitched, and he turned a strange shade. He hobbled three steps backward. "Gullary. And how did you come here?"

Arthur shrugged. "By truck." But Eleven didn't bother to listen. He hoofed it toward the prayer shed, took one glance back in our direction, and disappeared.

Stormi stared after him. "How *did* we come here, Jonah?"

Arthur stepped between us. "I think that's your question to answer, Stormi."

We were breaking apart, I felt it. Trust and mistrust fighting it out.

I hung my head, slowly wrung my hands, and Stormi continued. "Or would you like me to ask the ever-truthful Arthur?"

It was so complicated, it didn't matter anymore.

"Okay. The truth as I know it. It was Old Rickety. And then we were locked in and you were so furious and you wanted to get away and I wanted to get away and I wanted you to stop hating me, so I figured you might if you thought I knew a place. Then Arthur gave me this and I had a place to go." I reached in my pocket and brought out the chess piece, turned it over in my fingers. "It seemed as good a place as any. It felt like a mystery. Like maybe I knew something you didn't. For once you didn't know, it was secret between me and Arthur and—"

"Tres," she whispered.

"Tres. But I didn't know he was your grandpa, or that he was out to get us, or that we'd end up on a poster. Honest, it was just someplace to go."

Stormi started to pace. "So we're hiding from Tres in the place Tres wanted us to go."

"Indirectly," I said.

Arthur leaned over and offered his volume-packed whisper. "Technically speaking, it's a direct correlation."

"Thanks, Arthur."

He nodded curtly. "Stormi, Jonah has now told you everything. We wanted to reach Bishop, and Tres wanted us there. My question is, why are we *here*? A lot of this . . ." He gestured dramatically. "It seems to be a result of your doing. I don't think Jonah wanted to follow Winston at all."

I exhaled. "Accusations don't help, Arthur. I'll take it. My fault." I raised my hand. "I picked the town. Didn't know anything about this place. I don't know what I knew, seizures picking up as they are. But no matter how we got here, or who brought us here, we're here, right? We stick together. We stick—"

Stormi stepped toward me as if to strike, her violent Stormi eyes squinting with hate. Two inches from my chest, she took a sharp left and swooshed by me without a word. Even her breeze was pissed. She opened the cabin door, slamming it shut behind her.

Arthur winced. "I think perhaps I caused you some trouble just now and—"

I placed my hand over his mouth. "It's good it came out. From now on, maybe keep your wonderings about Stormi to yourself. Come on." I grabbed his arm and pulled. "We need to be gone long before this Q comes back, but first we're checking that shed."

"But you heard Eleven. It's illegal."

"Aren't you a little bit curious? Why an old man freaked when you mentioned Gullary?" I spun and grabbed both his shoulders, shaking gently. "Why a genius able to place you in zugzwang sent us to this spot?"

Arthur looked back toward the cabin, and when his face returned, it was all smiles. "A genius and his genius grand-daughter. This is Stormi's doing. But, yes, I'm curious."

Stormi exploded out the door, hand extended. "Not funny, Jonah! The truck keys. Now."

"I, uh, don't have your keys."

"They aren't where I left them. How are we supposed to leave if . . ." She froze, eyes frantic. "Give me five minutes." She raced around the side of the cabin.

Arthur and I glanced at each other.

He cleared his throat. "Doesn't that seem a bit odd to you?"

"She's been odd since the day we left. Don't know what that's about, but five minutes is all we need," I said, and walked toward the shed. We reached the door. Arthur turned the knob, and the wooden door swung open with force, catching me square on the kneecap, sending me to the dirt.

"Arthur, you idiot." I started to stand, and froze. There stood Q. I didn't need to be told. He was tall and strong, the muscles in his arms rippling with both power and years. Tanned, bald, and earringed, he looked like a pirate, or like Mr. Clean on Mom's disinfectant.

He stretched out an arm and pulled me to my feet as if I were a child.

"Not for you." He closed the door gently behind him. "My name is Michael Queene, and you may address me as such. Not Michael as my father did, nor Queene as acquaintances do. And though you will hear the men refer to me as Q, it is used only by those who know me well." He looked carefully from me to Arthur and back again. "The Hive functions because we have rules and trust. Do you understand these words?" Q folded his arms, and examined my back. "I asked if, as guests, you understand the importance of both those concepts. Have you not been taught?"

Arthur nodded and folded his hands. I swept the dirt off my jeans.

"My question was simple. Has your schooling not addressed issues of propriety?"

"My ma has . . . Michael Queene, sir," I answered.

"Which then begs the question: Why would you ignore your upbringing and the admonition of your own flesh and blood to do what you should not?"

"I guess I wanted to look."

"You are guessing. Turning a true false into a multiple choice. The command is clear—honor your father and mother that it may go well with you in the land. Why did you disobey your parents?"

His voice was deep and smooth, the kind of voice that places you at ease, even when you're certain you're in danger. Almost hypnotic, it was.

"I guess—"

"Do not begin with a guess, begin with the truth. Why did you choose rebellion over your Ma's instruction?"

"I'm a disobedient child?" I'd not before thought of myself as such, but there seemed little option. Q breathed deeply. "Stand up straight when you speak, posture matters. It communicates confidence."

"I can't."

By now we were so far afield, I no longer wanted anything but to see Stormi. Did I say her name out loud?

"The girl?" Q's voice penetrated.

"We don't know. She ran off," Arthur said.

"I see." Q sighed. "For her own good, I should find her. You should wait in the cabin."

"I think so too," Arthur said.

"Do not think. Let your yes be yes and your no be no. Say what you know, no more. Let's rehearse your sentiment again. You, Michael Queene, should go find her."

"Yes, you Michael Queene, should go find her."

Arthur was gone, trapped by Q's trance, but again the words from Tres's note rattled around inside me, took up residence, broke the spell.

Avoid Q to prevent more loss.

"It's time we leave." I rounded Arthur's shoulder with my arm and started a brisk walk toward the cabin. Michael Queene made no move to follow, watching us from the front of the shed.

"*We* need to find her, and find that Winston, and—"

Ahead, Stormi raced back into the courtyard. "It's bad. I hot-wired the truck. But they've drained the tank. I wired six more. All drained. Not a vehicle in that garage has a spit of gas in it. Jonah? What's happening?"

"I don't know." I turned and pointed at Q, slowly striding our way. "That's Michael Queene—first name, last name, use them both—and he's in charge of this hive, I know that. Be careful of his voice." I stared into Stormi's eyes. "We'll get out of here if we stick together."

I glanced back at Arthur. He was gone, walking quickly back toward Q. Soon, given Arthur's honesty, Q would know all our friend knew, which was pretty much everything.

"We don't leave without Arthur." I exhaled hard. "Agreed?"

Stormi let out a low whistle and drew close to my side. *"Arthurus hypnotizimus?"*

I forced a smile. "Yeah."

Okay Tres, why am I here?

CHAPTER 12

I sat with Stormi in silence. Hours alone in the cabin somehow separated us from each other, from ourselves. My mind floated back to her words, words of affection for me. How I would have soared to hear them in Gullary, but the winds had shifted, and she wasn't the same.

Maybe I wasn't either.

"You think he's all right?" Stormi spoke to nobody in particular. "He's been with that guy for hours."

"I don't reckon Arthur can get in too much trouble."

Outside, the muffled sound of men's voices surrounded the shed, and Stormi and I exchanged glances. "We stay together, no matter what," I said.

"Like we're together now?"

Stormi would never ask that. Not my Stormi, but I got up from Arthur's bed and sat down at her side, and lied. "We're fine."

The door swung open and Winston motioned us outside. "Come on."

I rose quickly and met him at the door. "Why'd you bring us? Why are you keeping us?"

"Keepin' you? You came on your own volition. No force used. Once here, we simply ask you to follow the rules set forth." He spun and strode toward the meeting hall.

"It's okay, Jonah." Stormi joined me, leaning her head against my shoulder. "I kind of freaked back there, but I've been thinking, being here has benefits. I don't think the police will find us. Cartwright won't find us. Tres doesn't seem eager to come, or he would have been here already. It's okay."

We walked hand-in-hand across the dusty ground.

Men streamed silently by us on all sides, either unaware of or uninterested in our presence. They lined up outside the hall. Perfect single file.

"Three, Seven, Eleven . . ."

They shouted numbers as they entered the doorway. "Fifty-two, Fifty-four, Sixty-one."

Stormi and I paused at the threshold, and then followed.

Two rows of picnic tables lined the length of the shadowy room. Three stained glass windows provided what little light there was. Arthur marched up to greet us.

"I'm glad to see you. I'm sorry I left. I told him everything, Jonah. Everything about you and Stormi and Tres. I told him everything. I had to. I'm sorry."

I shook my head. "It's all right."

"Sit." Q's word dropped all but the three of us onto the benches. We stood surrounded, like uncaged zoo animals. Q leaned back, folded his arms. He appeared more than happy; he was thrilled to make us a spectacle, to see us squirm, and

I hated him. I'd been a spectacle my entire life—in Gullary, it was my role. But no longer. Stormi stroked her necklace. She needed me, and here, far from the parents I had disobeyed, I felt a twinge of new, of strength.

I straightened as best I could and glared back at Q.

Stare away. I am Jonah Triumphus.

"Bow your heads."

"I will not bow to you," I whispered.

"Dear Lord," Q began.

Oh.

"Help us know right from wrong. Help us choose right."

The room erupted in unison, "Help us know right from wrong. Help us choose right."

"Amen." Q gestured to three chairs next to him, and soon we were seated, Arthur on his right, Stormi and me on his left.

Men spoke in hushed tones, ignoring us completely, all except for Winston. I caught him glancing our way.

"Jonah, where's Tres?" Q asked.

"I told you we don't know," Arthur interjected, and quickly fell silent.

"Who's Tres?" Stormi asked.

Q took a long drink. "There is a stupidity that comes off as simple ignorance. This is forgivable. Then there is a stupidity that is truly stupid. You, Stormi, are walking the path of the latter."

I cannot express how deeply his words shook me. Stormi had been called unnatural and odd, but nobody questioned her intelligence. She was the smartest one in every room, in control of all that transpired, and we all knew it. All but Michael Queene.

"Jonah, again, I ask you, where's Tres?"

"Who's Tres?" Stormi repeated, reaching for a roll.

How the question irked Q. The muscles around his face tightened, but only for a moment. Later, I would realize the battle Stormi waged here on my behalf, but we rarely understand such wars as they transpire.

Q dabbed his mouth with his napkin. "Are you familiar with King David and his prideful attempt to number his soldiers?"

Of course she wasn't. I knew David had whipped a pebble at a giant, but that was it. Stormi hadn't been to church, well, ever.

Stormi stood up. "I will tell you all a story."

I will not forget the next five minutes. A hall silent, except for Stormi, sharing a tale I'd never heard, of a general named Joab, charged by King David to count David's soldiers, a move which apparently displeased God mightily. So much so that God presented David with one of three calamities as punishment. Door number one: three years of famine. Door number two: three months of fleeing from David's enemies. And door number three: three days of a plague sent from the hand of God himself. David chose the plague, and seventy thousand men gave up the ghost. There likely would have been more casualties, but God held back the hand of one angry angel.

"Three days of plague," Stormi repeated, "that was it—three days. Then God showed mercy. We've been here one day now, after two more I expect to be mercifully released." She cast her terrible Stormi gaze at Q. "I would think you, Michael Queene, a man so bound by Scripture, would attempt to follow the principles found there, wouldn't you?"

Not a soul moved. Stormi sat down, reached for her water glass and took a sip. Q cleared his throat. "Tres's whereabouts are all that matter to me. You are here only until I know."

Stormi's eyes flashed. The space between sky and ground where lightning passes through? That's where I was. "Tres's whereabouts are all that matter to me as well, but I might have a better memory if you told me more about him."

"Have not your parents taught you to respect your elders?" Q regained his footing, and having slipped into his parental obedience quicksand myself, I stepped on Stormi's foot, tried to keep her from moving forth. She'd done so well.

She kicked me. "Orphans aren't taught. Dead people don't teach anything."

Stormi never spoke of her birth parents, except in an occasional stolen letter. Were they dead? Suddenly, I wanted to know.

"You've never been more wrong. I've simply been eager to speak with Tres for some time." Q shifted. "It's my understanding he's been unavailable."

"Not to Jonah." Arthur chose this moment to be Arthur.

I tossed a roll at his head, but Q intercepted it, placed it gently on his own plate.

"Jonah, you really don't know where you are, or why you're here, do you?" Q leaned back. "The Hive runs with precision and order. These two qualities bring my men comfort and some semblance of peace. This is my job, my calling. You can see why visitors may cause needless unease."

"Send us away, then." I leaned forward. "You want to find Tres, we don't. Send us away."

Q smiled. "To a young man, the remedy, of course, seems harmless enough, but you have only a small piece of the picture. I don't blame you. Even old men can be fools."

He glanced to his left, and I let my gaze follow. I blinked hard, and my heartbeat pounded. At a solitary table sat three men. I'd seen them only once, but their faces would not leave me. I knew them without their black suits, without their black hats.

One of them knew me.

I forced a smile. "I sure hope you find Tres soon. You know all we know. May we leave?"

"May we leave," Q repeated. "Perhaps both our desires are best met if you remain with us. Arthur mentioned Tres and Stormi's unique connection. If he's looking for you, it only makes sense that he will eventually come to us, at which point we both have what we want."

"Except that we don't want to see him," I said.

Q stood. "That appears to be inevitable. The question is, do you want to meet that criminal alone, or would it be safest for you here. I think the latter. Good night." He strode toward the door and again the room fell silent. The moment he exited, every man rose, calling his number as he too slipped into the night, which left the three of us alone.

"This Hive of yours is a cult, some kind of freakish place." Stormi slowly wandered to the center of the room. "Michael Queene's the leader, the rest a bunch of worker bees from who knows where." She quieted. "I don't know what's worse. Meeting Tres, or being stuck here."

I nodded, and then frowned. "What do you mean, Hive of mine? I didn't know anything about this place."

"You said you did."

"I said 'I know a place.' Generally, not specifically."

"Tres knew it."

"Technically and semantically, she's got you, Jonah." Arthur nodded.

"Yeah, well, I screwed up, okay? I screwed everything up. But it's not like I'm the only one who's been a little secretive."

"Technically, he's got you there, Stormi."

"Arthur, why don't you ask Jonah how *specifically* he plans on getting us out of here?"

Arthur looked confused. "She wants to know—"

I stood and stared at Stormi. "Tell her I'm working on an ingenious plan as we speak."

Arthur cleared his throat. "Apparently, Jonah is, even as we speak—"

"Tell Jonah that I wouldn't trust his ingenious plan if it was the only ingenious plan in existence."

Arthur opened his mouth and let it fall shut.

"Go on," Stormi said. "Tell him."

"Stormi—"

"Wait!" Stormi stepped forward. "Add in that I am working on my own ingenious plan, so he can give that brain of his a rest."

"Stormi—"

"Wait again."

Arthur sat back and folded his arms.

"Tell him that I still do."

"Your sentence is missing a few needed words, not that you would let me get to them," Arthur said.

I stepped around the table and walked toward Stormi. "You still do? 'Cause I kind of figured stuff changed. At least it felt like it had, or it felt like you had . . ."

"Still here," she said quietly, and stretched out her hand. I took it and drew her near, feeling her softness, suddenly wanting to feel much more.

"You two make absolutely no sense." Arthur shook his head and joined us. "So we're staying then? The food is good. Q seems nice enough."

"No, we're leaving," Stormi spoke into my chest. "Jonah's thinking of an ingenious plan."

She always did know what to say, and her trust kicked me back a few years.

"Wasn't that thing weird today?"

Stormi and I walked home from school, already the best of friends by third grade.

By "that thing," she meant the annual scoliosis screening. Girls visited privately with Nurse Loyna, but not the guys . . . oh no, every guy in Gullary Primary was shipped to the gym, where we stripped from the waist up, pressed our palms and leaned over, as if to touch our toes. A special doctor hired by the district slowly wandered behind our posteriors, staring at our spines. Principal Haynes walked beside him with a clipboard.

"Clear. Clear. Monitor. Clear. Clear."

His voice boomed. I didn't know who received the dreaded "monitor" labels, as I stared upside down back through my legs, but I pitied each one of them. The term *scoliosis* itself sounded terminal.

"Monitor. Clear. Clear." His voice strengthened. The guy was getting nearer. "Clear, Clear. What the—"

His shock occurred directly behind me, and the next thing I knew, he was tracing my lumbar with his thumbs. "Absolutely profound. Why hasn't this been caught?"

Haynes began fumbling about as if my back was a blight on his record. "It won't happen again," he managed.

"What's your name, son?"

"Jonah."

"You may straighten."

I did, and from the other side of the gym, somebody farted. The gym erupted, and several other gas bombs followed. I would have enjoyed it had I not been receiving a death sentence.

"Son, I've not seen a case of scoliosis this marked before. Do your parents know?"

"Am I going to die?" I asked.

"No."

"Then they don't know." I exhaled, thankful that I had caught something that would not lead to death, though right then, Peter Yallis and Riley Trew shuffled away from me. Who knew, scoliosis might be contagious.

I told Stormi about it on the way home.

"Well." She thought for some time. "If you have it, I want it too."

"No, you don't."

"You're the best-looking boy in third grade. Mom says so."

"Ms. P?"

"She's always saying how tall you are. She says how handsome that curly blond hair is. How strong you are."

"Strong? How would she know?"

Stormi looked off. "It's going to rain. We should hurry." She took off running.

"Stormi! Tell me about the strong part."

Yep, how early she knew what I needed to hear.

We slowly walked around the courtyard, Stormi's hand still tucked in mine. In the dark, it wasn't immediately clear which cabin was ours, but familiarity was already setting in, and the three of us quietly approached the door.

"Nobody else is up?"

"There's a curfew. Supper, then bed." Arthur stepped inside first. "Wow, dark in here."

We felt our way forward, plopping onto our beds. "So, tomorrow we figure out how to get out of here."

A voice from the direction of the desk: "You may not have that long."

CHAPTER 13

Some warnings cause the heart to beat with gusto. This warning coupled with a short shriek from Stormi nearly ended me.

I, surprisingly, was first to find a voice, speaking at the shape across the room. "What's going to happen to us?"

"I don't know."

Winston.

"It's the way of the Hive. Everyone knows a part. Keeps all of them from thinking too hard about what's being done."

"I don't understand," I continued.

"If you shoot someone dead to rights, you maybe feel it. But it don't hurt nothing if your job is only to buy bullets."

"And what's your job?" Stormi's voice shook.

"I ain't come to talk about me. I don't have much time before quarters are checked."

"You lied to us." I straightened and winced as my back expressed its displeasure. "You said there'd be nothing required, but we're stuck here now. You said we could leave whenever we wanted to and—"

He pushed his hands through his hair. "Shut up, I know what I said."

My eyes became one with the night, and I could see Winston rubbing his temples. Coming back here tonight hadn't been easy.

"Listen." Winston's voice dropped. "They will be coming, maybe tonight, maybe tomorrow night. But I think it's in their nature, so you best be ready."

"They?" whispered Stormi.

"The Hive. All of 'em. Didn't know what I was getting into when I took this job. 'Need a caretaker,' Queene said. 'The old caretaker has passed on and we need some young blood to help the older ones around here.' It was back in '09, and times were tough, so I took it. I took it. Only way I saw to feed my family."

"You have family here?"

"No, I ain't crazy, but they know where I live, where my young ones live. Queene has reminded me of this point several times. You ain't the only one who's as good as trapped." Winston leaned forward. "My job is food runs. Medicine runs. Whatever they need from the outside, that's what I get. Spend the weekends at home, the weeks out here in this accursed place."

"But you brought us here." Here, my naiveté showed bright, but I could not seem to overcome this point. People can be cruel and self-serving; I of all people should have known this.

"I did," Winston continued. "The Drinking Hole is the only business within twenty miles of this place. Queene wants me there, posts me there to listen. If I hear something unusual, he wants to have a look. The man hasn't left this compound for decades, but I reckon he knows more than anyone the ways of the outside."

"You're the eyes and ears, then. The hands and feet. Then you must know why he keeps us." Stormi hugged her arms, while outside the night winds howled.

"No." Winston shook his head. "Though I do know pieces are moving."

"Chess pieces?" Arthur asked.

"Sure, kid. Whatever. Listen, a few days ago, three of 'em came to me at night. Said they had a pass from Q. Said they needed to attend a family event. In short, they needed a ride. I was gassed and ready, so I took 'em to a tiny armpit town the other side of the state."

"Gullary," I said.

"Well, turns out they went without Queene's permission, and hell broke loose when we returned. The Hive turned inside out and Queene almost lost control."

"All because three men went to a funeral?" I asked.

"All because three men returned to Gullary."

The air grew thick. "Returned?"

"Ah, now you see the magnitude of a word. These aren't the first cells the men here in the Hive have occupied. You once had a prison in Gullary, filled with the most heinous humanity could offer. But a storm came, and their bonds broke away. True enough, some probably died beneath the rubble, but most didn't, and them that escaped came here."

Stormi pressed into my side, and Arthur joined us on the bed, breaking all his personal space rules.

I tried to clear my throat, but sound wouldn't come, and I swallowed hard instead. "We're living with rapists and murderers and—"

"Nobody here that's not done something worth being locked up for a lifetime. But credit Queene. He knew these violent inmates couldn't live as free men, at least not right off. He put them to work, gave 'em religion. Gave them a new purpose working in the Hive. Think of him as the new warden. He gives off confidence, demands order. Yeah, Queene looks calm, but he's never been, that's because of your friend Tres."

"Grandpa Tres," Stormi said softly.

"Grandpa?" Winston shook his head. "What a tangled web we weave. From stories pieced together, seems as there's one inmate left alive at storm's end but what refused to run with the rest. He chose to stay in Gullary though escape was offered."

"Grandpa Tres."

"And whatever kept your grandfather there, it's enough to keep Queene up at nights, or so the men whisper."

"But how do you know all this?" I asked. "You just buy the bullets."

"Sometimes, the unforeseen happens. Had a stowaway one weekend. Eighty-eight popped up his head and asked me to drive as far away from here as I could. I did what Queene told me, should that situation arise. We took off, slowly circled around, and I brought him back here, but on the way he told me more than I should know, what that now I'm telling you. About the men. Where they's been. About Tres and Q and—Oh, shoot, I will never forget his face when he saw me pull up to the garage. The sadness, and I didn't know. You got to believe me that I didn't know what they would do to him."

"What . . ." I realized I didn't need to know.

"Yeah, he gone. If the guilty three—that's what they call those that went back to Gullary—if Queene didn't keep them isolated from the others, they'd be gone too. I believe many of them got religion, found peace. But you can't force that. Many are here 'cause they're too scared to leave, but inside they're who they was. The ugly's just baked in a little harder."

"I still don't see why Tres worries anyone." Arthur spoke up. "It's not logical."

The door flew open. "Perhaps a bit too late for my caretaker to be paying my guests a social call."

Q stood in the doorway, large and imposing, and Winston shot up. "I miss my family, miss 'em something terrible. Seeing her about Jen's age, I needed to talk."

"Visiting hours are over." Q turned and vanished, leaving the door open.

Winston leaned over, his lips releasing little more than a breeze. "Go on now. Go."

He too disappeared, closing the door behind him. We huddled together.

"Why would Tres want us here?" I asked. "I don't care what anyone says, I spent time with him. He wouldn't want us dead. Stormi, this would be a really good time to know something that we don't."

"Do you believe him?" she asked quietly.

"Who? Winston? Yeah, I mean, don't you?"

"Didn't it all seem odd, him in here and Q showing up right then? He was so willing to tell us everything, but he's never gone to the authorities? There's the family explanation, but his cover was so thought out."

"It doesn't matter," I said. "If they check the cabins, we can't leave. All we have are a bunch of vehicles without gas."

"Nineteen."

We both looked at Arthur, who turned cheery. "Nineteen. He stores the gas. Thirty keeps the keys."

"How?" I asked.

"I know people think I'm stupid, you think I'm stupid, but didn't Michael Queene make you uncomfortable with that voice? I took it upon myself to find out what he knows, which you two couldn't do sitting in here, I might add."

I'd not felt the desire to kiss a guy before, but the urge overwhelmed and I planted one on his cheek. "You got Q to tell you all that. Ma would call you a blessed child."

Stormi stood and paced. "So we know who has what we need. We don't know which cell they're in. Unless you found that out too."

"No, I didn't. We need to stay awake tonight. One of us all the time." Arthur peeked out the door. "Knowing who's who doesn't help if we're dead. If we make it until morning, we go to work with the men. They yell their numbers on the way in to meals, so we should be able to figure out who the two are. We can track them back to their cells, and the next day when they go off, we grab what we need."

"And none of this goes to Winston, right?" Stormi grew excited. Hope returned to her words.

"Agreed." I sealed the matter, and then paused. "Arthur, I'm not sure what we'd do without you. Sorry for the way I made you feel small and stupid."

"I accept your apology, as long as you take the first watch." He jumped into bed. Stormi slapped my back and did the same, leaving me vertical—well, almost vertical. It could be worse. There was danger all around, but I was held fast by a true friend and a girl I loved.

Loved?

I walked toward the door, my mind fixed on that word, wondering when I should use it. Talk about danger.

CHAPTER 14

I stayed awake all night, my eyes peering out the cracked door and into the darkness. Truth had fallen from Winston's lips—the Hive was peaceful. Hard to fathom some great evil lurking about in the hearts of men, but then again, looks were deceiving. Even Gullary had turned, shifted, become less my home and more a quicksand. We'd only been away a few days, but the tether that had held me fast bound me no more. Now free floating, I could sense how secretive we'd been. Something lay under the surface.

Perhaps every place had its secrets.

My granddad and I crossed but briefly in this life.

Memories of him are light and vapory, more gas than solid. I remember his smell, and the Old Spice aroma that lingered in his car and his home. I remember his chair, brown and mahogany. How I wanted to sit in it. How I was warned not to.

I just can't remember his wife.

My grandmother had lived; the existence of Dad makes that a certainty. According to pieces gleaned from a hundred clipped conversations, she outlived Granddad by a mile. But that was all I knew. To our family, she was shadow. Never mentioned, her nothingness never explained.

Yes, I had asked.

"Sometimes your own kin chooses to vanish." This from Ma, who knelt in our backyard garden. She had glanced both ways before crossing this street.

"Vanish?" I was twelve, and the thought felt adventurous, holding the same terrible intrigue as a kidnapping. "Where is she now?"

Ma buried her trowel and pushed back to a sit. "The definition of vanish means she has disappeared."

"Do you know where she is?"

Ma reflected for a long time. "Ask your father."

From him I received nothing but a condescending smile, as if I had waded into territory too deep for me. Her chapter seemed closed.

Until a letter arrived two years later. Dad assembled Ma and me.

"Jonah, it appears that your grandma passed. The funeral has already been held." I recall him glancing sharply at Ma at this point, but thought nothing of it at the time. "I want you to know about this remarkable woman."

This dramatic 180 continued for months. Dad poured story after story into me, about the great travels of my historic grandma, the awful and tragic search she undertook through Mexico to find a treatment for Granddad's souring mind. She was a hero, Dad said. I should never forget that.

But she never showed the slightest interest in even seeing me, so the whole hero narrative never took. I would have liked to meet her.

"Did she know about my back?" I tapped my spine with the trowel. "Did she know about me?"

Ma adjusted the hose. "It's what she knew that kept her away."

I stayed awake all night.

In the dark of early morning, men bustled, and I carefully closed our cabin door. Time to move. "Stormi, Arthur, get up."

Minutes later we joined the comatose shuffling toward the dining hall, myself eager for a little coffee. Any adrenaline I had acquired from the day before had long since seeped away, and I blinked hard as I entered the building.

Arthur pulled me aside, my body offering little resistance. "You look awful. Why didn't you wake me?"

"I was doing fine until an hour ago." Remembering my family made me tired.

We took our seats at the head table, and neither Q nor any other man questioned us. All present waited in silence and darkness. I heard the prayer, but it did not enter; heard hushed conversation, but did not try to listen. Coffee. I drank coffee until we all rose.

We followed the group out into the courtyard, beyond the prayer shed, and onto a rough, stone-paved path that exited the ring of cells. It was too early to care where we walked; my body moved on caffeine and autopilot. The path quickly widened to a patio, and pulling up to it was a familiar squeal. A school bus hauling a beat-up trailer.

I exchanged hopeful glances with Stormi. Maybe we wouldn't need Arthur's plan, not if there was a gassed-up bus at the ready.

I followed Stormi on board and paused. Winston sat behind the wheel. Whatever crime he committed via his "secret" visit could not have been too heinous, and I doubted him all the more. Winston's hands did not shift on his lap, nor did his gaze stray from straight ahead, and we took the front two seats, Stormi and I backed by Arthur.

Loaded, the bus hissed and lurched forward.

An hour later the sun hinted its arrival and still we jarred onward. It felt doubtful that we were on any sanctioned road, given the lilt of our travel. The bounce and the rock grabbed my senses, pulled them back toward slumber, and when we finally stopped, I was barely coherent.

"Beautiful," Stormi whispered, divoting my side with her elbow.

I forced my eyes open. She was right.

I rose and stepped out into a garden. The sound of rushing water was the first thing I heard, the sudden explosion of trees and flowers the first thing I saw.

"Walk around, kids. See what old men hath wrought." Q's voice was low, but it turned on a dime. "To your stations, men. Tasks are set. Get to!"

Men scrambled and clumped near the trailer, grabbing hoes and shovels, shears and buckets.

"We don't have any clear direction," Arthur said.

Stormi took hold of my arm. "Sure we do. Walk around."

Here, I can only ask that you believe this account, though I'd understand if your faith is worn thin. Had I not seen it, I would not have believed such a place existed, certainly not in the barren of the panhandle.

That sound of water began in the garden's center, where a shallow lake rippled gently in the breeze. Given the hour, it reflected the red of morning. In the middle of that lake grew an island, tiny and perfect, home to nothing but two beautiful fruit trees.

Streams trickled out from the lake in four directions, and along the banks grew plants and flowers unseen in Gullary. Everywhere, the men tended and pruned, sculpted and watered.

The younger men worked the practical garden, alive with grains and vegetables. It was perfect. It was beautiful, and Winston's warnings felt remote.

Wish I had my camera.

We wandered the lakeshore. A rowboat waited, and Stormi nodded toward it.

"You think we can?"

"Once again, a child is thinking. This lack of certitude among the younger generation is concerning." Q stepped out of a thicket, pulled the boat into the water, and climbed aboard, beginning a slow row toward the island. "Do you want to join me, yes or no?"

"Yes," I said, and began walking toward him.

"Don't you *think* that's presumptuous? It's my island."

We watched him row clear out to the middle, climb out onto the tiny spit of land, and set up a rotating chair. From there, Q could spin around and see the entire group; he could monitor every move.

He could eat from the trees.

"This whole place is so bizarre." A hundred feet to our left, four men of near eighty fought with a huge tree, dragging it with fits and gasps toward a pre-dug hole. I started toward them to help, but Stormi grabbed my shoulder.

"I have to," I said. "They're not going to make it. They're busting in the heat, and Q's got it easy. It's not right." I turned to Stormi, who bit her lip.

"We need to get out of here," she said gently.

I broke free, jogged toward the men, and returned five minutes later, back on fire but staring at a vertical oak.

"We will. We will leave," I said while clapping the dirt off my hands, though I lacked conviction. "Of course, bizarre as it is, this garden is beautiful. If there weren't maybe murderers everywhere, I mean, we could live here. Right here."

Stormi sighed. "Describe what you see."

"Well, trees, water, pretty much an oasis. Four rivers, two trees."

"Garden of Eden."

"A bit over the top, Stormi."

"Maybe. Do you believe in the story? The Adam and Eve thing?"

"Ma does, Dad doesn't, so I'll go in fifty-fifty."

Stormi quieted. "Two trees were there. The tree of the knowledge of good and evil, and the tree of life. They ate from the knowledge tree—"

"And figured out they were nude. I remember that part."

Stormi nodded. "At that moment, sin entered this world. At that moment. What do you think would have happened if they ate from the tree of life after that? I'll tell you. They would have lived forever. Horrors committed in secret would have lived forever."

And here, I cannot tell you what came over her. She eased down to her knees, closed her eyes, and a wash of peace fell over her face. She was transfigured, to use the biggest Bible word I know.

She opened her eyes, stood, and breathed deep. I maintain that though she didn't tell me, it was at this moment that she figured it out. She knew what she would one day do.

"Secret horrors can't be allowed to live forever," she said.

"Yeah, well, I don't know about all that God stuff."

Stormi winked, returning in all her glory. "How about us? Do you know anything about us stuff?" She paused. "Say that we were alone. No Arthur, no Tres following, and no Gullary looking . . . If you and I were really a you and me, what would you do first?"

I thought a moment. Maybe it was the scenery, or Stormi's full attention. Maybe it was the urging of Genesis to be fruitful and multiply. "I'd, uh, I'd try, well, after asking, of course, to maybe kiss you. Maybe?"

"And second?"

"It would kind of depend on how the first thing went."

"Let's assume it went well. Very well."

"Huh." I puffed out air. "I don't let myself dwell on those type of moments. I'm not Connor, you know."

Moment lost. As I look back, this may be the most painful of them all.

Stormi bristled. It wasn't until twenty long paces stretched between us that I realized what I had done.

"Stormi, I, I didn't mean to say that. I mean, I shouldn't have brought him up, or to make you think about all that. Crap."

She was gone, gone from sight, and gone from hope.

"Kid, here's your shovel."

Don't need one. I'm digging deep on my own.

I turned, and a bald, fifty-something held out the tool. "Lots of work today. Good that you're here."

"Yeah, well, right now, I need to talk to Stormi before I can do anything else."

"Love waits. Q don't." He grabbed my arm and hauled me into the nearby field. Rich, black dirt gave easily beneath my feet, and I glanced over my shoulder in time to see Stormi reappear behind a clump of trees. She stopped and held my gaze.

"Move, kid. Planters are comin'. We got a hole to dig."

He plunged his shovel into the dirt, and straightened, leaning on the handle. "Your turn."

"So I dig anywhere?"

"No, fool, right there." He nodded downward, and I positioned my feet, bent, and dug out a scoop. My back throbbed.

I was too far away to flash Stormi an I'm-just-a-stupid-guy look, so I set my mind to digging. "What number do I call you?"

He glanced around. "No number while we're in a hole. Saul will do."

Another thrust, and another. Together we dug one foot. Three feet, widening as we dug. Sweat poured down, but I did not stop: Stormi was still watching. Half a day passed and the hole neared five feet deep, and a similar distance around.

"We planting another tree?" I paused, and crumpled, leaning down against the inside of the hole. Saul peeked over the edge and did the same.

"Ain't for us to know." He scratched in the dirt with his fingers, crusted red with Oklahoma earth. "Nothing asked, nothing required, exceptin' to dig." He stared up at the blue sky and sighed.

I leaned forward, silencing the scream of my vertebrae, searching for any question that'd buy me an extra minute before my next scoop. "How long you been here?"

"Long? Since the start. Some days, seems too long. Others, not long enough."

"Do you ever think of leaving?"

Saul's gaze searched me. He was looking for something; I felt it. But he didn't find it, and let his head fall back against the inside of the pit. "Every day, but there's nothing for me out there. Here, I got work to do."

"These holes?"

He scoffed. "Prayer work. Don't expect you to make sense of it."

"In the prayer shed."

Saul rubbed his face, gave the ground some light jabs with his shovel. "Some memories you don't dig up 'lessen you have to." He shifted, his face aging before my eyes. "I was so young, you know, the youngest. A dumb kid like you—no offense. Didn't know it would go down as it did. I don't think anyone really knew." He paused and looked off. "Maybe Q. Maybe Q knew."

"What went down? What happened? Was it in Gullary?"

He waggled his finger, and then gently backhanded my chest. "Sneaky, you are. Get an old man tired and unhinged in the heat." He slowly rose.

"Do you know Tres?"

Saul dropped down quickly to a knee. "Some names you best not say in the Hive. Come on, orders are to go down another foot."

Together we deepened and widened the hole. Moments later, a rope ladder was lowered and we climbed out. Dirty, smelly, but worked. And the work felt good. I felt good.

I followed Saul to the lake, took off my outer clothes and climbed in along with all the others. Arthur was washing some distance away; I didn't see Stormi, but believe me, I looked.

"What happened to you?"

Old fingers reached out and touched my spine. I recoiled. "That's not really your business." He nodded, offered a sympathetic smile and I softened.

"It's, uh, scoliosis. Bad case."

"Sorry, kid. Gotta be a painful way to live."

My eyes burned, and not from sweat. I plunged down beneath the surface. There, tears did come, and in a strange baptism, they were washed away. Some ancient hand had touched me, had compassion on me, and emotion overwhelmed. It came in splashes and waves unrecognizable. Sure, Stormi's hand brought comfort, but I tell you I'd never felt her fingers reach in that deep.

Ma would later say that I felt the touch of God. I don't know about that. I do know these old guys saw me, uncovered, and what they saw caused them to reach out, not run away.

When I finally brought myself to emerge, my wrinkled god was once again scrubbing, while a few nearby men offered sharp nods and safe glances. Yeah, I could live here with Stormi, surrounded by this new mercy. They may have been murderers and rapists, but they didn't violate my condition.

They left my heart intact.

A sudden splash of water struck my eyes, and when I opened them, the lake was spinning.

Not in water. Not . . . here.

I sloshed toward shore, but made it only two steps before Old Rick took me. Bubbles and gasping on the heels of a miracle. Then no more.

I came to in the cabin, dressed in oversized jeans and an undersized T-shirt. Stormi gently stroked my head, her words calming despite her message.

"Your seizures are stronger than they were. They take you longer and more often."

"Yeah."

"You could go . . . you could go back if you wanted to. Your seizures would improve if you did." Her voice quieted. "You belong there. You don't need to stay with me. I'm so sorry I dragged you into this."

"But it was Tres—"

"I don't think Tres cares much about you."

I slipped in and out of consciousness, but when next I woke, Old Rickety had released me. Stormi hadn't.

"I'm not going back. Not now." I winced my back into a different position. "I just got good at diggin' a hole. What'd you do today?"

"Nothing. But I stayed near you." She lowered her voice. "There's something disturbing here, even more than we were told. We shouldn't separate."

I thought about the hole, the kindness shown me in the lake. "Friendliest place I've ever been." I propped myself on an elbow. "Arthur, what'd they have you do?"

"Builder. They called me a builder." He raised his hand and showed off his callous. "It was basic, simple assembly-line organization. Choppers, planers, followed by builders. Guys chopped down a few trees. Others planed them into rough boards. Builders assembled and nailed the boards together into a crate."

Stormi bit her lip. "How big was your crate?"

"Big enough to lie down in."

"You built a coffin, Arthur." Stormi rubbed her forearms. "And Jonah, you dug the hole. What did you think was going to be planted there, a twenty-foot turnip?"

"I'm no gravedigger." I shook my head. "If that's what we were doing, Saul would have told me."

"If he knew," said Stormi.

Right. If he knew.

"Let's assume Stormi's right." Arthur scratched his head. "It would be logical that someone is going in the crate. Someone's going in the ground. It could be me. I pried information from Michael Queene."

"Or me." Stormi folded her hands. "It's me Tres is after."

"Or me."

I didn't really think it would be me. There was no reason to stick me in the hole, but it seemed the right thing to say.

We sat and thought in silence, until Stormi and I exchanged glances, and spoke in unison. "Winston."

"They have no need to get rid of us." Stormi stood. "We're the bait for Tres."

"Tres doesn't know if we're dead or not," I offered.

Stormi raised her eyebrows. "Doesn't he? He's coming. We need to leave. Tonight. Jonah, while you slept off your seizure, Arthur went to dinner. He knows which cell holds the keys. He knows where the gas is. We leave tonight."

Plans were changing so quickly. Besides, they didn't have all my information.

"Wait. There's another old guy here who touched my back, and I'm telling you neither Saul or him or the others at the lake would, well, they wouldn't hurt anyone!" I was suddenly furious, and took a deep breath. "The wrinkled one he . . . sort of changed me."

Stormi took my hand. "You're doing it again. You believe everything you hear or experience. You think the best of everyone. Snap out of it and assume the worst, please, for us."

"Don't fight. Let me collect what we need," Arthur said. "Jonah, upon further thought, it's my fault we're out here. I let Tres out of SMX. He's the one causing you all this trouble. I did that."

I shook my head, still stinging from Stormi.

"I'll see you soon with what we need." Arthur slowly slipped from the room.

"Where are you?" Stormi looked betrayed, her eyes holding less for me. "Still with me?"

"I'm sure I'm too naïve to answer that."

I, too, slipped out, powered by anger. So I trusted people. What was wrong with that? I paced a bit, slowing at the sight of the prayer shed. It had been taunting me since our arrival, since Q had denied me entrance.

For the first time, I moved through the compound without fear. Purpose gives a guy courage, and I reached the door and ducked inside.

Candlelight lit the room, a space large, simple, and without focus. The room presented no front or back. Church pews filled the shed, facing outward, worshiping each of the four walls. And on those walls, displayed in poster-sized frames, were photos. Pictures of teens. My-aged teens. Guys and girls.

Beneath each photo was a table, on which lay one knife, one bowl, and a towel. I marched right, and stopped in front of an especially beautiful girl, one I swore I'd seen before.

"You almost look Stormi-ish."

Behind me, the door creaked, and I dropped to the floor, crawling awkwardly beneath a pew. There I tried to straighten—to become parallel with the bench—as they provided little cover, but my hunch prevented me. Footsteps, slow and heavy, moved toward the far end of the room. Oak creaked, and I rolled over and sat up, my sight line skimming the top of the backrests. Even from behind, I knew the shape well.

I'd spent the day with him in a hole.

I relaxed. Saul was a friend. All day he showed kindness, certainly contrition. I thought to stand and join him. Then the sound started. Deep and sorrowful and filled with pain. A sob; he was sobbing. It wasn't a sob I had entertained in my life. This one came from a place I didn't know, and never wanted to visit. It was a sob from hell.

For ten minutes, it shook him, and it felt I was invading a moment not made for me. I could run out, but that would be more intrusive, so I grimaced my spine into a crouch and waited and watched, my eyes growing big.

Saul finally moved toward the table, pausing to glance at the girl he fronted, whose confident face smiled down upon him. He grabbed his sleeve, rolled it up to the elbow, and reached for the knife. He cut himself slowly, deeply, the blade moving easily through his fleshy forearm. I couldn't watch. I wanted him to stop, and my fingers clawed the bench.

He glanced up again, and in the soft glow of the candle, crimson dripped down his arm and into the bowl.

What is this place?

Finally, he took hold of the towel and applied pressure to his fresh wound. He stood, let his gaze rise to heaven and prayed, before shuffling toward the door and vanishing. I didn't dare stand, not for many minutes. But I could not remain; Arthur's plan was in motion. He and Stormi would likely be waiting on me. I finally rose and slipped out, bursting to tell Stormi what I saw, hoping she could make sense of something.

I made it halfway to the cabin, and heard more footsteps behind me. Arthur was running, a metal gas can clutched tight.

"Here!" He pressed the can into my gut and jammed a set of twenty keys into my hand. "One of these should start one of the cars parked in front. There's not enough gas in there to get far. I need to find where he stores the rest."

I'd not seen Arthur panicked before. The sight set my heart thumping. "Well, you'll never guess what I saw in the prayer shed. Saul, blood-letting in front of a girl, or a photo of a girl, I mean, there were a whole bunch—"

"Go, Jonah! Stormi's in the garage." He shoved me and raced back the way he came, quietly entering the cell across the courtyard from ours. My mind spun, caught hold of something solid, and I dashed toward Stormi.

She stood outside the garage, all doors gaping behind her.

"He did it?" Her eyes lit, and I handed her the gas can. She gave it a shake, and slumped. "There's not enough here."

"I know. He's getting more. But I have news too." I handed her the key ring. "Wait, how do you know which key goes to which?"

Stormi let her digits stroke the keys' notches, as old Mr. Fredricks had run fingers over his Braille books. She paused on a key. "Caddy. This is an old Caddy." She snaked through the garage, stopping at a rusted Cadillac parked in the front row. "This one. This one here. Fill it."

"But what if it doesn't—"

"It's parked in front. I know the key. Better idea?"

I didn't move.

"Fill it."

I popped the gas door and let a trickle ooze into the tank. Half spilled onto the ground, but I didn't tell Stormi.

"There's even less here than I thought," I called.

Stormi hopped out of the car. "We need Arthur. He'll bring more. He'll bring—"

Last July 4, Jimmy Kleinman waltzed over to his pyro-technic display and flicked his cigarette lighter. Gullary's designated fireworks man, his shows were large and unique, drawing folks all the way from Hinman to the spectacle.

But the last explosions of the night—the grand finale— did not take place hundreds of feet up, as desired. Nope, they blew right there on the ground with a shake that felt atomic to those of us gathered fifty feet away. The first fireball set off others, and folks screamed as the ground shook. Jimmy was not hurt, and local conversation rewrote the ending as the best finale ever.

The explosion that rocked the garage felt like that.

"Arthur!" I dropped my gas can and sprinted back into the compound, Stormi at my side. Men stumbled about, dazed, their faces glowing orange in the fireball that burned on the far side.

The cell Arthur had entered was engulfed, as were the adjacent ones.

"No," I whispered. "That was where he was!" I pointed. "He went in there!" Stormi shook and grabbed me by the arm. "This is our only chance."

I did not move.

"He's gone." She hugged me quick and hard. "He's gone for nothing if we don't get out."

"There's nothing left." My mind spun. "He was right here, talking to me. Just like back home on the bus. Gina was right there, and then she wasn't and now he isn't."

It makes little sense now, what I said and the hesitance I displayed, but explosions steal a mind's rational thought.

"I need you to snap out of this *now!*" Stormi yanked hard and I stumbled, falling backward toward freedom. "Maybe he made it out. Maybe he wasn't inside." I grabbed Stormi by the shoulder. "We said we wouldn't leave here without him!"

"There is no him to leave with!"

From behind the meeting room, Q appeared. "Water! Get water. Douse the houses on the west side! Douse, you fools!" His shocked gaze caught us, and he broke into a run.

"Come on!" Stormi shouted, and we turned our backs on our friend, my friend.

We jumped inside the Caddy, and Stormi fluttered the gas, the engine sputtering.

"God, now would be a really good time to show up," she hissed, and fluttered it again. The engine wheezed and coughed, and beneath her coaxing, roared to life. Stormi eased out, in front of a gasping Q, who slapped our trunk. With a near empty tank, conservation was more important than speed.

"He's dead." My own voice sounded far away.

Stormi checked her rearview and flicked the gas light on the console. "He knew it might happen."

"Did he tell you?"

"I just knew."

I glanced at Stormi. She knew and she let him go. She stopped the bus in Gullary, but let Arthur race to his death. How little I understood the ways of prophets.

CHAPTER 15

Echoes of the explosion played over in my mind.

The panic of our escape subsided, and was replaced by a sickening sense that I was the reason Arthur was no more. It was our friendship, not his and Stormi's, that drew him to his death, and I closed my eyes and saw his parents.

Arthur's dad was the tax guy in town, punching out numbers and pushing up glasses with oversized frames. He worked late into the night, every night, even on Christmas Eve. He was a joke in Gullary, his work ethic simultaneously appreciated and mocked.

He would be up now. Pushing his pencil and clattering his keys. Did he feel it? Did he feel a sudden hole in his world? Likely not. He probably readjusted those rims and kept on working.

"Arthur's dead," I said quietly.

Stormi peeked nervously in the rearview. "Yeah, a lot of people die."

How harsh the comment sounded, hanging all uncaring-like between us. Who was this girl?

"But not a lot of them are my friends."

Stormi's shoulders sagged, and she sighed. "I'll feel it soon. I will. I promise. It's just that right now, I need us to get as far away as possible."

The Cadillac was thankful for the sip, rewarding us with far more miles than I thought possible, but eventually it coughed and lurched. Once, and again.

"That's it." Stormi pounded the wheel and leaned back, gravel crackling beneath the last spin of rubber. "That's it."

We crunched to a stop. Far in the distance, a speck of light. The bar.

"Come on, Jonah. This is where we walk."

We left our getaway vehicle with the keys in the ignition, and moved awkwardly through the darkness. We weren't alone. The yowl of coyotes filled the night, and our pace quickened. But we had a beacon; how powerful was that one pinprick of light, drawing us forward.

Our conversation fell in staccato bursts.

"There are shrines back there," I said.

"Probably. It's like I told you, it's like a cult."

"Shrines to a bunch of teens."

Stormi thought a moment. "Probably teens like us that Winston brought in."

"I don't know. It doesn't matter now. Stormi, what do you want to do once we reach the place? Where do we go next?" My eyes grew suddenly heavy. "Arthur's parents, we need to tell them."

"We can call."

Stormi hummed, softly and peacefully. I thought of home, of Mom and Dad, and of Gullary. I missed it—no, not true. I missed what it was before. When Gina and Arthur were alive, and dreams of Stormi were only dreams, comfortable and out of reach. Now I felt like one of Tres's chess pieces, always moving, playing a game where kids die, Stormi could be mine, and my family was a memory. I felt older, stretched, unsettled.

Noise from the bar reached our ears. Little had changed. The explosion that rocked our ears must not have reached this oasis, though the flatness of earth made me wonder how it could have been missed. Cars roared and people shouted, maybe the same people as before, unaware that my friend was now dead.

We reached the crowd and again pushed inside. The bartender glanced up quickly and swore. "I did not think I'd be seein' you again." He glanced over our shoulder and toward the door. "There was three of ya, wasn't there?"

"Arthur," I said. "There was an acc—"

Stormi stepped hard on my foot. "He went home another way."

"Home, huh? You still have one? Then you best leave and you best leave now. Distance is your friend."

Stormi hung her shoulders. "We have no car, no truck."

"Then you're in a heap." He glanced at her sideways. "Unless you got something else you'd part with."

Stormi closed her eyes and reached beneath her top. "This." She stroked the gold necklace. "Can you help us?"

How willing she was to part with my gift. I shouldn't have been affected. My gut shouldn't have turned. Not after Arthur. Besides, the stupid thing was from Tres, and I was only the messenger. But, shoot, I *was* the messenger. It had come from my hand.

"I gave you that," I said softly.

"I'm listening now." The bartender held out his hand.

Stormi turned to me, but did not risk my gaze. "Take it off. Please. What else do we have?"

I slowly swept up her hair and fumbled with the clasp. Clumsy fingers finally achieved the goal, and I held it up before Stormi. She took hold and gently lay it on the bar.

He picked it up, turned it over in his hand. "Where'd it come from?"

That didn't follow as being important. "Probably a jewelry store," I muttered.

"I'm talking about the who of it. Who gave this to you?" He peered at Stormi, who pointed at me, and I winced.

"All right, um. It came from a guy I knew. A guy who wanted to share something with his granddaughter." I lowered my head. "Name's Tres, if you need to know."

"Tres." He slammed it down. "Nope. I won't take this. Don't want nothin' to do with this. Take it on out."

Stormi's face reddened; gone was any desire to hold on to the gift. Clearly she was deciding how mad to get. Fortunately, we had other problems to deal with. "We need transportation, and this must be worth—"

"More than you know." He lowered his voice and pushed the necklace toward me. I slipped it into my pocket.

We stood there, lost, stuck. I must have looked the part, as a minute passed and the bartender rolled his eyes and drummed his fingers.

"Fine. You didn't walk here," he continued. "What happened?"

"Our car is sitting in the road, out of gas."

"Make?"

"It's a Cadillac," Stormi said. "Low miles. New timing belt. They go first on those engines."

He looked off, dug in his pocket, and slammed down a set of keys. "Rusty Chevy truck parked around back. Old as the hills, but twice as tough. You take it. You'll need it. I'll have one of my guys outside pick up your ride. Keys in the ignition?"

"Yeah, thank you," I grabbed the keys. "Why are you helping like this? You don't know our names. I don't know yours."

The bartender closed his eyes. "Fourteen. For years, my name was Fourteen. You ain't the only ones to make it out. And if anyone else does, I'll be here."

We backed toward the door. Stormi wanted to leave, was trying to—I could see her tensing—but she lost her fight.

"What do you know about Tres, anyway?" she asked.

Fourteen broke into a broad smile. "Most honorable man I've ever met. And the angriest. I expect him to be back around soon. I'll tell him you passed through."

"Rather you didn't," Stormi said. And she was gone.

Fourteen chuckled. "She can't run forever, kid."

"How do you know all this?"

Fourteen picked up his paper and settled into his seat. "I'm a bartender. You hear quite a bit. That, and Tres was here not five hours before you came through the first time. Good man. On a mission, I'd say."

I turned and joined Stormi behind the bar. Who was this Tres? A nobody? That was the line in Gullary. A petty thief. One to pity, according to Mom. One to fear, according to Q and Stormi. One to respect, according to Fourteen.

I remembered all the days I treated him like a chore, as though he was hardly human.

"Keys." Stormi softened. "It's just us. Like I planned it. The road and us. A new vehicle the police won't be chasing. Tres likely thrown off our scent." She reached for the keys. "We might have our lives back."

"No. We'll never have them back," I muttered. "They've been purchased, right? Arthur, maybe Winston soon, once Q has his way. Our lives are worth more. They have to be."

We drove into the night, reached the highway, and Stormi soon took the fork north into Kansas. North felt broad and open, and with every mile, Stormi relaxed.

Maybe my Stormi.

That night I dreamed of Stormi, road trips, and the curves of each.

Unlike most journeys through the subconscious, the dream stuck with me into morning, plastered a goofy smile onto my face all day. The particulars will remain mine alone, but suffice it to say that it was filled with words of affection and melodramatic moments. We swore our devotion to each other, 'til death do us part.

'Til death do us part. It's an overused phrase, until death actually touches you.

Stormi tapped my leg. "Wake up. We'll stop here."

I worked my body upward. "Here?"

Morning had not come, and somewhere in the expanse that is western Kansas, guided by stars or gift, Stormi had turned off the highway and then turned again. She had found "here."

"We'll be safe for the night." She eased into a cleared expanse between fields. "Tomorrow, we can choose where to go, who to be."

"Given limited resources, I think I'll stay me." I lowered my window and listened to the sound of wheat rustling around us. Pushing out, I wandered the clearing, the unnatural clearing. There should have been a field here.

"This place feel off to you?" I called.

"It's over here, Jonah. Go turn on the headlamps."

Stormi's voice was caught up by the wind, but her form stood not far in the distance. I ducked inside the truck, did as instructed, and joined her.

She stood frozen in front of a cement cauldron. It was circular and massive, maybe fifty feet across, and who knew how deep.

Inside, in heaps and shadows, thousands of objects. Broken plastic and glass, twisted metal and a tennis ball, and thousands of things hid by the night. I glanced at Stormi, who nodded at the plaque on the cement:

WINDROW, KANSAS
May 23, 1998 Population: 410
May 24, 1998 Population: 0
Here we gathered after the storm.
Here we gathered all that we lost,
and moved on.

"I've heard of these. It's a storm cemetery. A tornado hit right here and the whole town took off." I glanced around. Four wooden structures stood nearby, bent with the weather, bent like me. A house, a garage, a silo, and a shed.

"Must have been a scary night," I whispered, recalling the images on the SMX museum's walls.

Stormi walked back to the truck and soon we stood in darkness. She returned and took my hand. "I think it was. For tonight, what do you pick—house or garage?"

I'd seen too many horror movies. "Garage. Unless it's filled with pitchforks and stuff, then the house."

The side door creaked open and we entered. The moon shone through where glass had been, and in its light I found a smooth stretch of ground, and lay down in the dirt. My back slowly loosened, and I found comfortable. Stormi shifted and rolled. Shifted and rolled. I found another dream, one where the darkness around me vanished into light, and a scream announced the breaking of dawn. I sat up quickly.

"Jonah. And hello, Stormi. It's been some time."

Tres wandered around the perimeter of the garage, pausing to peek out the cracks in the wall.

"Tres." I rubbed my eyes, trying to make sense of where we were, how the three of us found each other. "Are people out looking for you too?"

"No, Jonah, I done served my time long ago. I served it and then some."

Stormi pressed into me, her hand squeezing my thigh. "What do you want?"

Tres knelt on the ground and scribbled in the dirt before taking a seat. He reclined against the wall, resting forearms on his knees. "Guess I be wanting a lot of things."

"Arthur's dead," I said, and Tres's gaze shot up.

"Arthur, my chess friend. That is unfortunate. I'm sorry, Jonah." Tres shook his head. "That . . . I did not see that coming."

I knew I was supposed to be afraid of him—Stormi sure was—but his were the first comforting words I'd heard since the old guy from the Hive touched my back.

"Well, I'll get right to the wanting question, but first I need to tell you a story." Tres let his head thump back against the wall. "You two like stories?"

No and yes, Stormi and I answered simultaneously.

"This tale begins decades ago, with a man named Everett— Jonah Everett the first."

"My granddad."

"The same. Now shut up." He reached in his pocket and lit a cigarette, exhaling long and slow. "Your grandpa, the mayor of your fine town, grew sick and tired of all us miners and our rascally ways. Too much drinkin' and carousin' for his liking, too much petty theft in Gullary. So he and the town council, the Circle they was called, took matters into their own hands. They sectioned off a portion of the town jail for us 'petty offenders.' No trial, no judge. The Circle held folks as they saw fit."

"I always thought that was illegal," I said.

"Illegal don't always mean ineffective," Tres continued. "Gullary tilted crime free. And then the mines closed, most moved on, and there wasn't none left to commit crime. That's when SMX was built, and suddenly Gullary had all the criminals it could handle, safely locked away. Jobs returned, people returned, but so did petty crime, and your grandpa knew what to do. He grabbed a bucket of paint and smeared it crimson on a door. And the Circle begun again, stickin' good folks in SMX for a night."

"That's where you were."

"Two nights, that was my penalty for drunken conduct. Now, admittedly, drunk I was."

I struggled to wrap my head around the possibility. "*My* granddad threw *you* in there."

"He did, and the next night he threw in eighteen more. An underage drinking party. Probably purposed to fill 'm with the fear of God. Eighteen kids, in the cell right by mine."

"The big one. The foul one," I said.

"Yeah."

The night grew cold, and Stormi felt far away, though she pressed harder into my chest. It was Tres and me.

"I don't know how they got into the cell. How twenty hardened criminals broke free from the secure unit and got into our unmonitored wing, but they did. And the things done to those kids. I could hear it. Every cry. Every scream . . ."

So could I. I'd heard the screams mid-seizure.

"They killed them all. The senior class of Gullary vanished that day."

We sat for a while in the truth, a horror that filled in so many pieces, I didn't question it. Stormi didn't either.

"You'd think that justice would follow quick and sure, but guilt does strange things to a town," Tres continued. "Your grandpa convinced the Circle, the town, that every resident would be punished for the crime. And maybe he was right, as they all knew about the red door. He told the town that if the outside found out what'd been done, all would be held responsible, SMX would be closed, and their jobs would again disappear. The pressure to keep silent was great, especially from those who didn't lose nobody, and so the secret held, bound up inside Gullary."

"But you, you could have spoken. You heard it all," Stormi finally spoke, her voice vacant.

"Nobody would've heard me. Jonah the First done realized what I knew, and my punishment for drunkenness commuted from two days to a life sentence."

"No." I shook my head. The urge to protect your kin runs deep, and though I had no reason to doubt Tres, my objection spewed forth. "Granddad wouldn't have done that."

"Oh, it gets worse. When your dad took over, he left the system in place. He knows what transpired as well, son. I'm sorry, but your dad knows everything. He knows Cartwrights done lost a kid. Pickerings lost a kid. And he sure as hell knows he lost a daughter."

I flopped onto my back, staring up at rafters. Breath came shallow. A daughter. My sister. And my jaw tightened.

A monster. I'd always considered myself to be the family creature, hideous in form. I suddenly could not remain still and jumped up, because if true, if Tres told the truth, a more sinister monster roamed our trailer.

"I have a sister? Had a sister?" And here I asked the stupidest question I've ever heard, but grief dulls the mind. "Does my ma know?"

"I'm sorry, son. I am so sorry." Tres sounded like he cared, but he'd been sitting on this for months.

I rose and approached.

"Sit down, Jonah," Tres said.

I kept walking.

"Jonah, sit down."

"No. Not this time. You knew. This whole time I'm giving you food off my table, you knew I once had a sister and my dad knew I had a sister, and you just, you just . . . Screw you, Tres! Screw you!"

"How dare you question me, you arrogant child!" He rose, and we stood, pain to pain. But I couldn't hold it, my heart throbbed and I couldn't hold it. I no longer trusted anybody—not Stormi, not family, not Tres—and my legs buckled. Stormi eased me back to a sit, and minutes later, Tres too eased himself down.

We sat in silence. "Who were they?" Stormi asked. "The kids. Do you remember all their names?"

Tres stared at me. "You'll forgive me for not caring too much about Evangeline, your sister. Your dad has stolen my years, my life!" He rubbed his face hard. "I only think on one. Lanie. Her name was Lanie. And she was beautiful." Tres swallowed. "And she was mine."

"Your daughter?" Stormi asked.

He stiffened. "My girl. A man should never hear the sound of his girl being . . ." Tres cleared his throat. "So I sat and I waited for justice to fall, and it did. The storm came. Odd, the form 'justice' takes. Those that committed the crime survived. You met three of them at Gina's funeral. The rest, you probably encountered in the Hive. The twister threw open an escape hole and I stood, staring out at freedom, but I couldn't leave, couldn't throw my hat in with 'm, 'cause I heard their voices while they did what they did, and 'cause I knew help was comin' to Gullary." He looked sharply at Stormi. "A truth teller like me."

Tres shuffled in front of Stormi. "Why do you think you're here? Right here. Blind luck?"

Stormi had atrophied on the spot, like so much petri-fied wood.

"You drove, I'll bet. And you drove here. Well, welcome home. Windrow, it's where you was born. Born to my precious other daughter. Becky. Your mom's name. Died in the storm here, the same one that took Gullary, but you was spared. Spared for a specific purpose, I believe. To expose what'd been done, what's been hidden by the Circle. The Jonah Circle. That was your job in Gullary. You familiar with Exodus 20:5? Read up. But love for Jonah done blinded you. You was blinded by the pain you would cause Jonah if he knew, knew what his family was, and is."

"Love?" I asked.

"Shut up," Tres said. "It became clear Stormi needed a push. Consider this your push."

"What do you want me to do?" Stormi sounded small.

"Unearth what's been buried. Do right by all the kids, by my daughter. By your aunt. Nobody'll listen to a criminal, but you, if you go back and say what's been done, we'll see true justice fall."

"You really are my grandpa?"

"Sorry, darlin'. You don't get to choose family." He scooted back. "You also don't get to choose your gifts. You can see a little before, you can *see*. It was in your mother, which is why she left that God-forsaken town. It's in me." His face softened. "Which is the only reason I could best that Arthur in chess."

"The letters. The two halves that fit!" I said.

"Yeah, I could see hers, see the words, the shape. She likely could have seen mine, if she would've let herself."

Stormi shifted around, her back toward Tres. For minutes she sat in silence. When she spoke, I could barely make out her words.

"What if I don't return? What if Jonah and I move on?"

Tres stood, his voice terrible. "Then Jonah will never see his family again."

"I have no family," I hissed.

Tres paused. "I figured you'd say that. And hate me if you want, but I'm the only one telling you the truth. If Stormi don't go back, you'll die."

I felt a wallop of heat and light and the world spun. There was no aura, no warning that Old Rickety was here. He suddenly was, and in a moment, I wasn't.

I woke beside Stormi.

But she wasn't actually beside me. Always, her hands soothed me as Old Rick departed. Not this time. She sat, now her back turned to me, her hands in her lap.

"Stor, Stormi?"

She didn't answer.

My gaze flitted around the garage. "Where is he?"

"He blew out the way he came."

"Did I dream him? Did we both dream him?"

"No." She stroked her necklace, the one that should've been in my pocket. "Do you know where you got this?"

I closed my eyes. "I told you. Tres."

209

"He bought it for his Lanie, one day before. He was going to give it to her. He wanted me to have it."

"We don't have to go back," I said. "Old Rick isn't so bad."

Stormi swore, the first and last time I ever heard her do so. "I hate loving you."

CHAPTER 16

I woke with Stormi's words filling my thoughts, and I slowly rose, brushing myself off.

"Stormi?" I peeked out a crack in the wall, and my stomach sank. "Stormi!"

I ran outside, and slowed, my heartbeat finding its proper rhythm.

She was leaned over the cement wall, reaching for junk and setting the pieces on the concrete ledge.

I wandered to her side, but she did not slow.

"Whatcha up to?"

"I lived here." She retrieved a baby rattle, stared at it, then tossed it back. "When this happened, this was my home."

"Technically, you had blown away by the time they built this."

Stormi paused long enough to deliver a potent scowl.

"But yeah, I mean, you were here." I picked up one of her salvaged items, a musty book jacket. *Gone with the Wind.*

"Appropriate," I said.

"Why?" she asked. "Why do you think that's appropriate?"

"Well, the title and all."

"Ever read it?"

I shrugged. "Not all of it. I saw the movie."

"Scarlet's afraid to do what she must. To save what she loves, she thinks she'll lose herself."

"And that's you?"

"I think I lost myself long ago. I think I've been running from myself and I finally caught up. I need to go back."

I turned and walked back to the truck, and hopped inside. It would be a disaster to return. If half of what Tres said was true, an absolute disaster. All the guilt for Gina, for Tres's escape, and certainly Arthur's death, all of it would land on her. And I would be complicit. Dad and Ma wouldn't consider me involved in the diabolical, but I would be pegged as a mesmerized poodle, panting after Stormi and assisting her evil plans.

Yep, that would be me.

Here, far from Gullary, the seizures were intensifying, increasing in number, but I felt myself. As if I had control of myself, and it felt good. Plus, she said love. Or Tres said love and she didn't correct him. No, she had said it. She loved me. I loved her.

Away from Gullary, we loved each other.

I had no guarantees if we returned.

In time, Stormi joined me. "You understand why I can't stay here."

"Yeah, not here, but not Gullary either. I don't understand why you would think of going back to Connor and Ms. P and a bunch of people who think you're responsible for everything."

"Maybe I am."

I reached up and grabbed her hand. "You aren't." I sighed. "Listen, how about you give me a day? We don't talk about Gullary. We don't talk about Tres or Arthur. We live, we just live for a day. At the end, if you still want to go, we will."

I kissed her hand. "Give me one day."

Her gaze traveled from her hand to my eyes. "One day."

"It's only one day."

Ma picked me up from school and drove to the bus depot. At thirteen, my back had begun its most profound shift, and she was concerned, no, terrified.

"The International Scoliosis Association puts these camps on all over the country. You'll make friends. You'll feel normal."

Translated: You're such a loser.

When I arrived, a man bent beyond belief met me at the bus stop, offered a condescending smile, and herded me toward his car. Two other cottonwoods hunched in back, staring downward.

I slipped in the front and straightened as best I could, to prove I wasn't like them, that I didn't belong in this car or at this camp. To my discredit, I spent the entire next day ranking the angles of other kids' backs. By the time I left, I had assigned 101 kids a number. Me, I was 101.

I returned triumphant. I had seen how miserable others looked, and it made me feel good.

I ran over to Stormi's as soon as I got home. We went for a bike ride, and I told her about all the twisted, deformed kids at camp.

"Were you kind to them?"

Stormi sounded like Ma.

"I wasn't anything. Those kids are way bent. They're not like me."

Stormi let go of a handlebar, reached over, and stroked my back. My, she looked sad. At the time, I thought nothing of it, but already, she knew.

We drove into Harmony, Kansas, beneath a bluer sky.

Sure, it was all a ruse, a game, a trick to forget all that awaited us, but the fantasy took hold, likely because we wanted it to. We both wanted it to so badly.

"We should get married." Stormi glanced over, wild-eyed.

"Us? When? Wait, what? You actually want to?"

"More than I can say." She slowed the truck. "Do you?"

Well, shoot. I'd visited every situation pleasurable to a hormone-filled guy. But marriage, that lay in a different universe.

"I guess, someday."

"You guess? That's all the conviction you have?"

"No, Stormi, I can muster more, but leaping into marriage with me?" We pulled up in front of the post office. "Seems a tiny bit . . . monumental."

"I always knew we would." Storm leaned over and kissed my cheek, long and deep and real. Shivers visited the embarrassing parts, and I shifted in my seat.

"Come on." Her eyes twinkled. "Let's send our invitations."

We hopped out and Stormi took my hand and pushed into the post office. She pulled me to the counter, grabbed a few blank sheets from the recycle bin, and handed me a pen.

"Okay, we each should send one invitation. Who would you invite?"

I thought a moment. "My lying folks, I guess."

Stormi exhaled. "I'd invite Connor, so he could see it. Write to your folks. Tell them we eloped and got married."

"But we didn't."

"Now you're sounding like Arthur—" She paused and exhaled. "I'm sorry. I'm sorry. You can untell them tomorrow, but today, we celebrate."

I stared at my blank sheet.

Ma, Dad. I'm getting hitched. I'm getting married to Stormi, because I love her and she loves me, and I'm not some monstrous eunuch. Inside, I burned. *So you screwed up. You treated me like a castrated child, but you turned out dead wrong and now this is what you get, a prophetess for a daughter-in-law, and she knows everything you do.*

I dropped my pen. I could have kept going, but I didn't want them to spoil my engagement day.

Behind me, Stormi leaned over the counter, returning with two envelopes complete with licked stamps. She took my letter from the counter and inserted it without so much as glancing. She scribbled an address, and I watched my rage drop into the mail slot.

We exited and Stormi stretched. "We can't find a justice of the peace on such short notice, but we can skip that and get to the enjoyable part."

At this, I tell you my body trembled with a severe joy. What type of anticipation does this statement bring? Her and I. Us, together.

"Uh." My voice tripped over itself. "Where should we, you know?"

Stormi glanced around, and then pointed. "Right there."

I spun to see the location of my greatest desire. A frown spread over my face. "Culbertson's? That's a department store."

My love's eyes gleamed. "Think of all the things they'll have. Sheets. Bedding."

"Um, there are bound to be other people there. Certain firsts might be best done in private."

"It'll be a first for me too, you know."

Here, a twinge of sadness took me. *How can that be true?*

Stormi continued. "That's where we'll register. You and I. A full day of shopping together."

"So, shopping." I exhaled. "That's the enjoyable part?"

"What were you thinking?" She walked by me, elbowing me hard in the gut.

I grinned and watched her for a moment, before gaining momentum and following her across the street.

I do not know how long we were in that store.

My mind fogged over after ten minutes of towels and bedding and kitchenware. I only know we emerged to a sun low in the sky, with a sheet listing items to be purchased for the wedding of Stormi Pickering and Jonah Everett III.

"You know, Jonah, there are some things we really should talk about." She swung my arm and we strolled down Main Street. We took a left at the library and wandered into Harmony Park. She and I plunked into the swings, and rocked gently.

"Things like what?"

"Well, let's start with kids. Yes or no, and how many?"

"Seriously?"

She shot me such a doleful look; there'd be no ducking the question.

"Okay, yeah, well, I like kids, in general. It would just be hard to see a bent-over little person and think, I did that. I caused that. And I'd hate to pass on my *Floppicus on the flooricus* to a kid."

She slowly nodded. "You won't."

"Won't have kids or won't pass it on?"

"Depends on how you answer my question."

I puffed out air. "Okay, well, we should have kids. I mean, as long as they're girls and look like you. It would be a shame not to."

"I agree," she said, settled. "But they'd be boys. And I want at least three."

"Three? I can hardly take care of myself."

"Which brings us to another issue. How are you going to make a living? I don't want to work outside the home when our boys come." She paused. "That museum isn't exactly gainful employment."

"Right." I considered the alternatives. "Maybe I take a job at the DairyWhip?"

"Think bigger, for us."

"Bigger. Like an I-could-do-anything type of bigger?" I stopped my swing and felt a swell. "If there was nothing in my way, I'd go to art school. It'd take forever, but I could maybe be a photographer, though that's a tough way to earn money. For that, I'd be a pediatrician. There are enough idiots working with kids; there should be one decent one."

My, how Stormi beamed. "Yes. That will do. Dr. Everett, with photography as a side hobby." She swung higher, repeating that name, and with each repeating the idea fixed itself firmer in my mind.

Yeah, I'll be a doctor. I could do that. I could do that well.

Stormi scraped her feet against the pebbles, slowing her swing to a stop. "Lastly, religion. Do you have a feeling about that?"

"I don't think we need to nail that down yet. My folks still haven't."

"We do, because I need to know what *you* believe, not your parents. I'm not going to get into arguments in front of the kids."

I let my mouth gape to remind her there were, as of this time, no kids.

"Well, I think there is a God."

"Agreed."

"I think the Catholic versus Lutheran versus Baptist stuff is all kind of silly, though. I always wondered why Gullary divides three ways down the middle every Sunday morning. So I'm not sure about the denomination question."

"Good answer, so far we're right on. What about the Jesus question?"

"Jesus question."

"Yeah, do you believe in a God who floats around watching us like ants in an ant farm, or do you believe really personal? Do you believe in a Jesus who gets involved in the affairs of men?"

Once again, I slowed to a stop. "If he's watching us, it would be a pretty pathetic show. I hope he's involved, somehow."

"He is." Stormi loosened her shoe from her foot. "Totally, he is." She started to swing, higher, higher, and on a forward thrust she kicked, sending the shoe flying at least thirty feet.

"Beat that."

With pain, I bent over and untied my laces, but as I started swinging, my shoe was farthest from my mind. I was rehashing the Jesus question, and like my pediatrician dreams, the more I thought, the more fervent my opinion became. It was calcifying. By the time I reached full swing, I could have preached a sermon.

I shook the shoe forward an inch, shifted in the seat, and swooped down to outdistance my bride. I kicked, only to find my leg was too long for the maneuver. It wedged in the pebbly ground and my body lurched forward toward a mighty face plant. I recall thinking how much it would hurt, and then thinking that Jesus might have mercy on me, as he most certainly was involved in this event. But in the second between my thoughts and impact, Jesus left, and Old Rickety showed up.

I never felt the ground.

I awoke, my face on fire.

Stormi and I lay alone beneath a starry sky.

On the left was a bowl filled with water, and a wet towel streaked crimson. Stormi sat up slowly, peering down at me.

"Welcome back. I think I got the pebbles out. You ground them in there pretty deeply. There's a kind man in that blue house right there. He gave me all this." She glanced around the park. "Jonah, that was the strongest seizure I've seen. I was a little scared." She rested her head on my chest.

"I'm sorry for scaring you," I whispered. "And right after we solved all our problems."

Stormi scooted down and placed both elbows where her head had been. She lay smack on top of me. At any other moment, a thrill unspeakable would have taken me over, but not right after. Right after, rest was all I wanted.

"Well, I'm glad you came back to me. Though you did waste six hours of our day."

"Six hours?" I squeezed my eyes tight, and opened them slowly. The world still shifted slightly. "You wasted four hours shopping."

"Wasted? We need things, you know."

But the spell was broken. "Stormi, you don't need to keep pretending. I think I pretty much ruined the moment. It was fun dreaming though."

"It wasn't a dream. This day, this wasn't a dream. Wait for me, you'll see."

"Okay, Stormi." I closed my eyes again. "I'll wait."

When next I opened my eyes, strength had returned, and the morning sun splashed crimson across the horizon.

Stormi sat on the base of the slide, staring up at that sky.

"It's time, Jonah." She turned and forced a smile. "I wish you could have sat up with me last night, but it's too late now." She rose and walked over to where I sat and held out her hand. I took it, and we walked back to the truck.

On the windshield, a white slip was tucked beneath the wipers.

"Great," I said. "When did the police come by? I'll get our ticket."

Stormi nodded and started the engine. I snatched the citation, turned it over, reading the small letters scribbled in a writing that was faintly familiar.

Time to go to work, Stormi. Grandpa.

I stuffed it in my pocket, and joined Stormi in the truck.

CHAPTER 17

Less than a week.

We'd been gone a matter of days, but as we pulled into Gullary, there was no feeling of coming home, or even returning to the familiar. The trailer homes hadn't changed, SMX still stood, nestled in hills and fronted by enormous chat piles, and the Welcome to Gullary sign still boasted of the 1980 boys' basketball trip to state. Visually, it hadn't changed.

But it was not the Gullary I knew.

I grew angrier with each turn, a bubbly rage that felt like betrayal. There were secrets in Gullary. And I had spent all my time in the museum unwittingly guarding them, silencing a man who lost his daughter. Perpetuating a red door policy that killed my sister. I'd been used.

"How do we do this?" I asked.

"Tonight we'll settle in, I suppose. Tell your parents you're okay. Tomorrow, I start."

"You mean we."

Stormi slowed in front of my trailer, parking on the street. "No. I'm going to need you, but not to help me. I'm going to need you free to move. I think things will get quite restrictive for me soon."

I didn't know what she was talking about. "So, what exactly are you going to do? Take out an ad in the *Gazette*? How do you bring up what's been buried for so long?"

"You'll see in the morning." She nodded toward the door. "You should get out."

Strange. Stormi spoke with certainty again; our run-in with Tres brought back the confidence that had always marked her. I, though, felt no need to obey. This journey ended where it began, but I wouldn't.

I slowly stepped onto the street. I turned to close the door, and then paused. "You know something more than I do. Did Tres tell you something when I was . . . out?"

"Exodus 20:5. Jonah, I love you."

"I, uh, love you too."

Stormi pulled forward, taking the left toward Greasy Jake's. I listened to the engine quiet in the distance, and set my face toward my old home.

"Okay, Dad, here we go."

I strode to the door, threw it open, and stepped inside.

The trailer was still, still and foul. Small details like dead sisters and dead seniors no longer hid. All was in the light, and the place felt evil.

No one had waited up for my return. There was no candlelight vigil. What had I expected? Not sure, but the pit in my gut made clear that I did not receive it. And then I did.

The world erupted with motherly affection. Hugs and kisses, punctuated by tears and how-dare-I's, then more hugs and kisses. Half of her seemed thrilled to see me, while the other half was near ready to end my life for her worry.

Finally, the tempest stopped, and Ma rubbed her eyes with the heels of her hands. "So, aren't you going speak? You could explain where you been."

"Of course he will." Dad walked out from the back, a forced smile on his face. "Of course he will. I'm glad you're safe, more than you know, but things are set in motion here. Things you do not know."

"Hmm. Things I don't know."

I walked by him toward my bedroom. His fingers clamped around my forearm, but I yanked free.

"Let go," I said. Inside, the rage returned. I had no more filter. What rumbled fearsome inside spewed out. I hated him. For what he did to Tres. For what I did to Tres. I thought in that instant to tell him all I knew, but I kept silent, for Stormi. She had asked me too.

Dad folded his arms. "It seems my concern was unfounded, Ma. Our son is all grown up. He feels no need to include us in his life. How wise he has become." He walked slowly around me. "And to think I tried to protect him, defend him, but you already knew that, right?" He fisted the neckline of my shirt and drew me nearer.

Ma took a step. "Our son is home—"

Dad's other hand shot up. "Our son left. Whether he returned, well, that's yet to be seen." He slowly released me. Strange, throughout the transformation of my father, I felt no fear. In fact, he struck me as small.

Flattening my shirt, Dad continued. "Three questions is all I have, and you will answer them. Where did you go? Who were you with? Why did you come back?"

I glanced at Mom, who covered her mouth with a shaking hand. She shook her head, ever so slightly.

"Well, Dad, the truth is I got married."

Mom gasped, but Dad latched on to the only piece of my announcement that interested him.

"So you were with Stormi."

I shrugged. "It's less romantic when your spouse doesn't attend the ceremony. Yeah, I was with her. I reckon your invitation will arrive tomorrow."

"Anyone else?"

My thoughts bounced off Arthur and Tres, Michael Queene and Winston. Maybe time would soften this moment. Maybe there would be a right time to share, but not yet.

"Anyone else?" he thundered.

"Nobody you care about."

I backed toward my room, feeling my way down the hall with both hands, freezing at the entryway to the kitchen. On the table sat Ma's Bible.

I quick-stepped over to it and dug through the table of contents. I fumbled through the pages, as Ma and Dad stepped into the room. There it was, what I was searching for: Exodus 20:5.

"Please, Jonah. You can talk to us." Ma stepped forward. "What's gotten in to you?"

I read the verse twice, and then lifted my head. I stared from Ma to Dad, before reaching for Ma's marker and ringing the verse in crimson red:

For I, the Lord *your God, am a jealous God, punishing the children for the sin of the parents.*

My eyes stopped there. "Guess that covers it," I whispered.

I spun and disappeared into my room, shutting the door behind me. I would spend the rest of the evening sitting on my bed, staring out my bedroom window, hoping to see some shadow of Stormi behind her shades. But I did not. It crossed my mind that perhaps she did run after all. Perhaps she dropped me off and fled. It would be the cruelest of moves, but I'd heard of wives doing worse.

A tapping at my window.

I couldn't tell which side of consciousness called to me, though I guessed it to be the tail end of the strangest dream. In the darkness, Old Rickety had come to call, and I was in the thralls. Yet I was enjoying it, in the same way I imagined a kid loved a vomit-inducing roller coaster, though I'd never experienced one. Round and round spun the world, and I heaved and rocked.

Faster. Faster.

Somehow, I could speak. Somehow I wanted more. More intensity. More, just more.

Is that all you've got, Ricky?

Then I was taunting that seizure. Even laughing at him. He didn't take kindly to my lack of respect, and he hurled me through my unconscious. But the tapping, distinct and clear, pierced the muddled voice of Old Rick, and I awoke sitting up, staring at that window.

I rose without difficulty and walked toward the face that beckoned to me. Stormi.

"Come," she said.

I followed, as if it were the most natural of things to squeeze out of my window at 4 a.m.

Stormi spoke quickly, her breath heavy as we marched toward SMX.

"What did you tell your dad?"

"That we were married."

Stormi broke out laughing, loud enough and long enough that I felt a pang in my chest. Then she kissed my neck, and the pang vanished. "Brilliant. Mention Tres?"

I was stuck on *brilliant*. It wasn't a word I'd experienced before. "Who? Oh, Tres? No. I thought I was supposed to leave that to you. Wait, where were you last night? I looked."

"Where were you looking?"

"Through your window." She slowed and raised her eyebrows. "I mean, I glanced periodically in the general direction of your window, you know, to make sure you were fine. I wasn't peeking or snooping or anything."

She sighed, and slowed further. "I was at the shop all night. Jake keeps all his old school stuff there. I needed this."

Stormi had been carrying an oversized book throughout our walk, but only here did I notice it. She handed the year-book to me, opening to a dog-eared page. "I needed the names of those kids who died. Sure enough, according to the juniors listed the year before, there would have been eighteen in Gullary during Lanie's senior year. Ten boys, eight girls. Here they are."

My eyes first fell on Lanie, raven black hair and a face a bit like Stormi's. She was beautiful. "I've seen them, well, especially her. In the Hive. I told you, Saul was blood-letting in front of her. These photos are all in the Hive."

Part of me had been holding out, casting a hopeful line back to Granddad, wondering if in the crazy world of killers and prophets, somehow my innocent family was sucked in by mistake. But the yearbook sealed it, and I kicked at the stupid ground with my stupid Everett foot.

"I was named after a murderer."

"A lot of people are." Stormi closed the book and we turned the last corner to SMX. "Jonah, I brought you here because I want you to see what I did. I want you to see exactly what I did. Because I don't think they'll be here long, and then rumors will start and I, I want you to know I did it."

"Yeah. Okay."

My gaze followed Stormi's outstretched arm. Up, up, to the top of the two chat piles. In the light of the SMX yard bulb, eighteen crosses shone white against the lightening sky. Eight on one pile. Ten on the other.

"Tres said that's where they buried them. Quick. Beneath a mound nobody would ever move. I put their names on each one. I marked them all. I did it."

"You did." I wrapped my arm around her and we stood in silence, staring up at our undoing, at the act that would indeed set things in motion.

"We never said our vows," Stormi said softly.

"No, we didn't. But if we had, I would've meant them, and I would have kept them."

She pressed into my side and wrapped her arms around my middle. "I, Stormi, do solemnly swear to . . . Aw, forget that. Jonah Everett III." She turned to me and took hold of my hands. "You have me. All of me now. No matter what happens. You have me now. The only me that's worth having. The me that nobody else has ever had."

I knew it to be fact, and I didn't reckon she could promise me anything more. A life together? That wouldn't be more. Growing old together? She couldn't give me that either. But she could give me her now. Standing in front of two chat piles and before the remains of eighteen witnesses. She could give me that.

I took a deep breath. She was waiting for words, hoping, it was clear.

"Stormi, I'll wait for you."

I hoped it was enough. In truth, the sentence confused me each time I'd said it. Outside of her request, why would I need to wait? But she said I should, and I reckoned I should firm it in a vow.

Stormi leaped into my arms, and though my back screamed, my heart soared.

"I'll hold you to it," she whispered.

Slowly, she released me, and she pulled me away from the mounds.

"What now?" I asked.

Stormi shrugged. "Now's the big pause. We alone in this world know what I did. It's peaceful, isn't it?"

It was. Words amplified. Every moment was clearer, more distinct. Every second mattered.

"But what if nobody bothers to look up there?"

"Oh, they will." Stormi leaned into me and took my hand. "Can I stay with you the rest of the morning? I don't really want to bump into Connor just yet."

I didn't answer. Of course she could, though the where of it was unclear. Eventually, I led her silently back to my door. My room would be safe for our final hours. We quietly entered.

Dad stood in the foyer, coffee mug in hand, tongue planted firmly in cheek. "Been out all night." He took a sip. "Good to see you, Stormi."

Stormi squeezed my hand. "Mr. Everett."

"You've been gone for a time. How was your trip?"

"Informative."

Dad's hard face softened. There was a part of him that loved the competition, reveled in the talk. You don't rise to power without deriving a bit of twisted joy in crushing a worthy opponent. He never found his equal in this home, but Stormi was a handful, and he knew it.

"Informative," Dad repeated, gesturing us toward the kitchen table, where the Bible no longer rested. "Inform me."

Stormi didn't follow, and Dad turned, the hard returning to his face. Yeah, he loved the game, but he hated when he couldn't set the rules.

"I'm going to spend my last morning with Jonah. We're married, you know."

"So I've been told, though I admit the news takes on a little more gravity coming from you."

Stormi released my hand. "You don't know who you have in Jonah. But that's okay, because I do."

He set down his mug. "I know my boy inside and out."

It felt like there might be a fistfight, and I pulled her quickly into my room. "What are you doing? Are you trying to make him blow? Wait, you are, aren't you?"

She smiled, though tired covered her face. "Angry people make mistakes. The chess game isn't over, and pieces will move quickly once the sun rises. I need to be sure your dad is one of them."

I didn't completely understand, and the two of us lay down on the bed and held each other. I felt no urge for more. I only wanted to fast-forward a year or two, in hopes that we could skip whatever happened next.

Next came swiftly.

The door swung open and Dad and Mr. Cartwright pounded into the room, grabbing each of us by the arm and pulling us toward the door. No words were said, but I knew where we were heading.

CHAPTER 18

The chat piles.

We stood silently at the base, while Mr. Gurney slipped and stumbled about the top. He was a good choice. Mr. Gurney wandered homeless through Gullary. Unattached and widely considered mentally challenged in any number of ways, Gurney was rumored to have served our country well in Vietnam. This, and general human dignity, earned him a place at most any dinner table in Gullary. But when Gurney spoke, the man was ignored.

He caught sight of us and slowed. Three crosses lay across his arms, and he was fumbling with a fourth. After an unsuccessful tug, he straightened.

"Hey Jonah, Stormi! Say, Mayor, there's names on 'em. Why are there names on 'em?"

Dad shook me. "Be clear, Jonah. Is this your doing?"

"Yeah, it is."

"No," Stormi said sharply. "It isn't. It was my doing. The crosses were my idea. The inscriptions, well, they're Gullary's doing, but you already know that. Jonah knew nothing until this morning."

"I told you about her. Now you understand the threat." Mr. Cartwright hauled Stormi in front of Dad. "She buried my Gina, and now she's trying to raise—"

"Who?" Stormi called out, firm and strong. "Say your child's name. Who's under there? Doesn't it eat at you, Mr. Cartwright? Don't you wake up and go to sleep under a cloud? How about you, Mr. Everett?" She glanced at Dad, and peered into the sky. "I'm not blaming, I'm just saying. I bet losing a child destroys a man."

Dad's face changed a sickly shade of white and he looked to me. He knew that I knew about Evangeline.

Color returned, and Dad lowered his head. Slowly, he reached out and pried Cartwright's fingers from Stormi's arm. He was evil, but not cruel.

"Stormi," he spoke slowly, "you realize you waded into some things here that are before your time. Have you spoken with Tres lately?"

Here she smiled, soft and settled. "I've spoken with my grandpa."

Cartwright pushed her aside, and shook his head. He took hold of Dad's shoulders, but Dad's gears were spinning, his eyes fixed on the ground.

"Girl's lyin'. That ain't possible," Cartwright spoke. "Tres's lost girl was only eighteen. She had no child."

Dad's hands shook. "Tres had an older daughter. He did. She left here and Stormi could be hers." He cupped hands around his mouth. "Gurney! Get a move on!"

Gurney worked with speed, stumbling across the second chat ridge. He no longer gathered up the crosses, but rather pitched them down on the far side of the pile. On the ground, Dad's worry sent Cartwright into a frenzy. He paced back and forth, muttering as if his mind had soured.

I was watching the failure of Stormi's plan. A news ad would have been much more certain. There were better ways to spread word through a town.

Stormi eased toward me and winked, nodding toward the distance.

In the midst of all the confusion, a wind had picked up, swirling dust around the chat pile base. When the wind cleared, young Leonard, Kyle, and Colton, each eight years of curious, peered up at Gurney with gloves swinging from bike handlebars.

"What you doin', Mr. Gurney? Ain't you supposed to stay clear of them piles?" Leonard called.

Gurney froze, the words that fell from his lips doing more damage than any news ad could have done. "Hey, Leonard. I'm not rightly sure. Mr. Everett and Mr. Cartwright told me to dig the crosses out of the chat, and that's what I'm doing."

Secrets take a long time to construct and strengthen. It only takes two sentences to shatter them. Those boys shrugged, and then biked toward Gullary's ballfield, but Colton reached down and picked up two crosses on the way.

Dad and Cartwright took off after him, but Colton knew the rules; if an adult is in pursuit, you must possess something of value and you do not stop.

Mr. Gurney had a bird's-eye view of the whole affair, and glanced down at Stormi and me. "Do I keep on going?"

"No, sir," I shouted. "Leave those last two up there."

Gurney slid down. "Glad of that. Creepy business. And what of these other crosses on the ground here? Over ten of 'm."

"Did you recognize any of the names?" Stormi asked gently.

"Last names. Most folk in town."

Stormi took a deep breath. "Maybe deliver them for me, if it's not too much trouble."

Gurney started to pick them up. "Glad to, Stormi. Glad you're back. Gullary was mighty boring without you." He mouthed the name on the cross at his feet, bent over, and reached it to me. "Here you go. Easy enough. Evangeline Everett."

We watched him shuffle away, his arms filled with the past.

I clutched the cross in my hands.

"I'm sorry, Jonah. I really am." Stormi raked her fingers through her hair.

"You should leave here now," I begged. "Cartwright lost his head, but he'll come back. Dad too."

"They will. I'll be waiting right here." Stormi kissed me. "But you should go. I'll need you before this is done."

I glanced into the sky. Clouds had rolled in. "You know that for sure? Because I don't really want to leave you."

"You won't." Stormi pushed me away. "You promised."

I don't know which was more effective: three kids peddling Gurney's testimony, or the hand-delivered crosses. I suspect they worked in tandem. But the result was a scene I had not witnessed before.

My vantage point was the DairyWhip, filled with memories of Arthur. From an inside table, I watched the older residents of Gullary scurry into town, then vanish across the street into Orton's Drug. Folks went in. Dad and Ma went in. Three cones later, they had not emerged.

An hour passed, and Cartwright hopped from his truck, Stormi in tow. Again, he hauled her beneath the shoulder, though he needn't have done so. For her part, she looked at peace.

Why Orton's Drug, I did not know. There was nothing to distinguish the business from Gullary's other few establishments, other than its designation as Gullary's oldest. Once Orton's Drug Emporium, and before that Orton's Mercantile, Orton's had been a fixture in this part of Oklahoma for generations.

I rose and crossed the street. Though the store sign had been flipped to read *Sorry, We're Closed*, I slipped in. Mr. Orton was not seated behind the counter, nor was Roger, his mutt hound, usually wandering the aisles. Backroom voices raised, and I eased down the painting supply aisle toward the storeroom. The door was ajar and I ducked beneath the tarp rolls and peeked inside.

Women wept. Men wept. I thought I'd encountered every type of cry in Gullary, but those were normal cries. These reminded me of Saul's from the Hive. They were not of this earth.

"Quiet, all!" Dad said. "None of us thought we'd ever need to make use of the meeting place."

"But then, none of us knew that an unnatural would fly in!" Cartwright.

"But we all knew we had a hand in killing our babies."

For a moment, the weeping stopped; all sound, really. "You know it's true. I'll say now what we all know, but were too afraid to say then." I had never heard Ms. P silence a room.

"Martha's right. We did this. We allowed it. This falls on us, not Stormi."

Ma?

"There's nothing to revisit. We've worked through it. We survived." Mr. Cartwright took the floor. "The question at hand is what we do now. Our misfortune is barely contained. Leonard and Kyle especially are unconvinced. Now, they're but kids, but Gurney, the old coot, he's talking all over town."

"What is he saying?" Stormi's voice sounded peaceful, and I breathed deep.

Cartwright cleared his throat. "You've said enough."

"No, the question is valid." Ms. Utica, the English teacher, spoke up. "I'll tell you what he's saying, because he told me. He's saying that you and the mayor asked him to climb up on a toxic pile and remove a bunch of crosses, and that each cross bears the last name of someone from this town. Why treat Stormi like a criminal? Where's her part?"

I always liked Ms. Utica.

"Why are you here?" Dad asked. "You don't have anyone who . . ."

"Who what?" my teacher pressed.

And just like that, Ms. Utica was shoved from the room, and the door slammed.

"Look around! Make sure only the kids' families and those involved are here!" Cartwright boomed, and I stood. Ms. Utica grimaced and straightened her blouse.

"Something's afoot, Jonah. I followed the herd, and something's afoot."

"Two somethings, probably."

I stared at the wall, and the idea that my Stormi was trapped on the other side sickened me. I stayed because she asked me to, but it was all I could do to remain. On the wrong side of the door, a door I suddenly noticed had been painted red.

CHAPTER 19

Stormi was right.

The message spread.

With Ms. Utica, one of the few articulate people in town, asking questions, there was no way Dad could hide what had happened. He was a quick thinker, but he wasn't Houdini. I left Orton's and slowly walked down Main, turning onto C Street. The few nice homes in town stretched out before me, including the red brick beauty on the left. Arthur' house.

I took a deep breath, slowly climbed the steps, and rang the bell.

Arthur answered, but did not raise his gaze to meet mine.

"I was wondering when you would stop by. We went through an adventure. Wouldn't you say it was an adventure? Normally, people who go through adventures become friends. I thought that before our illegal adventure we might already have been friends. Certainly after, though."

I had no words. Death had been quick to take people of late, and I didn't reckon it planned on giving any back. But there Arthur stood, and then I was hugging him. He stiffened, not hugging me back.

I released him and stared and frowned and stared some more.

"Why didn't you tell me? You idiot! Do you know what I've been going through? I came here to tell your dad—"

His face lightened. "You thought I was caught up in the fire." He smiled broadly. "I wasn't." Arthur paused so long, I almost hit him. "I should have been. Absolutely, I should have been. But the gas keeper, number nineteen if you are referring to him by number . . . Isn't that strange that they used numbers? I think if I chose a number for myself, it would be twenty-eight, after my birthday, but it was probably taken, and then there would be two of me—"

"Arthur!"

"The gas keeper came running out right after I gave you the can, before I went in for more, and I couldn't go in then and I hid. Actually, I dropped onto the ground, but I'm quite flat and—"

"Arthur."

"He dashed into their prayer shack and came out with a candle, hurrying back to his cabin. He must have needed the flame to see, but gas and candles don't sit well together. Do you know about the laws of combustibility?"

I reached out, covered his mouth, then slowly uncovered it.

"He wasn't in there ten seconds before the explosion occurred. You were gone when I reached the garage. I thought you left me." He paused. "Why did you leave me?"

I opened my mouth. I had an answer, but it sounded flimsy and weak. Why does anyone leave anyone?

"It was my fault. I shouldn't have."

"So, I started walking. I walked twelve hours, and the next evening, I hitched back to Gullary. I thought I'd find you."

I nodded. "Yeah. We, uh, took a day off."

"A day off? I don't understand."

"It doesn't matter. Like I said, I came to tell your dad that you're dead." I placed my hand on his shoulder. "Glad you're not."

I turned to leave.

"Hang on. Do you want to come in? There are some strange events happening."

I'd never before been inside Arthur's house, a solid build with a wide foundation and a crawl space. It struck me how much I did want to stay here. Facing my parents felt hideous. Heading back to work at SMX even more so.

"Yeah, I'll hang out for a while."

I wish I could recall all of Arthur's room. The space miniatures and children's toys positioned on shelving units, the disassembled computer equipment strewn everywhere; this my mind still holds. But the knock downstairs came so forcefully, Dad's voice sounded so unsettling, that it filled all my brain's remaining memory.

"Jim, Margaret, the town's holding a gathering tonight at Jake's. We need you there."

The heat that night was overpowering. Not that we were strangers to sweat, but every few weeks an evening arrived with a vengeance that emptied streets and drove us into bought air.

But there was no space in Gullary large enough to fit the town. The Baptist church came close, but I wondered if a sanctuary meeting hit a nerve with Cartwright. Instead, an outdoor meeting was planned inside Greasy Jake's fenced yard. Three hundred plus heeded the call and filed into the dusty world where Stormi once lived

Seating proved tricky, the few decent chairs Jake owned reserved for the oldest and frailest among us. The rest grabbed tires and hubcaps and fenders, and plopped down. I stood against the fence, waiting for Stormi.

She didn't come.

Nor did anyone else of the young variety, and none that were in the Villa were wheeled in either. The few new families were also absent. This was a meeting of those who held power, and of this group, not a single head could I find missing.

Except Stormi.

Dad grabbed a wrench and pounded on a fender. Jake winced at the clang.

"Thank you for coming. We needed to speak to you all. Given the unfortunate events of this day, the Circle thought that perhaps you ought be aware of facts, so you can discern for yourself what is true and what is hearsay."

"Tell me why my neighbor had a cross planted in his yard!"

Bless Ms. Carlisle. The woman had no filter. A murmur went up, as many, especially on the outskirts, had their first encounter with today's activities.

"What cross?" Mr. Ingersoll, a hard-working farmer/hermit who we only saw every few months, folded meaty arms. He undoubtedly was inconvenienced by the meeting.

Dad raised his hands to no avail, and resorted again to the wrench.

"I'll get straight to it. Stormi Pickering, a girl we all know to be a bit—"

"Unnatural." Cartwright finished the sentence.

"By cloak of night, she planted crosses in our chat piles. If her confession is true, and I for one believe it, she needed a high-profile area to make her point." Dad shot me a glance. "I know a lot of you are close to Stormi. You've come to love her over the years she's been with us. I understand the sentiment. I'm still driving my Chrysler because of the care she put into it." He turned to Ms. Utica. "She sat in your classes, ate with your children, grew up in your homes."

At this, Ms. P. began a slow shake of the head. Connor sat still as stone beside her.

I wanted him dead.

"But Stormi, as you know, was never one of us. This, the extended culmination of her last school project, proves the point."

Dad was joined by the other members of the Circle. An ominous group of men, I might add. Cartwright stepped to the fore.

"Seems Stormi was taken with the plight of the Cherokee in Oklahoma. A worthy concern, to be sure, but one abnormally urged on by a book read right before school's end in literature class—ain't that right, Ms. Utica?"

Ms. Utica opened her mouth, but no words came out.

"*Hear My Flight*—wasn't that a book assigned in your class? Did not discussions about injustice follow? Was Stormi not most vocal in her outrage?"

Ms. Utica nodded, defeated.

"Well, it seems that Stormi felt obliged to do more than talk. The crosses on those chat piles, in your yards, based on a confession from her own lips, were meant to make you realize what it felt like for Cherokee families to lose their children. The names pulled from an old yearbook, like the one Jake reported missing not hours ago. Isn't that right, Jake?"

Jake was tortured. His face said it. "Missing, yeah, but she worked for me. She was privy to all I owned—"

"It was a cruel act by her, to be sure," Dad interrupted, "but one urged on by one of our community's most trusted teachers."

More murmurs. Ms. Utica hung her head, and Dad's gaze found me. *Do not speak, son.* I read it perfectly. *Do not speak.*

I watched as Dad's words took root, deepened in the fertile soil of a desperate town. I felt the Circle's hold tighten, deepen.

I'll need you before this is all over.

"That's a good story." I winced, my back screaming as I stepped into the ring. "A good story, Dad. Is there any more to it?" I stared at Ma. "Is there a chapter about Evangeline? Do you remember her? I don't. I don't remember my sister. I never got to meet my sister. I was never told about my sister."

Dad took a step toward me. "Enough, Jonah!"

"It's been long enough, all right. Today, by the chat piles, I finally saw her burial cross."

Ma's knees buckled and she toppled, caught on the way down by Ms. P. I turned slowly.

"Do any of you remember Lanie? She was beautiful. I've seen pictures. Daughter of Tres Cantor. She died the same night as my sister. There are sixteen more stories where those came from. Eighteen kids from this town are dead and buried beneath those mounds." I pointed at the piles in the distance. "Eight girls, ten guys, teens like me. Teens like me and Stormi. Let's tell their stories now!"

"That true?" Mr. Ingersoll asked. "That where they all went? There was no accident?"

Ms. Lowell burst into tears. "I can't. I do not care what happens to me, to us. I can't. It's true. Every word Jonah spoke is true. My Patricia, she's under there."

I did not stay to hear the rest, but hurried toward the gate as hundreds stood, confused and hollering.

I glanced over my shoulder, catching Dad's eyes, filled with both hatred and another emotion I scarcely recognized: admiration.

"Where is Stormi? We've got two stories, and I for one need to hear her intent!" Mr. Ingersoll's voice cut through the mayhem.

Where is Stormi? A sinking feeling struck me. *Where is Stormi?*

Oh, Lord.

I said my first real prayer.

CHAPTER 20

I lumbered home, snatched my gallery keys from the nail in my room, and hopped on my bike. Shouts in the distance made it clear the meeting had not ended, and I tore toward SMX in solitude.

I pulled past the guard tower, and a gust caught me. A loner. On a still night, from nowhere, a renegade wind nearly toppled the bike. It was gone as quickly as it had come.

"The Herald," I whispered.

Just legend, of course. But we'd seen enough tornadoes in our day to compile quite a body of twister lore. Some folks in town swore they could feel twisters coming in their bones, others looked to their pets for warning over the Tulsa weatherman.

We all treated our superstitions with a twinkle, knowing they were suspect at best. But not the Herald.

A wind born of nothing and heading nowhere. An orphan ghost too strong for the moment. I looked up. Not a cloud. Yet this only cemented the fear in my gut. A Herald had arrived.

A storm was coming.

I doubled my speed, dismounted while still coasting, and threw down my bike against the gallery door. A minute later, I was inside. Ten seconds more, I was in a familiar well-lit hall.

"Stormi? You here?"

"I am." She sounded frail, dispossessed.

"That you, Jonah? Your voice is a sound for these ears." An arm stuck out of the cell. Gurney continued. "What they done this for? Ain't done nothing but for 'm."

I jogged toward Stormi, sitting on the floor in Tres's old cell. Gurney was in the terror hold next on.

"Right back, I can get you out," I said.

"No." Stormi held up a hand.

"Yes!" Gurney kicked the bar. "Girl's gone loco in her brief confinement."

"Think, Jonah. If you let us out, you become a part of this. I told them you know nothing. I told them you were seizing while Tres told me what was done. They won't bother you. Right now, you can move freely."

"No, I don't think I can. See, a town meeting turned south. Dad and Cartwright shaded you as an activist on some activist cause. Not a bad cause really; in fact, it was doggone believable. So . . ."

"You spoke up."

"I spoke up."

"In front of the entire town."

I rubbed my forehead, wincing. "Pretty much."

"Pretty much?" Stormi broke into a wide smile. "Should I make your bed in here, or wait until they arrive? Jonah. You've changed." She reached out her hand. I grasped it. Yep. If there had been any doubt, it no longer lingered. I was messed up in love.

"Don't mean to interrupt, but it seems I could be let go without doing much additional harm. I didn't even know what I was doing."

"That's good, Mr. Gurney." Stormi stuck her lips out the bars. I wanted them, but let them move. "You not knowing was a good thing, but my guess is this might be the safest place for us to be. Jonah knows we're here. It'll take some time for them to figure out what to do with us. We'll wait it out, until maybe the storm dies down."

The storm.

"Stormi. I felt it on the way in. The Herald."

She stepped back, and then took her place near me. "Strong?"

"Almost took my bike."

"Sky?"

"Clear."

She rubbed her hands, and I could see her thinking. "Listen, it's coming. You need to get your dad to admit to what's been done. The truth needs to be said. The Herald didn't find you by accident. Gullary is out of chances, unless your dad— unless the *Circle*—confesses to what they did."

"How do I get him to do that? After tonight, he's not going to turn a listening ear."

Stormi stroked my cheek. "You are brave. You are changed. You'll figure it out. I've done my part, now finish it."

"You want *me* to finish it?"

Stormi gazed at me with eyes filled with pride. "Tres got this one thing wrong. He was waiting on me, when all this time you were the strong one. It's always been you."

I felt a smile sneak across my face. I would finish it. Me. *Floppicus bendicus*. It felt right. According to Tres, Stormi blew in to condemn this town, but now standing free on the outside, I reckoned she had a different purpose all along. She didn't come to change Gullary. She came to change me.

I straightened. "I guess I best head home. Dad is going to want to talk, I suppose."

"You sure I can't be of assistance?" My, Gurney looked pitiful. "Out there?"

"Sorry, Mr. Gurney. I'm sorry you were caught up in this. I'll be back to check on the both of you."

I left the way I came, pushing aside the doorstop and letting the door click behind me. It sounded so final, and in truth, I wasn't certain I would be able to return.

Still, the Herald chose me. I had no choice.

"You came back."

How dark our living room was.

How emotionless my dad's words.

I quietly shut the front door. Dad's outline sat black against the opened, moonlit window. He didn't turn to address me.

"Where else was I gonna go? This is home."

His shoulders rose and fell.

"It was a brave statement you made, there, in front of everybody. I give you that. Took some doing for me to get matters back under control."

"How could you lie?"

"How could I not?" Dad turned, and though his features were barely visible, he struck me as smaller, less imposing. "There are so many things you don't know."

I slowly sat down across from him. He was first to wade into the extended silence.

"I loved him, you know, your grandpa. Idolized him in every way, and there was reason to. Things were rough here. It wasn't safe for families. His family. Your family. It was his job to curb the violence poverty brings." Dad shook his head, continued speaking into the night. "He had the idea of using the prison in a secondary fashion. What was I to say? I was young. So you can be as mad as you want about whatever you're angry about. Cause as much trouble as you want for me, but that anger is all misplaced."

"But you knew about what happened. You said nothing."

Dad paused. "I don't know what you expected me to do. The system was in place. It worked. It had never failed. And then it did and it took my daughter and broke me, but I had a responsibility to protect the people of this town. I can't expect you to understand responsibility. You're like your mother that way, thinking with your heart instead of your brain."

I started to rise, pushed up halfway.

"Wait."

I eased back to a sit, and he continued. "You're sensitive, Jonah. But you're not as uninvolved as you think. Your back. Your seizures. I always reckoned those ailments were sent to smite me. A curse for what'd been done on your grandpa's watch, left undone on mine."

"My seizures aren't a curse. They just are."

"Yeah," Dad whispered. "But how I hated them, maybe you. I thought they were about me, and for that I'm sorry, Jonah. You deserved better."

The chain around my gut loosened. Dad had apologized. I couldn't remember hearing such from him before. Maybe there was hope, hope that the Herald could be silenced. "Why can't you apologize to everybody now? Like you did to me."

"Follow the thread if word gets out. The local press. Soon national news, son. We would be the story, and what would happen to us, Jonah? What would happen to our family? To other families living on grief? They would take good parents away from their children over wrongs committed twenty years ago. They would destroy more families. No, we can't go back."

Something like fog settled in that room, as Dad's logic took hold. I tried to find the right and the wrong, but they were muddled, lost in years and hurt.

"But Tres said the storm that took SMX, he said that was a judgment. He said the bus accident that took Gina was another one, stopped by Stormi. If that's true, I don't think you can run from this. Dad, I felt the Herald."

Dad shifted. "When?"

"Tonight. You were at Jake's. You know there was no wind. Not a trace."

A crack opened in Dad. I felt his wavering.

"Jonah, I'm not speaking about that superstition. When did you speak with Tres?"

"I brought him food forever; we talked then. A little more when he found Stormi and me, but that has nothing to do with what you need to do right now."

"I was under the impression that you were out of mind by the time he tracked you down." Dad hesitated. "At least that's what Stormi said. You contradict that story?"

The door opened and Cartwright filled the frame. I glanced back to Dad. The crack was filled.

"Yes. I mean no. Old Rick came right after Tres did, and when I came to, Tres was gone. I still don't know all he said to her."

Dad leaned forward. "Own up, son. Isn't it true that you knew all about the SMX incident before you left to find Stormi? You've long been planning to take out your anger on me." His voice sounded strained. "You and Stormi have been waiting for a chance."

"Don't turn this!" I softened. "When I left . . . When I left, you were my hero."

"I'm sorry, but sentiment aside, the boy is clearly part of the scheme." Cartwright stepped forward. "Partners with Tres from the start. He knows everything, and as long as he shows determined to fill the air with Tres's lies, for the greater good, he needs to be held. Come with me, Jonah."

"What lie am I telling?" I glanced at Dad, who fiddled with his lip. "Dad. Please."

His body slumped. "Do it quickly, Cartwright."

"No sir, let's take our time here awhile."

Our gazes spun toward the door, toward Tres. He looked large, imposing. Safe. "How you doin', kid?" Tres pushed right by Cartwright and strode to my chair.

"Honestly, I'm not sure. I think my dad is about to throw me in jail, and Stormi's already there, but aside from that, we're great."

"You did good, kid. Stormi did good." He turned to my Dad, now standing. "Do you really want to add to your legacy by pitchin' your own son into a cell? Why now? Because he knows a truth you need to speak?"

Silence.

"Nothin' to say to me? You have me in a prison for years without cause, and you feel no urge to make comment?"

"Tres, it wasn't that easy, and you know it."

"Oh, you're right on that. Let me tell you exactly how hard it was. Sitting in a cell while my daughter screamed not three feet away. Can you imagine hearing that?" Tres turned. "Can you imagine that, Mr. Cartwright?"

Cartwright slumped heavy into the wall, I imagine tilted by the weight of guilt.

"Do you want to know what Evangeline shrieked? Do you want to hear her words?"

"Please, no," Dad whispered.

"How about you, Cartwright? Care to hear what happened to Alan, what he said? Listen."

What Dad and Cartwright heard in the next minutes, I do not know. I myself heard nothing. But from the way they tore at their ears—the way Dad slumped from his chair—I reckon it was the stuff of nightmares. A child's last moments. Chilling.

"Now, the men who done that?" Tres continued. "I have three with me outside. For all we know, they was the ones to take my own girl from this earth. They's still payin' for the crime. Still in their cells, if you ask me." Tres's presence filled that dark room. "All I want, Mr. Everett, is for you to come clean on what's been done. Follow me out that door. Do it for the one you loved."

"Get out," Dad seethed, his breath heavy.

"This is your last opportunity, Mr. Everett."

"Get out!" Dad threw himself toward Tres, landing far short and on his knees, where he clawed at the carpet. I'd never seen Dad cry, and I admit that in that moment I wanted to throw myself beside him, grab hold of him, and rock him. I wanted to tell him everything was going to be all right. But I knew it wasn't.

"Come on, Jonah. I know what you said upon arrival, but this ain't no longer your home."

I rose on instinct and followed Tres away from everything I'd known. I didn't know the destination, but I knew the words were true. That wasn't my home. My home was with Stormi.

"So, now we get Stormi, right?"

"Now we wait. We see what your dad does. Gullary's last chance."

"Last chance?"

We stood across the street for five minutes. I glanced at the trailer, the town, Tres's face. The strength he'd shown was gone, and in his eyes was a sadness I'd never before witnessed. Tres became the old drifter. Without strength. Without anger.

Without hope.

He hung his head. "I just came from seeing Stormi. She told me the Herald's been sent. Time's up."

"And you left her in there?" I glanced around town, expecting to see some horror slowly advancing through our streets, but my gaze snagged on a small clump of men coming my way. They walked slowly, deliberately, three undertakers moving shoulder to shoulder in the middle of the street.

"These guys again? You brought them?"

"I brought them."

They reached us, and we stood awkward in the silence. One placed a hand on my back, but the thought of what that hand may have done years ago made me sick, and I jerked away.

"Jonah," the tall one said soberly.

"How did you three . . . What about Michael Queene? You got away again? Why come back?"

He cleared his throat. "There's living and there's living with yourself, and they aren't the same thing. In the Hive, we've been doing the first, but the second has proven elusive. Being back here, well, knowing perhaps there's a good part for us to play in this story, it's worth the risk."

"Part to play? What part?" The thought of Evangeline floated through my mind, tried to form, take shape. I could almost see her laughing—hear her telling me I was her favorite brother—and then she was gone, like so much vapor. "You've done enough here. Taken enough."

The tall one winced, as if struck. "It's a truth we live with. More confining than prison ever was. But maybe we can help others find their way out."

He glanced over his shoulder. A row of minivans and pick-ups snaked slowly along Main Street, their beds stacked high with boxes and picture frames, bicycles and small children. Lots of children. Seemed half the population was heading north out of town, but not just the young ones. Ms. Utica's yellow Jeep, Dr. Only-Doctor-in-Gullary's white Toyota Corolla—even Gurney's rusted moped tooled on by. Behind the main procession rolled a bus from the Villa, half filled.

"What's going on?"

Tres gave the tall undertaker's shoulder a squeeze and faced me. "Gullary's Exodus. Lot of innocents in this town. A lot of folks have clean hands and knew nothing of what was done. I brought my own heralds to give warning."

I couldn't break free from the straggling vehicles departing. Greasy Jake's roadster, Ms. P's station wagon . . .

Ms. P?

I grabbed Tres' arm.

"Ms. P's getting out? She knew! She knew everything about the red door and probably about Connor and what he was trying to do to Stormi and . . . why'd you tell her?"

Tres pried loose my fingers and patted my cheek as though I was a little child. "Mercy, Jonah. Even in this, look for it. We warned everybody." He forced a smile and tousled my hair. "Got a safe place you can go? You can come with us; we won't go far."

"For how long?"

"Until."

I thought a moment. Stormi was still here.

"I can't leave her."

Tres rolled his eyes. "She's not your concern anymore. Never was. Her purposes here are done." He leaned in. "Let. Her. Go."

I stared at this man, and started to laugh. I do not know where the joy came from, or why it came. Maybe nerves, but I wasn't anxious. Laughter bubbled up in waves and splashed out of me and over me and maybe I was going crazy, but in that moment I knew exactly my trajectory, and Tres, who knew everything, was clueless.

Finish this.

Wait for me.

"No."

Tres frowned. "No, what?"

"No, I'm not leaving her. As long as she is here, I'll be here. Easy as that."

"Do you have any idea what you're doing, boy?"

"None whatsoever!" And the cluelessness of love felt positively buoyant. "Don't worry, Tres. There's Arthur. I didn't see them leave. I could stay with him, I think, depending on his parents."

"So, the boy lived. That's good," Tres said. "Hard to find a suitable opponent these days." He smacked my back. It did not hurt. "So your choice is made. Okay. You find your way to Arthur's on your own?"

"I've lived here all my life. Gullary is my home."

"Good-bye, Jonah."

He gazed long at me, a remembering gaze of the uncomfortable kind. The kind you give when you are trying to make a memory.

The four of them walked toward a van parked across the street.

"Tres!" I rubbed my head. "I'm not going to see you again, am I?"

He leaned against the tailgate, mosquitoes buzzing him beneath the streetlight. "There's a little of Stormi in you, huh? You tell that girl I'm proud of her. Kiss my grandbaby . . . kiss Nayeli for me."

The van pulled out of town, and I watched it go.

Stormi. Nayeli.

I turned, knowing my job was to wait. I would give Dad three days to speak, and then I would find a way to finish it.

I didn't get three days.

For two hours, I wandered through an unnatural calm. The streets were deserted, and even the dogs and chickens held their breath. I alone moved in Gullary, a town once a movie, but now trapped in a still photo. Only the crunch of sneakers on gravel hinted that I was alive, that any of this was real.

Not a whisper of wind. Maybe I didn't feel the Herald after all—

The lost breeze heard my thoughts, and swept back into Gullary the moment my foot landed on A Street. By B Street, his brother had arrived, stiff and steady. But it was not until C Street, when Papa Gust showed up, that I felt fear.

Winds are not equal. Living in Oklahoma provides ample opportunity to study airflow. Winds blow straight, and winds spiral. They updraft and press a body down, like so much gravity. But they also carry emotion. Light and breezy, well, that's joy. Firm and forceful, there's a relentless strength to it, and it makes you say uncle. Oklahoma also is home to flirtatious, peek-a-boo winds, disappearing and reappearing with a wink and a nod.

And then there was the wind that hit on C Street. It came hard and fast and angry. There was a rage with it, no, *in* it. It was looking for something. Looking to do something. Something horrid. I ran to Arthur's buffeted by that wind. It grew in power so that I did not think of the hour upon arrival; I simply pounded the door.

The siren wail took care of the rest.

Arthur's dad threw open the screen. He fumbled with a robe and his glasses and the situation simultaneously, flattening down his hair and blinking hard.

"What?"

In that instant, my needs changed. Yeah, I had to find shelter, but Arthur's crawl space would not do.

"We need to go. Siren's up!"

"Gissy! Arthur! Grab and come!" His mind clicked on, and the words came rehearsed and urgent.

I turned toward the street, suddenly alive with motion. People scurried toward the underground community shelter, toward security.

Stormi.

I bolted toward SMX beneath the warning's throbbing wail. It cut through the gusts, but only slightly. When the siren sounded distant, Gullary knew, a storm was nearly upon us.

I fought forward, and at times sideways, but minutes later I reached the gallery. The front door banged open, and I raised my arms to protect my head and burst inside. Light on. Brick lodged against the red door.

Stormi slept.

I threw open her cell door with a clang. Stormi stretched and rolled over, sat up peacefully on her bed. The roof creaked. The roof of the impenetrable Supermax prison creaked.

"We need to go! There are sirens."

"You lead." Stormi stood and took my hand, and my heart-beat slowed. We would be okay. The storm would pass. We would be together.

After all, we were married.

We walked into the gallery, and pushed outside. Rain fell horizontal, and puddles raced across the prison yard.

We broke into a run, toward the shelter.

"I need to head home." Stormi's voice barely reached me. "I need something!"

"No time!" I tried to yank her, but she slipped free. "Bad idea! Really bad!" We veered down a street filled with rolling garbage cans and airborne tree branches, and slipped into Stormi's trailer. She disappeared into her bedroom.

The winds howled, and outside, metal and wood crashed against trailer walls.

"Hurry up, Stormi!" I ducked in after and froze.

Connor knelt on top of her. Groping in the storm.

Stormi fought, her screams swallowed up by the wind, and rage took me. I blinked and suddenly there were two Connors and two Stormis. The pre-seizure aura muddled my senses. I had little time. I lunged toward the nearest Connor, and felt my palms grasp solid neck, and then all feeling vanished, leaving only sound. The sound of wind and the screaming of children. My mind left this earth, as Old Rickety joined the storm and had his way with me.

But Old Rick must've known a big storm when he saw one. He didn't want to stick around either.

He departed as quickly as he had arrived. Uncharacteristic. And with his exit, my faculties returned, and I again felt skin. Connor's skin. I saw my hands still grasping his neck, and his body, limp on the ground.

"No." I released him and felt for a heartbeat, listened for breath. I found both, and fell back against Stormi's desk.

"He needs help. We need to tell someone what I did. I'm not covering this up, I'd be no better than Dad."

A tree limb crashed through the window, and Stormi hauled me to my feet. "Nobody will believe you, they'll think it was me." She tore at her dresser, grabbed a photo, and slid it into the back pocket of her jean shorts. "Okay! We need to get to the shelter."

"But we can't leave him!"

The front door flew open and crashed through the trailer, which rocked and settled.

"Now!" Stormi's voice was terrible.

I stumbled up and we pushed outside, arms crooked before our faces. A minute later, the leaves fell still. In that moment, silence. The world was unnatural.

"It's come," Stormi whispered, and I heard her. "Run!"

The roar surrounded. It was no train. It was alive, a creature, twisted and bent, come to gather up everything to itself. Hell was here. Stormi and I reached the shelter and dropped to our knees, pounding on the metal door to the underground bunker. It cracked, and then faces called to us from the dark. I descended, glanced up. Stormi was not following.

"Nope! Not today, Stormi!" I shouted. Hands grasped me from behind, but I broke free and joined Stormi back outside.

"Wait for me!" she called. "Please, wait for me to come home."

She kissed my neck, and around us the wind seemed to calm and the rain sprinkled a gentle note. I grabbed her with all I had. I kissed her, full and strong, searching for more. Stormi's eyes opened wide and then closed and for a time we were together. Completely. I lifted her from the earth and spun her, one with the winds around us. We would not leave one another. Ever.

Then she pushed hard, broke free and stumbled away. She ran into hell.

"Nayeli!" I dove to catch her, but grasped nothing, as the leftover seizure took me yet again. When next I came to, I huddled with all of Gullary in the dungeon, while the tornado raged overhead. Ma's hand gripped mine, but I knew the truth. I was alone.

CHAPTER 21

It's a strange thing, the workings of wind. What it takes, what it leaves, what it changes along the way.

As I sit on my step and gaze, I see little of what I knew. Gullary is gone, wiped clean, as it were. The chat piles, and I reckon those laying beneath, sucked back into the sky where they belong. Two years have passed since SMX was again reduced to foundation, though already talk in nearby towns has shifted to the importance of rebuilding the prison, a testament to pride, and to how hard it is for lessons to be learned.

Yep, Gullary is wiped clean. Except for one set of steps. Ours. And one bedroom. Mine. My photos were untouched, and those waiting to be hung rested undisturbed on my desk throughout the storm. Memories of her I treasure.

It is strange what the wind leaves. And though I've no illusions that my room will be spared future storms, it makes me feel good that it's lasted this long. Now, looking back, I'm also relieved that Connor was found pinned, but mostly whole, beneath his front door. Had he not survived, my weekly pilgrimages back to this place would have carried an entirely different feel.

Things taken? Seems Old Rick was a casualty. I've had not one hint of a seizure in the twenty-four months since the leveling.

The citizens, also. I've heard no eagerness to resurrect Gullary. Still, the familiar is tough to abandon, and most families migrated a mere seven miles or so to Waxton, with the balance moving deeper into the palm of the Ozarks, to the other side of Lake Gullary. The cement cauldron that remains marks what we once thought ours, and holds the sum of our lives in broken glass, brick, and cloth. Maybe my undertaking to write the record of what transpired will end up buried as well. I can't shake the feeling that I was central to the story for a reason, to record what killed this town, just as the truth was meant to give it one last chance.

Which brings me to Stormi. Of the living, she alone was swept away, though I believe this now to be her plan all along. In the months following the storm, I lost myself in the reporting of nearby towns, hoping for a breeze of news. What goes up generally does come down. Though I am not certain the laws of physics hold true for Stormi. I will, however, hold fast to her final words, and I will wait.

Foolish, my dad says, though he says little else. He wanders through his days a broken man. Ma waits for him to return, as I wait for Stormi.

Waiting, it gives purpose to time. Stormi said that once, so I will keep coming back, and someday, I will see her again.

I place my pen down as a cloud passes over the sun. Just one cloud, tiny and round, the only one in the sky. I stare at that cloud until it shifts and the heat of noon blazes once more. I think to add the cloud to my account and lower my gaze.

"Hello, Jonah."

Both of Me

Jonathan Friesen

It was supposed to be just another flight, another escape into a foreign place where she could forget her past, forget her attachments. Until Clara found herself seated next to an alluring boy named Elias Phinn—a boy who seems to know secrets she has barely been able to admit to herself for years.

When her carry-on bag is accidentally switched with Elias's identical pack, Clara uses the luggage tag to track down her things. At that address she discovers there is not one Elias Phinn, but two: the odd, paranoid, artistic, and often angry Elias she met on the plane, who lives in an imaginary world of his own making called Salem; and the kind, sweet, and soon irresistible Elias who greets her at the door, and who has no recollection of ever meeting Clara at all. As she learns of Elias's dissociative identity disorder, and finds herself quickly entangled in both of Elias's lives, Clara makes a decision that could change all of them forever. She is going to find out what the Salem Elias knows about her past, and how, even if it means playing along with his otherworldly quest. And she is going to find a way to keep the gentle Elias she's beginning to love from ever disappearing again.

Available in stores and online!

BLINK

Aquifer

Jonathan Friesen

Only He Can Bring What They Need to Survive.

In the year 2250, water is scarce, and those who control it control everything. Sixteen-year-old Luca has struggled with this truth, and what it means, his entire life. As the son of the Deliverer, he will one day have to descend to the underground Aquifer each year and negotiate with the reportedly ratlike miners who harvest the world's fresh water. But he has learned the true control rests with the Council aboveground, a group that has people following without hesitation, and which has forbidden all emotion and art in the name of keeping the peace. And this Council has broken his father's spirit, while also forcing Luca to hide every feeling that rules his heart.

But when Luca's father goes missing, everything shifts. Luca is forced underground, and discovers secrets, lies, and mysteries that cause him to reevaluate who he is and the world he serves. Together with his friends and a very alluring girl, Luca seeks to free his people and the Rats from the Council's control. But Luca's mission is not without struggle and loss, as his desire to uncover the truth could have greater consequences than he ever imagined.

Available in stores and online!

BLINK

Connect with Jonathan Friesen!

www.jonathanfriesen.com

 /AuthorJonathanFriesen

 @FriesenJonathan

 /friesenbooks

Summer 1999 Edition

COLLECTOR'S
VALUE GUIDE™

Ty® Beanie Babies®

Secondary Market Price Guide
& Collector Handbook

SEVENTH EDITION

Ty® Beanie Babies®

Front cover (left to right): Foreground – "Spangle™" – *Beanie Babies®*, "Almond™" – *Beanie Babies®*, "Schweetheart™" – *Beanie Babies®*
Background – "Eucalyptus™" – *Beanie Babies®*, "Clubby II™" – *Beanie Babies®*, "Paul™" – *Beanie Babies®*
Back cover (left to right): "Princess™" – *Beanie Buddies®*, "Princess™" – *Beanie Babies®*, "Neon™" – *Beanie Babies®*

Managing Editor:	Jeff Mahony	Art Director:	Joe T. Nguyen
Associate Editors:	Melissa A. Bennett	Production Supervisor:	Scott Sierakowski
	Jan Cronan	Senior Graphic Designers:	Carole Mattia-Slater
	Gia C. Manalio		Leanne Peters
	Paula Stuckart	Graphic Designers:	Jennifer J. Denis
Contributing Editor:	Mike Micciulla		Lance Doyle
Editorial Assistants:	Jennifer Filipek		Sean-Ryan Dudley
	Nicole LeGard Lenderking		Kimberly Eastman
	Christina Levere		Ryan Falis
	Joan C. Wheal		Jason C. Jasch
Research Assistants:	Timothy R. Affleck		David S. Maloney
	Priscilla Berthiaume		David Ten Eyck
	Heather N. Carreiro	Art Intern:	Janice Evert
	Beth Hackett		
	Victoria Puorro		
	Steven Shinkaruk		
Web Reporters:	Samantha Bouffard		
	Ren Messina		

CheckerBee PUBLISHING

(formerly Collectors' Publishing)
306 Industrial Park Road • Middletown, CT 06457

collectorbee.com

Contents

FROM THE BIGGEST TO THE SMALLEST, WELCOME ALL OF OUR NEW FRIENDS!

BEANIE BUDDIES®

BEANIE BABIES®

TEENIE BEANIE BABIES™

1999 March/April Releases:

5 Beanie Buddies®

16 Beanie Babies® (including "Clubby II")

16 Teenie Beanie Babies™ (including 4 International bears)

INTRODUCING THE COLLECTOR'S VALUE GUIDE™

*W*elcome to the latest edition of the Collector's Value Guide™ to Ty® Beanie Babies®, designed to help collectors – young and old, new and experienced – stay on top of the Ty collectibles market. We're pleased to bring you all the information that you have come to expect, packaged with exciting sections like a spotlight on how *Beanies* have been making headlines and an overview of the ever-growing club.

With the tremendous *Beanie Babies* craze – one that's sweeping the entire continent and even overseas – it's never been more important for collectors to know the real story behind these cuddly creatures. In the following pages, you'll find all the information and resources you need to keep up with the fast-paced and exciting world of Ty and to unravel its mysteries, including:

- The Newest Releases And Retirements Of *Beanie Babies*, *Beanie Buddies*® And *Teenie Beanie Babies*™

- The Most Current List Of The Top 10 Most Valuable *Beanie Babies*

- News Headlines From The World Of Ty

- A Comprehensive Look At *Beanie Babies* Variations

- Valuable Information About *Beanie Babies* And Their Presence On The Internet

- A Guide To Swing And Tush Tags

- A Lesson In Counterfeit *Beanies*

- And So Much More!

ℬeaniephile. Beanie-ologist. Beaniemaniac. Nicknames like these accurately describe today's avid – and amazingly zealous – collectors of H. Ty Warner's *Beanie Babies.* It seems the nicknames are popping up as fast as Ty's new creations. Though the toys were created for the children's market, the *Beanie Babies* craze has left collectors of all ages hungry for more, despite their sometimes staggering price tags, which can reach into the thousands on the secondary market.

Ty Warner couldn't possibly have imagined the impact of his venture when he first began. Warner started out selling stuffed animals for Dakin Inc. He stayed with the company until the mid-80s, when he left to travel overseas. Yet the call of the toys was great and after returning to the United States in 1986, Warner decided to create a toy company of his own. The initial product line of Ty Inc. consisted of a small litter of stuffed Himalayan cats and dogs which grew into a virtual jungle of animal species including bears, cows, pigs and the like. Building on their success and Warner's business-savvy, in 1993, Ty Inc. introduced a line of jointed, plush animals called *The Attic Treasures Collection*™. That same year, that vision of plush characters evolved into a smaller, child-friendly version: *Beanie Babies.*

In 1995, the *Pillow Pals*™, a line of baby-friendly, plush animals were added to Ty Inc.'s collection. Two years later, in 1997, miniature replicas of *Beanie Babies*, called *Teenie Beanie Babies*, were introduced through a special promotion with McDonald's fast-food restaurants. The Happy Meal promotion was so successful, Ty Inc. decided to do it again in 1998 and in 1999.

In fall 1998, larger, mirror-image counterparts to *Beanie Babies* were introduced: *Beanie Buddies.* Made of a material called Tylon®, these characters are known for their extra softness and coolness to the touch. Immediately, demand was high for the animals, however the production process is slow due to the long process involved in producing Tylon. Consequently, the availability of this plush was (and remains) low, creating an even higher demand and making the *Beanie Buddies* highly sought after.

The *Beanie Babies* fanfare began with nine unassuming characters at a Chicago trade show. Soon after, *Beanie Babies* began appearing in smaller stores and specialty gift shops. As Warner's business philosophy dictated, these retailers could only order limited amounts of product and large chain stores could not order them at all. And when the first three pieces retired, collectors were hooked and the hunt for the already hard-to-find *Beanies* was on, suddenly making these little bags of beans the biggest craze on the collectible scene.

Never wanting to disappoint collectors, Ty Inc. has kept up with the fast-paced environment of today's media-hungry world. *Beanie Babies* and *Beanie Buddies* have made charitable appearances on *The Rosie O'Donnell Show*, have offered some comfort on *ER* and have even become the subject of a legal debate on *Judge Judy*.

And aside from loving the spotlight, these characters are really quite charitable. Many *Beanie Babies* have lent themselves as featured promotions for several causes such as the Canadian Special Olympics, The For All Kids Foundation and the Diana, Princess Of Wales Memorial Fund. It is doubtful that Ty Warner knew what a humanitarian role his critters would play when he first created them.

But don't think for a minute that *Beanie Babies* are all about work, though – all work and no play makes a *Beanie Baby* a dull character! Starting in 1997, the plush creatures started making appearances at professional sporting events such as baseball, basketball, football and hockey games. Some *Beanie Babies* were even given away with commemorative cards. How successful was the promotion? Well, according to some "stats," these promotions were one hit after another. Now that's a batting record any player would be proud of.

And then in 1998 in conjunction with Cyrk Inc., the Beanie Babies® Official Club™ added another dimension to the fun of collecting *Beanie Babies*. The club offered its members special privileges and access to breaking *Beanie Babies* news. The club was a tremendous hit in its first year with the "Gold Kit," which was retired in March 1999. So drawing on the success of the charter year, Ty decided to issue a second club edition, the "Platinum Kit."

Beanie Babies have become a huge part of many people's lives and luckily for collectors, there doesn't seem to be any sign of slowing. Children and adults have found value in these plush toys that goes far beyond the price tag. Just remember to keep your eyes and ears open – there always seems to be something going on in the world of Ty.

ℬeanie Babies are popping up in all sorts of places, some of which you'd never guess. The following is a compilation of just a few examples of the hottest *Beanie* news. So kick back and enjoy the recap!

Not A Time To Diet! McDonald's restaurants, in conjunction with Ty Inc., will run a third *Teenie Beanie Babies* promotion from May 21st to June 3rd. Twelve new pieces, based on their full-sized *Beanie Babies* companions, will make their debut. This will be followed by a fourth promotion featuring four *Teenie Beanie Babies* International Bears. "Britannia," "Erin," "Glory" and "Maple" will be available for a small cost with any menu item purchase from June 4th to June 17th. Eat up!

Thanks Rosie! On the March 31 episode of *The Rosie O'Donnell Show*, the popular television host Rosie announced that she would be auctioning off a number of Ty products (donated by Ty Inc.) on *ebay.com* to benefit The All For Kids Foundation, a charity established by Rosie herself. The most impressive item auctioned off was a desk created from *Beanie Babies*. Talk about a plush office environment!

Money Does Talk? In order to help combat the problem of low stock at retail outlets, Ty Inc. has decided to reward some of the company's accounts with first-hand access to its products. The official word at *ty.com* is that shipments will be made first to the "most supportive" accounts. Upsell, upsell, upsell!

Third Time's A Charm! After much confusion over the spelling of "Millennium's" name, Ty has begun to issue tags with the recognized spelling "Millennium." So now the bear can be found in three versions. The most recent version has a tush tag and a swing tag with the corrected spelling. The previous version has a swing tag that is spelled with one "n" but a tush tag that is spelled with two. And the original version spells the name on both tags with one "n." So the question remains: Two "n"s or not two "n"s?

Log On! Don't miss the opportunity to register your name and password for the new "Official Ty Talk Cyberboard." It's a chance for *Beanie Babies* addicts to exchange information and swap rumors. Get chatting!

Stop Right There! Reports of burglaries of *Beanie Babies* have been surfacing. Apparently, the temptation to get their hands on those plush critters – and profit from the sale – is too much for some crooks to bear. *Beanie Babies* robbers have hit gift shops, homes, storage companies and even trade shows. Is that a *Beanie* in your pocket?

Going My Way? A look-alike "Inky" rose to celebrity status when he caught a free ride in a Volkswagen television commercial. The commercial featured a young boy tossing the bean bag at his father's head while he while he was driving. Don't worry, no people or octopi were hurt in the filming of this commercial.

"I Pledge Allegiance . . . " Back in 1996, Ty introduced three *Beanies* ("Libearty," "Lefty" and Righty") with American flags stitched to their bodies. This started a patriotic trend which has since spread to feature other countries on pieces like "Britannia," "Germania," "Maple " and "Osito." Being territorial has never been so adorable.

WHAT'S NEW FOR BEANIE BABIES®

*T*hrough a series of "crystal ball" images that appeared on the official Ty web site beginning on April 1, Ty introduced the world to the newest members of the family, including 15 *Beanie Babies* (there's also one new club bear) and five *Beanie Buddies*. There is something for everyone in the new releases, including a tie-dyed seahorse and a domestic tabby!

BRING ON THE BEANS

You'll go nuts over this adorable bear who is as sweet as honey! **"Almond,"** a beige-colored bruin, is one of four bears to march into the collection this season. Gentle as a lamb, she is sure to capture your heart as soon as you lay eyes on her!

"Amber," a "meow-velous" gold-furred beauty, promises to bring a little sunshine into your day! "Amber" and her gray counterpart "Silver" are excited to join the *Beanie Babies* family but hope to spend all nine of their lives with you and your family!

It's a jungle out there and **"Cheeks"** the baboon wants to be there to help guide you through thick and thin. This primate makes a great playmate, although that red snout is usually a sure giveaway during "hide and seek." Though the facial marks make "Cheeks" look a bit intimidating, you're sure to go "ape" over this sweetie!

Collectors who join the Beanie Babies® Official Club™ will receive the "Platinum" membership kit, which includes this eye-catching teddy. The second version of the official club mascot, **"Clubby II"** is just as stunning as his predecessor "Clubby" and features lavender fur specked with light blue highlights and a shiny silver neck ribbon.

Eucalyptus™

This Australian native follows "Mel" as the second koala in the collection. Named after his favorite food, **"Eucalyptus"** is a cuddly gray koala who would climb the highest tree to get to you! Collectors who want to add this adorable Aussie to their collection should hurry up before "Eucalyptus" goes "down under!"

Knuckles™

You won't find this pretty porker rolling around in the mud anytime soon. **"Knuckles,"** the prize pig, has meticulously brushed her fur and put on a shiny blue ribbon in hopes of charming you! She hopes that she's cleaned up her act enough to be welcomed into your collection!

Neon™

One of the most unique creatures to debut this season, **"Neon"** the tie-dyed seahorse is hard to miss! Born on April Fools' Day, this underwater beauty is a perfect companion to "Goochy" the jellyfish and is sure to light up your life with her electric colors!

Osito™

This patriotic teddy, who proudly wears the flag of Mexico on his chest, has travelled a long way from his homeland. **"Osito"** is a Spanish word meaning "little bear," and this bright red bruin promises that if you befriend him, he will remain your *amigo* forever!

"Paul" the walrus is in perfect tune with the lazy days of summer. Whether strolling across a road, playing in a strawberry field or marching with a band, this mod mammal is hip enough for any collection.

This little bruin is sweet as pie and makes the perfect bedtime companion. A great snuggler, **"Pecan,"** with her warm gold fur, will put you right to sleep. And while she will capture your heart with her Southern charm, she also makes a great protector, as one growl will let prowlers know that they shouldn't mess with you!

You'll "go bananas" over this schmall schweetie who has travelled from the depths of the jungle to be your friend! **"Schweetheart"** the orangutan and his buddy "Cheeks" become the fifth and sixth monkeys to join the *Beanie Babies* family. There's sure to be a lot of "monkey business" when this primate comes into your collection.

Night or day, **"Silver"** is always ready to play, play, play! And as every cloud has a silver lining, this frisky gray tabby will be the shining light in any collection. But he's sure to sell out fast, so sink your claws into him while you still can!

You'll see stars and stripes when you take a look at this bear! **"Spangle"** the American teddy is decked out in red, white and blue to help celebrate our country's birthday. Born on

Flag Day, he joins "Glory" and "Libearty" as the third patriotic American bear in the collection.

"Swirly" is unlike any other snail you might have seen – this snail is tickled pink! Carrying your home on your back is a tough job and "Swirly" isn't able to move very fast. However, you'll find that once you lay eyes on this friendly critter, you'll have no choice but to let "Swirly" slither into your heart very quickly!

Don't be concerned if you find this furry scavenger missing from your room at night! **"Tiptoe"** is probably silently tiptoeing through the house in search of a late-night snack! Anyone who has seen this creature avoiding the household feline in search of crumbs knows just how appropriate its name is!

Following in big brother "Wise's" footsteps, **"Wiser"** takes the stage this year as a proud member of the class of 1999 and gets an A+ for charm! Looking regal in a mortarboard, this striped owl is at the top of the class!

OH BUDDY, OH PAL

This golden bear was a hit as a *Beanie Baby* as collectors discovered that his heart is as golden as his special, soft fur. His success is sure to continue as **"Fuzz"** comes out of the shadows as the "Mystery Buddy" and into the light of the *Beanie Buddies* collection.

This saintly bear wants to be your guardian angel, watching over and protecting you from harm. And judging from the popularity of "Hope" the *Beanie Baby*, it is safe to say that you can never have too much hope with a **"Hope"** twice the size.

Any time you're starting to feel lonely, you can count on **"Jabber"** the parrot to save the day! His bright colors speak louder than words and are loud enough to cheer anyone up.

To help ring in the new century in a big way, Ty created this bigger version of **"Millennium."** "Millennium" is sure to be the life of the party on New Year's Eve as well as every eve before and after that!

Collectors who weren't able to purchase **"Princess"** the *Beanie Baby* before she retired are in luck! A larger, softer version of the bear is now available, as "Princess" the *Beanie Buddy* makes her debut! Continuing the tradition of the original "Princess" bear, all profits from the sale of this piece will be donated to the Diana, Princess Of Wales Memorial Fund.

WOULD YOU LIKE SOME BEANS WITH THAT?

Teenie Beanie Babies are back! Twelve new miniature versions of the popular *Beanie Babies* will make their debut for a third promotion at McDonald's restaurants nationwide, beginning on May 21st and running for a two week period. This year's featured stars will include **"Antsy," "Chip," "Claude,"**

"Freckles," "Iggy,"
"'Nook," "Nuts,"
"Rocket," "Smoochy,"
"Spunky," "Stretchy"
and **"Strut."**

But the treats don't stop there. In a fourth promotion, from June 4 to June 17, the release of four *Teenie Beanie Babies* International Bears will bring some exotic spice to the collection. During this time, **"Britannia," "Erin," "Glory"** and **"Maple"**will be available for purchase with the purchase of any regularly priced menu item.

We recommend that you get in line now, because this year's promotions are sure to be bigger and better than ever!

*I*f you haven't heard, there's a new edition of the Beanie Babies® Official Club™ – and you're going to love what it has to offer!

The "Platinum Edition Kit" includes "Clubby II," an adorable light purple bear with a metallic shine. The kit made its debut on *The Rosie O'Donnell Show* on March 31 and now collectors are rushing to get it from their favorite *Beanie Babies* retailer. The big news with this edition is that "Clubby II" is already included – there's no certificate to send in order to get your bear (although you do have to send in the registration form provided in the kit to become a "Platinum Edition" member).

"Clubby II" isn't the only thing you'll receive when you join. You also get three limited edition "Collector's Cards," a limited edition "Collector's Coin" featuring one of the original nine *Beanie Babies*, a "Platinum Edition" certificate and membership card, a checklist and a "Platinum Edition" newsletter. All of these exciting gifts come in a silver plastic carrying case with a clear front that allows you to see all your neat stuff and a back which features the official club logo.

Last year's "Gold Charter Members" who also become "Platinum Members" will be entitled to exclusive special offers and information.

So get your kit today and start enjoying the benefits!

On-line Face-lift

The Beanie Babies Official Club site will soon have a new look, promising lots of new and exciting things!

Look for more games, exclusive club information and pictures of your favorite Beanie Babies plush animals.

So be sure to keep your eye on *www.beaniebabyofficialclub.com*!

RECENT RETIREMENTS

*W*hile advance warnings on the Ty web site helped collectors to prepare for retirements in December and March, Ty surprised everyone with an unexpected retirement announcement in April 1999. Many collectors were left scrambling for "Princess," who on April 13th became the 44th *Beanie Baby* to be retired since December 31, 1998! In addition, two *Beanie Buddies* have been honored with retirement status since the end of December.

Following is a list of the recently retired *Beanie Babies* and *Beanie Buddies*, with their animal type, style number and issue year.

BEANIE BABIES®

RETIRED 4/13/99
Princess™ (bear, #4300, 1997)

RETIRED 3/31/99
Batty™ (bat, #4035, 1997)
Chip™ (cat, #4121, 1997)
Gobbles™ (turkey, #4034, 1997)
Hissy™ (snake, #4185, 1997)
Iggy™ (iguana, #4038, 1997)
Mel™ (bear, #4162, 1997)
Nanook™ (husky, #4104, 1997)
Pouch™ (kangaroo, #4161, 1997)
Pounce™ (cat, #4122, 1997)

RETIRED 3/31/99, cont.
Prance™ (cat, #4123, 1997)
Pugsly™ (pug dog, #4106, 1997)
Rainbow™ (chameleon, #4037, 1997)
Smoochy™ (frog, #4039, 1997)
Spunky™ (cocker spaniel, #4184, 1997)
Stretch™ (ostrich, #4182, 1997)
Strut™ (rooster, #4171, 1997)

RETIRED 3/15/99
Clubby™ (bear, N/A, 1998)

COLLECTOR'S
VALUE GUIDE™

RETIRED 12/31/98

1998 Holiday Teddy™
  (bear, #4204, 1998)
Ants™ (anteater, #4195, 1998)
Bongo™ (monkey, #4067, 1995)
Chocolate™ (moose, #4015, 1994)
Claude™ (crab, #4083, 1997)
Congo™ (gorilla, #4160, 1996)
Curly™ (bear, #4052, 1996)
Doby™ (Doberman, #4110, 1997)
Dotty™ (dalmatian, #4100, 1997)
Fetch™ (golden retriever,
  #4189, 1998)
Fleece™ (lamb, #4125, 1997)
Freckles™ (leopard, #4066, 1996)

RETIRED 12/31/98, cont.

Glory™ (bear, #4188, 1998)
Nuts™ (squirrel, #4114, 1997)
Pinky™ (flamingo, #4072, 1995)
Pumkin'™ (pumpkin, #4205, 1998)
Roary™ (lion, #4069, 1997)
Santa™ (Santa, #4203, 1998)
Scoop™ (pelican, #4107, 1996)
Snip™ (Siamese cat, #4120, 1997)
Spike™ (rhinoceros, #4060, 1996)
Stinger™ (scorpion, #4193, 1998)
Tuffy™ (terrier, #4108, 1997)
Valentino™ (bear, #4058, 1995)
Wise™ (owl, #4187, 1998)
Zero™ (penguin, #4207, 1998)

BEANIE BUDDIES®

RETIRED 3/31/99
Beak™ (kiwi, #9301, 1998)

RETIRED 12/31/98
Twigs™ (giraffe, #9308, 1998)

TY® SWING TAGS AND TUSH TAGS

TAGS

*U*pon entering the world of *Beanie Babies*, collectors quickly become aware of the importance of the trademark heart-shaped tag. Although the tags on these miniature bean bag creatures come with instructions to remove them, complying may also remove the majority of the animal's secondary market value.

In order to attain the highest price on the secondary market, both of the tags on a *Beanie Baby* should be in mint condition. The **swing tag**, also referred to as the hang tag, is the paper, heart-shaped tag which is affixed with a plastic attachment to the animal. The **tush tag** is a smaller cloth tag near the animal's posterior. Ripped or wrinkled tags can significantly reduce the animal's value on the secondary market, sometimes making it difficult to re-sell the piece.

1st Generation

The Beanie Babies Collection
Brownie ™ style 4010
© 1993 Ty Inc. Oakbrook, IL. USA
All Rights Reserved. Caution:
Remove this tag before giving
toy to a child. For ages 5 and up.
Handmade in Korea.
Surface
Wash.

Why are tags so important? By looking carefully at the tag, collectors can identify which "generation" it is and determine approximately when that piece was produced. *Beanie Babies* have had a total of five hang tags since the line's introduction in 1994 and pieces with older tags are generally worth more than those with more recent tags.

BEANIE BABIES® SWING TAGS

Generation 1 (Early 1994-Mid 1994):
These single sheet tags feature a single red heart with "ty" printed on the front in skinny lettering. The animal's name, style number, reference to "The Beanie Babies Collection" and company information all appear on the back.

2nd Generation

The Beanie Babies Collection
© 1993 Ty Inc. Oakbrook IL. USA
All Rights Reserved, Caution:
Remove this tag before giving
toy to a child. For ages 3 and up.
Handmade in China
Surface
Wash.

Chilly ™ style 4012
to _____
from _____
with
love

Generation 2 (Mid 1994-Early 1995):
While the outside is identical to the first generation tag, this tag opens like a book. The inside contains the animal's name and style number, a "to/from/with love" section for

COLLECTOR'S
VALUE GUIDE™

20

gift giving, a reference to "The Beanie Babies Collection," plus care, cautionary and company information.

3rd Generation

Generation 3 (Early 1995-Early 1996): Unlike previous tags, the "ty" logo on this generation tag is puffy. All of the same information is provided on the inside of the tag, with the addition of a trademark symbol and Ty's three corporate addresses.

> The Beanie Babies ™ Collection
> ℗ Ty Inc.
> Oakbrook IL. U.S.A.
> ℗ Ty UK Ltd.
> Waterlooville, Hants
> PO8 8HH
> ℗ Ty Deutschland
> 90008 Nürnberg
> Handmade in China
>
> Garcia ™ style 4051
> to _____
> from _____
> with
> love

4th Generation

Generation 4 (Early 1996-Late 1997): A yellow star containing the words "Original Beanie Baby" was added to the front of this tag. Also, the inside of this tag underwent major format changes as a poem and birthdate were added for each animal, as well as the Ty web site address.

> The Beanie Babies™Collection
> ℗Ty Inc.
> Oakbrook IL. U.S.A.
> ℗Ty UK Ltd.
> Fareham, Hants
> PO15 5TX
> ℗Ty Deutschland
> 90008 Nürnberg
> Handmade in China
>
> Doodle™ style 4171
> DATE OF BIRTH : 3 - 8 - 96
> Listen closely to "cock-a-doodle-doo"
> What's the rooster saying to you?
> Hurry, wake up sleepy head
> We have lots to do, get out of bed!
> Visit our web page!!!
> http://www.ty.com

5th Generation

Generation 5 (Late 1997-Current): While the only change on the outside of the 5th generation tag is the typeface of the phrase "Original Beanie Baby," the inside of the tag is significantly different. The birthday is written out rather than abbreviated, while "http://" is removed from the Internet address. The piece's style number is deleted (it can be found in the last four digits of the UPC code) and the corporate offices of Ty UK and Ty Deutschland are consolidated as Ty Europe. Also, the name "Beanie Babies Collection" became registered (®).

> The Beanie Babies Collection®
> ℗ Ty Inc.
> Oakbrook, IL. U.S.A.
> ℗ Ty Europe Ltd.
> Fareham, Hants
> PO15 5TX. U.K.
> ℗ Ty Canada
> Aurora, Ontario
> Handmade in China
>
> Pinky™
> DATE OF BIRTH: February 13, 1995
> Pinky loves the everglades
> From the hottest pink she's made
> With floppy legs and big orange beak
> She's the Beanie that you seek !
> www.ty.com

New Generation?

> The Beanie Babies Collection®
> ℗Ty Inc.
> Oakbrook. IL. U.S.A.
> ℗Ty Europe Ltd.
> Fareham. Hants
> PO15 5TX. U.K.
> ℗Ty Canada
> Aurora, Ontario
> Handmade in China
>
> 1998 Holiday Teddy ™
> DATE OF BIRTH : December 25, 1998
> Dressed in his P.J's. and ready for bed
> Hugs given, good nights said
> This little Beanie will stay close at night
> Ready for a hug at first morning light!
> www.ty.com

A New Generation?: In the summer of 1998, some *Beanie Babies* tags began appearing with slight differences. The writing in the star logo has a different font, making the word "Original" appear smaller and the letters of the word "Baby" closer together. The font used on the inside of the tag is larger and darker, as is the writing on the back of the tag. Also, in January 1999, the Ty Europe Ltd. address was changed to "Ty Europe, Gasport, Hampshire, U.K." While some collectors speculate that these changes could be the birth of a new generation, others insist that they are merely modifications to the current swing tag generation.

BEANIE BABIES® TUSH TAGS

Version 1: The first *Beanie Babies* tush tags are white with black printing and list company and production information.

Version 2: The red heart Ty logo is added and the information on the tush tag is printed in red.

Version 3: This tag features the addition of the name of the animal below the Ty heart and "The Beanie Babies Collection™" above the heart.

Version 4: This tush tag sports a small red star on the upper left-hand side of the Ty heart logo. On some tags, a clear sticker with the star was placed next to the Ty logo.

Version 5: In late 1997, these tags began to appear with a registration mark (®) after "Beanie Babies" in the collection's name and a trademark (™) after the animal's name.

Version 6: These tags feature another slight change in trademark symbols. The registration mark in the collection's name moved from after "Beanie Babies" to after "Collection." Some of the recent tush tags have also noted a change to "P.E." pellets from "P.V.C."

Also, in mid-1998, a red stamp began to appear inside some *Beanie Babies'* tush tags. The stamp is an oval containing numbers and Chinese writing.

Version 7: The latest version features a hologram on the tush tag, as well as a red heart printed in disappearing ink.

BEANIE BUDDIES® SWING TAGS

Generation 1: So far, there is only one generation of swing tag for the *Beanie Buddies*. It's the same size as the *Beanie Babies* tags and, on the outside, looks like a *Beanie Baby* 5th generation swing tag (with the exception of the word "Buddy" instead of "Baby" in the yellow star). The inside of the tag has the name of the animal and a fact about its *Beanie Baby* counterpart.

BEANIE BUDDIES® TUSH TAGS

Version 1: The first *Beanie Buddies* tush tags are white with a red heart containing the word "ty" in white letters. The back of the tag gives the company name and fabric information in black writing.

Version 2: The newest *Beanie Buddies* have "The Beanie Buddies Collection®" written in red lettering above the heart. The back gives the company name and fabric information written in red.

*T*he secondary market values on these pages demonstrate just how valuable many *Beanie Babies* have become. This "Top Ten" list ranks the *Beanie Babies* according to their values on the secondary market. Because the market constantly fluctuates, the values of these pieces can quickly change; however, the most valuable *Beanie Babies* are typically those that retired quickly, are rare variations or were not released to the general public. Are you lucky enough to own any of the *Beanie Babies* on this list?

#1 BEAR™ (Sales Rep Gift, Special Tag)
Market Value: $10,000

Ty Inc. presented "#1 Bear" to each of its sales reps in December 1998 for helping to make *Beanie Babies* the number one collectible. The tags feature a special message and the date of the conference and Warner signed and numbered each gift himself.

PEANUT™ (Dark Blue)
Market Value: ❸ – $4,700

Introduced in June 1995, this *Beanie Baby* was a factory error. Only about 2,000 dark blue elephants were produced before the color was changed to light blue, making this original "Peanut" highly sought after.

NANA™
Market Value: ❸ – $4,000

"Nana" is a hard-to-find *Beanie Baby* whose name was changed shortly after he was introduced in June 1995. Although "Nana" wasn't around long, his namesake "Bongo" hung around until December 1998.

TEDDY™ (Violet, Employee Bear, No Swing Tag)
Market Value: $3,800

A gift from Ty Inc. to its employees in September 1996, this bear was not available to the general public. Similar to "Teddy" (violet, new face), this version has no swing tag and wears either a red or green ribbon.

BROWNIE™
Market Value: ❶ – $3,700
One of the original nine *Beanie Babies* introduced in January 1994, "Brownie" was only available for a short time before his name was changed to "Cubbie." This makes "Brownie" quite rare and very valuable.

BILLIONAIRE BEAR™
(Employee Bear, Special Swing Tag)
Market Value: $3,400

In the fall of 1998, Ty Inc. gave two of these bears to each of its employees as a token of gratitude for a job well done. Unavailable to the general public, these bears include Ty Warner's signature on every swing tag!

DERBY™ (No Star/Fine Mane)
Market Value: ❸ – $3,300
Since his introduction in June 1995, "Derby" has undergone three dramatic changes. However, it is the original "Derby" that collectors seek for their collections, making him the most valuable horse in the stable.

PINCHERS™ ("Punchers™" Swing Tag)
Market Value: ❶ – $3,200
When this little lobster made his debut with the original nine *Beanie Babies* in January 1994, some of his swing tags read "Punchers." What a wonderful mistake for collectors who managed to trap this guy early!

TEDDY™ (Brown, Old Face)
Market Value: ❶ – $2,700
When this "old face" bear joined the *Beanie Babies* family in June 1995, his antique look quickly won the hearts of collectors young and old alike. This brown fellow is also the only "Teddy" that was ever available with a birthdate and a poem.

HUMPHREY™
Market Value: ❶ – $2,300
Collectors barely noticed when this doleful dromedary entered the *Beanie Babies* world in June 1994. But when he became one of the first three *Beanie Babies* to be honored with retirement status, his popularity began to soar.

How To Use Your Collector's Value Guide™

There are five simple steps in determining the current market value of your *Beanie Babies* collection:

1 Record the price paid and the date purchased for each *Beanie Babies* piece that you own in the allotted space.

2 Use the swing tag generation chart on the right to help you identify the generation of your *Beanie Baby* tag (for more information on tag generations, see pages 20-23).

TY® TAG KEY

5 – 5th Generation
4 – 4th Generation
3 – 3rd Generation
2 – 2nd Generation
1 – 1st Generation

3 Find the value of the piece by looking at the dollar amount listed next to the corresponding heart. For current *Beanie Babies* with a fifth generation tag, fill in the current market value, which is usually the price you paid. If a piece's value is not established, it is listed as "N/E." Sports Promotion *Beanie Babies* are listed beginning on page 131 and are marked in the Value Guide with the appropriate symbol. *Beanie Buddies* begin on page 135, while the *Teenie Beanie Babies* section begins on page 143.

SPORTS PROMOTION BEANIE BABIES® KEY

Canadian Special Olympics
Major League Baseball
National Basketball Association
National Football League
National Hockey League
Women's National Basketball Association

4 Add the "Market Value" for each *Beanie Baby* you own and write the sum in the "Value Totals" box at the bottom of each page. Use a pencil so you can make changes as your collection grows.

5 Write in your totals from each Value Guide page on page 150-151 and add the sums together to get the "Grand Total" of your *Beanie Babies* collection.

Catch The Beanie Wave!

The wave of *Beanie Babies* introduced this year has given collectors a thrilling ride. First introduced in 1994, the market is now exploding with the bean-stuffed animals! While most *Beanie Babies* maintain a value close to their original price, others go zooming off the secondary market charts! In this Value Guide, you'll find all *Beanie Babies* released, as well as information from stock numbers to birthdates to the range of difficulty in locating those that are still current.

Degree Of Difficulty Ratings
Just Released
Easy To Find
Moderate To Find
Hard To Find
Very Hard To Find
Impossible To Find

1

#1 Bear™
(exclusive Ty sales representative gift)

Bear · N/A
Issued: December 12, 1998
Not Available In Retail
Stores – Impossible To Find

Market Value:
Special Tag – $10,000

Dedication Appearing On Special Tag
In appreciation of selling over several Billion dollars in 1998 and achieving the industry ranking of #1 in Gift sales, #1 in Collectible sales, #1 in Cash register area sales, #1 in Markup %, I present to you This Signed and Numbered bear!

Birthdate: N/A
Price Paid: $_____
Date Purchased: _____
Tag Generation: _____

#1

2

1997 Teddy™

Bear · #4200
Issued: October 1, 1997
Retired: December 31, 1997

Market Value:
❹ – $55

Birthdate: December 25, 1996
Price Paid: $_____
Date Purchased: _____
Tag Generation: _____

Beanie Babies are special no doubt
All filled with love – inside and out
Wishes for fun times filled with joy
Ty's holiday teddy is a magical toy!

3

1998 Holiday Teddy™

Bear · #4204
Issued: September 30, 1998
Retired: December 31, 1998

Market Value:
❺ – $55

Birthdate: December 25, 1998
Price Paid: $_____
Date Purchased: _____
Tag Generation: _____

Dressed in his PJ's, and ready for bed
Hugs given, good nights said
This little Beanie will stay close at night
Ready for a hug at first morning light!

Value Totals _____

COLLECTOR'S
VALUE GUIDE™

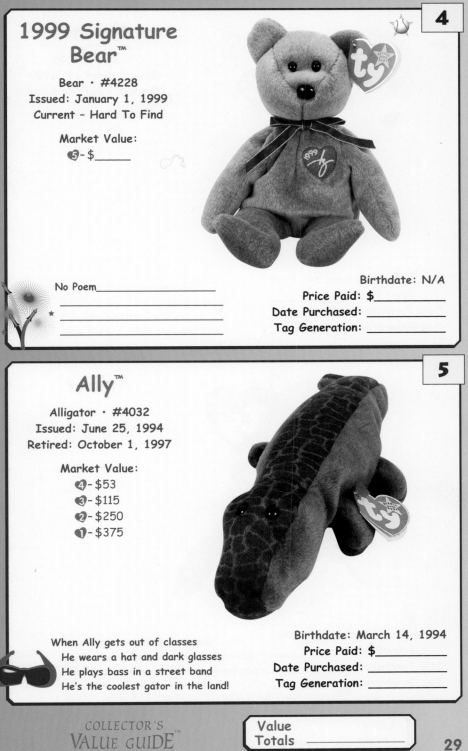

4

1999 Signature Bear™

Bear · #4228
Issued: January 1, 1999
Current – Hard To Find

Market Value:
[5]- $_____

No Poem

Birthdate: N/A
Price Paid: $__________
Date Purchased: __________
Tag Generation: __________

5

Ally™

Alligator · #4032
Issued: June 25, 1994
Retired: October 1, 1997

Market Value:
[4]- $53
[3]- $115
[2]- $250
[1]- $375

When Ally gets out of classes
He wears a hat and dark glasses
He plays bass in a street band
He's the coolest gator in the land!

Birthdate: March 14, 1994
Price Paid: $__________
Date Purchased: __________
Tag Generation: __________

Value Totals __________

6

NEW!

Almond™

Bear · #4246
Issued: April 19, 1999
Current – Just Released

Market Value:
[5]- $_____

Birthdate: April 14, 1999
Price Paid: $__________
Date Purchased: __________
Tag Generation: __________

Leaving her den in early spring
So very hungry, she'll eat anything
Nuts, fruit, berries and fish
Mixed together make a great dish!

7

NEW!

Amber™

Cat · #4243
Issued: April 20, 1999
Current – Just Released

Market Value:
[5]- $_____

Birthdate: February 21, 1999
Price Paid: $__________
Date Purchased: __________
Tag Generation: __________

Sleeping all day and up all night
Waiting to pounce and give you a fright
She means no harm, just playing a game
She's very lovable and quite tame!

Value Totals __________

8

Ants™

Anteater · #4195
Issued: May 30, 1998
Retired: December 31, 1998

Market Value:
[5]- $12

Most anteaters love to eat bugs
But this little fellow gives big hugs
He'd rather dine on apple pie
Than eat an ant or harm a fly!

Birthdate: November 7, 1997
Price Paid: $__________
Date Purchased: __________
Tag Generation: __________

9

Baldy™

Eagle · #4074
Issued: May 11, 1997
Retired: May 1, 1998

Market Value:
[5]- $18
[4]- $23

Hair on his head is quite scant
We suggest Baldy get a transplant
Watching over the land of the free
Hair in his eyes would make it hard to see!

Birthdate: February 17, 1996
Price Paid: $__________
Date Purchased: __________
Tag Generation: __________

Value Totals __________

10

B

Batty™

Bat · #4035
Issued: October 1, 1997
Retired: March 31, 1999

A

Market Value:

A. Tie-dye
(Jan. 99-March 99)
[5]- $26

B. Brown
(Est. Oct. 97-Jan. 99)
[5]- $13
[4]- $18

Birthdate: October 29, 1996
Price Paid: $__________
Date Purchased: __________
Tag Generation: __________

Bats may make some people jitter
Please don't be scared of this critter
If you're lonely or have nothing to do
This Beanie Baby would love to hug you!

11

Beak™

Kiwi · #4211
Issued: September 30, 1998
Current - Easy To Find

Market Value:
[5]- $_____

Birthdate: February 3, 1998
Price Paid: $__________
Date Purchased: __________
Tag Generation: __________

Isn't this just the funniest bird?
When we saw her, we said "how absurd"
Looks aren't everything, this we know
Her love for you, she's sure to show!

Value Totals __________

12

Bernie™

St. Bernard · #4109
Issued: January 1, 1997
Retired: September 22, 1998

Market Value:
[5]- $12
[4]- $15

This little dog can't wait to grow
To rescue people lost in the snow
Don't let him out – keep him on your shelf
He doesn't know how to rescue himself!

Birthdate: October 3, 1996
Price Paid: $__________
Date Purchased: __________
Tag Generation: __________

13

Bessie™

Cow · #4009
Issued: June 3, 1995
Retired: October 1, 1997

Market Value:
[4]- $65
[3]- $135

Bessie the cow likes to dance and sing
Because music is her favorite thing
Every night when you are counting sheep
She'll sing you a song to help you sleep!

Birthdate: June 27, 1995
Price Paid: $__________
Date Purchased: __________
Tag Generation: __________

Value Totals __________

14

Billionaire Bear™

(exclusive Ty employee gift)

Bear · N/A

Issued: September 26, 1998

Not Available In Retail Stores – Impossible To Find

Market Value:

Special Tag – $3,400

Birthdate: N/A

Price Paid: $__________

Date Purchased: __________

Tag Generation: __________

Dedication Appearing On Special Tag

In recognition of value and
contributions in shipping over
a billion dollars since Jan '98,
I present to you this exclusive
signed bear!

15

Blackie™

Bear · #4011

Issued: June 25, 1994

Retired: September 15, 1998

Market Value:

[5] - $17

[4] - $20

[3] - $105

[2] - $240

[1] - $350

Birthdate: July 15, 1994

Price Paid: $__________

Date Purchased: __________

Tag Generation: __________

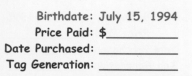

Living in a national park
He only played after dark
Then he met his friend Cubbie
Now they play when it's sunny!

Value Totals __________

16

Blizzard™

Tiger · #4163
Issued: May 11, 1997
Retired: May 1, 1998

Market Value:
[5] - $22
[4] - $26

In the mountains, where it's snowy and cold
Lives a beautiful tiger, I've been told
Black and white, she's hard to compare
Of all the tigers, she is most rare!

Birthdate: December 12, 1996
Price Paid: $__________
Date Purchased: __________
Tag Generation: __________

17

Bones™

Dog · #4001
Issued: June 25, 1994
Retired: May 1, 1998

Market Value:
[5] - $21
[4] - $24
[3] - $110
[2] - $240
[1] - $320

Bones is a dog that loves to chew
Chairs and tables and a smelly old shoe
"You're so destructive" all would shout
But that all stopped, when his teeth
Fell out!

Birthdate: January 18, 1994
Price Paid: $__________
Date Purchased: __________
Tag Generation: __________

Value Totals __________

18

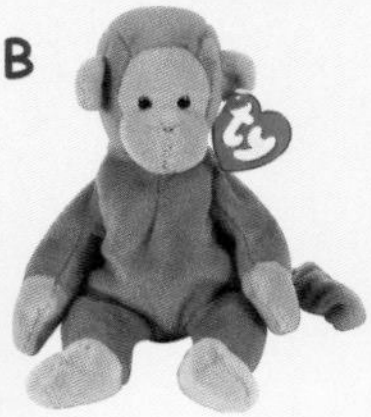
B

A

Bongo™

(name changed from "Nana™")

Monkey · #4067

Issued: June 3, 1995

Retired: December 31, 1998

Market Value:

A. Tan Tail
(June 95-Dec. 98)
[5]-$12
[4]-$15
[3]-$140

B. Brown Tail
(Feb. 96-June 96)
[4]-$64
[3]-$150

Birthdate: August 17, 1995
Price Paid: $__________
Date Purchased: __________
Tag Generation: __________

Bongo the monkey lives in a tree
The happiest monkey you'll ever see
In his spare time he plays the guitar
One of these days he will be a big star!

19

Britannia™

(exclusive to Great Britain)

Bear · #4601

Issued: December 31, 1997

Current - Impossible To Find

Market Value
(in U.S. market):
[5]-$330

Birthdate: December 15, 1997
Price Paid: $__________
Date Purchased: __________
Tag Generation: __________

Britannia the bear will sail the sea
So she can be with you and me
She's always sure to catch the tide
And wear the Union Flag with pride

Value
Totals __________

20

Bronty™

Brontosaurus • #4085
Issued: June 3, 1995
Retired: June 15, 1996

Market Value:
❸– $1,000

No Poem_____
_____
_____
_____

Birthdate: N/A
Price Paid: $_____
Date Purchased: _____
Tag Generation: _____

21

Brownie™

(name changed to "Cubbie™")
Bear • #4010
Issued: January 8, 1994
Retired: 1994

Market Value:
❶– $3,700

ORIGINAL NINE

No Poem_____
_____
_____
_____

Birthdate: N/A
Price Paid: $_____
Date Purchased: _____
Tag Generation: _____

22

Bruno™

Dog · #4183
Issued: December 31, 1997
Retired: September 18, 1998

Market Value:
[5]- $12

Birthdate: September 9, 1997
Price Paid: $__________
Date Purchased: __________
Tag Generation: __________

Bruno the dog thinks he's a brute
But all the other Beanies think he's cute
He growls at his tail and runs in a ring
And everyone says, "Oh, how darling!"

23

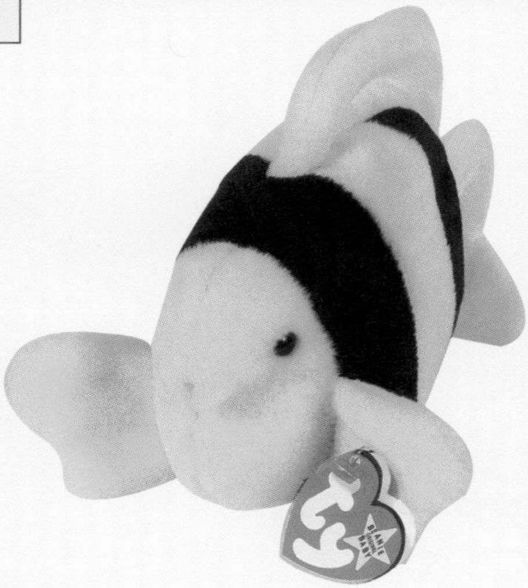

Bubbles™

Fish · #4078
Issued: June 3, 1995
Retired: May 11, 1997

Market Value:
[4]- $152
[3]- $215

Birthdate: July 2, 1995
Price Paid: $__________
Date Purchased: __________
Tag Generation: __________

All day long Bubbles likes to swim
She never gets tired of flapping her fins
Bubbles lived in a sea of blue
Now she is ready to come home with you!

Value Totals __________

24

Bucky™

Beaver · #4016
Issued: January 7, 1996
Retired: December 31, 1997

Market Value:
- ❹ – $35
- ❸ – $110

Bucky's teeth are as shiny as can be
Often used for cutting trees
He hides in his dam night and day
Maybe for you he will come out and play!

Birthdate: June 8, 1995
Price Paid: $_____
Date Purchased: _____
Tag Generation: _____

25

Bumble™

Bee · #4045
Issued: June 3, 1995
Retired: June 15, 1996

Market Value:
- ❹ – $620
- ❸ – $580

Bumble the bee will not sting you
It is only love that this bee will bring you
So don't be afraid to give this bee a hug
Because Bumble the bee is a love-bug.

Birthdate: October 16, 1995
Price Paid: $_____
Date Purchased: _____
Tag Generation: _____

Value
Totals _____

26

Butch™

Bull Terrier · #4227
Issued: January 1, 1999
Current - Moderate To Find

Market Value:
[5]-$_____

Birthdate: October 2, 1998
Price Paid: $__________
Date Purchased: __________
Tag Generation: __________

Going to the pet shop to buy dog food
I ran into Butch in a good mood
"Come to the pet shop down the street"
"Be a good dog, I'll buy you a treat!"

27

Canyon™

Cougar · #4212
Issued: September 30, 1998
Current - Easy To Find

Market Value:
[5]-$_____

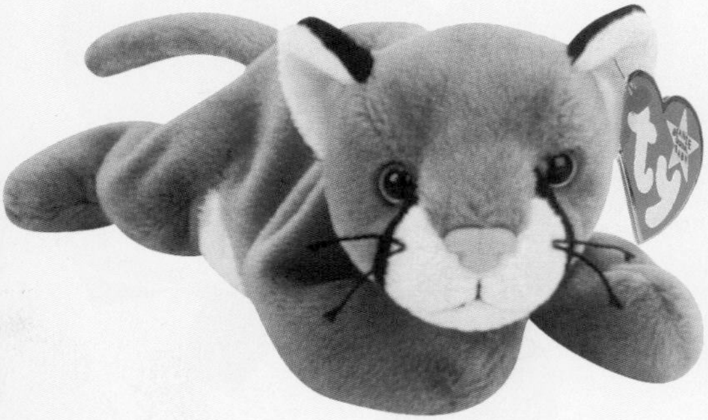

Birthdate: May 29, 1998
Price Paid: $__________
Date Purchased: __________
Tag Generation: __________

I climb rocks and really run fast
Try to catch me, it's a blast
Through the mountains, I used to roam
Now in your room, I'll call home!

Value Totals __________

28

Caw™

Crow • #4071
Issued: June 3, 1995
Retired: June 15, 1996

Market Value:
❸ – $675

No Poem_____

_____

_____

_____

Birthdate: N/A
Price Paid: $_____
Date Purchased: _____
Tag Generation: _____

29

NEW!

Cheeks™

Baboon • #4250
Issued: April 17, 1999
Current – Just Released

Market Value:
❺ – $_____

Don't confuse me with an ape
I have a most unusual shape
My cheeks are round and ty-dyed red
On my behind as well as my head!

Birthdate: May 10, 1999
Price Paid: $_____
Date Purchased: _____
Tag Generation: _____

Value
Totals _____

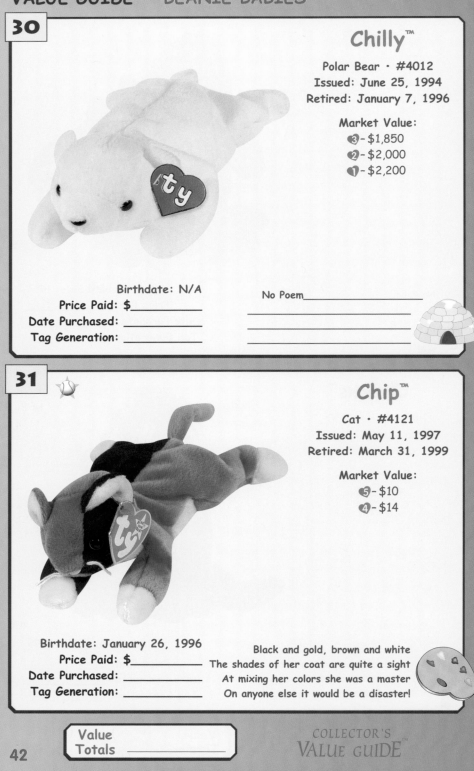

30

Chilly™

Polar Bear • #4012
Issued: June 25, 1994
Retired: January 7, 1996

Market Value:
3 – $1,850
2 – $2,000
1 – $2,200

Birthdate: N/A
Price Paid: $_____
Date Purchased: _____
Tag Generation: _____

No Poem _____
_____
_____
_____

31

Chip™

Cat • #4121
Issued: May 11, 1997
Retired: March 31, 1999

Market Value:
5 – $10
4 – $14

Birthdate: January 26, 1996
Price Paid: $_____
Date Purchased: _____
Tag Generation: _____

Black and gold, brown and white
The shades of her coat are quite a sight
At mixing her colors she was a master
On anyone else it would be a disaster!

Value Totals _____

COLLECTOR'S
VALUE GUIDE™

32

Chocolate™

9 ORIGINAL NINE

Moose · #4015
Issued: January 8, 1994
Retired: December 31, 1998

Market Value:
[5]-$12
[4]-$15
[3]-$132
[2]-$340
[1]-$525

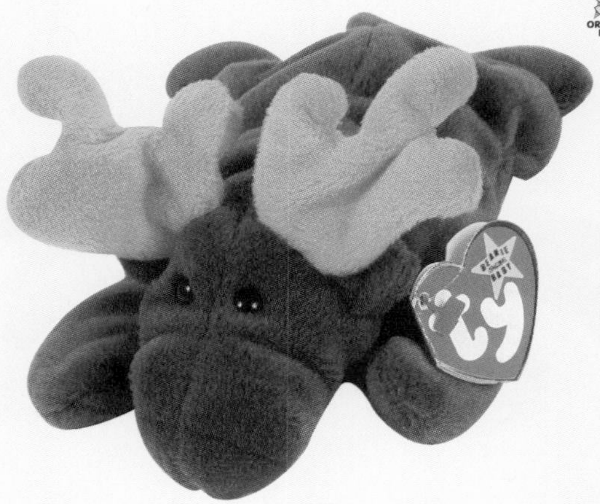

Licorice, gum and peppermint candy
This moose always has these handy
There is one more thing he likes to eat
Can you guess his favorite sweet?

Birthdate: April 27, 1993
Price Paid: $__________
Date Purchased: __________
Tag Generation: __________

33

Chops™

Lamb · #4019
Issued: January 7, 1996
Retired: January 1, 1997

Market Value:
[4]-$185
[3]-$250

Chops is a little lamb
This lamb you'll surely know
Because every path that you may take
This lamb is sure to go!

Birthdate: May 3, 1996
Price Paid: $__________
Date Purchased: __________
Tag Generation: __________

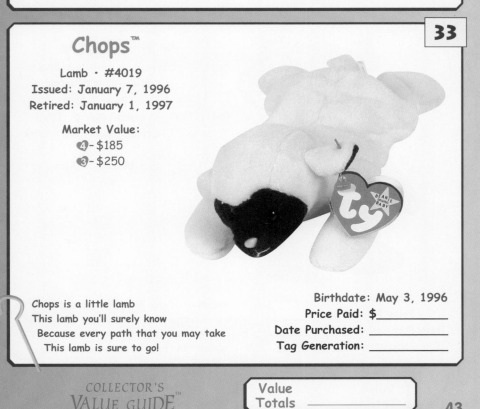

Value Totals __________

34

Claude™

Crab · #4083
Issued: May 11, 1997
Retired: December 31, 1998

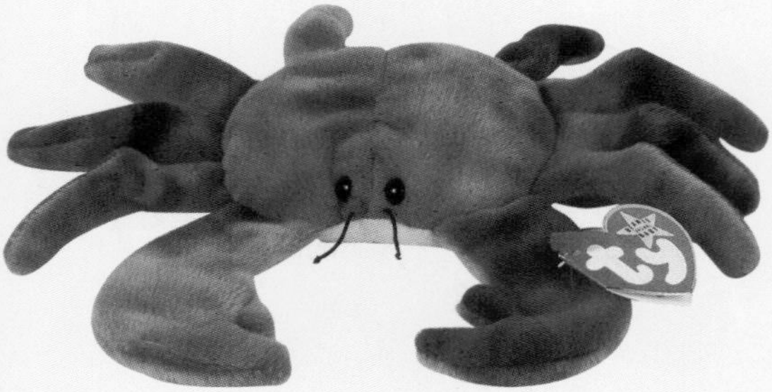

Market Value:
[5] - $14
[4] - $17

Birthdate: September 3, 1996
Price Paid: $__________
Date Purchased: __________
Tag Generation: __________

Claude the crab paints by the sea
A famous artist he hopes to be
But the tide came in and his paints fell
Now his art is on his shell!

35

Clubby™

(exclusive to Beanie Babies® Official Club™ members)
Bear · N/A
Issued: May 1, 1998
Retired: March 15, 1999

Market Value:
[5] - $55

Birthdate: July 7, 1998
Price Paid: $__________
Date Purchased: __________
Tag Generation: __________

Wearing his club pin for all to see
He's a proud member like you and me
Made especially with you in mind
Clubby the bear is one of a kind!

Value Totals __________

36

NEW!

Clubby II™

(exclusive to Beanie Babies® Official Club™ members)

Bear · N/A
Issued: March 31, 1999
Current – Just Released

Market Value:
[5]-$_____

A proud club member, named Clubby II
My color is special, a purplish hue
Take me along to your favorite place
Carry me in my platinum case!

Birthdate: March 9, 1999
Price Paid: $__________
Date Purchased: __________
Tag Generation: __________

37

Congo™

Gorilla · #4160
Issued: June 15, 1996
Retired: December 31, 1998

Market Value:
[5]-$12
[4]-$14

Black as the night and fierce is he
On the ground or in a tree
Strong and mighty as the Congo
He's related to our Bongo!

Birthdate: November 9, 1996
Price Paid: $__________
Date Purchased: __________
Tag Generation: __________

Value Totals __________

38

Coral™

Fish · #4079
Issued: June 3, 1995
Retired: January 1, 1997

Market Value:
4 – $185
3 – $250

Birthdate: March 2, 1995
Price Paid: $_____
Date Purchased: _____
Tag Generation: _____

Coral is beautiful, as you know
Made of colors in the rainbow
Whether it's pink, yellow or blue
These colors were chosen just for you!

39

Crunch™

Shark · #4130
Issued: January 1, 1997
Retired: September 24, 1998

Market Value:
5 – $12
4 – $14

Birthdate: January 13, 1996
Price Paid: $_____
Date Purchased: _____
Tag Generation: _____

What's for breakfast? What's for lunch?
Yum! Delicious! Munch, munch, munch!
He's eating everything by the bunch
That's the reason we named him Crunch!

Value
Totals _____

COLLECTOR'S
VALUE GUIDE™

40

Cubbie™

(name changed from "Brownie™")

Bear · #4010

Issued: January 8, 1994

Retired: December 31, 1997

Market Value:

[5]- $30

[4]- $30

[3]- $165

[2]- $350

[1]- $525

Cubbie used to eat crackers and honey
And what happened to him was funny
He was stung by fourteen bees
Now Cubbie eats broccoli and cheese!

Birthdate: November 14, 1993

Price Paid: $__________

Date Purchased: __________

Tag Generation: __________

41

Curly™

Bear · #4052

Issued: June 15, 1996

Retired: December 31, 1998

Market Value:

[5]- $25

[4]- $30

A bear so cute with hair that's Curly
You will love and want him surely
To this bear always be true
He will be a friend to you!

Birthdate: April 12, 1996

Price Paid: $__________

Date Purchased: __________

Tag Generation: __________

Value Totals __________

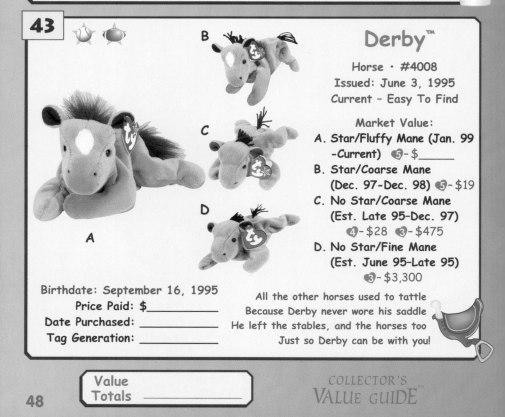

42

Daisy™

Cow · #4006
Issued: June 25, 1994
Retired: September 15, 1998

Market Value:
[5]-$13
[4]-$17
[3]-$130
[2]-$250
[1]-$355

Birthdate: May 10, 1994
Price Paid: $__________
Date Purchased: __________
Tag Generation: __________

Daisy drinks milk each night
So her coat is shiny and bright
Milk is good for your hair and skin
What a way for your day to begin!

43

Derby™

B

A

C

D

Horse · #4008
Issued: June 3, 1995
Current – Easy To Find

Market Value:
A. Star/Fluffy Mane (Jan. 99 -Current) [5]-$_____
B. Star/Coarse Mane (Dec. 97-Dec. 98) [5]-$19
C. No Star/Coarse Mane (Est. Late 95-Dec. 97) [4]-$28 [3]-$475
D. No Star/Fine Mane (Est. June 95-Late 95) [3]-$3,300

Birthdate: September 16, 1995
Price Paid: $__________
Date Purchased: __________
Tag Generation: __________

All the other horses used to tattle
Because Derby never wore his saddle
He left the stables, and the horses too
Just so Derby can be with you!

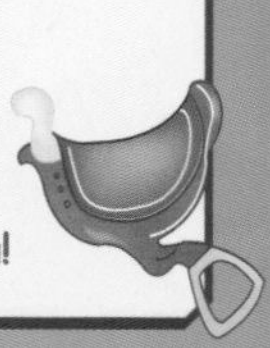

Value Totals __________

44

Digger™

B

Crab · #4027
Issued: June 25, 1994
Retired: May 11, 1997

Market Value:
A. Red (June 95-May 97)
④- $120
❸- $240
B. Orange (June 94-June 95)
❸- $700
❷- $780
❶- $900

A

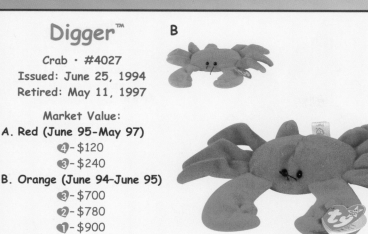

Digging in the sand and walking sideways
That's how Digger spends her days
Hard on the outside but sweet deep inside
Basking in the sun and riding the tide!

Birthdate: August 23, 1995
Price Paid: $_____
Date Purchased: _____
Tag Generation: _____

45

Doby™

Doberman · #4110
Issued: January 1, 1997
Retired: December 31, 1998

Market Value:
❺- $12
④- $14

This dog is little but he has might
Keep him close when you sleep at night
He lays around with nothing to do
Until he sees it's time to protect you!

Birthdate: October 9, 1996
Price Paid: $_____
Date Purchased: _____
Tag Generation: _____

46

Doodle™
(name changed to "Strut™")

Rooster · #4171
Issued: May 11, 1997
Retired: 1997

Market Value:
❹- $45

Birthdate: March 8, 1996
Price Paid: $_____
Date Purchased: _____
Tag Generation: _____

Listen closely to "cock-a-doodle-doo"
What's the rooster saying to you?
Hurry, wake up sleepy head
We have lots to do, get out of bed!

47

Dotty™

Dalmatian · #4100
Issued: May 11, 1997
Retired: December 31, 1998

Market Value:
❺- $13
❹- $15

Birthdate: October 17, 1996
Price Paid: $_____
Date Purchased: _____
Tag Generation: _____

The Beanies all thought it was a big joke
While writing her tag, their ink pen broke
She got in the way, and got all spotty
So now the Beanies call her Dotty!

Value
Totals _____

COLLECTOR'S
VALUE GUIDE™

48

Early™

Robin · #4190
Issued: May 30, 1998
Current – Easy To Find

Market Value:
5 – $_____

Early is a red breasted robin
For a worm he'll soon be bobbin'
Always known as a sign of spring
This happy robin loves to sing!

Birthdate: March 20, 1997
Price Paid: $_____
Date Purchased: _____
Tag Generation: _____

49

Ears™

Rabbit · #4018
Issued: January 7, 1996
Retired: May 1, 1998

Market Value:
5 – $15
4 – $18
3 – $100

He's been eating carrots so long
Didn't understand what was wrong
Couldn't see the board during classes
Until the doctor gave him glasses!

Birthdate: April 18, 1995
Price Paid: $_____
Date Purchased: _____
Tag Generation: _____

50

Echo™

Dolphin · #4180
Issued: May 11, 1997
Retired: May 1, 1998

Market Value:
[5] - $18
[4] - $22

Birthdate: December 21, 1996
Price Paid: $__________
Date Purchased: __________
Tag Generation: __________

Echo the dolphin lives in the sea
Playing with her friends, like you and me
Through the waves she echoes the sound
"I'm so glad to have you around!"

51

Eggbert™

Chick · #4232
Issued: January 1, 1999
Current – Moderate To Find

Market Value:
[5] - $_____

Birthdate: April 10, 1998
Price Paid: $__________
Date Purchased: __________
Tag Generation: __________

Cracking her shell taking a peek
Look, she's playing hide and seek
Ready or not, here I come
Take me home and have some fun!

Value Totals __________

52

Erin™

Bear · #4186
Issued: January 31, 1998
Current – Hard To Find

Market Value:

🌀- $_____

Named after the beautiful Emerald Isle
This Beanie Baby will make you smile,
A bit of luck, a pot of gold,
Light up the faces, both young and old!

Birthdate: March 17, 1997
Price Paid: $_____
Date Purchased: _____
Tag Generation: _____

53

NEW!

Eucalyptus™

Koala · #4240
Issued: April 8, 1999
Current – Just Released

Market Value:

🌀- $_____

Koalas climb with grace and ease
  To the top branches of the trees
  Sleeping by day under a gentle breeze
  Feeding at night on two pounds of leaves!

Birthdate: April 28, 1999
Price Paid: $_____
Date Purchased: _____
Tag Generation: _____

54

Ewey™

Lamb · #4219
Issued: January 1, 1999
Current – Moderate To Find

Market Value:
[5]- $_____

Birthdate: March 1, 1998
Price Paid: $__________
Date Purchased: __________
Tag Generation: __________

Needles and yarn, Ewey loves to knit
Making sweaters with perfect fit
Happy to make one for you and me
Showing off hers, for all to see!

55

Fetch™

Golden Retriever · #4189
Issued: May 30, 1998
Retired: December 31, 1998

Market Value:
[5]- $18

Birthdate: February 4, 1997
Price Paid: $__________
Date Purchased: __________
Tag Generation: __________

Fetch is alert at the crack of dawn
Walking through dew drops on the lawn
Always golden, loyal and true
This little puppy is the one for you!

Value Totals __________

56

Flash™

Dolphin · #4021
Issued: January 8, 1994
Retired: May 11, 1997

Market Value:
- ❹ – $120
- ❸ – $195
- ❷ – $340
- ❶ – $480

You know dolphins are a smart breed
Our friend Flash knows how to read
Splash the whale is the one who taught her
Although reading is difficult under the water!

Birthdate: May 13, 1993
Price Paid: $_____
Date Purchased: _____
Tag Generation: _____

57

Fleece™

Lamb · #4125
Issued: January 1, 1997
Retired: December 31, 1998

Market Value:
- ❺ – $12
- ❹ – $14

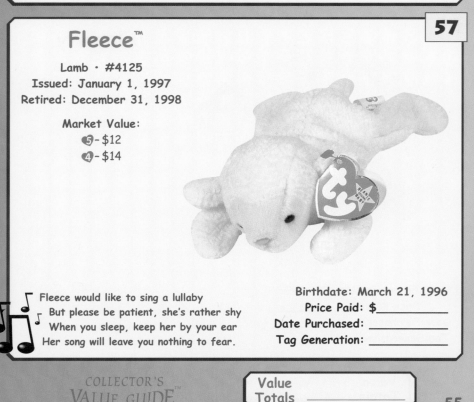

Fleece would like to sing a lullaby
But please be patient, she's rather shy
When you sleep, keep her by your ear
Her song will leave you nothing to fear.

Birthdate: March 21, 1996
Price Paid: $_____
Date Purchased: _____
Tag Generation: _____

58

Flip™

Cat · #4012
Issued: January 7, 1996
Retired: October 1, 1997

Market Value:
❹ - $36
❸ - $120

Birthdate: February 28, 1995
Price Paid: $_____
Date Purchased: _____
Tag Generation: _____

Flip the cat is an acrobat
She loves playing on her mat
This cat flips with such grace and flair
She can somersault in mid air!

59

Floppity™

Bunny · #4118
Issued: January 1, 1997
Retired: May 1, 1998

Market Value:
❺ - $18
❹ - $21

Birthdate: May 28, 1996
Price Paid: $_____
Date Purchased: _____
Tag Generation: _____

Floppity hops from here to there
Searching for eggs without a care
Lavender coat from head to toe
All dressed up and nowhere to go!

Value
Totals _____

COLLECTOR'S
VALUE GUIDE™

Flutter™

60

Butterfly · #4043
Issued: June 3, 1995
Retired: June 15, 1996

Market Value:
❸- $1,075

No Poem_____
_____
_____
_____

Birthdate: N/A
Price Paid: $_____
Date Purchased: _____
Tag Generation: _____

Fortune™

61

Panda · #4196
Issued: May 30, 1998
Current – Moderate To Find

Market Value:
❺- $_____

Nibbling on a bamboo tree
This little panda is hard to see
You're so lucky with this one you found
Only a few are still around!

Birthdate: December 6, 1997
Price Paid: $_____
Date Purchased: _____
Tag Generation: _____

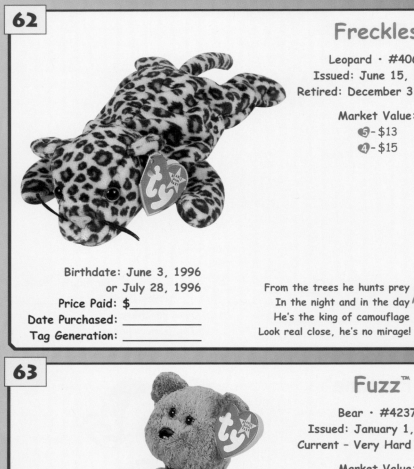

62

Freckles™

Leopard · #4066
Issued: June 15, 1996
Retired: December 31, 1998

Market Value:
[5] - $13
[4] - $15

Birthdate: June 3, 1996
or July 28, 1996
Price Paid: $__________
Date Purchased: __________
Tag Generation: __________

From the trees he hunts prey
In the night and in the day
He's the king of camouflage
Look real close, he's no mirage!

63

Fuzz™

Bear · #4237
Issued: January 1, 1999
Current - Very Hard To Find

Market Value:
[5] - $_____

Birthdate: July 23, 1998
Price Paid: $__________
Date Purchased: __________
Tag Generation: __________

Look closely at this handsome bear
His texture is really quite rare.
With golden highlights in his hair
He has class, style and flair!

Value Totals __________

64

Garcia™

Bear · #4051
Issued: January 7, 1996
Retired: May 11, 1997

Market Value:
[4] - $190
[3] - $260

The Beanies use to follow him around
Because Garcia traveled from town to town
He's pretty popular as you can see
Some even say he's legendary!

Birthdate: August 1, 1995
Price Paid: $__________
Date Purchased: __________
Tag Generation: __________

65

Germania™

(exclusive to Germany)

Bear · #4236
Issued: January 1, 1999
Current - Impossible To Find

Market Value
(in U.S. market):
[5] - $400

Poem Translation
Unity and Justice and Freedom
Is the song of German unity.
All good little girls and boys
Should love this little German bear.

Einigkeit und Recht und Freiheit
ist der Deutschen Einheistlied.
Allen Kindern brav und fein
soll dieser Bär das Liebste sein.

Geburtstag: Oktober 3, 1990
Price Paid: $__________
Date Purchased: __________
Tag Generation: __________

Value Totals __________

66

GiGi™

Poodle · #4191
Issued: May 30, 1998
Current – Easy To Find

Market Value:
[5]-$_____

Birthdate: April 7, 1997
Price Paid: $__________
Date Purchased: __________
Tag Generation: __________

Prancing and dancing all down the street
Thinking her hairdo is oh so neat
Always so careful in the wind and rain
She's a dog that is anything but plain!

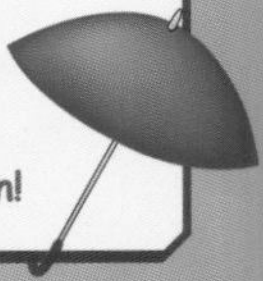

67

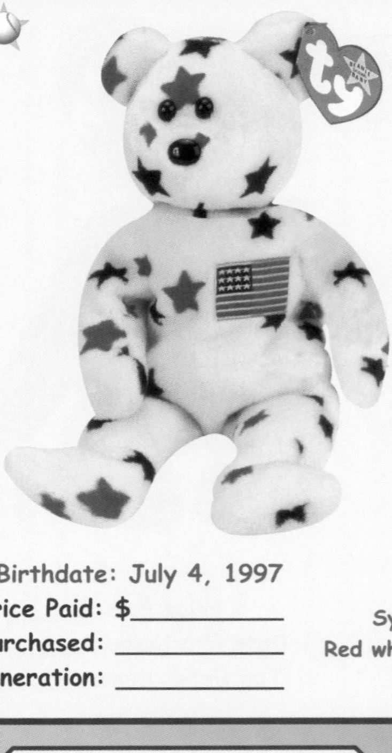

Glory™

Bear · #4188
Issued: May 30, 1998
Retired: December 31, 1998

Market Value:
[5]-$38

Birthdate: July 4, 1997
Price Paid: $__________
Date Purchased: __________
Tag Generation: __________

Wearing the flag for all to see
Symbol of freedom for you and me
Red white and blue – Independence Day
Happy Birthday USA!

Value Totals __________

68

Goatee™

Mountain Goat · #4235
Issued: January 1, 1999
Current – Moderate To Find

Market Value:
[5]- $_____

Though she's hungry, she's in a good mood
Searching through garbage, tin cans for food
For Goatee the goat, it's not a big deal
Anything at all makes a fine meal!

Birthdate: November 4, 1998
Price Paid: $__________
Date Purchased: __________
Tag Generation: __________

69

Gobbles™

Turkey · #4034
Issued: October 1, 1997
Retired: March 31, 1999

Market Value:
[5]- $12
[4]- $15

Gobbles the turkey loves to eat
Once a year she has a feast
I have a secret I'd like to divulge
If she eats too much her tummy will bulge!

Birthdate: November 27, 1996
Price Paid: $__________
Date Purchased: __________
Tag Generation: __________

Value Totals __________

70

Goldie™

Goldfish · #4023
Issued: June 25, 1994
Retired: December 31, 1997

Market Value:
[5]- $45
[4]- $45
[3]- $120
[2]- $240
[1]- $410

Birthdate: November 14, 1994
Price Paid: $__________
Date Purchased: __________
Tag Generation: __________

She's got rhythm, she's got soul
What more to like in a fish bowl?
Through sound waves Goldie swam
Because this goldfish likes to jam!

71

Goochy™

Jellyfish · #4230
Issued: January 1, 1999
Current – Moderate To Find

Market Value:
[5]- $_____

Birthdate: November 18, 1998
Price Paid: $__________
Date Purchased: __________
Tag Generation: __________

Swirl, swish, squirm and wiggle
Listen closely, hear him giggle
The most ticklish jellyfish you'll ever meet
Even though he has no feet!

Value Totals __________

72

Gracie™

Swan · #4126
Issued: January 1, 1997
Retired: May 1, 1998

Market Value:
[5] - $17
[4] - $19

As a duckling, she was confused,
Birds on the lake were quite amused.
Poking fun until she would cry,
Now the most beautiful swan at Ty!

Birthdate: June 17, 1996
Price Paid: $__________
Date Purchased: __________
Tag Generation: __________

73

Grunt™

Razorback · #4092
Issued: January 7, 1996
Retired: May 11, 1997

Market Value:
[4] - $155
[3] - $225

Some Beanies think Grunt is tough
No surprise, he's scary enough
But if you take him home you'll see
Grunt is the sweetest Beanie Baby!

Birthdate: July 19, 1995
Price Paid: $__________
Date Purchased: __________
Tag Generation: __________

Value Totals __________

74

Halo™

Angel Bear · #4208
Issued: September 30, 1998
Current - Moderate To Find

Market Value:
[5]- $_____

Birthdate: August 31, 1998
Price Paid: $__________
Date Purchased: __________
Tag Generation: __________

When you sleep, I'm always here
Don't be afraid, I am near
Watching over you with lots of love
Your guardian angel from above!

75

B

A

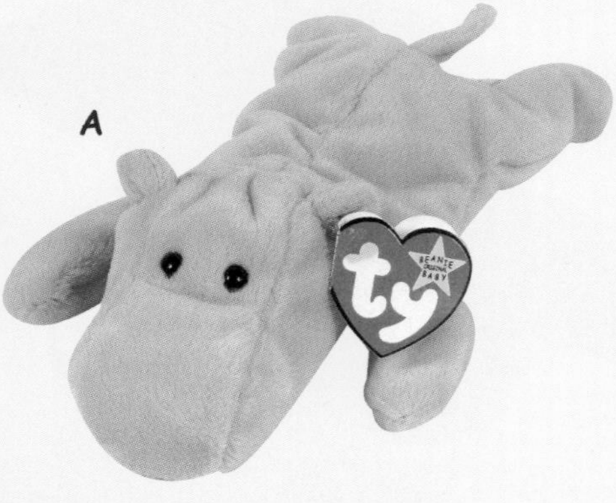

Happy™

Hippo · #4061
Issued: June 25, 1994
Retired: May 1, 1998

Market Value:
A. Lavender (June 95-May 98)
[5]- $25
[4]- $30
[3]- $225
B. Gray (June 94–June 95)
[3]- $630
[2]- $725
[1]- $825

Birthdate: February 25, 1994
Price Paid: $__________
Date Purchased: __________
Tag Generation: __________

Happy the Hippo loves to wade
In the river and in the shade
When Happy shoots water out of his snout
You know he's happy without a doubt!

Value Totals __________

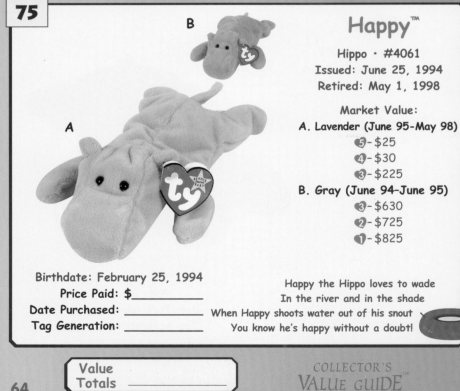

76

Hippie™

Bunny • #4218
Issued: January 1, 1999
Current - Moderate To Find

Market Value:
5 - $_____

Hippie fell into the dye, they say
While coloring eggs, one spring day
From the tips of his ears, down to his toes
Colors of springtime, he proudly shows!

Birthdate: May 4, 1998
Price Paid: $_____
Date Purchased: _____
Tag Generation: _____

77

Hippity™

Bunny • #4119
Issued: January 1, 1997
Retired: May 1, 1998

Market Value:
5 - $20
4 - $23

Hippity is a cute little bunny
Dressed in green, he looks quite funny
Twitching his nose in the air
Sniffing a flower here and there!

Birthdate: June 1, 1996
Price Paid: $_____
Date Purchased: _____
Tag Generation: _____

COLLECTOR'S
VALUE GUIDE™

Value
Totals _____

78

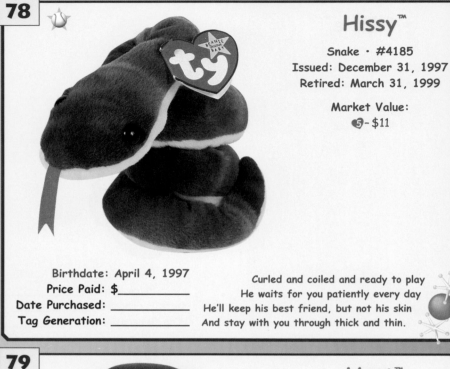

Hissy™

Snake · #4185
Issued: December 31, 1997
Retired: March 31, 1999

Market Value:
5 – $11

Birthdate: April 4, 1997
Price Paid: $_____
Date Purchased: _____
Tag Generation: _____

Curled and coiled and ready to play
He waits for you patiently every day
He'll keep his best friend, but not his skin
And stay with you through thick and thin.

79

Hoot™

Owl · #4073
Issued: January 7, 1996
Retired: October 1, 1997

Market Value:
4 – $43
3 – $110

Birthdate: August 9, 1995
Price Paid: $_____
Date Purchased: _____
Tag Generation: _____

Late to bed, late to rise
Nevertheless, Hoot's quite wise
Studies by candlelight, nothing new
Like a president, do you know Whooo?

Value
Totals _____

COLLECTOR'S
VALUE GUIDE™

80

Hope™

Bear · #4213
Issued: January 1, 1999
Current - Moderate To Find

Market Value:
[5]- $_____

Every night when it's time for bed
Fold your hands and bow your head
An angelic face, a heart that's true
You have a friend to pray with you!

Birthdate: March 23, 1998
Price Paid: $__________
Date Purchased: __________
Tag Generation: __________

81

Hoppity™

Bunny · #4117
Issued: January 1, 1997
Retired: May 1, 1998

Market Value:
[5]- $18
[4]- $21

Hopscotch is what she likes to play
If you don't join in, she'll hop away
So play a game if you have the time,
She likes to play, rain or shine!

Birthdate: April 3, 1996
Price Paid: $__________
Date Purchased: __________
Tag Generation: __________

Value Totals __________

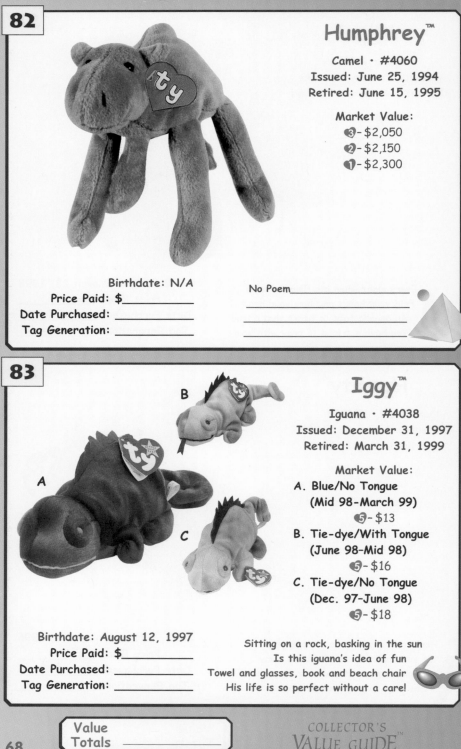

82

Humphrey™

Camel · #4060
Issued: June 25, 1994
Retired: June 15, 1995

Market Value:
❸- $2,050
❷- $2,150
❶- $2,300

Birthdate: N/A
Price Paid: $_____
Date Purchased: _____
Tag Generation: _____

No Poem_____
_____
_____
_____

83

B

Iggy™

Iguana · #4038
Issued: December 31, 1997
Retired: March 31, 1999

Market Value:
A. Blue/No Tongue
   (Mid 98–March 99)
   ❺- $13
B. Tie-dye/With Tongue
   (June 98–Mid 98)
   ❺- $16
C. Tie-dye/No Tongue
   (Dec. 97–June 98)
   ❺- $18

A

C

Birthdate: August 12, 1997
Price Paid: $_____
Date Purchased: _____
Tag Generation: _____

Sitting on a rock, basking in the sun
Is this iguana's idea of fun
Towel and glasses, book and beach chair
His life is so perfect without a care!

Value
Totals _____

COLLECTOR'S
VALUE GUIDE™

84

Inch™

Inchworm · #4044
Issued: June 3, 1995
Retired: May 1, 1998

Market Value:

A. Yarn Antennas (Oct. 97-May 98)
[5]-$24
[4]-$27

B. Felt Antennas (June 95–Oct. 97)
[4]-$150
[3]-$190

B

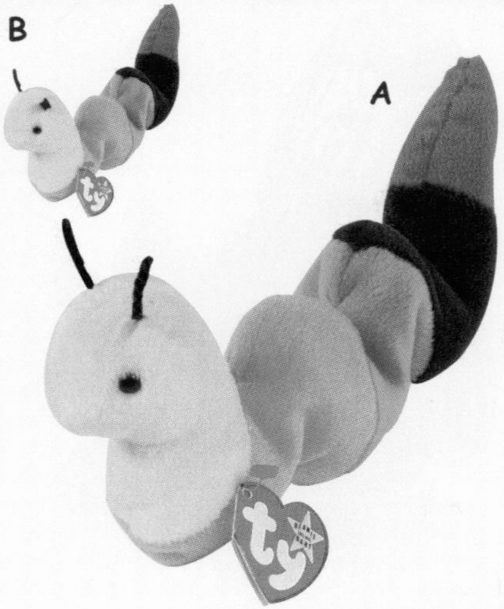

A

Inch the worm is a friend of mine
He goes so slow all the time
Inching around from here to there
Traveling the world without a care!

Birthdate: September 3, 1995
Price Paid: $________
Date Purchased: ________
Tag Generation: ________

85

Inky™

Octopus · #4028
Issued: June 25, 1994
Retired: May 1, 1998

Market Value:

A. Pink (June 95-May 98)
[5]-$32 [4]-$35 [3]-$215

B. Tan With Mouth (Sept. 94–June 95)
[3]-$610 [2]-$680

C. Tan Without Mouth (June 94–Sept. 94)
[2]-$775 [1]-$850

B

C

A

Inky's head is big and round
As he swims he makes no sound
If you need a hand, don't hesitate
Inky can help because he has eight!

Birthdate: November 29, 1994
Price Paid: $________
Date Purchased: ________
Tag Generation: ________

86

Jabber™

Parrot • #4197
Issued: May 30, 1998
Current – Easy To Find

Market Value:
5 – $_____

Birthdate: October 10, 1997
Price Paid: $_____
Date Purchased: _____
Tag Generation: _____

Teaching Jabber to move his beak
A large vocabulary he now can speak
Jabber will repeat what you say
Teach him a new word everyday!

87

Jake™

Mallard Duck • #4199
Issued: May 30, 1998
Current – Easy To Find

Market Value:
5 – $_____

Birthdate: April 16, 1997
Price Paid: $_____
Date Purchased: _____
Tag Generation: _____

Jake the drake likes to splash in a puddle
Take him home and give him a cuddle
Quack, Quack, Quack, he will say
He's so glad you're here to play!

Value
Totals _____

COLLECTOR'S
VALUE GUIDE™

88

Jolly™

Walrus • #4082
Issued: May 11, 1997
Retired: May 1, 1998

Market Value:
[5]- $16
[4]- $18

Jolly the walrus is not very serious
He laughs and laughs until he's delirious
He often reminds me of my dad
Always happy, never sad!

Birthdate: December 2, 1996
Price Paid: $________
Date Purchased: ________
Tag Generation: ________

89

Kicks™

Bear • #4229
Issued: January 1, 1999
Current - Moderate To Find

Market Value:
[5]- $_____

The world cup is his dream
Kicks the bear is the best on his team
He hopes that one day he'll be the pick
First he needs to improve his kick!

Birthdate: August 16, 1998
Price Paid: $________
Date Purchased: ________
Tag Generation: ________

Value Totals ________

90

Kiwi™

Toucan · #4070
Issued: June 3, 1995
Retired: January 1, 1997

Market Value:
[4] - $170
[3] - $240

Birthdate: September 16, 1995
Price Paid: $__________
Date Purchased: __________
Tag Generation: __________

Kiwi waits for the April showers
Watching a garden bloom with flowers
There trees grow with fruit that's sweet
I'm sure you'll guess his favorite treat!

91

NEW!

Knuckles™

Pig · #4247
Issued: April 14, 1999
Current – Just Released

Market Value:
[5] - $_____

Birthdate: March 25, 1999
Price Paid: $__________
Date Purchased: __________
Tag Generation: __________

In the kitchen working hard
Using ingredients from the yard
No one will eat it, can you guess why?
Her favorite recipe is for mud pie!

Value Totals __________

KuKu™

92

Cockatoo · #4192
Issued: May 30, 1998
Current – Easy To Find

Market Value:
☺- $_____

This fancy bird loves to converse
He talks in poems, rhythms and verse
So take him home and give him some time
You'll be surprised how he can rhyme!

Birthdate: January 5, 1997
Price Paid: $_____
Date Purchased: _____
Tag Generation: _____

Lefty™

93

Donkey · #4085
Issued: June 15, 1996
Retired: January 1, 1997

Market Value:
④- $250

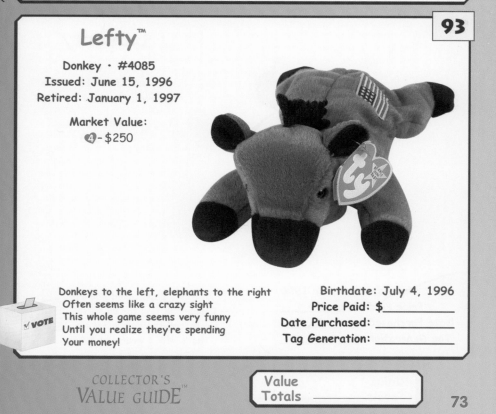

Donkeys to the left, elephants to the right
Often seems like a crazy sight
This whole game seems very funny
Until you realize they're spending
Your money!

Birthdate: July 4, 1996
Price Paid: $_____
Date Purchased: _____
Tag Generation: _____

94

ORIGINAL NINE 9

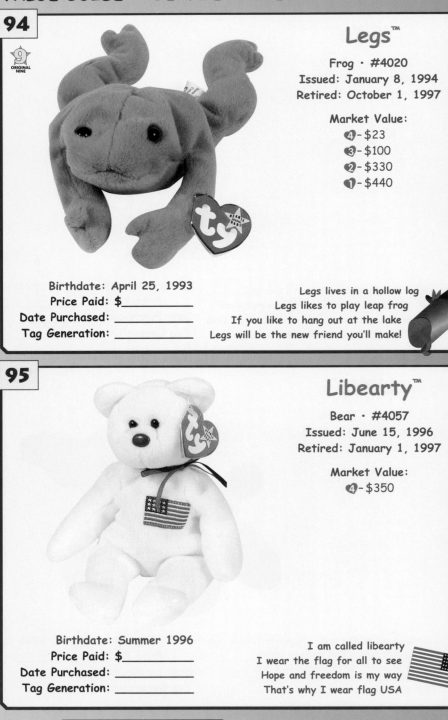

Legs™

Frog · #4020
Issued: January 8, 1994
Retired: October 1, 1997

Market Value:
4 – $23
3 – $100
2 – $330
1 – $440

Birthdate: April 25, 1993
Price Paid: $_____
Date Purchased: _____
Tag Generation: _____

Legs lives in a hollow log
Legs likes to play leap frog
If you like to hang out at the lake
Legs will be the new friend you'll make!

95

Libearty™

Bear · #4057
Issued: June 15, 1996
Retired: January 1, 1997

Market Value:
4 – $350

Birthdate: Summer 1996
Price Paid: $_____
Date Purchased: _____
Tag Generation: _____

I am called libearty
I wear the flag for all to see
Hope and freedom is my way
That's why I wear flag USA

Value
Totals _____

COLLECTOR'S
VALUE GUIDE™

96

Lizzy™

B

A

Lizard · #4033
Issued: June 3, 1995
Retired: December 31, 1997

Market Value:
A. Blue (Jan. 96-Dec. 97)
[5]- $28
[4]- $28
[3]- $275
B. Tie-dye (June 95–Jan. 96)
[3]- $975

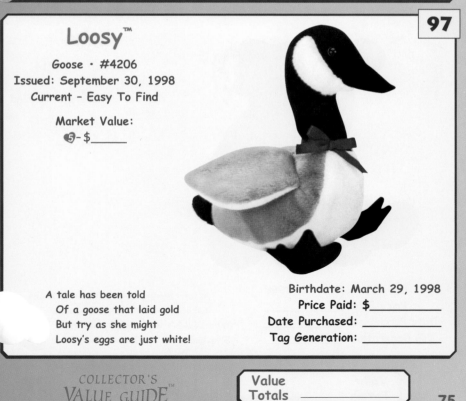

Lizzy loves Legs the frog
She hides with him under logs
Both of them search for flies
Underneath the clear blue skies!

Birthdate: May 11, 1995
Price Paid: $__________
Date Purchased: __________
Tag Generation: __________

97

Loosy™

Goose · #4206
Issued: September 30, 1998
Current - Easy To Find

Market Value:
[5]- $_____

A tale has been told
Of a goose that laid gold
But try as she might
Loosy's eggs are just white!

Birthdate: March 29, 1998
Price Paid: $__________
Date Purchased: __________
Tag Generation: __________

Value Totals __________

98

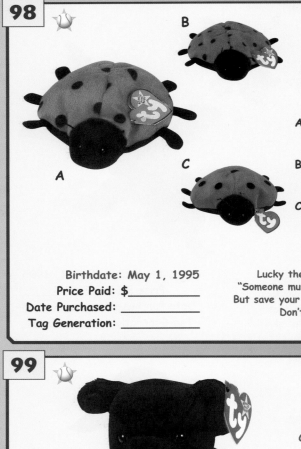

Lucky™

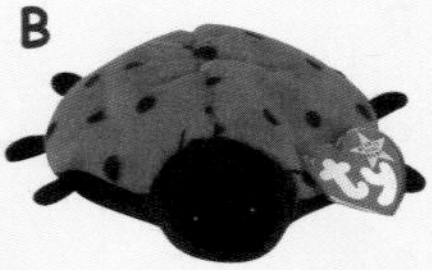

B

A

C

Ladybug · #4040
Issued: June 25, 1994
Retired: May 1, 1998

Market Value:

A. **Approx. 11 Printed Spots (Feb. 96–May 98)**
[5]-$23 [4]-$25

B. **Approx. 21 Printed Spots (Est. Mid 96–Late 96)**
[4]-$440

C. **Approx. 7 Felt Glued-On Spots (June 94–Feb. 96)**
[3]-$205 [2]-$370
[1]-$550

Birthdate: May 1, 1995
Price Paid: $__________
Date Purchased: __________
Tag Generation: __________

Lucky the lady bug loves the lotto
"Someone must win" that's her motto
But save your dimes and even a penny
Don't spend on the lotto and
You'll have many!

99

Luke™

Black Lab · #4214
Issued: January 1, 1999
Current - Moderate To Find

Market Value:
[5]-$_____

Birthdate: June 15, 1998
Price Paid: $__________
Date Purchased: __________
Tag Generation: __________

After chewing on your favorite shoes
Luke gets tired, takes a snooze
Who wouldn't love a puppy like this?
Give him a hug, he'll give you a kiss!

Value Totals __________

100

Mac™

Cardinal · #4225
Issued: January 1, 1999
Current – Moderate To Find

Market Value:
[5]-$_____

Mac tries hard to prove he's the best
Swinging his bat harder than the rest
Breaking records, enjoying the game
Hitting home runs is his claim to fame!

Birthdate: June 10, 1998
Price Paid: $__________
Date Purchased: __________
Tag Generation: __________

101

Magic™

Dragon · #4088
Issued: June 3, 1995
Retired: December 31, 1997

Market Value:
A. Pale Pink Thread
(June 95-Dec. 97)
[4]-$46
[3]-$135
B. Hot Pink Thread
(Est. Mid 96–Early 97)
[4]-$63

B

A

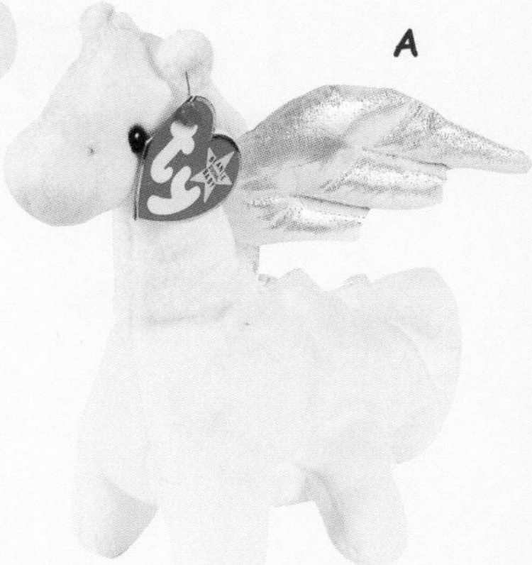

Magic the dragon lives in a dream
The most beautiful that you have ever seen
Through magic lands she likes to fly
Look up and watch her, way up high!

Birthdate: September 5, 1995
Price Paid: $__________
Date Purchased: __________
Tag Generation: __________

Value
Totals __________

102

Manny™

Manatee · #4081
Issued: January 7, 1996
Retired: May 11, 1997

Market Value:
❹ – $160
❸ – $220

Birthdate: June 8, 1995
Price Paid: $_____
Date Purchased: _____
Tag Generation: _____

Manny is sometimes called a sea cow
She likes to twirl and likes to bow
Manny sure is glad you bought her
Because it's so lonely under water!

103

B

The Beanie Babies Collection™
ty®
Pride
HANDMADE IN CHINA
© 1996 TY INC.
OAKBROOK IL U.S.A.
SURFACE WASHABLE
ALL NEW MATERIAL
POLYESTER FIBER
& PVC PELLETS CE
REG. NO. PA. 1965(KR)

A

Maple™
(exclusive to Canada)

Bear · #4600
Issued: January 1, 1997
Current – Impossible To Find

Market Value
(in U.S. market):
A. "Maple™" Tush Tag
(Est. Early 97-Current)
❺ – $200
❹ – $230
B. "Pride™" Tush Tag
(Est. Early 97)
❹ – $625

Birthdate: July 1, 1996
Price Paid: $_____
Date Purchased: _____
Tag Generation: _____

Maple the bear likes to ski
With his friends, he plays hockey.
He loves his pancakes and eats every crumb
Can you guess which country he's from?

Value
Totals _____

COLLECTOR'S
VALUE GUIDE™

104

Mel™

Koala · #4162
Issued: January 1, 1997
Retired: March 31, 1999

Market Value:
[5] - $11
[4] - $13

How do you name a Koala bear?
It's rather tough, I do declare!
It confuses me, I get into a funk
I'll name him Mel, after my favorite hunk!

Birthdate: January 15, 1996
Price Paid: $__________
Date Purchased: __________
Tag Generation: __________

105

Millennium™

Bear · #4226
Issued: January 1, 1999
Current – Hard To Find

Market Value:

A. "Millennium™" On Both Tags (Early 99–Current)
[5] - $______

B. "Millenium™" Swing Tag & "Millennium™" Tush Tag (Early 99)
[5] - $28

C. "Millenium™" On Both Tags (Jan. 99–Early 99)
[5] - $28

B

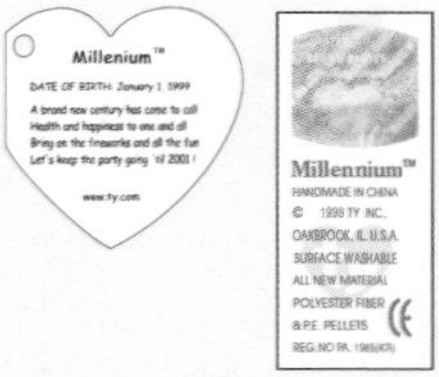
Millenium™
DATE OF BIRTH: January 1, 1999
A brand new century has come to call
Health and happiness to one and all
Bring on the fireworks and all the fun
Let's keep the party going 'til 2001!
www.ty.com
Millennium™
HANDMADE IN CHINA
© 1998 TY INC.,
OAKBROOK, IL. U.S.A.
SURFACE WASHABLE
ALL NEW MATERIAL
POLYESTER FIBER
& P.E. PELLETS
REG. NO PA. 1965(KR)

C

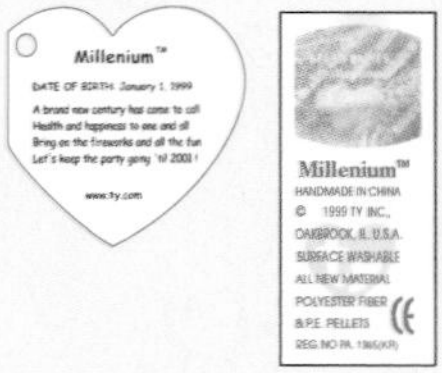
Millenium™
DATE OF BIRTH: January 1, 1999
A brand new century has come to call
Health and happiness to one and all
Bring on the fireworks and all the fun
Let's keep the party going 'til 2001!
www.ty.com
Millenium™
HANDMADE IN CHINA
© 1999 TY INC.,
OAKBROOK, IL. U.S.A.
SURFACE WASHABLE
ALL NEW MATERIAL
POLYESTER FIBER
& P.E. PELLETS
REG. NO PA. 1965(KR)

A

A brand new century has come to call
Health and happiness to one and all
Bring on the fireworks and all the fun
Let's keep the party going 'til 2001!

Birthdate: January 1, 1999
Price Paid: $__________
Date Purchased: __________
Tag Generation: __________

Value Totals __________

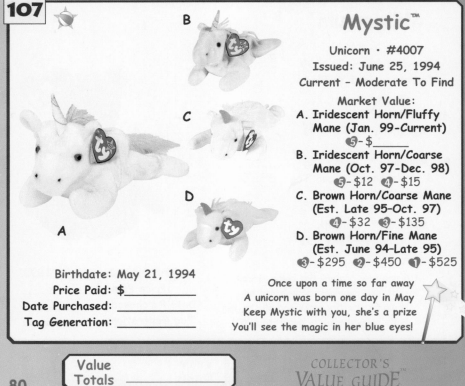

106

Mooch™

Spider Monkey · #4224
Issued: January 1, 1999
Current – Moderate To Find

Market Value:
[5]-$_____

Birthdate: August 1, 1998
Price Paid: $__________
Date Purchased: __________
Tag Generation: __________

Look in the treetops, up towards the sky
Swinging from branches way up high
Tempt him with a banana or fruit
When he's hungry, he acts so cute!

107

B

A

C

D

Mystic™

Unicorn · #4007
Issued: June 25, 1994
Current – Moderate To Find

Market Value:

A. Iridescent Horn/Fluffy Mane (Jan. 99-Current)
[5]-$_____

B. Iridescent Horn/Coarse Mane (Oct. 97-Dec. 98)
[5]-$12 [4]-$15

C. Brown Horn/Coarse Mane (Est. Late 95–Oct. 97)
[4]-$32 [3]-$135

D. Brown Horn/Fine Mane (Est. June 94–Late 95)
[3]-$295 [2]-$450 [1]-$525

Birthdate: May 21, 1994
Price Paid: $__________
Date Purchased: __________
Tag Generation: __________

Once upon a time so far away
A unicorn was born one day in May
Keep Mystic with you, she's a prize
You'll see the magic in her blue eyes!

Value Totals __________

108

Nana™
(name changed to "Bongo™")

Monkey · #4067
Issued: June 3, 1995
Retired: 1995

Market Value:
❸– $4,000

No Poem_____
_____
_____

Birthdate: N/A
Price Paid: $_____
Date Purchased: _____
Tag Generation: _____

109

Nanook™

Husky · #4104
Issued: May 11, 1997
Retired: March 31, 1999

Market Value:
❺– $12
❹– $14

Nanook is a dog that loves cold weather
To him a sled is light as a feather
Over the snow and through the slush
He runs at hearing the cry of "mush"!

Birthdate: November 21, 1996
Price Paid: $_____
Date Purchased: _____
Tag Generation: _____

COLLECTOR'S
VALUE GUIDE™

Value
Totals _____

110

NEW!

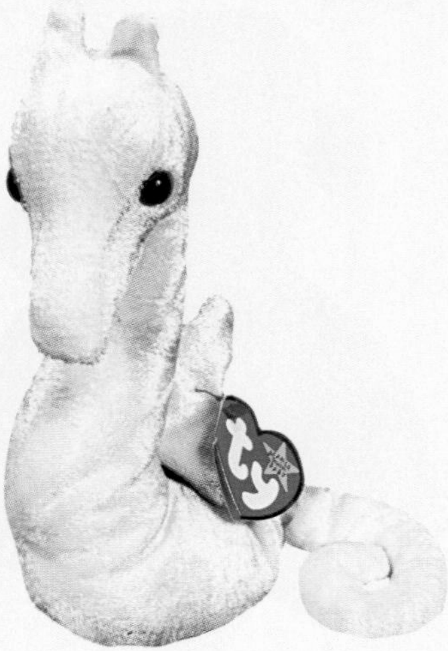

Neon™

Seahorse · #4239
Issued: April 8, 1999
Current – Just Released

Market Value:
[5]-$_____

Birthdate: April 1, 1999
Price Paid: $__________
Date Purchased: __________
Tag Generation: __________

Born in shallow water in a sea grass bay
Their eyes can swivel and look every way
Walk down the beach on a bright sunny day
Jump into the sea and watch them play!

111

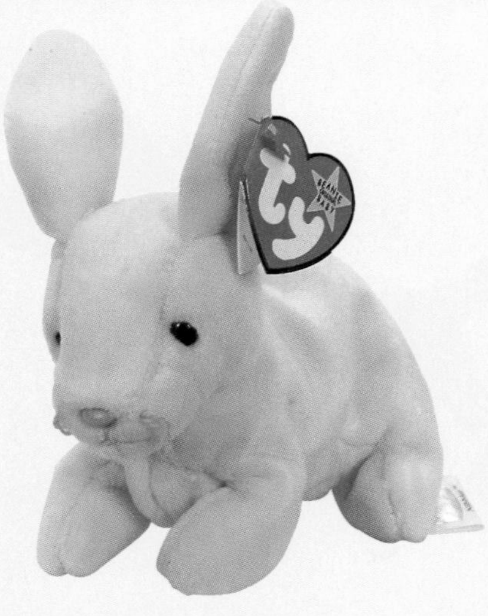

Nibbler™

Rabbit · #4216
Issued: January 1, 1999
Current – Moderate To Find

Market Value:
[5]-$_____

Birthdate: April 6, 1998
Price Paid: $__________
Date Purchased: __________
Tag Generation: __________

Twitching her nose, she looks so sweet
Small in size, she's very petite
Soft and furry, hopping with grace
She'll visit your garden, her favorite place!

Value Totals __________

112

Nibbly™

Rabbit · #4217
Issued: January 1, 1999
Current – Moderate To Find

Market Value:
[5]-$_____

Wonderful ways to spend a day
Bright and sunny in the month of May
Hopping around as trees sway
Looking for friends, out to play!

Birthdate: May 7, 1998
Price Paid: $__________
Date Purchased: __________
Tag Generation: __________

113

Nip™

Cat · #4003
Issued: January 7, 1995
Retired: December 31, 1997

Market Value:
A. White Paws
(March 96–Dec. 97)
[5]-$25 [4]-$25 [3]-$280
B. All Gold
(Jan. 96–March 96)
[3]-$870
C. White Face
(Jan. 95–Jan. 96)
[3]-$500 [2]-$525

B

C

A

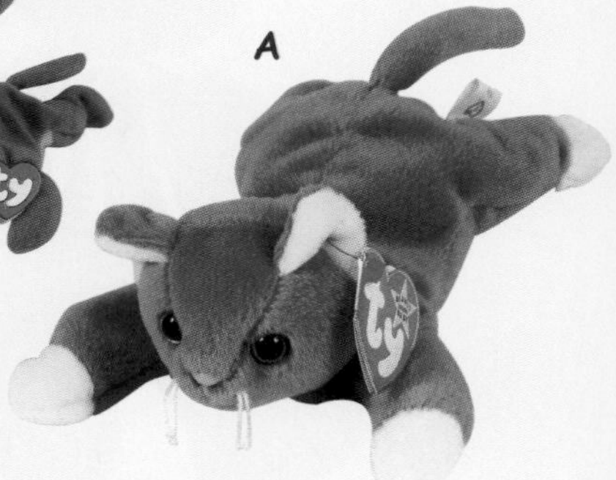

His name is Nipper, but we call him Nip
His best friend is a black cat named Zip
Nip likes to run in races for fun
He runs so fast he's always number one!

Birthdate: March 6, 1994
Price Paid: $__________
Date Purchased: __________
Tag Generation: __________

Value Totals __________

114

Nuts™

Squirrel · #4114
Issued: January 1, 1997
Retired: December 31, 1998

Market Value:
[5]- $12
[4]- $14

Birthdate: January 21, 1996
Price Paid: $__________
Date Purchased: __________
Tag Generation: __________

With his bushy tail, he'll scamper up a tree
The most cheerful critter you'll ever see,
He's nuts about nuts, and he loves to chat
Have you ever seen a squirrel like that?

115

NEW!

Osito™

Bear · #4244
Issued: April 17, 1999
Current - Just Released

Market Value:
[5]- $_____

Birthdate: February 5, 1999
Price Paid: $__________
Date Purchased: __________
Tag Generation: __________

Across the waters of the Rio Grande
Lies a beautiful and mystic land
A place we all should plan to go
Known by all as Mexico!

Value Totals __________

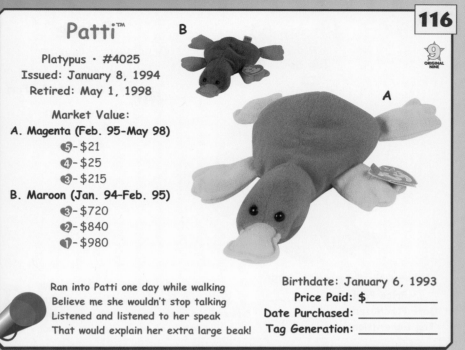

116

Patti™

Platypus · #4025
Issued: January 8, 1994
Retired: May 1, 1998

B

A
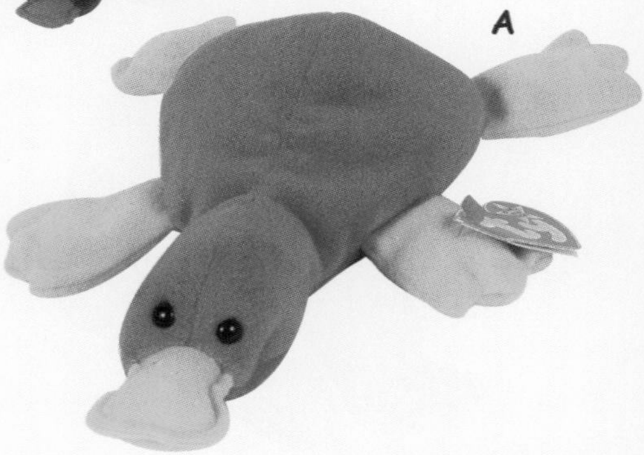

Market Value:

A. Magenta (Feb. 95-May 98)

[5]-$21
[4]-$25
[3]-$215

B. Maroon (Jan. 94-Feb. 95)

[3]-$720
[2]-$840
[1]-$980

Ran into Patti one day while walking
Believe me she wouldn't stop talking
Listened and listened to her speak
That would explain her extra large beak!

Birthdate: January 6, 1993
Price Paid: $__________
Date Purchased: __________
Tag Generation: __________

117

Paul™

NEW!

Walrus · #4248
Issued: April 12, 1999
Current – Just Released

Market Value:

[5]-$_____

Traveling the ocean in a submarine
Singing and playing a tambourine
One day hoping to lead a band
First he needs to find dry land!

Birthdate: February 23, 1999
Price Paid: $__________
Date Purchased: __________
Tag Generation: __________

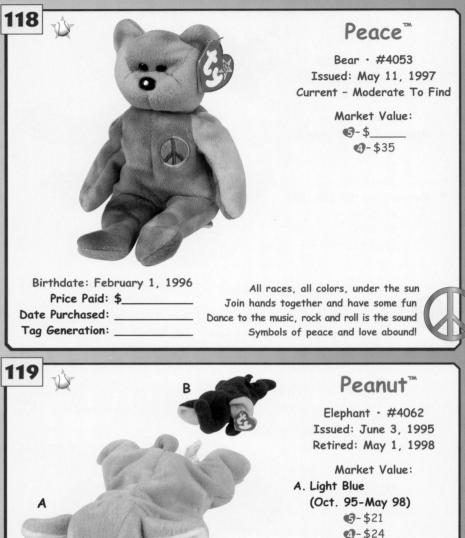

118

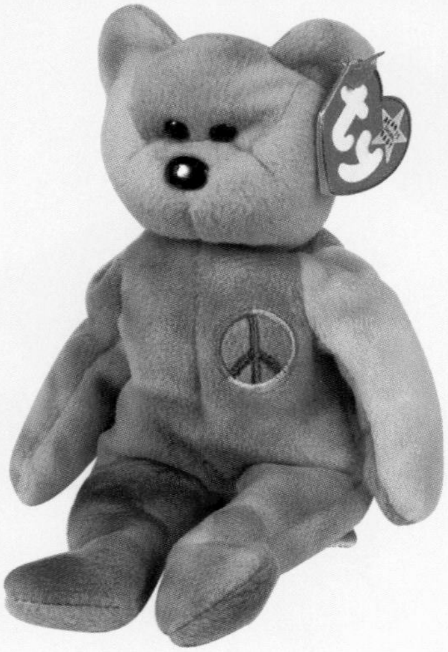

Peace™

Bear · #4053
Issued: May 11, 1997
Current – Moderate To Find

Market Value:
[5]-$_____
[4]-$35

Birthdate: February 1, 1996
Price Paid: $__________
Date Purchased: __________
Tag Generation: __________

All races, all colors, under the sun
Join hands together and have some fun
Dance to the music, rock and roll is the sound
Symbols of peace and love abound!

119

B

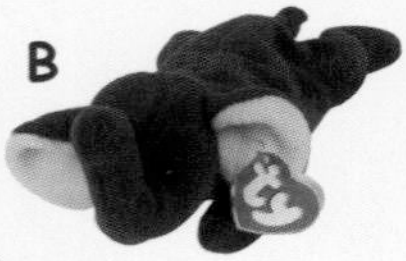

A

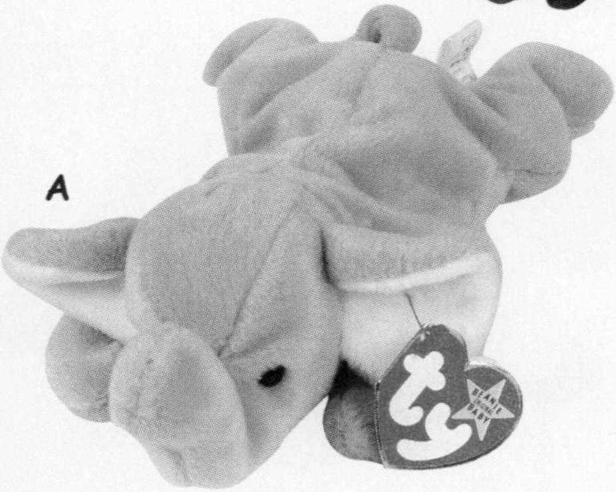

Peanut™

Elephant · #4062
Issued: June 3, 1995
Retired: May 1, 1998

Market Value:

A. Light Blue
(Oct. 95–May 98)
[5]-$21
[4]-$24
[3]-$875

B. Dark Blue
(June 95–Oct. 95)
[3]-$4,700

Birthdate: January 25, 1995
Price Paid: $__________
Date Purchased: __________
Tag Generation: __________

Peanut the elephant walks on tip-toes
Quietly sneaking wherever she goes
She'll sneak up on you and a hug
You will get
Peanut is a friend you won't soon forget!

Value Totals __________

120

NEW!

Pecan™

Bear • #4251
Issued: April 8, 1999
Current - Just Released

Market Value:
[5]- $_____

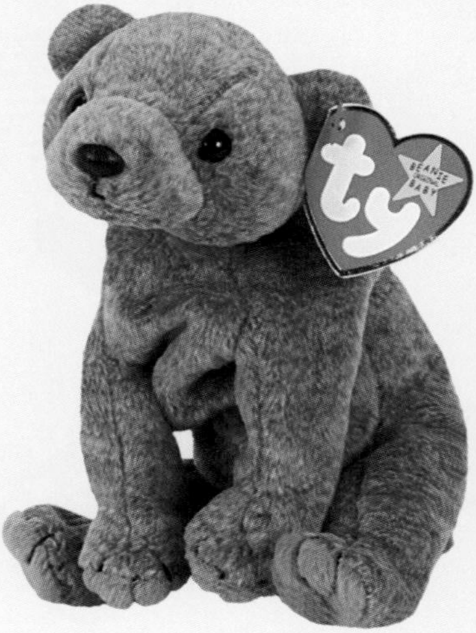

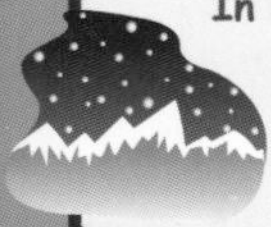

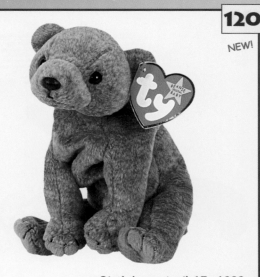

In late fall, as wind gusts blow
Pecan hibernates before winter snow
In early spring, sweet scent of a flower
Wakes her up to take a shower!

Birthdate: April 15, 1999
Price Paid: $__________
Date Purchased: __________
Tag Generation: __________

121

Peking™

Panda • #4013
Issued: June 25, 1994
Retired: January 7, 1996

Market Value:
[3]- $1,900
[2]- $2,100
[1]- $2,200

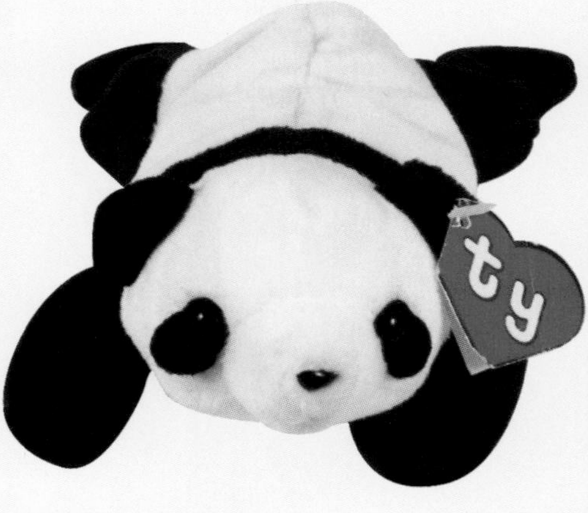

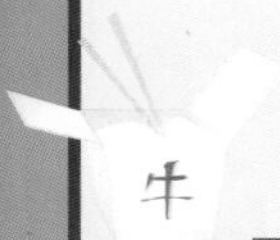

No Poem__________

Birthdate: N/A
Price Paid: $__________
Date Purchased: __________
Tag Generation: __________

Value Totals __________

122

ORIGINAL NINE

B

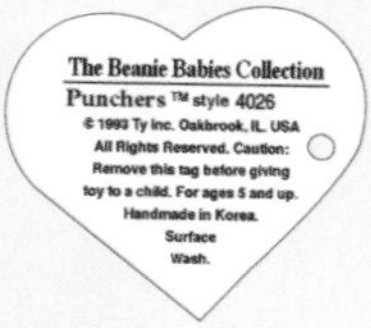
The Beanie Babies Collection
Punchers ™ style 4026
© 1993 Ty Inc. Oakbrook, IL. USA
All Rights Reserved. Caution:
Remove this tag before giving
toy to a child. For ages 5 and up.
Handmade in Korea.
Surface
Wash.

A

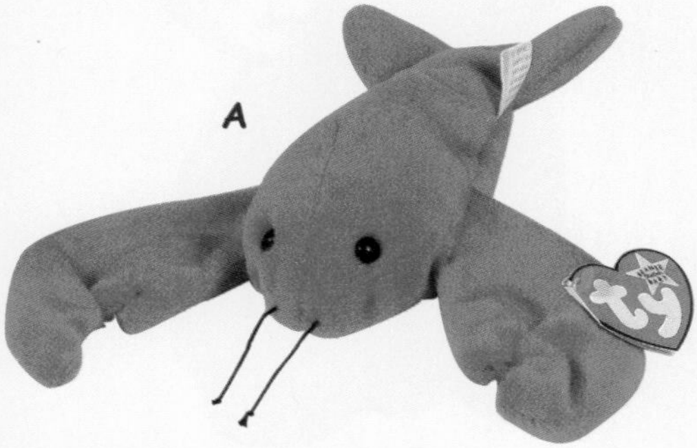

Pinchers™

Lobster · #4026
Issued: January 8, 1994
Retired: May 1, 1998

Market Value:
A. "Pinchers™" Swing Tag
(Jan. 94-May 98)
[5]-$22
[4]-$25
[3]-$120
[2]-$365
[1]-$700
B. "Punchers™" Swing Tag
(Est. Early 94)
[1]-$3,200

Birthdate: June 19, 1993
Price Paid: $__________
Date Purchased: __________
Tag Generation: __________

This lobster loves to pinch
Eating his food inch by inch
Balancing carefully with his tail
Moving forward slow as a snail!

123

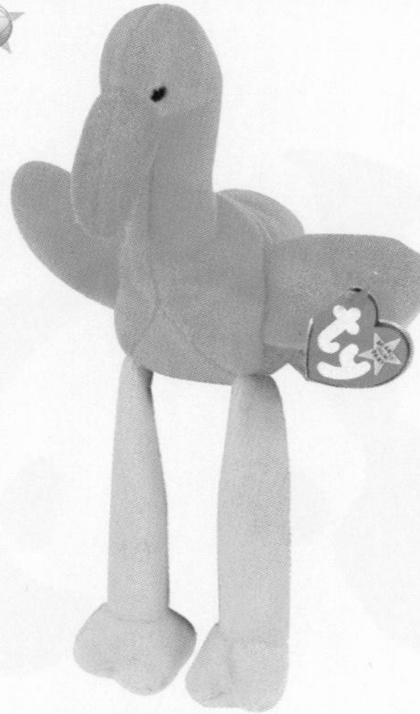

Pinky™

Flamingo · #4072
Issued: June 3, 1995
Retired: December 31, 1998

Market Value:
[5]-$12
[4]-$14
[3]-$130

Birthdate: February 13, 1995
Price Paid: $__________
Date Purchased: __________
Tag Generation: __________

Pinky loves the everglades
From the hottest pink she's made
With floppy legs and big orange beak
She's the Beanie that you seek!

Value Totals __________

124

Pouch™

Kangaroo · #4161
Issued: January 1, 1997
Retired: March 31, 1999

Market Value:
[5] - $11
[4] - $14

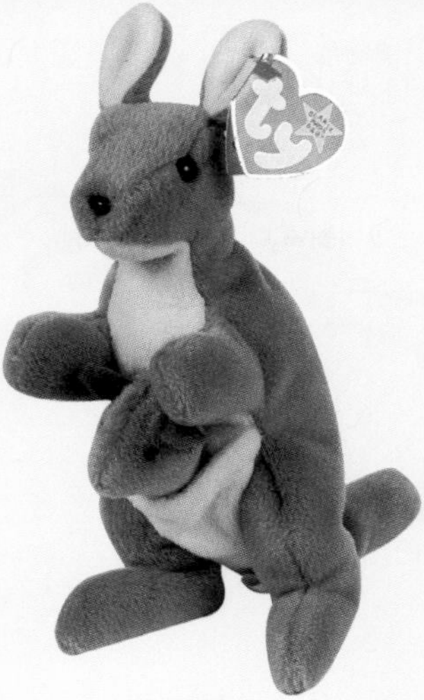

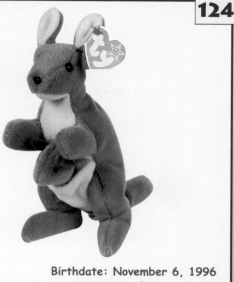

My little pouch is handy I've found
It helps me carry my baby around
I hop up and down without any fear
Knowing my baby is safe and near.

Birthdate: November 6, 1996
Price Paid: $__________
Date Purchased: __________
Tag Generation: __________

125

Pounce™

Cat · #4122
Issued: December 31, 1997
Retired: March 31, 1999

Market Value:
[5] - $11

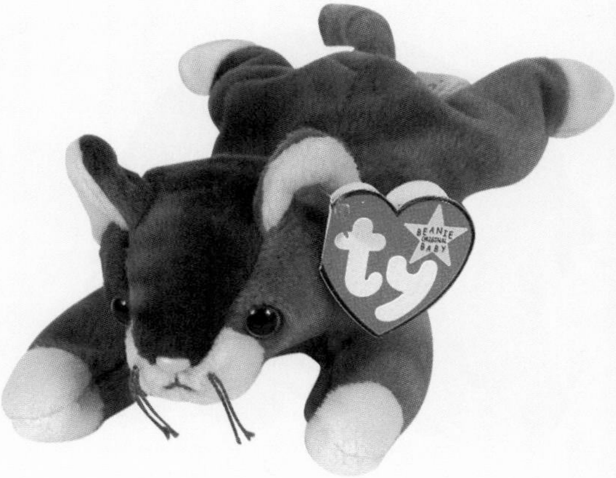

Sneaking and slinking down the hall
To pounce upon a fluffy yarn ball
Under the tables, around the chairs
Through the rooms and down the stairs!

Birthdate: August 28, 1997
Price Paid: $__________
Date Purchased: __________
Tag Generation: __________

Value Totals __________

126

Prance™

Cat · #4123
Issued: December 31, 1997
Retired: March 31, 1999

Market Value:
[5] - $11

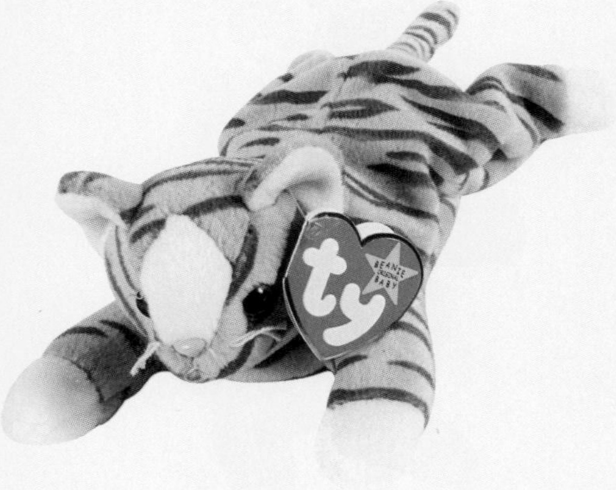

Birthdate: November 20, 1997
Price Paid: $__________
Date Purchased: __________
Tag Generation: __________

She darts around and swats the air
Then looks confused when nothing's there
Pick her up and pet her soft fur
Listen closely, and you'll hear her purr!

127

Prickles™

Hedgehog · #4220
Issued: January 1, 1999
Current – Moderate To Find

Market Value:
[5] - $_____

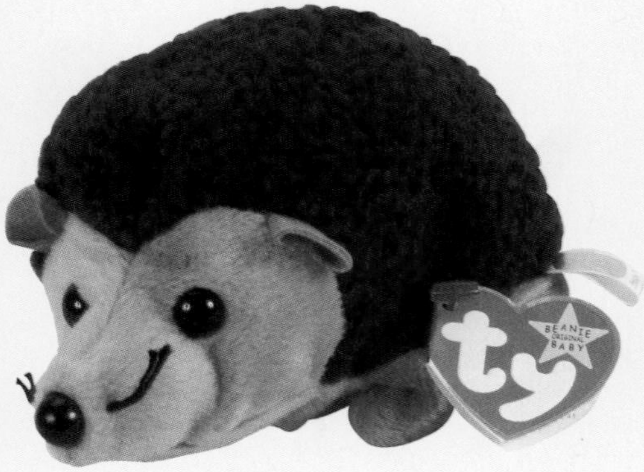

Birthdate: February 19, 1998
Price Paid: $__________
Date Purchased: __________
Tag Generation: __________

Prickles the hedgehog loves to play
She rolls around the meadow all day
Tucking under her feet and head
Suddenly she looks like a ball instead!

Value Totals __________

128

Princess™

B

Bear · #4300
Issued: October 29, 1997
Retired: April 13, 1999

Market Value:
A. "P.E. Pellets" On Tush Tag
(Est. Late 97-April 99)
❹ – $30
B. "P.V.C. Pellets" On Tush
Tag (Est. Late 97)
❹ – $130

A

Like an angel, she came from heaven above
She shared her compassion, her pain, her love
She only stayed with us long enough to teach
The world to share, to give, to reach.

Birthdate: N/A
Price Paid: $_____
Date Purchased: _____
Tag Generation: _____

129

Puffer™

Puffin · #4181
Issued: December 31, 1997
Retired: September 18, 1998

Market Value:
❺ – $12

What in the world does a puffin do?
We're sure that you would like to know too
We asked Puffer how she spends her days
Before she answered, she flew away!

Birthdate: November 3, 1997
Price Paid: $_____
Date Purchased: _____
Tag Generation: _____

Value
Totals _____

130

Pugsly™

Pug Dog · #4106
Issued: May 11, 1997
Retired: March 31, 1999

Market Value:
[5]-$11
[4]-$13

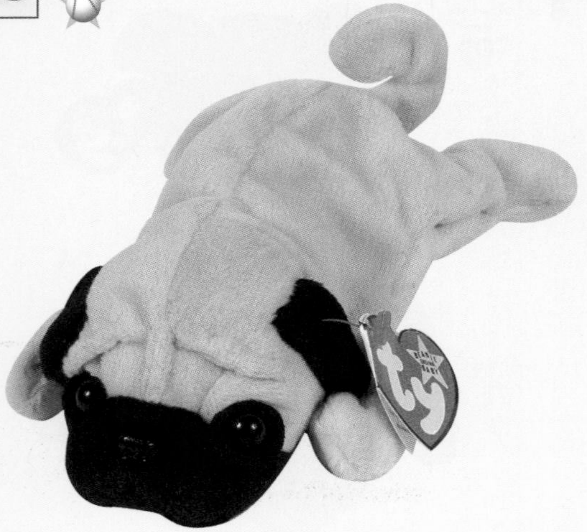

Birthdate: May 2, 1996
Price Paid: $__________
Date Purchased: __________
Tag Generation: __________

Pugsly is picky about what he will wear
Never a spot, a stain or a tear
Image is something of which he'll gloat
Until he noticed his wrinkled coat!

131

Pumkin'™

Pumpkin · #4205
Issued: September 30, 1998
Retired: December 31, 1998

Market Value:
[5]-$33

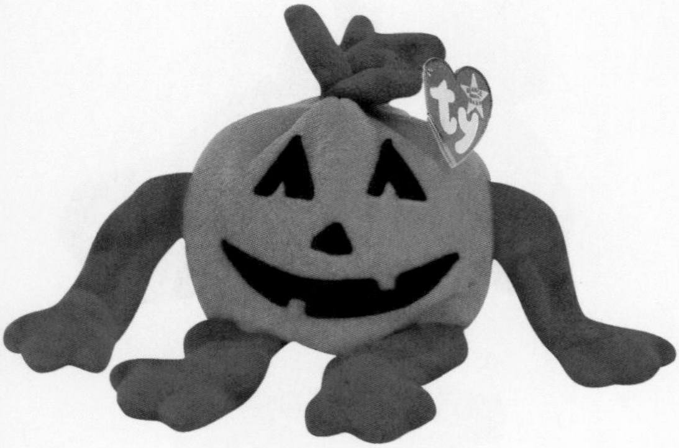

Birthdate: October 31, 1998
Price Paid: $__________
Date Purchased: __________
Tag Generation: __________

Ghost and goblins are out tonight
Witches try hard to cause fright
This little pumpkin is very sweet
He only wants to trick or treat!

Value Totals __________

132

Quackers™

Duck · #4024
Issued: June 25, 1994
Retired: May 1, 1998

Market Value:
A. "Quackers™" With Wings
(Jan. 95–May 98)
5–$17 **4**–$20
3–$115 **2**–$760
B. "Quacker™" Without
Wings (June 94–Jan. 95)
2–$2,100 **1**–$2,250

B

A

There is a duck by the name of Quackers
Every night he eats animal crackers
He swims in a lake that's clear and blue
But he'll come to the shore to be with you!

Birthdate: April 19, 1994
Price Paid: $_____
Date Purchased: _____
Tag Generation: _____

133

Radar™

Bat · #4091
Issued: September 1, 1995
Retired: May 11, 1997

Market Value:
4–$165
3–$200

Radar the bat flies late at night
He can soar to an amazing height
If you see something as high as a star
Take a good look, it might be Radar!

Birthdate: October 30, 1995
Price Paid: $_____
Date Purchased: _____
Tag Generation: _____

134

B

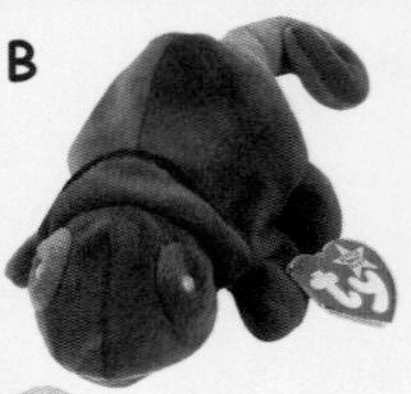

A

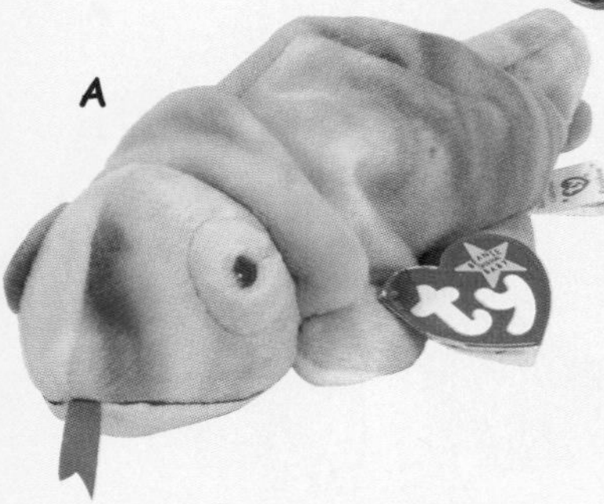

Rainbow™

Chameleon · #4037
Issued: December 31, 1997
Retired: March 31, 1999

Market Value:
A. Tie-dye/With Tongue
(Mid 98-March 99)
[5]- $15
B. Blue/No Tongue
(Dec. 97-Mid 98)
[5]- $19

Birthdate: October 14, 1997
Price Paid: $__________
Date Purchased: __________
Tag Generation: __________

Red, green, blue and yellow
This chameleon is a colorful fellow.
A blend of colors, his own unique hue
Rainbow was made especially for you!

135

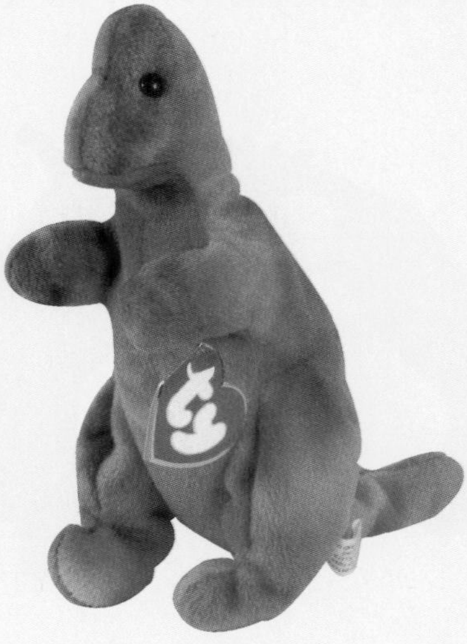

Rex™

Tyrannosaurus · #4086
Issued: June 3, 1995
Retired: June 15, 1996

Market Value:
[3]- $900

Birthdate: N/A
Price Paid: $__________
Date Purchased: __________
Tag Generation: __________

No Poem__________

Value Totals __________

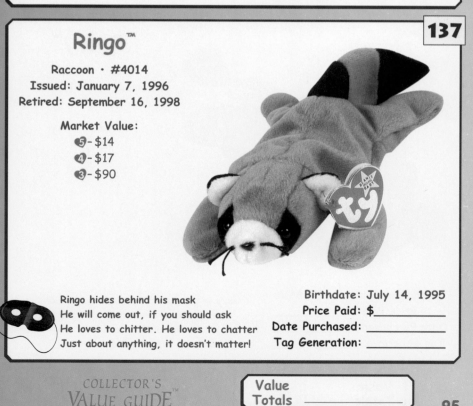

136

Righty™

Elephant · #4086
Issued: June 15, 1996
Retired: January 1, 1997

Market Value:
[4]- $250

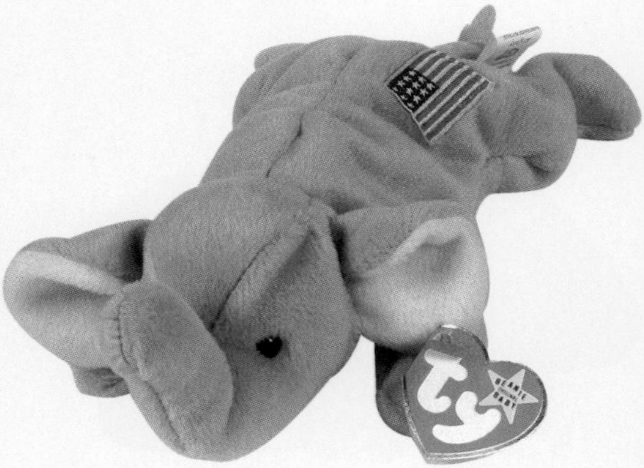

Donkeys to the left, elephants to the right
Often seems like a crazy sight
This whole game seems very funny
Until you realize they're spending
Your money!

Birthdate: July 4, 1996
Price Paid: $__________
Date Purchased: __________
Tag Generation: __________

137

Ringo™

Raccoon · #4014
Issued: January 7, 1996
Retired: September 16, 1998

Market Value:
[5]- $14
[4]- $17
[3]- $90

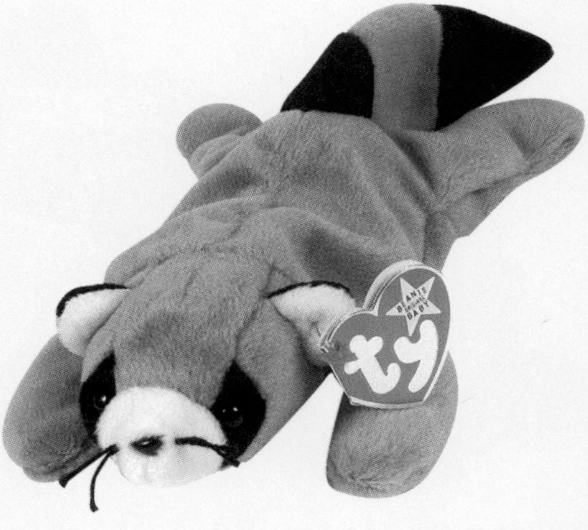

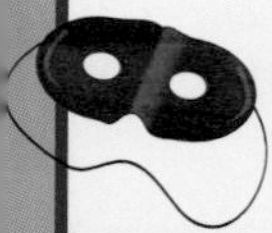

Ringo hides behind his mask
He will come out, if you should ask
He loves to chitter. He loves to chatter
Just about anything, it doesn't matter!

Birthdate: July 14, 1995
Price Paid: $__________
Date Purchased: __________
Tag Generation: __________

Value Totals __________

138

Roam™

Buffalo · #4209
Issued: September 30, 1998
Current – Easy To Find

Market Value:
[5]- $_____

Birthdate: September 27, 1998
Price Paid: $__________
Date Purchased: __________
Tag Generation: __________

Once roaming wild on American land
Tall and strong, wooly and grand
So rare and special is this guy
Find him quickly, he's quite a buy!

139

Roary™

Lion · #4069
Issued: May 11, 1997
Retired: December 31, 1998

Market Value:
[5]- $13
[4]- $15

Birthdate: February 20, 1996
Price Paid: $__________
Date Purchased: __________
Tag Generation: __________

Deep in the jungle they crowned him king
But being brave is not his thing
A cowardly lion some may say
He hears his roar and runs away!

Value Totals __________

140

Rocket™

Blue Jay · #4202
Issued: May 30, 1998
Current – Easy To Find

Market Value:
[5]-$_____

Rocket is the fastest blue jay ever
He flies in all sorts of weather
Aerial tricks are his specialty
He's so entertaining for you and me!

Birthdate: March 12, 1997
Price Paid: $__________
Date Purchased: __________
Tag Generation: __________

141

Rover™

Dog · #4101
Issued: June 15, 1996
Retired: May 1, 1998

Market Value:
[5]-$23
[4]-$27

This dog is red and his name is Rover
If you call him he is sure to come over
He barks and plays with all his might
But worry not, he won't bite!

Birthdate: May 30, 1996
Price Paid: $__________
Date Purchased: __________
Tag Generation: __________

Value Totals __________

142

Sammy™

Bear · #4215
Issued: January 1, 1999
Current – Moderate To Find

Market Value:
[5]-$_____

Birthdate: June 23, 1998
Price Paid: $__________
Date Purchased: __________
Tag Generation: __________

As Sammy steps up to the plate
The crowd gets excited, can hardly wait
We know Sammy won't let us down
He makes us the happiest fans in town!

143

Santa™

Santa · #4203
Issued: September 30, 1998
Retired: December 31, 1998

Market Value:
[5]-$38

Birthdate: December 6, 1998
Price Paid: $__________
Date Purchased: __________
Tag Generation: __________

Known by all in his suit of red
Piles of presents on his sled
Generous and giving, he brings us joy
Peace and love, plus this special toy!

Value Totals __________

144

Scat™

Cat · #4231
Issued: January 1, 1999
Current – Moderate To Find

Market Value:
[5]- $_____

Newborn kittens require lots of sleep
Shhh...it's naptime, don't make a peep
Touch her fur, it feels like silk
Wake her up to drink mother's milk!

Birthdate: May 27, 1998
Price Paid: $__________
Date Purchased: __________
Tag Generation: __________

145

Schweetheart™

NEW!

Orangutan · #4252
Issued: April 11, 1999
Current – Just Released

Market Value:
[5]- $_____

Of all the jungles filled with vines
Traveling about, you came to mine
Because of all the things you said
I can't seem to get you otta my head!

Birthdate: January 23, 1999
Price Paid: $__________
Date Purchased: __________
Tag Generation: __________

Value Totals __________

146

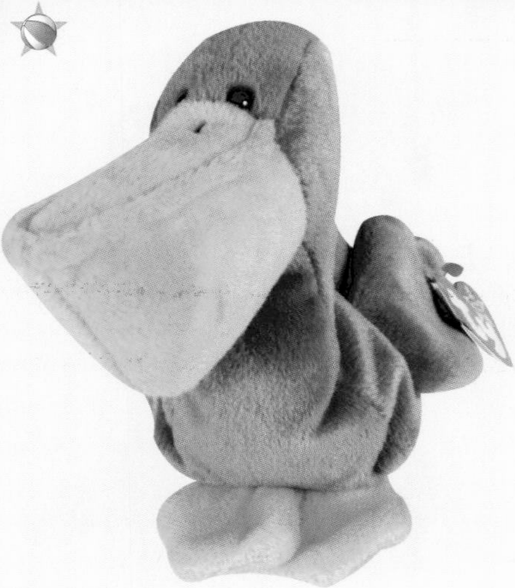

Scoop™

Pelican · #4107
Issued: June 15, 1996
Retired: December 31, 1998

Market Value:
[5] - $12
[4] - $15

Birthdate: July 1, 1996
Price Paid: $__________
Date Purchased: __________
Tag Generation: __________

All day long he scoops up fish
To fill his bill, is his wish
Diving fast and diving low
Hoping those fish are very slow!

147

Scorch™

Dragon · #4210
Issued: September 30, 1998
Current - Moderate To Find

Market Value:
[5] - $_____

Birthdate: July 31, 1998
Price Paid: $__________
Date Purchased: __________
Tag Generation: __________

A magical mystery with glowing wings
Made by wizards and other things
Known to breathe fire with lots of smoke
Scorch is really a friendly ol' bloke!

Value Totals __________

148

Scottie™

Scottish Terrier • #4102
Issued: June 15, 1996
Retired: May 1, 1998

Market Value:
[5]- $23
[4]- $27

Birthdate: June 3, 1996
or June 15, 1996
Price Paid: $__________
Date Purchased: __________
Tag Generation: __________

Scottie is a friendly sort
Even though his legs are short
He is always happy as can be
His best friends are you and me!

149

Seamore™

Seal • #4029
Issued: June 25, 1994
Retired: October 1, 1997

Market Value:
[4]- $130
[3]- $180
[2]- $380
[1]- $570

Birthdate: December 14, 1996
Price Paid: $__________
Date Purchased: __________
Tag Generation: __________

Seamore is a little white seal
Fish and clams are her favorite meal
Playing and laughing in the sand
She's the happiest seal in the land!

Value Totals __________

150

Seaweed™

Otter · #4080
Issued: January 7, 1996
Retired: September 19, 1998

Market Value:
[5]- $24
[4]- $28
[3]- $100

Birthdate: March 19, 1996
Price Paid: $__________
Date Purchased: __________
Tag Generation: __________

Seaweed is what she likes to eat
It's supposed to be a delicious treat
Have you tried a treat from the water
If you haven't, maybe you "otter"!

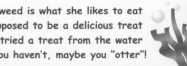

151

NEW!

Silver™

Cat · #4242
Issued: April 21, 1999
Current – Just Released

Market Value:
[5]- $_____

Birthdate: February 11, 1999
Price Paid: $__________
Date Purchased: __________
Tag Generation: __________

Curled up, sleeping in the sun
He's worn out from having fun
Chasing dust specks in the sunrays
This is how he spends his days!

Value Totals __________

152

Slippery™

Seal · #4222
Issued: January 1, 1999
Current – Moderate To Find

Market Value:
[5]- $_____

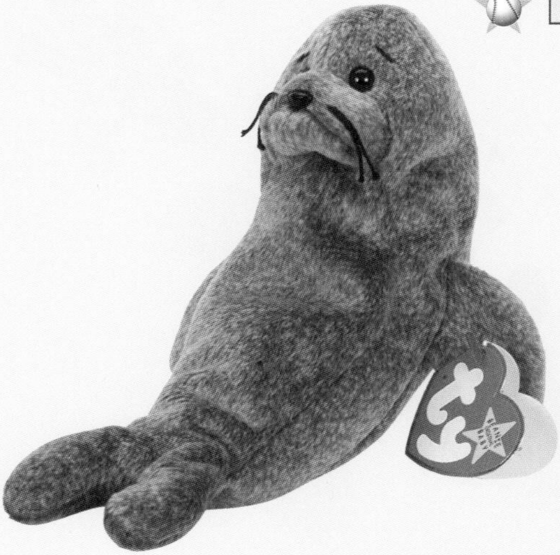

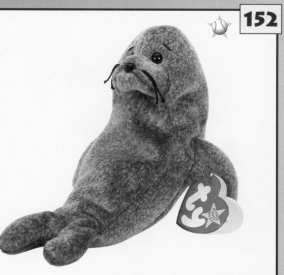

In the ocean, near a breaking wave
Slippery the seal acts very brave
On his surfboard, he sees a swell
He's riding the wave! Oooops...he fell!

Birthdate: January 17, 1998
Price Paid: $__________
Date Purchased: __________
Tag Generation: __________

153

Slither™

Snake · #4031
Issued: June 25, 1994
Retired: June 15, 1995

Market Value:
[3]- $1,800
[2]- $2,000
[1]- $2,150

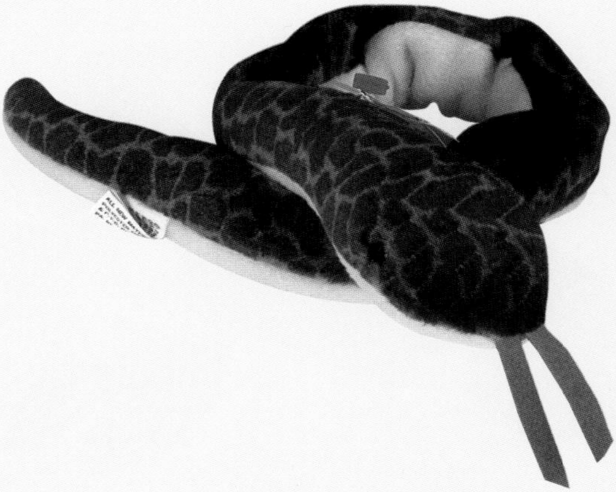

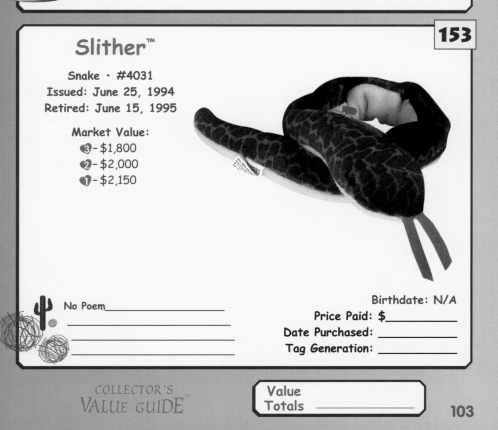

No Poem

Birthdate: N/A
Price Paid: $__________
Date Purchased: __________
Tag Generation: __________

Value Totals __________

154

Sly™

Fox · #4115
Issued: June 15, 1996
Retired: September 22, 1998

A

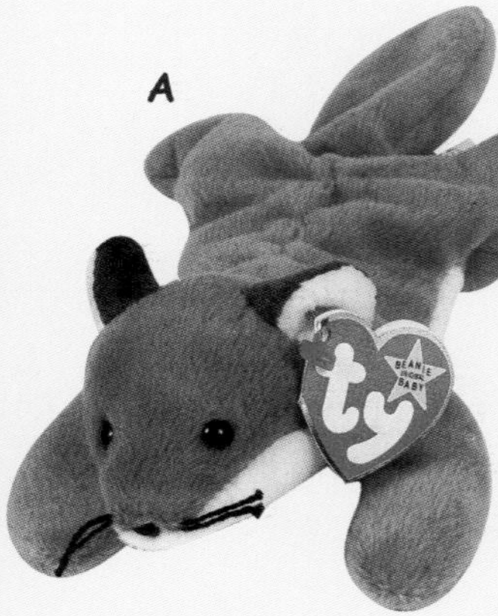

B

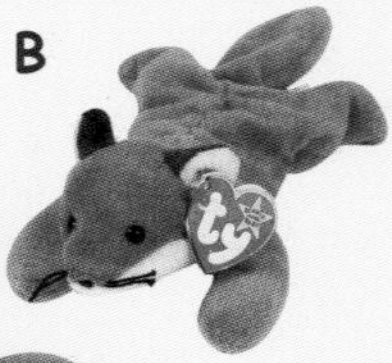

Market Value:
A. White Belly
(Aug. 96-Sept. 98)
[5]- $13
[4]- $16
B. Brown Belly
(June 96-Aug. 96)
[4]- $160

Birthdate: September 12, 1996
Price Paid: $__________
Date Purchased: __________
Tag Generation: __________

Sly is a fox and tricky is he
Please don't chase him, let him be
If you want him, just say when
He'll peek out from his den!

155

Smoochy™

Frog · #4039
Issued: December 31, 1997
Retired: March 31, 1999

Market Value:
[5]- $11

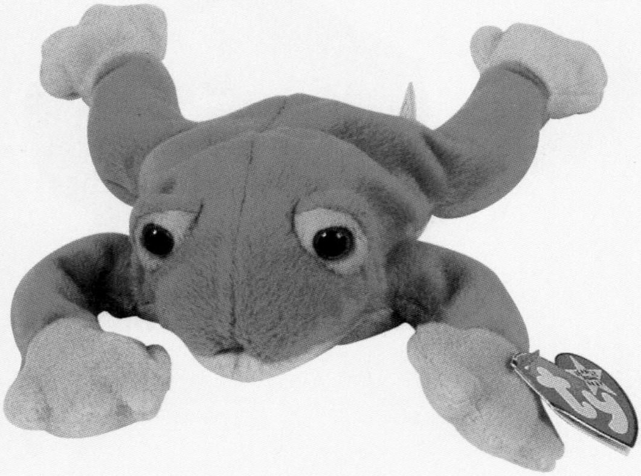

Birthdate: October 1, 1997
Price Paid: $__________
Date Purchased: __________
Tag Generation: __________

Is he a frog or maybe a prince?
This confusion makes him wince
Find the answer, help him with this
Be the one to give him a kiss!

Value Totals __________

156

Snip™

Siamese Cat · #4120
Issued: January 1, 1997
Retired: December 31, 1998

Market Value:
- 5 – $13
- 4 – $16

Snip the cat is Siamese
She'll be your friend if you please
So toss her a toy or a piece of string
    Playing with you is her favorite thing!

Birthdate: October 22, 1996
Price Paid: $_____
Date Purchased: _____
Tag Generation: _____

157

Snort™

Bull · #4002
Issued: January 1, 1997
Retired: September 15, 1998

Market Value:
- 5 – $13
- 4 – $16

Although Snort is not so tall
He loves to play basketball
He is a star player in his dreams
Can you guess his favorite team?

Birthdate: May 15, 1995
Price Paid: $_____
Date Purchased: _____
Tag Generation: _____

158

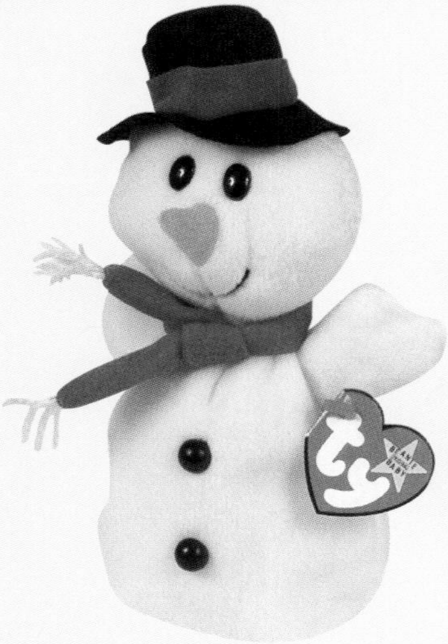

Snowball™

Snowman · #4201
Issued: October 1, 1997
Retired: December 31, 1997

Market Value:
[4] - $44

Birthdate: December 22, 1996
Price Paid: $__________
Date Purchased: __________
Tag Generation: __________

There is a snowman, I've been told
That plays with Beanies out in the cold
What is better in a winter wonderland
Than a Beanie snowman in your hand!

159

NEW!

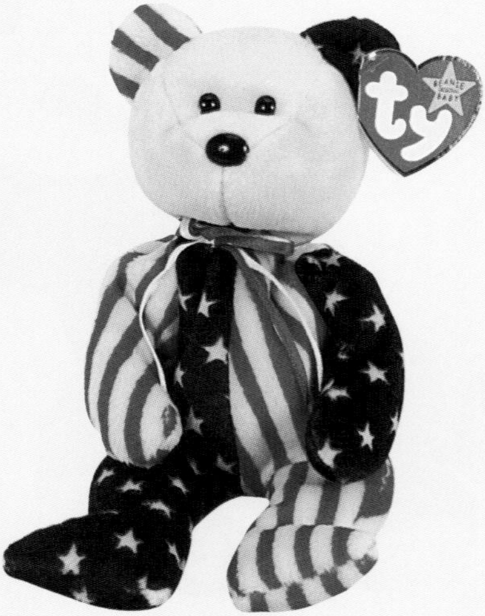

Spangle™

Bear · #4245
Issued: April 24, 1999
Current – Just Released

Market Value:
[5] - $_____

Birthdate: June 14, 1999
Price Paid: $__________
Date Purchased: __________
Tag Generation: __________

Stars and stripes he wears proudly
Everywhere he goes he says loudly
"Hip hip hooray, for the land of the free
There's no place on earth I'd rather be!"

Value Totals __________

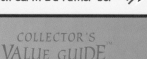

160

Sparky™

Dalmatian · #4100
Issued: June 15, 1996
Retired: May 11, 1997

Market Value:
④–$132

Sparky rides proud on the fire truck
Ringing the bell and pushing his luck
He gets under foot when trying to help
He often gets stepped on and
Lets out a yelp!

Birthdate: February 27, 1996
Price Paid: $_____
Date Purchased: _____
Tag Generation: _____

161

Speedy™

Turtle · #4030
Issued: June 25, 1994
Retired: October 1, 1997

Market Value:
④–$35
③–$120
②–$250
①–$425

Speedy ran marathons in the past
Such a shame, always last
Now Speedy is a big star
After he bought a racing car!

Birthdate: August 14, 1994
Price Paid: $_____
Date Purchased: _____
Tag Generation: _____

162

Spike™

Rhinoceros · #4060
Issued: June 15, 1996
Retired: December 31, 1998

Market Value:
[5]-$11
[4]-$14

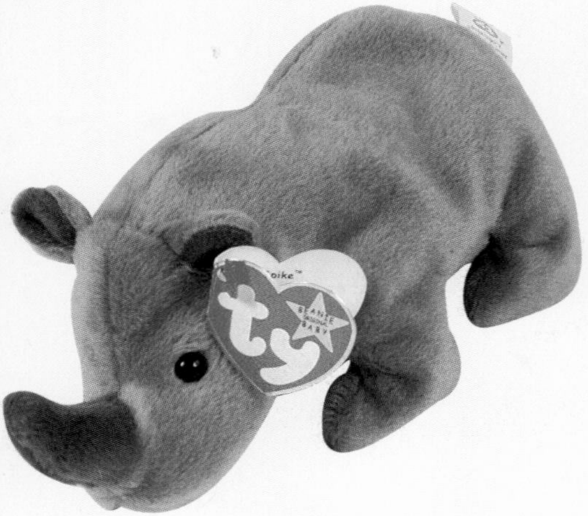

Birthdate: August 13, 1996
Price Paid: $__________
Date Purchased: __________
Tag Generation: __________

Spike the rhino likes to stampede
He's the bruiser that you need
Gentle to birds on his back and spike
You can be his friend if you like!

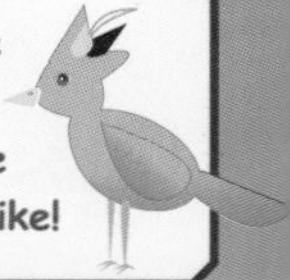

163

Spinner™

Spider · #4036
Issued: October 1, 1997
Retired: September 19, 1998

Market Value:
A. "Spinner™" Tush Tag
(Oct. 97-Sept. 98)
[5]-$13
[4]-$17
B. "Creepy™" Tush Tag
(Est. Late 97-Sept. 98)
[5]-$65

B

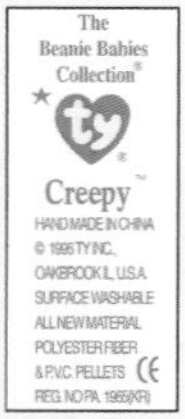
The
Beanie Babies
Collection®
ty
Creepy™
HAND MADE IN CHINA
© 1996 TY INC.
OAKBROOK IL. U.S.A.
SURFACE WASHABLE
ALL NEW MATERIAL
POLYESTER FIBER
& P.V.C. PELLETS
REG. NO PA. 1965(KR)

A

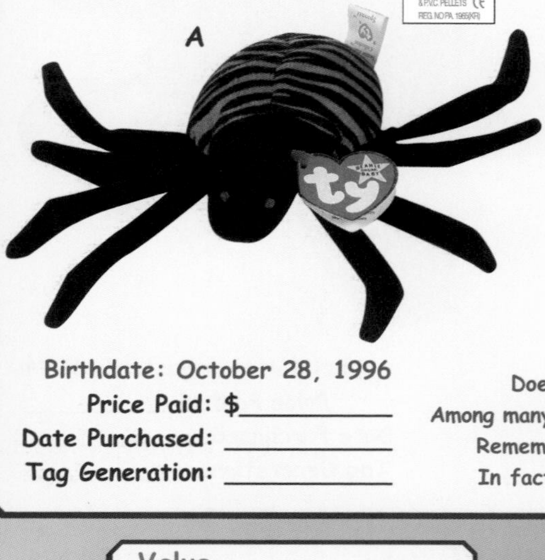

Birthdate: October 28, 1996
Price Paid: $__________
Date Purchased: __________
Tag Generation: __________

Does this spider make you scared?
Among many people that feeling is shared
Remember spiders have feelings too
In fact, this spider really likes you!

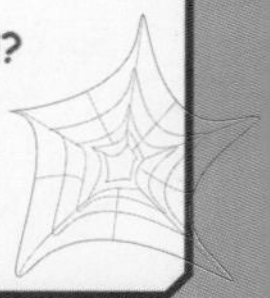

Value
Totals __________

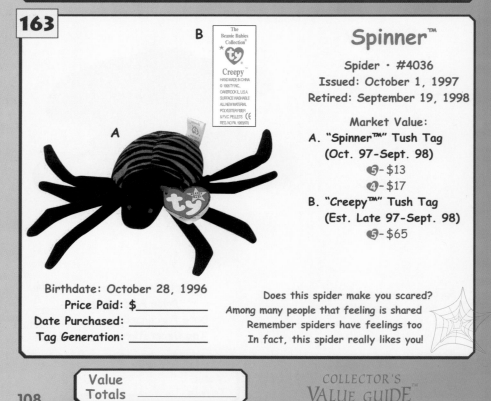

164

Splash™

Whale · #4022
Issued: January 8, 1994
Retired: May 11, 1997

Market Value:
❹ – $120
❸ – $160
❷ – $370
❶ – $575

Splash loves to jump and dive
He's the fastest whale alive
He always wins the 100 yard dash
With a victory jump he'll make a splash!

Birthdate: July 8, 1993
Price Paid: $_____
Date Purchased: _____
Tag Generation: _____

165

Spooky™

B

Ghost · #4090
Issued: September 1, 1995
Retired: December 31, 1997

Spook ™ style 4090
to _____
from _____
with
love

Market Value:
A. "Spooky™" Swing Tag
   (Est. Late 95-Dec. 97)
   ❹ – $36
   ❸ – $160
B. "Spook™" Swing Tag
   (Est. Sept. 95-Late 95)
   ❸ – $480

A

Ghosts can be a scary sight
But don't let Spooky bring you any fright
Because when you're alone, you will see
The best friend that Spooky can be!

Birthdate: October 31, 1995
Price Paid: $_____
Date Purchased: _____
Tag Generation: _____

166

ORIGINAL NINE

B

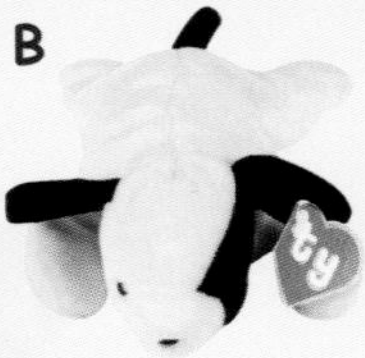

A

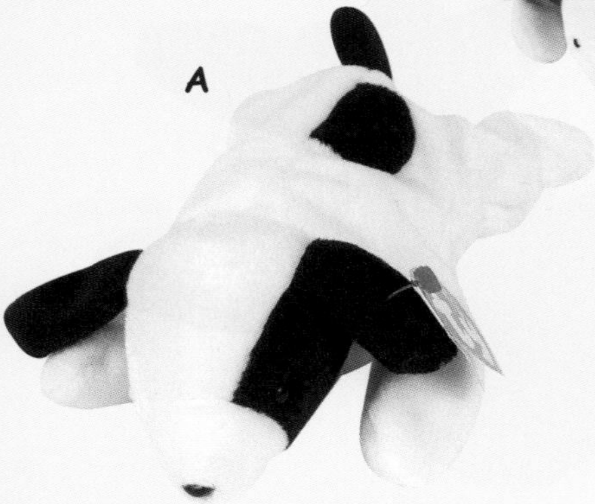

Spot™

Dog · #4000
Issued: January 8, 1994
Retired: October 1, 1997

Market Value:
A. With Spot
(April 94-Oct. 97)
[4]-$55
[3]-$140
[2]-$700
B. Without Spot
(Jan. 94–April 94)
[2]-$1,850
[1]-$2,250

Birthdate: January 3, 1993
Price Paid: $__________
Date Purchased: __________
Tag Generation: __________

See Spot sprint, see Spot run
You and Spot will have lots of fun
Watch out now, because he's not slow
Just stand back and watch him go!

167

Spunky™

Cocker Spaniel · #4184
Issued: December 31, 1997
Retired: March 31, 1999

Market Value:
[5]-$12

Birthdate: January 14, 1997
Price Paid: $__________
Date Purchased: __________
Tag Generation: __________

Bouncing around without much grace
To jump on your lap and lick your face
But watch him closely he has no fears
He'll run so fast he'll trip over his ears

Value Totals __________

168

Squealer™

Pig · #4005
Issued: January 8, 1994
Retired: May 1, 1998

Market Value:
[5]-$28
[4]-$32
[3]-$105
[2]-$285
[1]-$500

Squealer likes to joke around
He is known as class clown
Listen to his stories awhile
There is no doubt he'll make you smile!

Birthdate: April 23, 1993
Price Paid: $__________
Date Purchased: __________
Tag Generation: __________

169

Steg™

Stegosaurus · #4087
Issued: June 3, 1995
Retired: June 15, 1996

Market Value:
[3]-$950

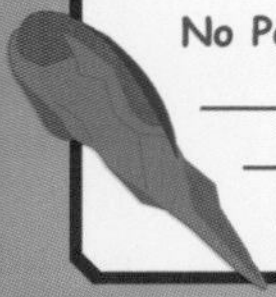

No Poem__________________
____
____
____

Birthdate: N/A
Price Paid: $__________
Date Purchased: __________
Tag Generation: __________

Value Totals __________

170

Stilts™

Stork • #4221
Issued: January 1, 1999
Current – Easy To Find

Market Value:
❺-$_____

Birthdate: June 16, 1998
Price Paid: $_____
Date Purchased: _____
Tag Generation: _____

Flying high over mountains and streams
Fulfilling wishes, hopes and dreams
The stork brings parents bundles of joy
The greatest gift, a girl or boy!

171

Sting™

Stingray • #4077
Issued: June 3, 1995
Retired: January 1, 1997

Market Value:
❹-$170
❸-$255

Birthdate: August 27, 1995
Price Paid: $_____
Date Purchased: _____
Tag Generation: _____

I'm a manta ray and my name is Sting
I'm quite unusual and this is the thing
Under the water I glide like a bird
Have you ever seen something so absurd?

Value
Totals _____

COLLECTOR'S
VALUE GUIDE™

172

Stinger™

Scorpion · #4193
Issued: May 30, 1998
Retired: December 31, 1998

Market Value:
[5] - $14

Stinger the scorpion will run and dart
But this little fellow is really all heart
So if you see him don't run away
Say hello and ask him to play!

Birthdate: September 29, 1997
Price Paid: $__________
Date Purchased: __________
Tag Generation: __________

173

Stinky™

Skunk · #4017
Issued: June 3, 1995
Retired: September 28, 1998

Market Value:
[5] - $15
[4] - $17
[3] - $92

Deep in the woods he lived in a cave
Perfume and mints were the gifts he gave
He showered every night in the kitchen sink
Hoping one day he wouldn't stink!

Birthdate: February 13, 1995
Price Paid: $__________
Date Purchased: __________
Tag Generation: __________

174

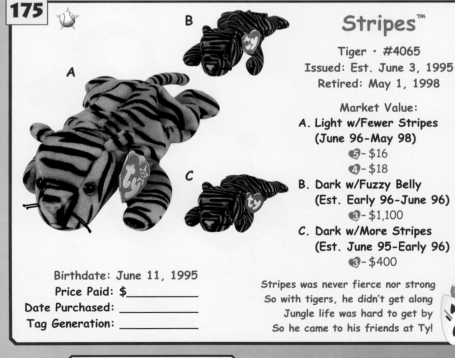

Stretch™

Ostrich · #4182
Issued: December 31, 1997
Retired: March 31, 1999

Market Value:
[5] - $12

Birthdate: September 21, 1997
Price Paid: $__________
Date Purchased: __________
Tag Generation: __________

She thinks when her head is underground
The rest of her body can't be found
The Beanie Babies think it's absurd
To play hide and seek with this bird!

175

B

A

C

Stripes™

Tiger · #4065
Issued: Est. June 3, 1995
Retired: May 1, 1998

Market Value:
A. Light w/Fewer Stripes (June 96-May 98)
[5] - $16
[4] - $18
B. Dark w/Fuzzy Belly (Est. Early 96-June 96)
[3] - $1,100
C. Dark w/More Stripes (Est. June 95-Early 96)
[3] - $400

Birthdate: June 11, 1995
Price Paid: $__________
Date Purchased: __________
Tag Generation: __________

Stripes was never fierce nor strong
So with tigers, he didn't get along
Jungle life was hard to get by
So he came to his friends at Ty!

Value Totals __________

176

Strut™

(name changed from "Doodle™")

Rooster · #4171
Issued: July 12, 1997
Retired: March 31, 1999

Market Value:
[5] - $12
[4] - $16

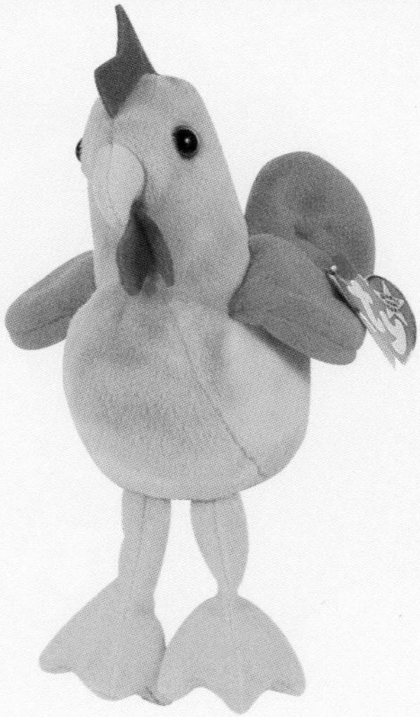

Listen closely to "cock-a-doodle-doo"
What's the rooster saying to you?
Hurry, wake up sleepy head
We have lots to do, get out of bed!

Birthdate: March 8, 1996
Price Paid: $__________
Date Purchased: __________
Tag Generation: __________

177

NEW!

Swirly™

Snail · #4249
Issued: April 14, 1999
Current – Just Released

Market Value:
[5] - $_____

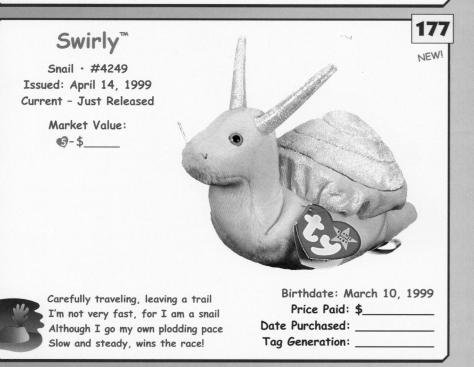

Carefully traveling, leaving a trail
I'm not very fast, for I am a snail
Although I go my own plodding pace
Slow and steady, wins the race!

Birthdate: March 10, 1999
Price Paid: $__________
Date Purchased: __________
Tag Generation: __________

Value Totals __________

178

Tabasco™

Bull · #4002
Issued: June 3, 1995
Retired: January 1, 1997

Market Value:
④ – $175
③ – $215

Birthdate: May 15, 1995
Price Paid: $_____
Date Purchased: _____
Tag Generation: _____

Although Tabasco is not so tall
He loves to play basketball
He is a star player in his dream
Can you guess his favorite team?

179

Tank™

B

A

C

Armadillo · #4031
Issued: Est. January 7, 1996
Retired: October 1, 1997

Market Value:
A. 9 Plates/With Shell
(Est. Late 96-Oct. 97)
④ – $76
B. 9 Plates/Without Shell
(Est. Mid 96-Late 96)
④ – $215
C. 7 Plates/Without Shell
(Est. Jan 96-Mid 96)
③ – $190

Birthdate: February 22, 1995
Price Paid: $_____
Date Purchased: _____
Tag Generation: _____

This armadillo lives in the South
Shoving Tex-Mex in his mouth
He sure loves it south of the border
Keeping his friends in good order!

Value
Totals _____

COLLECTOR'S
VALUE GUIDE™

180

Teddy™ (brown)

B

Bear · #4050
Issued: June 25, 1994
Retired: October 1, 1997

Market Value:
A. New Face (Jan. 95-Oct. 97)
④- $100
③- $375
②- $800
B. Old Face (June 94-Jan. 95)
②- $2,500
①- $2,700

A

Teddy wanted to go out today
All of his friends went out to play
But he'd rather help whatever you do
After all, his best friend is you!

Birthdate: November 28, 1995
Price Paid: $_____
Date Purchased: _____
Tag Generation: _____

181

Teddy™ (cranberry)

B

Bear · #4052
Issued: June 25, 1994
Retired: January 7, 1996

Market Value:
A. New Face (Jan. 95-Jan. 96)
③- $1,800
②- $1,900
B. Old Face (June 94-Jan. 95)
②- $1,800
①- $1,900

A

No Poem_____
_____
_____
_____

Birthdate: N/A
Price Paid: $_____
Date Purchased: _____
Tag Generation: _____

Value
Totals _____

182

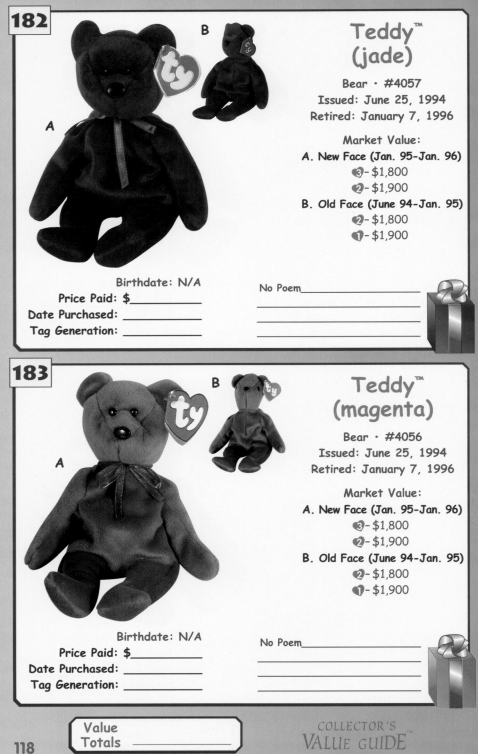

B

A

Teddy™ (jade)

Bear • #4057
Issued: June 25, 1994
Retired: January 7, 1996

Market Value:
A. New Face (Jan. 95-Jan. 96)
❸- $1,800
❷- $1,900
B. Old Face (June 94-Jan. 95)
❷- $1,800
❶- $1,900

Birthdate: N/A
Price Paid: $_____
Date Purchased: _____
Tag Generation: _____

No Poem_____
_____
_____

183

B

A

Teddy™ (magenta)

Bear • #4056
Issued: June 25, 1994
Retired: January 7, 1996

Market Value:
A. New Face (Jan. 95-Jan. 96)
❸- $1,800
❷- $1,900
B. Old Face (June 94-Jan. 95)
❷- $1,800
❶- $1,900

Birthdate: N/A
Price Paid: $_____
Date Purchased: _____
Tag Generation: _____

No Poem_____
_____
_____

Value
Totals _____

COLLECTOR'S
VALUE GUIDE™

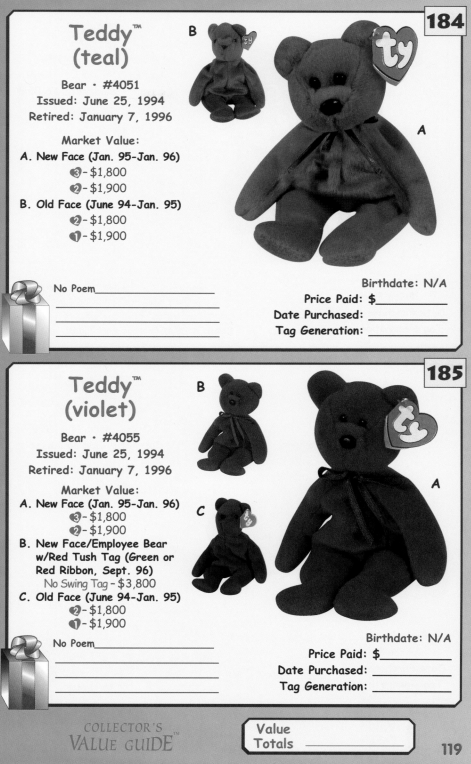

184

Teddy™ (teal)

Bear · #4051
Issued: June 25, 1994
Retired: January 7, 1996

Market Value:
A. New Face (Jan. 95-Jan. 96)
③ - $1,800
② - $1,900
B. Old Face (June 94-Jan. 95)
② - $1,800
① - $1,900

No Poem _____
_____
_____
_____

Birthdate: N/A
Price Paid: $ _____
Date Purchased: _____
Tag Generation: _____

185

Teddy™ (violet)

Bear · #4055
Issued: June 25, 1994
Retired: January 7, 1996

Market Value:
A. New Face (Jan. 95-Jan. 96)
③ - $1,800
② - $1,900
B. New Face/Employee Bear
w/Red Tush Tag (Green or
Red Ribbon, Sept. 96)
No Swing Tag - $3,800
C. Old Face (June 94-Jan. 95)
② - $1,800
① - $1,900

No Poem _____
_____
_____
_____

Birthdate: N/A
Price Paid: $ _____
Date Purchased: _____
Tag Generation: _____

Value
Totals _____

186

Tiny™

Chihuahua · #4234
Issued: January 1, 1999
Current – Moderate To Find

Market Value:
[5]-$_____

Birthdate: September 8, 1998
Price Paid: $__________
Date Purchased: __________
Tag Generation: __________

South of the Border, in the sun
Tiny the Chihuahua is having fun
Attending fiestas, breaking piñatas
Eating a taco, or some enchiladas!

187

NEW!

Tiptoe™

Mouse · #4241
Issued: April 16, 1999
Current – Just Released

Market Value:
[5]-$_____

Birthdate: January 8, 1999
Price Paid: $__________
Date Purchased: __________
Tag Generation: __________

Creeping quietly along the wall
Little foot prints fast and small
Tiptoeing through the house with ease
Searching for a piece of cheese!

Value Totals __________

188

Tracker™

Basset Hound · #4198
Issued: May 30, 1998
Current – Easy To Find

Market Value:
[5] - $_____

Sniffing and tracking and following trails
Tracker the basset always wags his tail
It doesn't matter what you do
He's always happy when he's with you!

Birthdate: June 5, 1997
Price Paid: $__________
Date Purchased: __________
Tag Generation: __________

189

Trap™

Mouse · #4042
Issued: June 25, 1994
Retired: June 15, 1995

Market Value:
[3] - $1,440
[2] - $1,550
[1] - $1,700

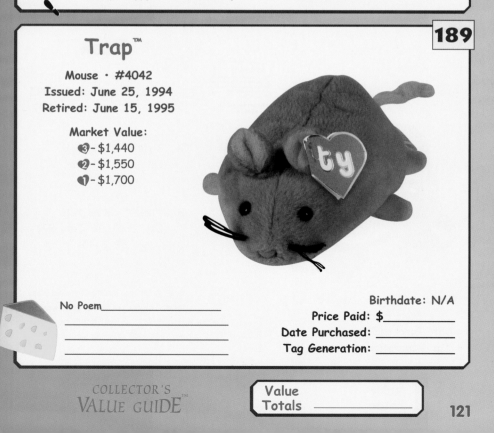

No Poem__________________

Birthdate: N/A
Price Paid: $__________
Date Purchased: __________
Tag Generation: __________

190

Tuffy™

Terrier · #4108
Issued: May 11, 1997
Retired: December 31, 1998

Market Value:
[5] - $12
[4] - $15

Birthdate: October 12, 1996
Price Paid: $__________
Date Purchased: __________
Tag Generation: __________

Taking off with a thunderous blast
Tuffy rides his motorcycle fast
The Beanies roll with laughs and squeals
He never took off his training wheels!

191

Tusk™

Walrus · #4076
Issued: Est. June 3, 1995
Retired: January 1, 1997

B

Tuck™ style 4076
DATE OF BIRTH : 9-18-95
Tusk brushes his teeth everyday
To keep them shiny, it's the only way
Teeth are special, so you must try
And they will sparkle when
You say "Hi"!
Visit our web page!!!
http://www.ty.com

A

Market Value:
A. "Tusk™" Swing Tag
(Est. June 95-Jan. 97)
[4] - $130
[3] - $185
B. "Tuck™" Swing Tag
(Est. Early 96-Jan. 97)
[4] - $145

Birthdate: September 18, 1995
Price Paid: $__________
Date Purchased: __________
Tag Generation: __________

Tusk brushes his teeth everyday
To keep them shiny, it's the only way
Teeth are special, so you must try
And they will sparkle when
You say "Hi"!

TOOTHPASTE

Value Totals __________

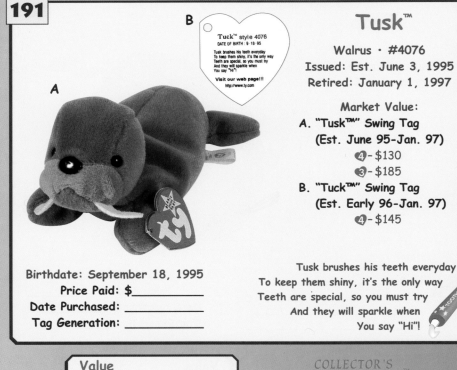

192

Twigs™

Giraffe · #4068
Issued: January 7, 1996
Retired: May 1, 1998

Market Value:
[5]-$23
[4]-$25
[3]-$105

Twigs has his head in the clouds
He stands tall, he stands proud
With legs so skinny they wobble and shake
What an unusual friend he will make!

Birthdate: May 19, 1995
Price Paid: $________
Date Purchased: ________
Tag Generation: ________

193

Valentina™

Bear · #4233
Issued: January 1, 1999
Current – Hard To Find

Market Value:
[5]-$_____

Flowers, candy and hearts galore
Sweet words of love for those you adore
With this bear comes love that's true
On Valentine's Day and all year through!

Birthdate: February 14, 1998
Price Paid: $________
Date Purchased: ________
Tag Generation: ________

Value Totals ________

194

Valentino™

Bear · #4058
Issued: January 7, 1995
Retired: December 31, 1998

Market Value:
[5]-$26
[4]-$30
[3]-$150
[2]-$260

Birthdate: February 14, 1994
Price Paid: $__________
Date Purchased: __________
Tag Generation: __________

His heart is red and full of love
He cares for you so give him a hug
Keep him close when feeling blue
Feel the love he has for you!

195

Velvet™

Panther · #4064
Issued: June 3, 1995
Retired: October 1, 1997

Market Value:
[4]-$33
[3]-$105

Birthdate: December 16, 1995
Price Paid: $__________
Date Purchased: __________
Tag Generation: __________

Velvet loves to sleep in the trees
Lulled to dreams by the buzz of the bees
She snoozes all day and plays all night
Running and jumping in the moonlight!

Value Totals __________

196

Waddle™

Penguin · #4075
Issued: June 3, 1995
Retired: May 1, 1998

Market Value:
[5]-$22
[4]-$25
[3]-$100

Waddle the Penguin likes to dress up
Every night he wears his tux
When Waddle walks, it never fails
He always trips over his tails!

Birthdate: December 19, 1995
Price Paid: $__________
Date Purchased: __________
Tag Generation: __________

197

Waves™

Whale · #4084
Issued: May 11, 1997
Retired: May 1, 1998

Market Value:
[5]-$18
[4]-$22

Join him today on the Internet
Don't be afraid to get your feet wet
He taught all the Beanies how to surf
Our web page is his home turf!

Birthdate: December 8, 1996
Price Paid: $__________
Date Purchased: __________
Tag Generation: __________

Value Totals __________

198

Web™

Spider · #4041
Issued: June 25, 1994
Retired: January 7, 1996

Market Value:
❸- $1,300
❷- $1,400
❶- $1,600

Birthdate: N/A

Price Paid: $_____
Date Purchased: _____
Tag Generation: _____

No Poem_____
_____
_____
_____

199

Weenie™

Dachshund · #4013
Issued: January 7, 1996
Retired: May 1, 1998

Market Value:
❺- $30
❹- $34
❸- $120

Birthdate: July 20, 1995
Price Paid: $_____
Date Purchased: _____
Tag Generation: _____

Weenie the dog is quite a sight
Long of body and short of height
He perches himself high on a log
And considers himself to be top dog!

TOP DOG

Value
Totals _____

COLLECTOR'S
VALUE GUIDE™

200

Whisper™

Deer • #4194
Issued: May 30, 1998
Current – Easy To Find

Market Value:
[5]- $_____

She's very shy as you can see
When she hides behind a tree
With big brown eyes and soft to touch
This little fawn will love you so much!

Birthdate: April 5, 1997
Price Paid: $__________
Date Purchased: __________
Tag Generation: __________

201

Wise™

Owl • #4187
Issued: May 30, 1998
Retired: December 31, 1998
Market Value:
[5]- $32

Wise is at the head of the class
With A's and B's he'll always pass
He's got his diploma and feels really great
Meet the newest graduate: Class of '98!

Birthdate: May 31, 1997
Price Paid: $__________
Date Purchased: __________
Tag Generation: __________

Value Totals __________

202

NEW!

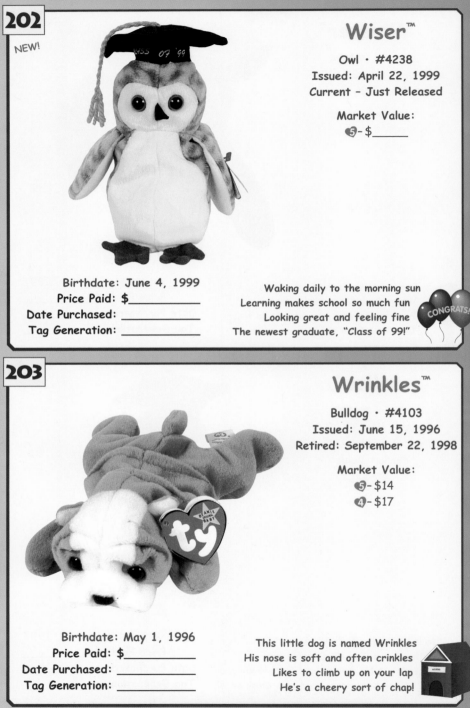

Wiser™

Owl · #4238
Issued: April 22, 1999
Current – Just Released

Market Value:
[5]-$_____

Birthdate: June 4, 1999
Price Paid: $__________
Date Purchased: __________
Tag Generation: __________

Waking daily to the morning sun
Learning makes school so much fun
Looking great and feeling fine
The newest graduate, "Class of 99!"

203

Wrinkles™

Bulldog · #4103
Issued: June 15, 1996
Retired: September 22, 1998

Market Value:
[5]-$14
[4]-$17

Birthdate: May 1, 1996
Price Paid: $__________
Date Purchased: __________
Tag Generation: __________

This little dog is named Wrinkles
His nose is soft and often crinkles
Likes to climb up on your lap
He's a cheery sort of chap!

Value Totals __________

204

Zero™

Penguin · #4207
Issued: September 30, 1998
Retired: December 31, 1998

Market Value:
[5]- $30

Penguins love the ice and snow
Playing in weather twenty below
Antarctica is where I love to be
Splashing in the cold, cold sea!

Birthdate: January 2, 1998
Price Paid: $__________
Date Purchased: __________
Tag Generation: __________

205

Ziggy™

Zebra · #4063
Issued: June 3, 1995
Retired: May 1, 1998

Market Value:
[5]- $22
[4]- $24
[3]- $100

Ziggy likes soccer - he's a referee
That way he watches the games for free
The other Beanies don't think it's fair
But Ziggy the Zebra doesn't care!

Birthdate: December 24, 1995
Price Paid: $__________
Date Purchased: __________
Tag Generation: __________

Value Totals __________

206

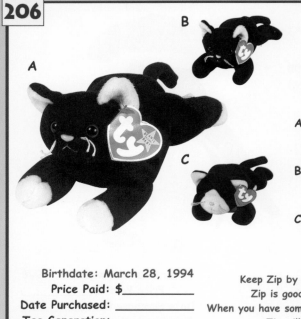

Zip™

Cat · #4004
Issued: January 7, 1995
Retired: May 1, 1998

A

B

C

Market Value:

A. White Paws
(March 96–May 98)
[5]-$38 [4]-$42 [3]-$390

B. All Black
(Jan. 96–March 96)
[3]-$1,200

C. White Face
(Jan. 95–Jan. 96)
[3]-$460 [2]-$535

Birthdate: March 28, 1994
Price Paid: $__________
Date Purchased: __________
Tag Generation: __________

Keep Zip by your side all the day through
Zip is good luck, you'll see it's true
When you have something you need to do
Zip will always believe in you!

WELCOME TO ALL OF OUR NEW FRIENDS!

Value Totals __________

SPORTS PROMOTION BEANIE BABIES®

Beanie Babies have become hot promotional items in the United States and Canada. They're showing up on fields, courts and rinks, as well as at events like the Special Olympics.

SPORTS PROMOTION BEANIE BABIES® KEY

Canadian Special Olympics	National Football League
Major League Baseball	National Hockey League
National Basketball Association	Women's National Basketball Association

1 1999 Signature Bear™
New York Yankees
5/9/99 • N/A
Market Value: N/E

2 Baldy™
Philadelphia 76ers
1/17/98 • LE-5,000
Market Value: $220

3 Baldy™
Washington Capitals
2/20/99 • LE-5,000
Market Value: N/E

4 Batty™
Milwaukee Brewers
5/31/98 • LE-12,000
Market Value: $115

5 Batty™
New York Mets
7/12/98 • LE-30,000
Market Value: $115

6 Batty™
Seattle Mariners
5/29/99 • LE-15,000
Market Value: N/E

7 Blackie™
Boston Bruins
10/12/98 • LE-5,000
Market Value: $110

8 Blackie™
Chicago Bears
In Club Kits • LE-20,000
Market Value: $100

9 Blackie™
Chicago Bears
11/8/98 • LE-8,000
Market Value: $110

10 Blizzard™
Chicago White Sox
7/12/98 • LE-20,000
Market Value: $115

11 Bones™
Chicago Blackhawks
10/24/98 • LE-5,000
Market Value: $100

12 Bones™
New York Yankees
3/10/98 • N/A
Market Value: $200

13 Bongo™
Charlotte Sting
7/17/98 • LE-3,000
Market Value: $185

14 Bongo™
Cleveland Cavaliers
4/5/98 • LE-5,000
Market Value: $175

15 Chip™
Atlanta Braves
8/19/98 • LE-12,000
Market Value: $105

16 Chocolate™
Dallas Cowboys
9/6/98 • LE-10,000
Market Value: $125

17 Chocolate™
Denver Nuggets
4/17/98 • LE-5,000
Market Value: $140

18 Chocolate™
Seattle Mariners
9/5/98 • LE-10,000
Market Value: $105

19 Chocolate™
Tennessee Oilers
10/18/98 • LE-7,500
Market Value: $95

20 Chocolate™
Toronto Maple Leafs
1/2/99 • LE-3,000
Market Value: $95

21 Claude™
Sacramento Kings
3/14/99 • LE-5,000
Market Value: N/E

22 Cubbie™
Chicago Cubs
1/15-1/17/99 • N/A
Market Value: N/E

SPORTS PROMOTION BEANIE BABIES®

	Price Paid	Value of My Collection
1.		
2.		
3.		
4.		
5.		
6.		
7.		
8.		
9.		
10.		
11.		
12.		
13.		
14.		
15.		
16.		
17.		
18.		
19.		
20.		
21.		
22.		
PENCIL TOTALS		

(23) Cubbie™
Chicago Cubs
1/16-1/18/98 • LE-100
Market Value: $480

(24) Cubbie™
Chicago Cubs
5/18/97 • LE-10,000
Market Value: $165

(25) Cubbie™
Chicago Cubs
9/6/97 • LE-10,000
Market Value: $140

(26) Curly™
Charlotte Sting
6/15/98 • LE-5,000
Market Value: $180

(27) Curly™
Chicago Bears
12/20/98 • LE-10,000
Market Value: $100

(28) Curly™
Cleveland Rockers
8/15/98 • LE-3,200
Market Value: $145

(29) Curly™
New York Mets
8/22/98 • LE-30,000
Market Value: $95

(30) Curly™
San Antonio Spurs
4/27/98 • LE-2,500
Market Value: $150

(31) Daisy™
Chicago Cubs
5/3/98 • LE-10,000
Market Value: $375

(32) Derby™
Houston Astros
8/16/98 • LE-15,000
Market Value: $105

(33) Derby™
Indianapolis Colts
10/4/98 • LE-10,000
Market Value: $100

(34) Dotty™
Los Angeles Sparks
7/31/98 • LE-3,000
Market Value: $145

(35) Early™
Milwaukee Brewers
6/12/99 • LE-12,000
Market Value: N/E

(36) Ears™
Oakland A's
3/15/98 • LE-1,500
Market Value: $240

(37) Erin™
Chicago Cubs
8/5/99 • LE-12,000
Market Value: N/E

(38) Fortune™
Kansas City Royals
6/6/99 • LE-10,000
Market Value: N/E

(39) Glory™
All-Star Game
7/7/98 • LE-52,000 approx.
Market Value: $200

(40) Goatee™
Arizona Diamondbacks
7/8/99 • LE-10,000
Market Value: N/E

(41) Gobbles™
Phoenix Coyotes
11/26/98 • LE-5,000
Market Value: N/E

(42) Gobbles™
St. Louis Blues
11/24/98 • LE-7,500
Market Value: $95

(43) Goochy™
Tampa Bay Devil Rays
4/10/99 • LE-10,000
Market Value: N/E

(44) Gracie™
Chicago Cubs
9/13/98 • LE-10,000
Market Value: $145

(45) Hippie™
Minnesota Twins
6/18/99 • LE-10,000
Market Value: N/E

(46) Hippie™
St. Louis Blues
3/22/99 • LE-7,500
Market Value: N/E

(47) Hissy™
Arizona Diamondbacks
6/14/98 • LE-6,500
Market Value: $90

(48) KuKu™
Detroit Tigers
7/11/99 • LE-10,000
Market Value: N/E

(49) Lucky™
Minnesota Twins
7/31/99 • LE-10,000
Market Value: $110

(50) Luke™
Texas Rangers
9/5/99 • LE-15,000
Market Value: N/E

(51) Mac™
St. Louis Cardinals
6/14/99 • LE-20,000
Market Value: N/E

(52) Maple™
Canadian Special Olympics
8/97 & 12/97 • N/A
Market Value: $400

SPORTS PROMOTION BEANIE BABIES®

	Price Paid	Value of My Collection
23.		
24.		
25.		
26.		
27.		
28.		
29.		
30.		
31.		
32.		
33.		
34.		
35.		
36.		
37.		
38.		
39.		
40.		
41.		
42.		
43.		
44.		
45.		
46.		
47.		
48.		
49.		
50.		
51.		
52.		
PENCIL TOTALS		

(53) **Mel™** Anaheim Angels 9/6/98 • LE-10,000 **Market Value: $115**	**(54)** **Mel™** Detroit Shock 7/25/98 • LE-5,000 **Market Value: $110**

(53) **Mel™** Anaheim Angels — 9/6/98 • LE-10,000 — **Market Value: $115**

(54) **Mel™** Detroit Shock — 7/25/98 • LE-5,000 — **Market Value: $110**

(55) **Millennium™** Chicago Cubs — 9/26/99 • LE-40,000 — **Market Value: N/E**

(56) **Millennium™** New York Yankees — 8/15/99 • N/A — **Market Value: N/E**

(57) **Mystic™** Los Angeles Sparks — 8/3/98 • LE-5,000 — **Market Value: $135**

(58) **Mystic™** Washington Mystics — 7/11/98 • LE-5,000 — **Market Value: $160**

(59) **Peace™** Oakland A's — 5/1/99 • LE-10,000 — **Market Value: N/E**

(60) **Peanut™** Oakland A's — 8/1/98 • LE-15,000 — **Market Value: $95**

(61) **Peanut™** Oakland A's — 9/6/98 • LE-15,000 — **Market Value: $95**

(62) **Pinky™** San Antonio Spurs — 4/29/98 • LE-2,500 — **Market Value: $160**

(63) **Pinky™** Tampa Bay Devil Rays — 8/23/98 • LE-10,000 — **Market Value: $80**

(64) **Pugsly™** Atlanta Braves — 9/2/98 • LE-12,000 — **Market Value: $90**

(65) **Pugsly™** Texas Rangers — 8/4/98 • LE-10,000 — **Market Value: $105**

(66) **Roam™** Buffalo Sabres — 2/19/99 • LE-5,000 — **Market Value: $95**

(67) **Roary™** Kansas City Royals — 5/31/98 • LE-13,000 — **Market Value: $100**

(68) **Rocket™** Toronto Blue Jays — 9/6/98 • LE-12,000 — **Market Value: $105**

(69) **Rover™** Cincinnati Reds — 8/16/98 • LE-15,000 — **Market Value: $85**

(70) **Sammy™** Chicago Cubs — 1/15-1/17/99 • N/A — **Market Value: N/E**

(71) **Sammy™** Chicago Cubs — 4/25/99 • LE-12,000 — **Market Value: N/E**

(72) **Scoop™** Houston Comets — 8/6/98 • LE-5,000 — **Market Value: $145**

(73) **Scorch™** Cincinnati Reds — 6/19/99 • LE-10,000 — **Market Value: N/E**

(74) **Slippery™** San Francisco Giants — 4/11/99 • LE-15,000 — **Market Value: N/E**

(75) **Sly™** Arizona Diamondbacks — 8/27/98 • LE-10,000 — **Market Value: $90**

(76) **Smoochy™** St. Louis Cardinals — 8/14/98 • LE-20,000 — **Market Value: $110**

(77) **Snort™** Chicago Bulls — 4/10/99 • LE-5,000 — **Market Value: N/E**

(78) **Spunky™** Buffalo Sabres — 10/23/98 • LE-5,000 — **Market Value: $90**

(79) **Stretch™** New York Yankees — 8/9/98 • N/A — **Market Value: $105**

(80) **Stretch™** St. Louis Cardinals — 5/22/98 • LE-20,000 — **Market Value: $105**

(81) **Stripes™** Detroit Tigers — 5/31/98 • LE-10,000 — **Market Value: $100**

(82) **Stripes™** Detroit Tigers — 8/8/98 • LE-10,000 — **Market Value: $95**

SPORTS PROMOTION BEANIE BABIES®

	Price Paid	Value of My Collection
53.		
54.		
55.		
56.		
57.		
58.		
59.		
60.		
61.		
62.		
63.		
64.		
65.		
66.		
67.		
68.		
69.		
70.		
71.		
72.		
73.		
74.		
75.		
76.		
77.		
78.		
79.		
80.		
81.		
82.		
PENCIL TOTALS		

83		84		85		86	

Strut™
Indiana Pacers
4/2/98 • LE-5,000
Market Value: $120

Tiny™
Houston Astros
7/18/99 • LE-20,000
Market Value: N/E

Tuffy™
New Jersey Devils
10/24/98 • LE-5,000
Market Value: $100

Tuffy™
San Francisco Giants
8/30/98 • LE-10,000
Market Value: $110

87		88		89		90	

Valentina™
New York Mets
5/30/99 • LE-18,000
Market Value: N/E

Valentino™
Canadian Special Olympics
6/98, 9/98 & 10/98 • N/A
Market Value: $235

Valentino™
New York Yankees
5/17/98 • LE-10,000
Market Value: $180

Waddle™
Pittsburgh Penguins
10/24/98 • LE-7,000
Market Value: $85

91		92		93		94	

Waddle™
Pittsburgh Penguins
11/21/98 • LE-7,000
Market Value: $85

Waves™
San Diego Padres
8/14/98 • LE-10,000
Market Value: $105

Weenie™
Tampa Bay Devil Rays
7/26/98 • LE-15,000
Market Value: $95

Whisper™
Milwaukee Bucks
2/28/99 • LE-5,000
Market Value: N/E

SPORTS PROMOTION BEANIE BABIES®

	Price Paid	Value of My Collection
83.		
84.		
85.		
86.		
87.		
88.		
89.		
90.		
91.		
92.		
93.		
94.		
PENCIL TOTALS		

The Big Ones

This group of giant *Beanie* look-alikes keeps getting bigger. With five new releases for summer, there are now 28 *Beanie Buddies*. On April Fools' Day, "Fuzz" was revealed as the Mystery *Beanie Buddy*. Also among the new releases is "Princess," perhaps the most anticipated of them all!

1

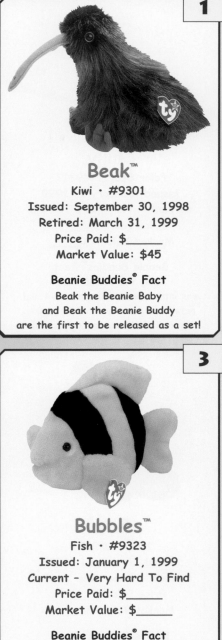

Beak™
Kiwi · #9301
Issued: September 30, 1998
Retired: March 31, 1999
Price Paid: $_____
Market Value: $45

Beanie Buddies® Fact
Beak the Beanie Baby
and Beak the Beanie Buddy
are the first to be released as a set!

2

Bongo™
Monkey · #9312
Issued: January 1, 1999
Current – Hard To Find
Price Paid: $_____
Market Value: $_____

Beanie Buddies® Fact
Bongo the Beanie Baby
was first named Nana.
Ty Warner liked the name Bongo better
because he plays the Bongos!

3

Bubbles™
Fish · #9323
Issued: January 1, 1999
Current – Very Hard To Find
Price Paid: $_____
Market Value: $_____

Beanie Buddies® Fact
Bubbles the Beanie Baby made
in the swimming position was
quite a challenge to manufacture.

4

Chilly™
Polar Bear · #9317
Issued: January 1, 1999
Current – Very Hard To Find
Price Paid: $_____
Market Value: $_____

Beanie Buddies® Fact
Chilly the Beanie Baby
was introduced in June of 1994 and
retired in January of 1996 making
him one of the most sought after!

5

Chip™
Cat · #9318
Issued: January 1, 1999
Current – Hard To Find
Price Paid: $_____
Market Value: $_____

Beanie Buddies® Fact
Chip the Beanie Baby
due to the variety of colors and pattern shapes,
is one of the most difficult to produce.
It takes over 20 pieces to make Chip!

6

Erin™
Bear · #9309
Issued: January 1, 1999
Current – Impossible To Find
Price Paid: $_____
Market Value: $_____

Beanie Buddies® Fact
Erin the Beanie Baby is the first bear to
represent a country but not wear the
country's flag!

7

NEW!

Fuzz™
Bear · #9328
Issued: April 1, 1999
Current – Just Released
Price Paid: $_____
Market Value: $_____

Beanie Buddies® Fact
Fuzz the Beanie Baby is made with Tylon®
that is crimped under extremely high
temprature.

Value
Totals _____

COLLECTOR'S
VALUE GUIDE™

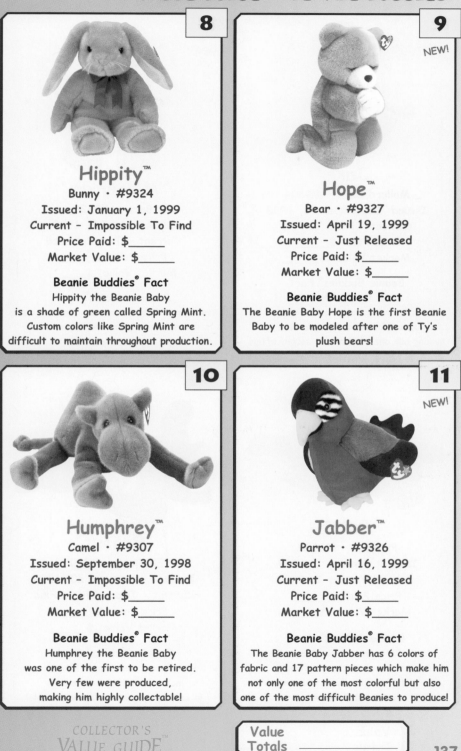

8

Hippity™
Bunny • #9324
Issued: January 1, 1999
Current – Impossible To Find
Price Paid: $_____
Market Value: $_____

Beanie Buddies® Fact
Hippity the Beanie Baby
is a shade of green called Spring Mint.
Custom colors like Spring Mint are
difficult to maintain throughout production.

9

NEW!

Hope™
Bear • #9327
Issued: April 19, 1999
Current – Just Released
Price Paid: $_____
Market Value: $_____

Beanie Buddies® Fact
The Beanie Baby Hope is the first Beanie
Baby to be modeled after one of Ty's
plush bears!

10

Humphrey™
Camel • #9307
Issued: September 30, 1998
Current – Impossible To Find
Price Paid: $_____
Market Value: $_____

Beanie Buddies® Fact
Humphrey the Beanie Baby
was one of the first to be retired.
Very few were produced,
making him highly collectable!

11

NEW!

Jabber™
Parrot • #9326
Issued: April 16, 1999
Current – Just Released
Price Paid: $_____
Market Value: $_____

Beanie Buddies® Fact
The Beanie Baby Jabber has 6 colors of
fabric and 17 pattern pieces which make him
not only one of the most colorful but also
one of the most difficult Beanies to produce!

12

Jake™
Mallard Duck · #9304
Issued: September 30, 1998
Current – Hard To Find
Price Paid: $_____
Market Value: $_____

Beanie Buddies® Fact
Jake the Beanie Baby
due to his numerous colors
was difficult to manufacture
making him one of the most sought after!

13

NEW!

Millennium™
Bear · #9325
Issued: April 9, 1999
Current – Just Released
Price Paid: $_____
Market Value: $_____

Beanie Buddies® Fact
The Beanie Baby Millennium commemorates
the new millennium and therefore is
highly collectible!

14

Patti™
Platypus · #9320
Issued: January 1, 1999
Current – Hard To Find
Price Paid: $_____
Market Value: $_____

Beanie Buddies® Fact
Patti the Beanie Baby
was one of the original nine.
Patti was available in both
maroon and magenta!

15

Peanut™
Elephant · #9300
Issued: September 30, 1998
Current – Impossible To Find
Price Paid: $_____
Market Value: $_____

Beanie Buddies® Fact
Peanut the Beanie Baby
made in this royal blue color
is extremely rare and very valuable!

Value
Totals _____

COLLECTOR'S
VALUE GUIDE™

16

Peking™
Panda • #9310
Issued: January 1, 1999
Current – Very Hard To Find
Price Paid: $_____
Market Value: $_____

Beanie Buddies® Fact
Peking the Beanie Baby
was the first Panda made by Ty.
He was retired after only six months
making him highly collectible!

17

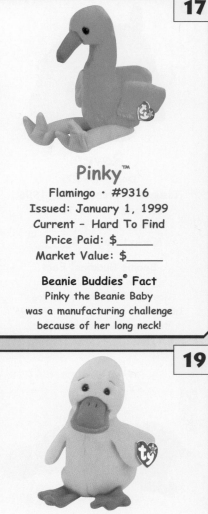

Pinky™
Flamingo • #9316
Issued: January 1, 1999
Current – Hard To Find
Price Paid: $_____
Market Value: $_____

Beanie Buddies® Fact
Pinky the Beanie Baby
was a manufacturing challenge
because of her long neck!

18

NEW!

Princess™
Bear • #9329
Issued: April 23, 1999
Current – Just Released
Price Paid: $_____
Market Value: $_____

Beanie Buddies® Fact
N/A

19

Quackers™
Duck • #9302
Issued: September 30, 1998
Current – Hard To Find
Price Paid: $_____
Market Value: $_____

Beanie Buddies® Fact
Quackers the Beanie Baby
retired in May 1998,
was once made without wings!

Value
Totals _____

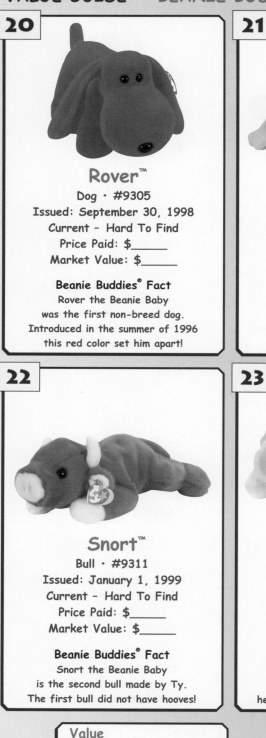

20

Rover™
Dog · #9305
Issued: September 30, 1998
Current – Hard To Find
Price Paid: $_____
Market Value: $_____

Beanie Buddies® Fact
Rover the Beanie Baby
was the first non-breed dog.
Introduced in the summer of 1996
this red color set him apart!

21

Smoochy™
Frog · #9315
Issued: January 1, 1999
Current – Hard To Find
Price Paid: $_____
Market Value: $_____

Beanie Buddies® Fact
Smoochy the Beanie Baby
is the second Beanie Baby frog
made by Ty!

22

Snort™
Bull · #9311
Issued: January 1, 1999
Current – Hard To Find
Price Paid: $_____
Market Value: $_____

Beanie Buddies® Fact
Snort the Beanie Baby
is the second bull made by Ty.
The first bull did not have hooves!

23

Squealer™
Pig · #9313
Issued: January 1, 1999
Current – Hard To Find
Price Paid: $_____
Market Value: $_____

Beanie Buddies® Fact
Squealer the Beanie Baby
was one of the original nine.
Squealer was so popular that
he didn't retire for over four years!

Value
Totals _____

COLLECTOR'S
VALUE GUIDE™

24

Stretch™
Ostrich · #9303
Issued: September 30, 1998
Current – Hard To Find
Price Paid: $_____
Market Value: $_____

Beanie Buddies® Fact
Stretch the Beanie Baby
is one of the most difficult to produce
due to her long neck and numerous parts!

25

Teddy™
Bear · #9306
Issued: September 30, 1998
Current – Impossible To Find
Price Paid: $_____
Market Value: $_____

Beanie Buddies® Fact
Teddy the Beanie Baby
was made in six colors.
A very limited number were produced
in this special cranberry color!

26

Tracker™
Basset Hound · #9319
Issued: January 1, 1999
Current – Hard To Find
Price Paid: $_____
Market Value: $_____

Beanie Buddies® Fact
Tracker the Beanie Baby
has the most expressive eyes.
Close attention to this detail
means limited production.

27

Twigs™
Giraffe · #9308
Issued: September 30, 1998
Retired: January 1, 1999
Price Paid: $_____
Market Value: $125

Beanie Buddies® Fact
Twigs the Beanie Baby
was manufactured in fabric
created exclusively for Ty
and was retired in May 1998!

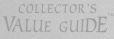

28

Waddle™

Penguin · #9314
Issued: January 1, 1999
Current – Hard To Find
Price Paid: $_____
Market Value: $_____

Beanie Buddies® Fact
Waddle the Beanie Baby
was the first of two penguins
to be made by Ty.
He was retired in April of 1998!

Value
Totals _____

COLLECTOR'S
VALUE GUIDE™

1

1997 Teenie Beanie Babies™ Complete Set (set/10)
Issued: April 11, 1997
Retired: May 15, 1997
Price Paid: $_____
Market Value: $165

2

1998 Teenie Beanie Babies™ Complete Set (set/12)
Issued: May 22, 1998
Retired: June 12, 1998
Price Paid: $_____
Market Value: $70

3

NEW!

1999 Teenie Beanie Babies™ Complete Set (set/12)
Issued: May 21, 1999
Retired: June 3, 1999
Price Paid: $_____
Market Value: N/E

4

NEW!

1999 Teenie Beanie Babies™ International Bears (set/4)
Issued: June 4, 1999
Retired: June 17, 1999
Price Paid: $_____
Market Value: N/E

5

NEW!

Antsy™
Anteater • 3rd Promotion
Issued: May 21, 1999
Retired: June 3, 1999
Price Paid: $_____
Market Value: N/E

6

Bones™
Dog • 2nd Promotion, #9 of 12
Issued: May 22, 1998
Retired: June 12, 1998
Price Paid: $_____
Market Value: $7

Value
Totals _____

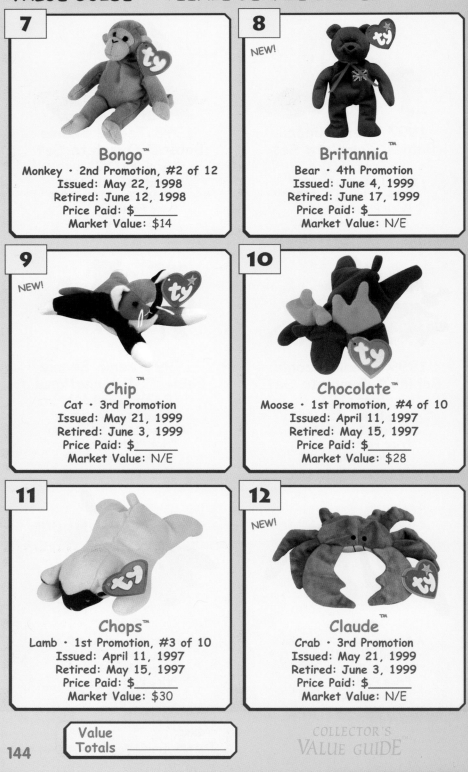

7

Bongo™
Monkey • 2nd Promotion, #2 of 12
Issued: May 22, 1998
Retired: June 12, 1998
Price Paid: $_____
Market Value: $14

8

NEW!

Britannia™
Bear • 4th Promotion
Issued: June 4, 1999
Retired: June 17, 1999
Price Paid: $_____
Market Value: N/E

9

NEW!

Chip™
Cat • 3rd Promotion
Issued: May 21, 1999
Retired: June 3, 1999
Price Paid: $_____
Market Value: N/E

10

Chocolate™
Moose • 1st Promotion, #4 of 10
Issued: April 11, 1997
Retired: May 15, 1997
Price Paid: $_____
Market Value: $28

11

Chops™
Lamb • 1st Promotion, #3 of 10
Issued: April 11, 1997
Retired: May 15, 1997
Price Paid: $_____
Market Value: $30

12

NEW!

Claude™
Crab • 3rd Promotion
Issued: May 21, 1999
Retired: June 3, 1999
Price Paid: $_____
Market Value: N/E

Value
Totals _____

COLLECTOR'S
VALUE GUIDE™

13

Doby™
Doberman • 2nd Promotion, #1 of 12
Issued: May 22, 1998
Retired: June 12, 1998
Price Paid: $_____
Market Value: $14

14

NEW!

Erin™
Bear • 4th Promotion
Issued: June 4, 1999
Retired: June 17, 1999
Price Paid: $_____
Market Value: N/E

15

NEW!

Freckles™
Leopard • 3rd Promotion
Issued: May 21, 1999
Retired: June 3, 1999
Price Paid: $_____
Market Value: N/E

16

NEW!

Glory™
Bear • 4th Promotion
Issued: June 4, 1999
Retired: June 17, 1999
Price Paid: $_____
Market Value: N/E

17

Goldie™
Goldfish • 1st Promotion, #5 of 10
Issued: April 11, 1997
Retired: May 15, 1997
Price Paid: $_____
Market Value: $23

18

Happy™
Hippo • 2nd Promotion, #6 of 12
Issued: May 22, 1998
Retired: June 12, 1998
Price Paid: $_____
Market Value: $7

COLLECTOR'S
VALUE GUIDE™

Value
Totals _____

19

NEW!

Iggy™
Iguana • 3rd Promotion
Issued: May 21, 1999
Retired: June 3, 1999
Price Paid: $_____
Market Value: N/E

20

Inch™
Inchworm • 2nd Promotion, #4 of 12
Issued: May 22, 1998
Retired: June 12, 1998
Price Paid: $_____
Market Value: $7

21

Lizz™
Lizard • 1st Promotion, #10 of 10
Issued: April 11, 1997
Retired: May 15, 1997
Price Paid: $_____
Market Value: $20

22

NEW!

Maple™
Bear • 4th Promotion
Issued: June 4, 1999
Retired: June 17, 1999
Price Paid: $_____
Market Value: N/E

23

Mel™
Koala • 2nd Promotion, #7 of 12
Issued: May 22, 1998
Retired: June 12, 1998
Price Paid: $_____
Market Value: $7

24

NEW!

'Nook™
Husky • 3rd Promotion
Issued: May 21, 1999
Retired: June 3, 1999
Price Paid: $_____
Market Value: N/E

Value
Totals _____

COLLECTOR'S
VALUE GUIDE™

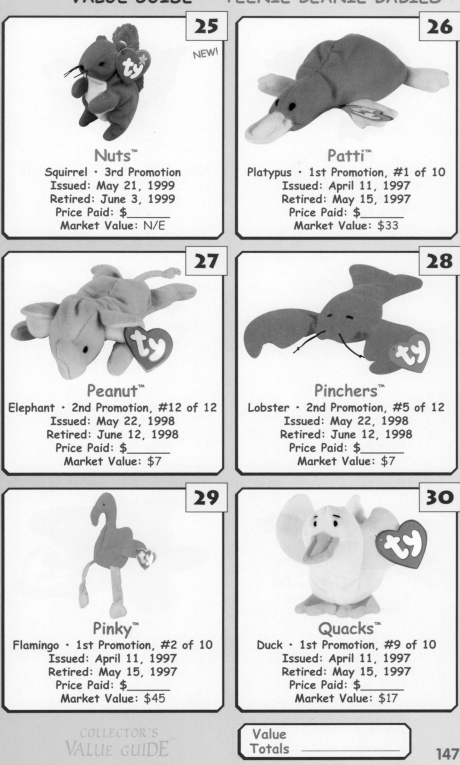

25 NEW!

Nuts™
Squirrel • 3rd Promotion
Issued: May 21, 1999
Retired: June 3, 1999
Price Paid: $_____
Market Value: N/E

26

Patti™
Platypus • 1st Promotion, #1 of 10
Issued: April 11, 1997
Retired: May 15, 1997
Price Paid: $_____
Market Value: $33

27

Peanut™
Elephant • 2nd Promotion, #12 of 12
Issued: May 22, 1998
Retired: June 12, 1998
Price Paid: $_____
Market Value: $7

28

Pinchers™
Lobster • 2nd Promotion, #5 of 12
Issued: May 22, 1998
Retired: June 12, 1998
Price Paid: $_____
Market Value: $7

29

Pinky™
Flamingo • 1st Promotion, #2 of 10
Issued: April 11, 1997
Retired: May 15, 1997
Price Paid: $_____
Market Value: $45

30

Quacks™
Duck • 1st Promotion, #9 of 10
Issued: April 11, 1997
Retired: May 15, 1997
Price Paid: $_____
Market Value: $17

31

NEW!

Rocket™
Blue Jay • 3rd Promotion
Issued: May 21, 1999
Retired: June 3, 1999
Price Paid: $_____
Market Value: N/E

32

Scoop™
Pelican • 2nd Promotion, #8 of 12
Issued: May 22, 1998
Retired: June 12, 1998
Price Paid: $_____
Market Value: $7

33

Seamore™
Seal • 1st Promotion, #7 of 10
Issued: April 11, 1997
Retired: May 15, 1997
Price Paid: $_____
Market Value: $26

34

NEW!

Smoochy™
Frog • 3rd Promotion
Issued: May 21, 1999
Retired: June 3, 1999
Price Paid: $_____
Market Value: N/E

35

Snort™
Bull • 1st Promotion, #8 of 10
Issued: April 11, 1997
Retired: May 15, 1997
Price Paid: $_____
Market Value: $15

36

Speedy™
Turtle • 1st Promotion, #6 of 10
Issued: April 11, 1997
Retired: May 15, 1997
Price Paid: $_____
Market Value: $22

Value
Totals _____

37

NEW!

Spunky™
Cocker Spaniel • 3rd Promotion
Issued: May 21, 1999
Retired: June 3, 1999
Price Paid: $_____
Market Value: N/E

38

NEW!

Stretchy™
Ostrich • 3rd Promotion
Issued: May 21, 1999
Retired: June 3, 1999
Price Paid: $_____
Market Value: N/E

39

NEW!

Strut™
Rooster • 3rd Promotion
Issued: May 21, 1999
Retired: June 3, 1999
Price Paid: $_____
Market Value: N/E

40

Twigs™
Giraffe • 2nd Promotion, #3 of 12
Issued: May 22, 1998
Retired: June 12, 1998
Price Paid: $_____
Market Value: $13

41

Waddle™
Penguin • 2nd Promotion, #11 of 12
Issued: May 22, 1998
Retired: June 12, 1998
Price Paid: $_____
Market Value: $7

42

Zip™
Cat • 2nd Promotion, #10 of 12
Issued: May 22, 1998
Retired: June 12, 1998
Price Paid: $_____
Market Value: $8

COLLECTOR'S
VALUE GUIDE™

Value
Totals _____

TOTAL VALUE OF MY COLLECTION

BEANIE BABIES® VALUE TOTALS	BEANIE BABIES® VALUE TOTALS	BEANIE BABIES® VALUE TOTALS
Page 27	Page 50	Page 73
Page 28	Page 51	Page 74
Page 29	Page 52	Page 75
Page 30	Page 53	Page 76
Page 31	Page 54	Page 77
Page 32	Page 55	Page 78
Page 33	Page 56	Page 79
Page 34	Page 57	Page 80
Page 35	Page 58	Page 81
Page 36	Page 59	Page 82
Page 37	Page 60	Page 83
Page 38	Page 61	Page 84
Page 39	Page 62	Page 85
Page 40	Page 63	Page 86
Page 41	Page 64	Page 87
Page 42	Page 65	Page 88
Page 43	Page 66	Page 89
Page 44	Page 67	Page 90
Page 45	Page 68	Page 91
Page 46	Page 69	Page 92
Page 47	Page 70	Page 93
Page 48	Page 71	Page 94
Page 49	Page 72	Page 95
Subtotal	Subtotal	Subtotal

Page Totals _____

COLLECTOR'S
VALUE GUIDE™

BEANIE BABIES® *Value Totals*	BEANIE BABIES® *Value Totals*	BEANIE BUDDIES® *Value Totals*
Page 96	Page 119	Page 135
Page 97	Page 120	Page 136
Page 98	Page 121	Page 137
Page 99	Page 122	Page 138
Page 100	Page 123	Page 139
Page 101	Page 124	Page 140
Page 102	Page 125	Page 141
Page 103	Page 126	Page 142
Page 104	Page 127	
Page 105	Page 128	Subtotal
Page 106	Page 129	TEENIE BEANIE BABIES™ *Value Totals*
Page 107	Page 130	
Page 108		Page 143
Page 109	Subtotal	Page 144
Page 110	SPORTS PROMOTION BEANIE BABIES® *Value Totals*	Page 145
Page 111		Page 146
Page 112		Page 147
Page 113	Page 131	Page 148
Page 114	Page 132	Page 149
Page 115	Page 133	
Page 116	Page 134	
Page 117		
Page 118		
Subtotal	Subtotal	Subtotal

COLLECTOR'S VALUE GUIDE™

GRAND TOTAL _____

*I*t didn't take long for the *Beanie Babies* craze to catch on. Since their introduction in 1994, the now famous under-stuffed plush animals have become the hottest items on the collectibles landscape. Not only do children love to collect them, but adults are known to search high and low for their favorites. *Beanie Babies* seem to be everywhere and nowhere at the same time. They can be found (in limited supply) at a wide variety of gift shops, boutiques, candy stores, airport shops and more, but if you're looking for a rare or retired *Beanie*, your best best is the secondary market.

The secondary market is created when pieces become difficult to find. This may occur for a number of reasons. First, stores often have trouble keeping enough stock to meet the desires of their customers and availability of particular pieces may run low. Therefore, collectors often choose to pay inflated prices for a *Beanie Baby* that may eventually turn up at their local store at issue price. And as with most collectible lines, the retirement of a *Beanie Baby* creates demand as collectors scramble to purchase the remaining stock through retail stores. Once the supply is depleted, these pieces become highly sought after on the secondary market.

The secondary market can be found in several different places. For *Beanie Babies*, the most popular is the Internet. Once you're on-line, you can find everything from bulletin boards that list pieces for sale, to auction sites where you can bid on *Beanie*s. With Internet access, you can literally search the world for the *Beanie Babies* you want, but always remember to exercise caution when making transactions on the web.

More and more, advertisements for *Beanie Babies* are showing up in the classified sections of newspapers. Sometimes they are listed in the collectibles section, other times in their very own section. Also, most collecting magazines feature classified ads in the back section.

While most retailers are not active in the secondary market, they are a great resource. Your local retailer may be able to connect you with other collectors who are buying or selling pieces. Your retailer may also be able to direct you to trade shows (local and national) and swap & sells (which they may actually sponsor).

If you plan to buy your *Beanie Babies* on the secondary market, be sure you know what to look for. In the *Beanie Babies* world, the condition of the piece (and its swing and tush tags) plays a big role in the animal's value. Some *Beanie* lovers don't mind wear and tear, but to most, a perfect, or "mint" piece is extremely important. Expect the secondary market value for a *Beanie* in poor condition or without a tag to significantly drop. The value can also be affected by the generation of tag the animal wears (*see Ty® Swing Tags And Tush Tags on page 20*).

Another element that drives up the values of *Beanie Babies* are variations (*see Variations on page 156*). Valuable variations that affect the secondary market price include physical or color changes and printed mistakes. "Happy" the hippo, for instance, originally featured a gray body, but the fabric was later changed to lavender. When collectors realized the first version was no longer available, the gray hippo became a hot commodity on the secondary market.

So while discovering a variation or finding a retired piece can be really exciting, it is nearly impossible to know which ones will actually command a high value on the secondary market. So allow this search to be fun, but try not to allow it to become the center of your collecting universe.

BEANIE BABIES® AND THE INTERNET

The Internet

If you need any proof of the success of Ty Warner's *Beanie Babies*, look no further than your own computer. On any given day, collectors can find hundreds of thousands of web sites featuring the plush critters. Though Ty Inc. started its own web site, *www.ty.com*, in 1996, collectors have found that one site simply isn't enough to satisfy their cravings for *Beanie Babies* information.

If you're looking for first-hand information and pictures though, your first on-line stop should be *www.ty.com*. There, you'll find official information on all your favorite Ty collectibles. There's also a monthly diary by the "Info Beanie" where *Beanie Babies* characters come alive through reports of their daily activities (and every so often they divulge clues about the goings-on in the world of Ty). Members of the Beanie Babies Official Club have further access to privileged on-line information when they type in their membership number. Whether a club member or not, with one click of the mouse, savvy web surfers can be way ahead of the collecting game.

For those collectors who have decided to skip the crowds and craze of actual stores, the Internet offers convenient shopping and on-line auctions. Plug in a number and a few hours later you may be the proud new owner of an elusive retired or newly released piece One popular auction site is *www.ebay.com* (known as "eBay"). Talk-show host Rosie O'Donnell chose to use this location when she auctioned off a number of *Beanie Babies* donated by Ty Inc. With traffic on the Internet and the demand for *Beanie Babies* at an all-time high, there are a wealth of options open to you.

While there are numerous benefits to on-line *Beanie Babies* browsing, Internet users should always use caution. This is easy if you just exercise patience. Become well acquainted with the site that you are using and only use secure sites for on-line transactions. Also, be sure to thoroughly check a site's references to ensure they are reputable. When you do find an on-line site you trust, exercise good collectible judgement. Also, always be sure to set a limit and stick to it, whether purchasing one *Beanie* or an entire collection. And if you're feeling overwhelmed by it all, there are plenty of on-line chat rooms for those collectors who are looking for friends in the collecting community. For some, browsing the Internet in search of Ty collectibles has become a full-time hobby.

Internet resources for *Beanie Babies* are sprouting up all over the place and they can add many dimensions to the enjoyment of collecting. If you can't find exactly what you're looking for on-line, though, have some fun and create your own site. It's a great chance to showcase your favorite *Beanie Babies* and make some new friends as well.

THE HOTTEST SITE AROUND!

www.collectorbee.com

Be sure to check out all of the latest news about Ty's *Beanie Babies* on our web site, www.collectorbee.com.

You'll find the most updated information about new releases, retirements and the latest scoop on not just all your favorite Ty lines, but the rest of the collectibles industry as well.

Variations

$\mathcal{S}$ ince their introduction in 1994, *Beanie Babies* have grown to enormous heights in the collecting world. Whether your collection consists of every *Beanie* or just a few, it's possible there could be some variations among them. The noted variations on the secondary market are those that have significant differences such as changes to name, color or material, or mistakes made in the factory such as incorrect tags.

NAME CHANGES

The Beanie Babies Collection
Brownie ™ style 4010
© 1993 Ty Inc. Oakbrook, IL. USA
All Rights Reserved. Caution:
Remove this tag before giving
toy to a child. For ages 5 and up.
Handmade in Korea.
Surface
Wash.

The Beanie Babies Collection
Cubbie ™ style 4010
© 1993 Ty Inc. Oakbrook, IL. USA
All Rights Reserved. Caution:
Remove this tag before giving
toy to a child. For ages 5 and up.
Handmade in Korea.
Surface
Wash.

Brownie™/Cubbie™: You'd think "Brownie" would be the perfect name for this little bear but soon after his release in 1994, he decided "Cubbie" was more catchy.

Creepy™/Spinner™: This spider liked scaring people more than spinning webs, so he took it upon himself to change the name on his tush tag to "Creepy." But the ploy to re-name himself didn't last long and his tag was corrected to read "Spinner."

The Beanie Babies Collection
★ **ty** ®
Creepy ™
HAND MADE IN CHINA
© 1996 TY INC.
OAKBROOK IL, U.S.A.
SURFACE WASHABLE
ALL NEW MATERIAL
POLYESTER FIBER
& P.V.C. PELLETS (CE)
REG. NO PA. 1965(KR)

The Beanie Babies Collection
★ **ty** ®
Spinner ™
HAND MADE IN CHINA
© 1996 TY INC.
OAKBROOK IL, U.S.A.
SURFACE WASHABLE
ALL NEW MATERIAL
POLYESTER FIBER
& P.V.C. PELLETS (CE)
REG. NO PA. 1965(KR)

Doodle™/Strut™: Singing "Cock-A-'Doodle'-Doo" was all this rooster did when he was first released . . . that is until the day he started strutting around the barnyard. That's when his friends at Ty decided to change his name to "Strut" to fit his new personality.

Doodle ™ style 4171
DATE OF BIRTH : 3 - 8 - 96
Listen closely to "cock-a-doodle-doo"
What's the rooster saying to you?
Hurry, wake up sleepy head
We have lots to do, get out of bed!
Visit our web page!
http://www.ty.com

Strut ™ style 4171
DATE OF BIRTH : 3 - 8 - 96
Listen closely to "cock-a-doodle-doo"
What's the rooster saying to you?
Hurry, wake up sleepy head
We have lots to do, get out of bed!
Visit our web page!!!
http://www.ty.com

Millenium™/Millennium™:

This bear almost entered the next century with a spelling error in his name that collectors caught on to immediately! Both tags had only one "n" in the name but the spelling was quickly corrected on the tush tag and finally on the swing tag.

Millenium™
DATE OF BIRTH: January 1, 1999
A brand new century has come to call
Health and happiness to one and all
Bring on the fireworks and all the fun
Let's keep the party going 'til 2001 !
www.ty.com

Millennium™
OF BIRTH: January 1, 1999
A brand new century has come to call
Health and happiness to one and all
Bring on the fireworks and all the fun
's keep the party going 'til 2001 !
www.ty.com

Nana™/Bongo™:

"Nana" was just monkeying around when he asked Ty to change his name to "Bongo." But much to his surprise, the new name was well-liked and "Bongo" it was!

Nana ™ style 4067
to _____
from _____
with
love

Bongo ™ style 4067
to _____
from _____
with
love

Pride™/Maple™:

The "Pride" version of this Canadian bear was a mistake. The name "Pride" was changed to "Maple" before his release in 1997 but some "Pride" tags made it onto some of the bears anyway, making those an extremely rare find.

The
Beanie Babies
Collection™

ty®

Pride
HAND MADE IN CHINA
© 1996 TY INC.
OAKBROOK IL, U.S.A.
SURFACE WASHABLE
ALL NEW MATERIAL
POLYESTER FIBER
& P.V.C. PELLETS CE
REG. NO PA. 1965(KR)

The
Beanie Babies
Collection™

★ ty®

Maple
HAND MADE IN CHINA
© 1996 TY INC.
OAKBROOK IL, U.S.A.
SURFACE WASHABLE
ALL NEW MATERIAL
POLYESTER FIBER
& P.V.C. PELLETS CE
REG. NO PA. 1965(KR)

Punchers™/Pinchers™:

This bright red lobster got his claws on the wrong name for a brief time. Some "Pinchers" were caught with the name "Punchers" on their swing tags. The mistake was corrected though before the next batch of lobsters were released.

The Beanie Babies Collection
Punchers ™ style 4026
© 1993 Ty Inc. Oakbrook, IL. USA
All Rights Reserved. Caution:
Remove this tag before giving
toy to a child. For ages 5 and up.
Handmade in Korea.
Surface
Wash.

The Beanie Babies Collection
Pinchers ™ style 4026
© 1993 Ty Inc. Oakbrook, IL. USA
All Rights Reserved. Caution:
Remove this tag before giving
toy to a child. For ages 5 and up.
Handmade in Korea.
Surface
Wash.

Spook™/Spooky™: Actually, this little ghost isn't spooky at all; in fact, when "Spooky" first began appearing in stores, his swing tag said "Spook." A spell was cast shortly after and the incorrect "Spook" tags disappeared.

Spook ™ style 4090

to _____
from _____
with
love

Spooky™ style 4090
DATE OF BIRTH : 10 - 31 - 95

Ghosts can be a scary sight
But don't let Spooky bring you any fright
Because when you're alone, you will see
The best friend that Spooky can be!

Visit our web page!!!
http://www.ty.com

Tuck™/Tusk™: As if having tusks didn't catch enough attention, this little walrus has been known to feature two different spellings on his swing tags. Most tags read "Tusk" (the correct version), while others appears as "Tuck."

Tuck™ style 4076
DATE OF BIRTH : 9 -18 -95

Tusk brushes his teeth everyday
To keep them shiny, it's the only way
Teeth are special, so you must try
And they will sparkle when
You say "Hi"!

Visit our web page!!!
http://www.ty.com

Tusk™ style 4076
DATE OF BIRTH : 9 -18 -95

Tusk brushes his teeth everyday
To keep them shiny, it's the only way
Teeth are special, so you must try
And they will sparkle when
You say "Hi"!

Visit our web page!!!
http://www.ty.com

COLOR CHANGES

Batty™: This guy is a bit "Batty" indeed. Just before he retired in March 1999, he decided to be more like his ocean-dwelling friend, "Claude," and change his look to tie-dye.

Digger™: "Digger" decided soon after her release that she looked much better in red. So, in the summer of 1995, she changed her color from the original orange to bright red.

Happy™: The gray color of this *Beanie* did not go with its name, so shortly after his release in 1994, his color was changed to a much happier lavender.

Inky™: "Inky" was so unhappy with his tan color that he actually had no smile. But one day, he found his smile and he became so happy that he turned a bright shade of pink.

Lizzy™: When "Lizzy" heard her friend "Claude" was coming to town soon, she knew the two would look the same in their tie-dyed outfits. That's when "Lizzy" decided to become blue with black spots.

Patti™: "Patti" thought she would be noticed more if she were a brighter color. She was very satisfied when her original darker maroon color became magenta . . . and hard to miss!

Peanut™: With most elephants, it's their trunk that's the attention-getter. But not with this one! Collecting turned into a circus when "Peanut" escaped from the factory with royal blue material, instead of the planned light blue.

DESIGN CHANGES

Bongo™: Along with a name change, this curious monkey decided to change his tail color, too! So, "Nana" not only became "Bongo," but his tail went from brown to tan.

D e r b y ™ : "Derby" has experienced many "laps around the track!" First he had a fine mane, then a coarse mane, then he added a star to his forehead. Now, the latest version has a fluffy mane.

Iggy™: Collectors became quite confused over this creature. He was first introduced with rainbow fabric. He then began appearing with a tongue. Finally, his fabric was corrected to the dark blue that used to clothe "Rainbow."

Inch™: This colorful inchworm's antennas underwent a fabric change from felt to yarn.

Lucky™: Luck may not be one of the things this ladybug had, but spots sure were! When she was introduced, she only had seven spots that were glued onto her shell. Later, the spots were printed on her fabric and she went from having 21 to only having 11.

Magic™: In the land of magic, everything is noticed, even a minor thread change on "Magic." The color went from pale pink to hot pink, then back to pale pink.

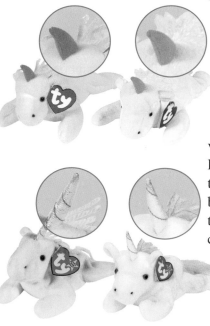

Mystic™: "Mystic" noticed all the fun her horse friend "Derby" was having, so she decided to join him with multiple variations. She originally had a fine mane and a tan horn. Her mane then became coarse. She then turned her horn iridescent and finally fluffed her mane a little bit.

VARIATIONS

Nip™ and Zip™: These two cats decided it would be fun to play the variation game together. When they were first introduced, their faces and bellies were white, then they changed to solid tan ("Nip") and black ("Zip"). Finally they put on white boots with which they used to walk into retirement.

Quackers™: Although ducks can't fly without wings, "Quackers" thought he was different. When he was first hatched he was wingless, but that changed just a few months later.

Rainbow™: The dark blue color of this *Beanie* didn't match up with his name when he was first released, causing collectors to confuse him with "Iggy" who was at that time, rainbow colored. Finally the confusion ended when "Rainbow" was given his tie-dyed color and a tongue!

Sly™: Perhaps this is where "sly as a fox" comes from, because this *Beanie Baby* knew how to get attention. Soon after his release, he changed his solid-colored tan belly to white, making him two-toned!

Spot™: Believe it or not, "Spot" was first released with no spots! After feeling a bit silly because of what his name implied, he added a big spot right on his back.

Stripes™: This little tiger was a darker orange with plenty of black stripes when he was first released. But over time, his fur became fuzzy, he lost some stripes, and his color turned much brighter.

Tank™: "Tank" was first produced with seven "plates" on his back, but no shell. Then he added two plates, forgetting the shell, again. Finally, with help of a little stitching, his shell was added.

Teddy™: These teddy bears (in six different colors) came together and took on a whole new look. They were first introduced with a pointed nose and eyes that were far apart. But soon they were given a "new face" which featured lower noses and closer eyes.

Princess™: "Princess" can be found with the two different pellet types listed on her tush tag: "P.V.C" and "P.E." The more coveted style in the secondary market is the one with the "P.V.C." pellets.

The Beanie Babies Collection®
★ ty ®
Princess™
HANDMADE IN CHINA
© 1997 TY INC.,
OAKBROOK, IL. U.S.A.
SURFACE WASHABLE
ALL NEW MATERIAL
ESTER FIBER
V.C. PELLETS CE
REG. NO PA. 1965(KR)

The Beanie Babies Collection®
★ ty ®
Princess™
HANDMADE IN CHINA
© 1997 TY INC.,
OAKBROOK, IL. U.S.A.
SURFACE WASHABLE
ALL NEW MATERIAL
POLYESTER FIBER
& P.E. PELLETS CE
REG. NO PA. 1965(KR)

Counterfeit Alert!

COUNTERFEIT

*W*ould you be able to tell a fake *Beanie Baby* from an authentic one? Most counterfeits look so much like the real thing it is sometimes impossible for the unsuspecting collector to tell the difference. But with a little bit of knowledge and common sense, the hunt for your favorite *Beanie Babies* can be worry-free!

Counterfeit *Beanie Babies* began showing up in 1996, just as the craze for the understuffed toys began to heat up. At first, it was relatively easy to tell the difference, but as *Beanie Babies* became more popular, fakes became more sophisticated. So how can you tell if you have a counterfeit animal? Here are some common problems to look for:

Tags – Swing tags are a good place to start. On the outside of a counterfeit, the gold trim is rarely even around the entire tag and often has an orange tint. It may also look like foil.

COUNTERFEIT

The writing in the star also tends to run out of the bounds of the graphic. On the inside of the tag, you'll often find the red coloring from the front has bled through and the black type is smeared. There are often extra spaces, and trademarks and registration marks are sometimes missing or in the wrong place. There are also some easy to overlook things such as no umlaut over the "u" on the word "Nürnberg."

COUNTERFEIT

Billionaire™
HANDMADE IN CHINA

As for tush tags, many times they are wider than the real ones and have blurry or runny type. Also, many are not even the correct generation. "Billionaire's" tush tag should be the sixth version but, on some fakes, it resembles a seventh version tag. It doesn't stop there – the makeshift hologram is often actually just a gray-colored square.

Poor Quality – Most counterfeits are made poorly. Look for imperfections in the stitching, eyes that are too far apart or too close together, ears and noses that are square instead of round or even fur that is too long or shiny. In a detailed piece such as "Glory," the fake is easy to spot. On some, the stars are painted on (you can feel them) and can flake, the flag has white stitching rather than transparent and there is a red ribbon and a blue ribbon around the neck. Most *Beanies* also have a seam down their backs. If there are two colors of material at a seam, make sure they are even. One "Peking" imposter does not have a matching seam.

COUNTERFEIT

AUTHENTIC

Wrong Colors – Wrong colors can often slip by. Sometimes specific areas are the wrong color like a nose that is brown when it should be black (or vice versa). In some instances, the entire *Beanie* is the wrong color. Collectors are finding "Billionaire" with

COUNTERFEIT   AUTHENTIC   a solid brown fur, rather than speckled fur like "Kicks." The dollar sign can also be wrong – it's usually a mint green rather than the actual dark green. The light blue version of "Peanut" the elephant may show up as turquoise, with bright pink ears and a white belly, where the real "Peanut" is solid baby blue and has very pastel pink ears.

Extra Accessories – Since some of the *Beanie Babies* have ribbons, you should familiarize yourself with which ones do. Many "Glory" and "Erin" look-alikes do have ribbons, while the real ones should not.

Keep in mind, making yourself better aware of what to look for will help you collect the real thing!

COUNTERFEIT   AUTHENTIC

Beanie Babies® Aren't The Only Counterfeits!

It's been discovered that fake Ty® Beanie Babies® trading cards are also being passed off as real.

One of the more common reproductions is of the special (and extremely rare) cards with Ty Warner's signature on them. While the real signature is in gold ink, like that of a paint pen, the fakes are written in plain black ink.

If it's the cards you're after, you should make sure they're real, too!

JANUARY

Jan. 1, 1999 - Millennium™
Jan. 2, 1998 - Zero™
Jan. 3, 1993 - Spot™
Jan. 5, 1997 - KuKu™
Jan. 6, 1993 - Patti™
Jan. 8, 1999 - Tiptoe™
Jan. 13, 1996 - Crunch™
Jan. 14, 1997 - Spunky™

Jan. 15, 1996 - Mel™
Jan. 17, 1998 - Slippery™
Jan. 18, 1994 - Bones™
Jan. 21, 1996 - Nuts™
Jan. 23, 1999 - Schweetheart™
Jan. 25, 1995 - Peanut™
Jan. 26, 1996 - Chip™

FEBRUARY

Feb. 1, 1996 - Peace™
Feb. 3, 1998 - Beak™
Feb. 4, 1997 - Fetch™
Feb. 5, 1999 - Osito™
Feb. 11, 1999 - Silver™
Feb. 13, 1995 - Pinky™
Feb. 13, 1995 - Stinky™
Feb. 14, 1994 - Valentino™
Feb. 14, 1998 - Valentina™

Feb. 17, 1996 - Baldy™
Feb. 19, 1998 - Prickles™
Feb. 20, 1996 - Roary™
Feb. 20, 1997 - Early™
Feb. 21, 1999 - Amber™
Feb. 22, 1995 - Tank™
Feb. 23, 1999 - Paul™
Feb. 25, 1994 - Happy™
Feb. 27, 1996 - Sparky™
Feb. 28, 1995 - Flip™

MARCH

March 1, 1998 - Ewey™
March 2, 1995 - Coral™
March 6, 1994 - Nip™
March 8, 1996 - Doodle™
March 8, 1996 - Strut™
March 9, 1999 - Clubby II™
March 10, 1999 - Swirly™
March 12, 1997 - Rocket™
March 14, 1994 - Ally™

March 17, 1997 - Erin™
March 19, 1996 - Seaweed™
March 20, 1997 - Early™
March 21, 1996 - Fleece™
March 23, 1998 - Hope™
March 25, 1999 - Knuckles™
March 28, 1994 - Zip™
March 29, 1998 - Loosy™

APRIL

April 1, 1999 - Neon™

April 3, 1996 - Hoppity™

April 4, 1997 - Hissy™

April 5, 1997 - Whisper™

April 6, 1998 - Nibbler™

April 7, 1997 - GiGi™

April 10, 1998 - Eggbert™

April 12, 1996 - Curly™

April 14, 1999 - Almond™

April 15, 1999 - Pecan™

April 16, 1997 - Jake™

April 18, 1995 - Ears™

April 19, 1994 - Quackers™

April 23, 1993 - Squealer™

April 25, 1993 - Legs™

April 27, 1993 - Chocolate™

April 28, 1999 - Eucalyptus™

MAY

May 1, 1995 - Lucky™

May 1, 1996 - Wrinkles™

May 2, 1996 - Pugsly™

May 3, 1996 - Chops™

May 4, 1998 - Hippie™

May 7, 1998 - Nibbly™

May 10, 1994 - Daisy™

May 10, 1999 - Cheeks™

May 11, 1995 - Lizzy™

May 13, 1993 - Flash™

May 15, 1995 - Snort™

May 15, 1995 - Tabasco™

May 19, 1995 - Twigs™

May 21, 1994 - Mystic™

May 27, 1998 - Scat™

May 28, 1996 - Floppity™

May 29, 1998 - Canyon™

May 30, 1996 - Rover™

May 31, 1997 - Wise™

JUNE

June 1, 1996 - Hippity™

June 3, 1996 - Freckles™

June 3, 1996 - Scottie™

June 4, 1999 - Wiser™

June 5, 1997 - Tracker™

June 8, 1995 - Bucky™

June 8, 1995 - Manny™

June 10, 1998 - Mac™

June 11, 1995 - Stripes™

June 14, 1999 - Spangle™

June 15, 1996 - Scottie™

June 15, 1998 - Luke™

June 16, 1998 - Stilts™

June 17, 1996 - Gracie™

June 19, 1993 - Pinchers™

June 23, 1998 - Sammy™

June 27, 1995 - Bessie™

JULY

July 1, 1996 - Maple™
July 1, 1996 - Scoop™
July 2, 1995 - Bubbles™
July 4, 1996 - Lefty™
July 4, 1996 - Righty™
July 4, 1997 - Glory™
July 7, 1998 - Clubby™

July 8, 1993 - Splash™
July 14, 1995 - Ringo™
July 15, 1994 - Blackie™
July 19, 1995 - Grunt™
July 20, 1995 - Weenie™
July 23, 1998 - Fuzz™
July 28, 1996 - Freckles™
July 31, 1998 - Scorch™

AUGUST

Aug. 1, 1995 - Garcia™
Aug. 1, 1998 - Mooch™
Aug. 9, 1995 - Hoot™
Aug. 12, 1997 - Iggy™
Aug. 13, 1996 - Spike™
Aug. 14, 1994 - Speedy™

Aug. 16, 1998 - Kicks™
Aug. 17, 1995 - Bongo™
Aug. 23, 1995 - Digger™
Aug. 27, 1995 - Sting™
Aug. 28, 1997 - Pounce™
Aug. 31, 1998 - Halo™

SEPTEMBER

Sept. 3, 1995 - Inch™
Sept. 3, 1996 - Claude™
Sept. 5, 1995 - Magic™
Sept. 8, 1998 - Tiny™
Sept. 9, 1997 - Bruno™
Sept. 12, 1996 - Sly™

Sept. 16, 1995 - Derby™
Sept. 16, 1995 - Kiwi™
Sept. 18, 1995 - Tusk™
Sept. 21, 1997 - Stretch™
Sept. 27, 1998 - Roam™
Sept. 29, 1997 - Stinger™

OCTOBER

Oct. 1, 1997 - Smoochy™	Oct. 16, 1995 - Bumble™
Oct. 2, 1998 - Butch™	Oct. 17, 1996 - Dotty™
Oct. 3, 1996 - Bernie™	Oct. 22, 1996 - Snip™
Oct. 3, 1990 - Germania™	Oct. 28, 1996 - Spinner™
Oct. 9, 1996 - Doby™	Oct. 29,1996 - Batty™
Oct. 10, 1997 - Jabber™	Oct. 30, 1995 - Radar™
Oct. 12, 1996 - Tuffy™	Oct. 31, 1995 - Spooky™

NOVEMBER

Nov. 3, 1997 - Puffer™	Nov. 14, 1994 - Goldie™
Nov. 4, 1998 - Goatee™	Nov. 18, 1998 - Goochy™
Nov. 6, 1996 - Pouch™	Nov. 20, 1997 - Prance™
Nov. 7, 1997 - Ants™	Nov. 21, 1996 - Nanook™
Nov. 9, 1996 - Congo™	Nov. 27, 1996 - Gobbles™
Nov. 14, 1993 - Cubbie™	Nov. 28, 1995 - Teddy™ (br.)
	Nov. 29, 1994 - Inky™

DECEMBER

Dec. 2, 1996 - Jolly™	Dec. 16, 1995 - Velvet™
Dec. 6, 1997 - Fortune™	Dec. 19, 1995 - Waddle™
Dec. 6, 1998 - Santa™	Dec. 21, 1996 - Echo™
Dec. 8, 1996 - Waves™	Dec. 22, 1996 - Snowball™
Dec. 12, 1996 - Blizzard™	Dec. 24, 1995 - Ziggy™
Dec. 14, 1996 - Seamore™	Dec. 25, 1996 - 1997 Teddy™
Dec. 15, 1997 - Britannia™	Dec. 25, 1998 - 1998 Teddy™

COLLECTOR'S CHECKLIST

On this handy list, you can check off which Beanie Babies are in your collection. You can also circle the numbered heart that corresponds with the tag that your Beanie Baby is wearing. Current pieces are listed first, followed by retired pieces, and each variation is listed separately.

Current Beanie Babies®

- ❑ 1999 Signature Bear™ . ⑤
- ❑ Almond™ . . . . ⑤
- ❑ Amber™ . . . . ⑤
- ❑ Beak™ . . . . ⑤
- ❑ Britannia™ . . . . ⑤
- ❑ Butch™ . . . . ⑤
- ❑ Canyon™ . . . . ⑤
- ❑ Cheeks™ . . . . ⑤
- ❑ Clubby II™ . . . . ⑤
- ❑ Derby™
  (star/fluffy mane) . . . ⑤
- ❑ Early™ . . . . ⑤
- ❑ Eggbert™ . . . . ⑤
- ❑ Erin™ . . . . ⑤
- ❑ Eucalyptus™ . . . . ⑤
- ❑ Ewey™ . . . . ⑤
- ❑ Fortune™ . . . . ⑤
- ❑ Fuzz™ . . . . ⑤
- ❑ Germania™ . . . . ⑤
- ❑ GiGi™ . . . . ⑤
- ❑ Goatee™ . . . . ⑤
- ❑ Goochy™ . . . . ⑤
- ❑ Halo™ . . . . ⑤
- ❑ Hippie™ . . . . ⑤
- ❑ Hissy™ . . . . ⑤

- ❑ Hope™ . . . . ⑤
- ❑ Jabber™ . . . . ⑤
- ❑ Jake™ . . . . ⑤
- ❑ Kicks™ . . . . ⑤
- ❑ Knuckles™ . . . . ⑤
- ❑ KuKu™ . . . . ⑤
- ❑ Loosy™ . . . . ⑤
- ❑ Luke™ . . . . ⑤
- ❑ Mac™ . . . . ⑤
- ❑ Maple™ ("Maple™"
  tush tag) . . . . ④ ⑤
- ❑ Millennium™
  ("Millennium™" on
  both tags) . . . . ⑤
- ❑ Mooch™ . . . . ⑤
- ❑ Mystic™ (iridescent
  horn/fluffy mane) . . . . ⑤
- ❑ Neon™ . . . . ⑤
- ❑ Nibbler™ . . . . ⑤
- ❑ Nibbly™ . . . . ⑤
- ❑ Osito™ . . . . ⑤
- ❑ Paul™ . . . . ⑤
- ❑ Peace™ . . . . ④ ⑤
- ❑ Pecan™ . . . . ⑤
- ❑ Prickles™ . . . . ⑤
- ❑ Roam™ . . . . ⑤
- ❑ Rocket™ . . . . ⑤
- ❑ Sammy™ . . . . ⑤
- ❑ Scat™ . . . . ⑤
- ❑ Schweetheart™ . . . . . . ⑤
- ❑ Scorch™ . . . . ⑤
- ❑ Silver™ . . . . ⑤
- ❑ Slippery™ . . . . ⑤
- ❑ Spangle™ . . . . ⑤
- ❑ Stilts™ . . . . ⑤
- ❑ Swirly™ . . . . ⑤
- ❑ Tiny™ . . . . ⑤
- ❑ Tiptoe™ . . . . ⑤
- ❑ Tracker™ . . . . ⑤

- ❑ Valentina™ . . . . ⑤
- ❑ Whisper™ . . . . ⑤
- ❑ Wiser™ . . . . ⑤

Retired Beanie Babies®

- ❑ #1 Bear™ . . . . **Special Tag**
- ❑ 1997 Teddy™ . . . . ④
- ❑ 1998 Holiday Teddy™ . ⑤
- ❑ Ally™ . . . . ❶ ❷ ❸ ④
- ❑ Ants™ . . . . ⑤
- ❑ Baldy™ . . . . ④ ⑤
- ❑ Batty™ (brown) . . . . ④ ⑤
- ❑ Batty™ (tie-dye) . . . . . . ⑤
- ❑ Bernie™ . . . . ④ ⑤
- ❑ Bessie™ . . . . ❸ ④
- ❑ Billionaire
  Bear™ . . . . **Special Tag**
- ❑ Blackie™ . . ❶ ❷ ❸ ④ ⑤
- ❑ Blizzard™ . . . . ④ ⑤
- ❑ Bones™ . . . ❶ ❷ ❸ ④ ⑤
- ❑ Bongo™
  (tan tail) . . . . . . ❸ ④ ⑤
- ❑ Bongo™
  (brown tail) . . . . ❸ ④
- ❑ Bronty™ . . . . ❸
- ❑ Brownie™ . . . . ❶
- ❑ Bruno™ . . . . ⑤
- ❑ Bubbles™ . . . . ❸ ④
- ❑ Bucky™ . . . . ❸ ④
- ❑ Bumble™ . . . . ❸ ④
- ❑ Caw™ . . . . ❸
- ❑ Chilly™ . . . . ❶ ❷ ❸
- ❑ Chip™ . . . . ④ ⑤
- ❑ Chocolate™ . ❶ ❷ ❸ ④ ⑤
- ❑ Chops™ . . . . ❸ ④
- ❑ Claude™ . . . . ④ ⑤
- ❑ Clubby™ . . . . ⑤
- ❑ Congo™ . . . . ④ ⑤

☐ Coral™ .... [3] [4]
☐ Crunch™ .... [4] [5]
☐ Cubbie™ .. [1] [2] [3] [4] [5]
☐ Curly™ .... [4] [5]
☐ Daisy™ ... [1] [2] [3] [4] [5]
☐ Derby™ (no star/ coarse mane) ...... [3] [4]
☐ Derby™ (no star/fine mane) ... [3]
☐ Derby™ (star/coarse mane) ... [5]
☐ Digger™ (orange) .... [1] [2] [3]
☐ Digger™ (red) ...... [3] [4]
☐ Doby™ .... [4] [5]
☐ Doodle™ .... [4]
☐ Dotty™ .... [4] [5]
☐ Ears™ .... [3] [4] [5]
☐ Echo™ .... [4] [5]
☐ Fetch™ .... [5]
☐ Flash™ ...... [1] [2] [3] [4]
☐ Fleece™ .... [4] [5]
☐ Flip™ .... [3] [4]
☐ Floppity™ .... [4] [5]
☐ Flutter™ .... [3]
☐ Freckles™ .... [4] [5]
☐ Garcia™ .... [3] [4]
☐ Glory™ .... [5]
☐ Gobbles™ .... [4] [5]
☐ Goldie™ ... [1] [2] [3] [4] [5]
☐ Gracie™ .... [4] [5]
☐ Grunt™ .... [3] [4]
☐ Happy™ (gray) .. [1] [2] [3]
☐ Happy™ (lavender) ...... [3] [4] [5]
☐ Hippity™ .... [4] [5]
☐ Hoot™ .... [3] [4]
☐ Hoppity™ .... [4] [5]
☐ Humphrey™ ..... [1] [2] [3]
☐ Iggy™ (blue/no tongue) ...... [5]
☐ Iggy™ (tie-dye/no tongue) ... [5]
☐ Iggy™ (tie-dye/with tongue) . [5]
☐ Inch™ (felt antennas) .... [3] [4]
☐ Inch™ (yarn antennas) .... [4] [5]
☐ Inky™ (pink) .... [3] [4] [5]
☐ Inky™ (tan/ with mouth) .... [2] [3]
☐ Inky™ (tan/ without mouth) .... [1] [2]
☐ Jolly™ .... [4] [5]
☐ Kiwi™ .... [3] [4]
☐ Lefty™ .... [4]
☐ Legs™ .... [1] [2] [3] [4]
☐ Libearty™ .... [4]
☐ Lizzy™ (blue) ... [3] [4] [5]
☐ Lizzy™ (tie-dye) ...... [3]
☐ Lucky™ (7 spots) ...... [1] [2] [3]
☐ Lucky™ (11 spots) .. [4] [5]
☐ Lucky™ (21 spots) ..... [4]
☐ Magic™ (hot pink thread) ..... [4]
☐ Magic™ (pale pink thread) . [3] [4]
☐ Manny™ .... [3] [4]
☐ Maple™ ("Pride™" tush tag) .... [4]
☐ Mel™ .... [4] [5]
☐ Millennium™ ("Millenium™" swing tag & "Millennium™" tush tag) .... [5]
☐ Millennium™ ("Millenium™" on both tags) .... [5]
☐ Mystic™ (iridescent horn/coarse mane). [4] [5]
☐ Mystic™ (brown horn/coarse mane). [3] [4]
☐ Mystic™ (brown horn/fine mane). [1] [2] [3]
☐ Nana™ .... [3]
☐ Nanook™ .... [4] [5]
☐ Nip™ (all gold) .... [3]
☐ Nip™ (white face) .. [2] [3]
☐ Nip™ (white paws) .... [3] [4] [5]
☐ Nuts™ .... [4] [5]
☐ Patti™ (magenta) ...... [3] [4] [5]
☐ Patti™ (maroon) . [1] [2] [3]
☐ Peanut™ (dark blue) ... [3]
☐ Peanut™ (light blue) ..... [3] [4] [5]
☐ Peking™ .... [1] [2] [3]
☐ Pinchers™ ("Pinchers™" swing tag). [1] [2] [3] [4] [5]
☐ Pinchers™ ("Punchers™" swing tag) .... [1]
☐ Pinky™ .... [3] [4] [5]
☐ Pouch™ .... [4] [5]
☐ Pounce™ .... [5]
☐ Prance™ .... [5]
☐ Princess™ (P.E. pellets). [4]
☐ Princess™ (P.V.C. pellets) ...... [4]
☐ Puffer™ .... [5]
☐ Pugsly™ .... [4] [5]

COLLECTOR'S CHECKLIST

- ❏ Pumkin™ . . . . ❺
- ❏ Quackers™ ("Quackers™"/ w/wings) . . . . ❷ ❸ ❹ ❺
- ❏ Quackers™ ("Quacker™"/ without wings) . . . . . ❶ ❷
- ❏ Radar™ . . . . ❸ ❹
- ❏ Rainbow™ (blue/no tongue) . . . . . . ❺
- ❏ Rainbow™ (tie-dye/with tongue) . ❺
- ❏ Rex™ . . . . ❸
- ❏ Righty™ . . . . ❹
- ❏ Ringo™ . . . . ❸ ❹ ❺
- ❏ Roary™ . . . . ❹ ❺
- ❏ Rover™ . . . . ❹ ❺
- ❏ Santa™ . . . . ❺
- ❏ Scoop™ . . . . ❹ ❺
- ❏ Scottie™ . . . . ❹ ❺
- ❏ Seamore™ . . ❶ ❷ ❸ ❹
- ❏ Seaweed™ . . . . . . ❸ ❹ ❺
- ❏ Slither™ . . . . ❶ ❷ ❸
- ❏ Sly™ (brown belly) . . . . ❹
- ❏ Sly™ (white belly) . . ❹ ❺
- ❏ Smoochy™ . . . . ❺
- ❏ Snip™ . . . . ❹ ❺
- ❏ Snort™ . . . . ❹ ❺
- ❏ Snowball™ . . . . ❹
- ❏ Sparky™ . . . . ❹
- ❏ Speedy™ . . . . ❶ ❷ ❸ ❹
- ❏ Spike™ . . . . ❹ ❺
- ❏ Spinner™ ("Creepy™" tush tag) . . . . ❺
- ❏ Spinner™ ("Spinner™" tush tag) . . . . ❹ ❺
- ❏ Splash™ . . . . . ❶ ❷ ❸ ❹
- ❏ Spooky™ ("Spook™" swing tag) . . . . ❸

- ❏ Spooky™ ("Spooky™" swing tag) . . . . ❸ ❹
- ❏ Spot™ (with spot) . . . . . ❷ ❸ ❹
- ❏ Spot™ (without spot) . . . . . ❶ ❷
- ❏ Spunky™ . . . . ❺
- ❏ Squealer™ . ❶ ❷ ❸ ❹ ❺
- ❏ Steg™ . . . . ❸
- ❏ Sting™ . . . . ❸ ❹
- ❏ Stinger™ . . . . ❺
- ❏ Stinky™ . . . . ❸ ❹ ❺
- ❏ Stretch™ . . . . ❺
- ❏ Stripes™ (dark w/ fuzzy belly) . . . . ❸
- ❏ Stripes™ (dark w/ more stripes) . . . . ❸
- ❏ Stripes™ (light w/ fewer stripes) . . . . ❹ ❺
- ❏ Strut™ . . . . ❹ ❺
- ❏ Tabasco™ . . . . ❸ ❹
- ❏ Tank™ (7 plates/ without shell) . . . . ❸
- ❏ Tank™ (9 plates/shell) . . . . ❹
- ❏ Tank™ (9 plates/ without shell) . . . . ❹
- ❏ Teddy™ (brown/ new face) . . . . . . ❷ ❸ ❹
- ❏ Teddy™ (brown/ old face) . . . . ❶ ❷
- ❏ Teddy™ (cranberry/ new face) . . . . ❷ ❸
- ❏ Teddy™ (cranberry/ old face) . . . . ❶ ❷
- ❏ Teddy™ (jade/new face) . . . ❷ ❸
- ❏ Teddy™ (jade/old face) . . . . ❶ ❷

- ❏ Teddy™ (magenta/ new face) . . . . ❷ ❸
- ❏ Teddy™ (magenta/ old face) . . . . ❶ ❷
- ❏ Teddy™ (teal/new face) . . . . ❷ ❸
- ❏ Teddy™ (teal/old face) . . . . ❶ ❷
- ❏ Teddy™ (violet/new face) . . ❷ ❸
- ❏ Teddy™ (violet/ new face employee bear w/red tush tag) . . . **No Swing Tag**
- ❏ Teddy™ (violet/old face) . . . ❶ ❷
- ❏ Trap™ . . . . ❶ ❷ ❸
- ❏ Tuffy™ . . . . ❹ ❺
- ❏ Tusk™ ("Tuck™" swing tag) . . . ❹
- ❏ Tusk™ ("Tusk™" swing tag) . ❸ ❹
- ❏ Twigs™ . . . . ❸ ❹ ❺
- ❏ Valentino™ . . . ❷ ❸ ❹ ❺
- ❏ Velvet™ . . . . ❸ ❹
- ❏ Waddle™ . . . . ❸ ❹ ❺
- ❏ Waves™ . . . . ❹ ❺
- ❏ Web™ . . . . ❶ ❷ ❸
- ❏ Weenie™ . . . . ❸ ❹ ❺
- ❏ Wise™ . . . . ❺
- ❏ Wrinkles™ . . . . ❹ ❺
- ❏ Zero™ . . . . ❺
- ❏ Ziggy™ . . . . ❸ ❹ ❺
- ❏ Zip™ (all black) . . . . ❸
- ❏ Zip™ (white face) . . ❷ ❸
- ❏ Zip™ (white paws) . . . ❸ ❹ ❺

Current Beanie Buddies®

- ❑ Bongo™
- ❑ Bubbles™
- ❑ Chilly™
- ❑ Chip™
- ❑ Erin™
- ❑ Fuzz™
- ❑ Hippity™
- ❑ Hope™
- ❑ Humphrey™
- ❑ Jabber™
- ❑ Jake™
- ❑ Millennium™
- ❑ Patti™
- ❑ Peanut™
- ❑ Peking™
- ❑ Pinky™
- ❑ Princess™
- ❑ Quackers™
- ❑ Rover™
- ❑ Smoochy™
- ❑ Snort™
- ❑ Squealer™
- ❑ Stretch™
- ❑ Teddy™
- ❑ Tracker™
- ❑ Waddle™

Retired Beanie Buddies®

- ❑ Beak™
- ❑ Twigs™

Current Teenie Beanie Babies™
(To Be Retired: June 3, 1999)

- ❑ 1999 Teenie Beanie Babies™ Complete Set
- ❑ Antsy™
- ❑ Chip™
- ❑ Claude™
- ❑ Freckles™
- ❑ Iggy™
- ❑ 'Nook™
- ❑ Nuts™
- ❑ Rocket™
- ❑ Smoochy™
- ❑ Spunky™
- ❑ Stretchy™
- ❑ Strut™

Current Teenie Beanie Babies™
(To Be Retired: June 17, 1999)

- ❑ 1999 Teenie Beanie Babies™ International Bears
- ❑ Britannia™
- ❑ Erin™
- ❑ Glory™
- ❑ Maple™

Retired Teenie Beanie Babies™

- ❑ 1997 Teenie Beanie Babies™ Complete Set
- ❑ 1998 Teenie Beanie Babies™ Complete Set
- ❑ Bones™
- ❑ Bongo™
- ❑ Chocolate™

- ❑ Chops™
- ❑ Doby™
- ❑ Goldie™
- ❑ Happy™
- ❑ Inch™
- ❑ Lizz™
- ❑ Mel™
- ❑ Patti™
- ❑ Peanut™
- ❑ Pinchers™
- ❑ Pinky™
- ❑ Quacks™
- ❑ Scoop™
- ❑ Seamore™
- ❑ Snort™
- ❑ Speedy™
- ❑ Twigs™
- ❑ Waddle™
- ❑ Zip™

ALPHABETICAL INDEX

Below is an alphabetical listing of the Beanie Babies, Beanie Buddies and Teenie Beanie Babies, and the pages on which you can find them in the Value Guide!

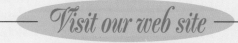